**She knew he was t[** was at least two or mor[ this vantage point—dir[

*very* tall. She could smell the starch of his shirt mixed with a faint whiff of smoke and possibly brandy. She slid her gaze over the shirt and waistcoat to his cravat— a conservatively tied Oriental—to the firm, slightly cleft chin, moving on to the lips, very swiftly past those, and finally resting on his eyes. Pure molten gold. Yes, exactly like those of the Burmese tiger she had seen at a menagerie in Paris. His bearing was just as predatory.

"It would appear, sir, in order for me to *move*, as you require, you will have to bestir yourself as well."

She thought she saw one side of his mouth shift ever so slightly upward into what might have been the merest twitch of a smile. She could not be one hundred percent sure because, to do so, she would have to look at his lips. The duke shifted his weight and made a small bow. Her shoulder brushed the superfine of his midnight blue jacket as she hurriedly squeezed past him.

She strode almost to the mirrors before wheeling around and giving him what she hoped was an accusatory look.

"Well, Your Grace. I hope you are satisfied."

"Satisfied, Mrs. Weston?" He raised that infernal eyebrow. "Oh no, madam, I am very far from satisfied. However, I am hopeful I will be, in the not so distant future." Again his gaze raked over her. "Yes, I do live in hope."

## Praise for Jess Russell

*THE DRESSMAKER'S DUKE* came in first in the Fool for Love Contest, Golden Apple Awards' Secret Craving Contest, the Indiana Golden Opportunity Contest, and the Golden Rose Contest (also winning the award for Best of the Best), and finaled in the Great Beginnings, Emerald City Opener, and the Lone Star Contests.

# The Dressmaker's Duke

by

Jess Russell

This is a work of fiction. Names, characters, places, and incidents are either the product of the author's imagination or are used fictitiously, and any resemblance to actual persons living or dead, business establishments, events, or locales, is entirely coincidental.

**The Dressmaker's Duke**

COPYRIGHT © 2014 by Jess Russell

All rights reserved. No part of this book may be used or reproduced in any manner whatsoever without written permission of the author or The Wild Rose Press, Inc. except in the case of brief quotations embodied in critical articles or reviews.
Contact Information: info@thewildrosepress.com

Cover Art by *Debbie Taylor*

The Wild Rose Press, Inc.
PO Box 708
Adams Basin, NY 14410-0708
Visit us at www.thewildrosepress.com

Publishing History
First English Tea Rose Edition, 2014
Print ISBN 978-1-62830-475-6
Digital ISBN 978-1-62830-476-3

Published in the United States of America

# Dedication

To my mother, Doris Rausch,
who was my first gentle reader.

## Acknowledgements

It takes a village to write a book. I am blessed with incredibly generous friends and family who shored me up when my doubts threatened to raze my fragile story to rubble.

So, first up, is Mom, to whom I gave the beginning pages, "to check for grammar." Then to Rita, who can appreciate every nuance and detail in anything, then to my lovely sis, Jenn, and her gals, KK and Meg, and on to dearest friends, Ash, Veronique, Mary, Kris, Margaret, and Jackie.

Along this journey I met new friends. At the top of that list is Amber Belldene who, in essence, took off my training wheels and steered me to tell my story. To Addison Fox for our shared glasses of wine and her unfailing mentorship. To Lise Horton for her hand-holding through contracts, and the Hon. J. Kevin McKay for his litigious insights. To Tina Constable for pointing me in the right direction (several times). To the RWANYC and the Beau Monde Chapters of Romance Writers of America for just about anything a girl could need, from encouragement to how to address a duke. To Collette Cameron for making things better, always. To Cynthia Young for her deep caring and attention to detail. And to The Wild Rose Press, most especially Susan Yates and Nicole D'Arienzo, my editors, for whom no question was too silly and no "adjustment" too small.

Finally, to the men in my life, Patrick and Aidan, my real life Heroes. And to my dad who, I believe, would have been proud.

Chapter One

*London, England*
*Late March 1810*

*Good God, did she not see the carriage?*

Rhys Merrick's expelled breath fogged the shop window in a silent shout. Heart pounding, he rubbed the glass.

The carriage careened by and—there she was. Intact.

Silly female, she could have caused all manner of damage by her folly. She certainly had ruined her gown, her backside now liberally daubed with street filth and wet. But what was more singular, the woman seemed oblivious to her near escape, still wrestling to close an ancient-looking umbrella. Another gust of wind caught its underbelly, and Rhys was certain this time it would take flight, but the woman held on, only to have the thing turn itself inside out for her trouble. Ribs dangling, it now resembled a large, black, extremely dead bird.

"Mr. Merrick, I will only be a moment longer." The shopkeeper's moon like face and bulging eyes appeared from around the door at the back of the shop. Twin shocks of glossy over-long hair lapped his ears, framing his huge eyes and snub nose.

Remarkable. If the man were shrunk and glazed, he

would make a very fine Staffordshire dog.

"While you are waiting, you may like to look at that fine temple clock on the table against the far wall." The shopkeeper's enthusiasm begged for only a pink tongue and wagging tail.

Rhys turned back to the window, but the woman was gone.

*Blasted rain.*

Passing the giant Egyptian sarcophagus, which stood as a kind of sentinel to the left of the shop's door—Horus, perhaps?—Rhys moved to the back of the room and the temple clock.

The front door bell jangled.

A gust of fresh air blew in, carrying a scent of lemon mixed with some smell he could not immediately identify. The aroma rose like a high note over the heavy dank and must of the shop. The door swung shut, sealing out the noise of the street and rain.

Rhys pressed himself into the farthest corner of the long narrow room. Likely he would never be recognized dressed as he was, especially in this part of town, but he did not want to chance the inevitable fawning that would take place should someone recognize him as the Duke of Roydan.

It was the woman with the umbrella—or rather, *without* the umbrella. She stood frozen, as if now that she had come in out of the wet, she had lost all momentum. Rhys watched for the moment she would notice the huge falcon head of Horus looming above her and pick up her sopping skirts and leave. Then he might have the shop to himself again.

This particular shop was not for the faint of heart. Mr. Crup specialized in the macabre. The window boasted several shrunken heads and the skeleton of some unknown creature with a sign looped about its neck identifying it as a Celtic Dragon.

However, Crup's oddities appeared to have no effect on this woman. Either she was too numb or too jaded to respond. He could not be sure. A dark lace veil hung limply over the front of her bonnet, obscuring her features.

"Mr. Merrick?" The shopkeeper yapped sharply. Rhys held his breath and pressed further into the shadows. The man emerged a moment later, scanning the shop. "Oh, shite." He set a small object on the counter. "Your pardon, ma'am, but a chap goes to all this trouble and for what?"

Rhys turned away to examine the temple clock.

"Good afternoon, sir."

The woman's voice crept into the space right between his shoulder blades. Surprised, he turned to confront her. But no, her attention was firmly on the shopkeeper.

"Filthy weather we're having," she said, shaking drops of rain from her shawl. Her voice was a viola, soft and deeply rounded. It seemed to roll through her, pulling her spine straighter, her shoulders back, and chin up. No longer a bedraggled, bespattered woman, she was a lady.

However, she was definitely one who existed in that dubious state known as genteel poverty. Even in the dim light, Rhys could see her dress was several seasons old—had to be, for him to notice—and slightly short. The hem turned one too many times, exposing her muddy boots.

"I swear I would not be surprised to see

mushrooms sprouting from between my toes these days," she said.

Rhys's head jerked up, but the woman was still turned toward Crup. A trickle of laughter seeped from beneath her veil, but it seemed forced, like a gaudy ribbon added at the last moment to prettify a gift.

"I must say, Mr. Crup, I have never—" She looked above her and into Horus's great falcon eyes and then reached up to touch the god's huge curved beak.

Rhys had the notion she did so as a kind of good luck charm. Absurd.

"You are Mr. Crup, the proprietor, are you not?" she asked turning back to the little man.

Crup nodded, and scratched behind his ear.

She wove her way across the shop to the counter. "Yes, I thought you looked the part. A distinguished man, for a distinguished shop." She tilted her head charmingly.

She was laying it on a bit thick. No sane person would ever connect "distinguished" with this shopkeeper. Rhys felt certain that beneath her veil, one would see a completely different picture than the one she was taking pains to create. "It is so rare to find someone who obviously knows quality when he sees it." Mr. Crup's gaze tracked from the woman's sodden bonnet and veil down to her muddied hem.

She cleared her throat and straightened her shoulders. "But I fear I have interrupted a sale?"

Crup waved a hand dismissively. "Well, madam, I am known in some circles as having the rarest and finest treasures."

"I am relieved to hear you say so. Which is why I am sure you will be very interested in what I have to show you."

Rhys's weight shifted to his toes as she dug into a small bag and carefully unwrapped some silver items. Only a brush and mirror set. What a show for nothing. Still, she'd even had him craning to see her tripe.

"Looks to be only plate," said Crup.

"Oh, but note the deep bevel…"

Their voices faded as Rhys picked up the temple clock and turned it over looking for marks. Nothing. And it should be heavier. Likely made of inferior wood and the carvings were crude. He returned it to the table.

*What was that combination of smells?* It was extremely distracting.

Perhaps he would slip out if the rain had stopped. He glanced toward the pair to determine if escape was possible.

The shopkeeper pushed the items back across the counter. "You might try Leicester's down the road." And he turned away.

Rhys started for the door. But not before the woman sagged, as if the shopkeeper's attention was the only thing holding her up. Undoubtedly she had been to Leicester's along with most of the other more reputable shops.

Her hand covered her veiled face. She swayed.

*Blistering Hell, she was not going to faint?* He did not want to reveal his presence, to play the hero. Nonetheless, he primed himself, ready to spring into action.

However when Crup turned back, her spine snapped straight as a flagpole, and her veil fluttered with her breath. Rhys relaxed a degree.

"Very well, sir, you have left me no choice but to

bring out the real artillery." She dipped her hand into her pocket and withdrew something wrapped in a handkerchief, placing it gently on the counter.

"What's this?" He plucked at the handkerchief and a heavy object clunked to the counter. The woman's shoulders jerked with the sound.

The meager light fell precisely on the pierced case of a watch as if a stage had been set for its unveiling.

*Dear God, it looked to be heart-shaped.*

The guts of a rare, late seventeenth-century Tompion watch sat in an ivory box on a shelf in his library at Roydan House. Its case had eluded him.

*If only he could see clearly...*

Crup took up a loop and held it to his eye covering the watch with his paw. His tongue poked out over his lower lip as he wound the screw. *Gently, man.*

"Pretty enough, but it don't seem to work." And he looked up, straight into Rhys's eyes. "Ah, Mr. Merrick, you did not leave."

Too late, Rhys realized he was halfway across the shop. The woman's hand flew up to her veil as she turned away.

"I have that crystal I was telling you about." Crup moved down the long counter, the woman now forgotten.

Rhys ignored the man along with his urge to remain uninvolved. "Might I have a look, madam?"

She turned back to him and startled. *His eyes. Why could his eyes not be a sensible brown like every other fellow?* But after a moment, she nodded.

His fingers ached to brush over the enameled case—a fantasy of scrolled flourishes in various shades of blue—but he made himself painstakingly pull each finger of his gloves and then lay them precisely, one on top of the other, on the counter.

A bit of enamel was worn away near the left side of the heart's deep V. He carefully thumbed open the case. Yes, the minute hand was intact, and the gold illuminated numerals clear as the day it was made. He flipped it over. There was the mark, a conjoined ND.

He mentally opened its back and imagined his Tompion works nestled within this beautiful shell. However, the rest of his body was entirely focused on the woman beside him.

She must have moved closer, her spicy scent stronger. He would swear he could feel her breathing. His skin prickled.

"Pity it don't work." Crup's pudgy fingers drummed on the counter. "Still it's a pretty little trinket. I'll give you three quid for the thing."

The woman was still too close, her arm but a whisper from his own. His heart migrated higher in his chest, far too close to his throat. Likely from the thrill of the hunt.

*Ballocks.* As fine as the case was, it was useless to believe certain stirrings in his body were simply the result of a watch—one that did not even work.

Rhys made himself release the watch, setting it back on the counter. "I am sorry to interfere; I will leave you to your dealings." He stepped away, restoring the space she had invaded, if not his breathing.

"So little?" she turned toward Rhys as if he might provide some small miracle.

"Look here." Crup's odor of onions and mackerel overwhelmed her delicate perfume. "The thing don't work. How am I to sell a bauble that don't work? Three quid is my final offer."

She reached for the watch to take it back. Rhys almost hoped she would, she seemed so distressed. But her hand stopped, then fisted, and finally she tucked it beneath her paisley shawl, leaving the watch on the counter.

It was not his place to interfere. He had a strict code of ethics when dealing with these shops, and he never deviated from his rules.

"Mr. Crup, I believe the gold itself is worth five pounds." Rhys clenched his teeth.

"Look here, Mr. Merrick—"

Rhys raised an eyebrow, one of his surest weapons, and gave the man his most ducal look. It never failed him and didn't now as the shopkeeper blinked, his mouth gapping open. Besides, Rhys was going to buy the thing, at a reasonable profit, just as soon as the woman left the shop. No one would be cheated.

Rhys turned back to the woman. *What was beyond that cursed veil?* Only a tease of her lips and the line of her nose. Nothing of her eyes. Her neck was very long and white. Was that a wisp of dark hair? He needed to get out of this shop, but his foot was in the stirrup, so to speak, and he could not cede the field until the woman was satisfied.

"Would five pounds be acceptable, madam?"

Her lips parted beneath the lace; only a hint of white as she caught her bottom lip with her teeth. She touched the worn bit of blue on the watch, tracing the left curve. A final farewell? The bump of a ring under her glove on her third finger had Rhys imagining the man who had been attached to that watch, and to this woman. What kind of man could command such reverence?

"Very well, sir," she said. Rhys released his breath. She clasped her hands together and turned to Mr. Crup. "I will accept your offer at five pounds."

The little man's eyes darted to Rhys as if needing his final approval. Rhys gave the shopkeeper a nod and the man turned back to her. "That's a fine paisley you're wearing. I might be willing to pay something for that as well."

"Oh no, I will not part with this."

Crup shrugged at the woman's sudden vehemence.

She pulled the shawl about her like a shield and turned away to the window. Streaks of weak sun hit a few last drops of rain that hung from the eaves.

"Now, Mr. Merrick. I do have that crystal you was asking about—"

"How much?" Rhys scarcely recognized her voice; it had diminished from warm fervor to breathless nothing.

"How much for the shawl?" she repeated.

Mr. Crup sniffed and shook his head like a dog with a flea. "I'll only be a moment, Mr. Merrick." He gestured to her to come nearer. Lifting the edge of the shawl, he rubbed it between his blunt fingers. She stiffened but endured his fondling. Rhys put his own hand behind his back to be imprisoned by the other. He could almost feel the soft wool brush his cheeks and nose.

"Eight guineas."

Her head snapped up. "It's worth at least twenty." The woman didn't know a thing about watches but obviously knew the worth of fine wool.

"Naw, eight is all I can give," he said, squaring off

9

to her.

Dash it all, at this point Rhys would give her fifty guineas to save her bloody shawl and his peace of mind.

"Then I will only sell the watch, sir," she said firmly.

"As you please. If you would sign your name to this receipt, madam."

She dipped the pen and briskly wrote her name. Her long neck arched, exposing the nape. *Yes, definitely dark hair.* Rhys swallowed.

"Very good, Mrs. Weston." Crup blotted the paper and handed it to her.

*Mrs. Weston...*

She put the receipt in her reticule and turned to Rhys. He steeled himself for her thanks. He did not want it.

"Mr. Merrick, I am in your debt. Thank you for your assistance."

*You can thank me by lifting your veil so I might see you are just an ordinary woman with ordinary cares. Or, perhaps you would allow me to dip my head to the space between your neck and shoulder to ascertain if that intoxicating smell is merely attached to your shawl or to your actual person?*

In contrast to his heated thoughts, he was sure his face was a mask of frozen disdain. It usually was whenever he felt such discomfort. She held his gaze far longer than he'd expected—certainly no mealy-mouthed miss. But sure enough, after teetering a moment, she turned to leave. He had successfully repelled her.

"Here, don't you want your money?" Crup rushed

forward, his gaze darting to Rhys. "I won't have you say later I cheated you."

Mrs. Weston's veil fluttered with her gasp, and her hands covered her heart. She murmured something he could not catch and shook her head at the floor.

Then she laughed. Not the small nervous titter of earlier, but a full-throated, out-and-out laugh.

Rhys's teeth cut into the inner flesh of his cheeks.

"Well, it looks as if the rain has stopped, Mrs. Weston." Crup stood by the door. "Best take advantage."

She started toward the door and then hesitated. Her fingertips touched her mouth, and her shadowed gaze turned back to Rhys.

A swell of unbidden emotion surged against his dam of control. *What? Speak. Anything but thanks.* Her head cocked and lips parted. A smile?

He strained to think of something to say; anything to keep her light near him. But his words remained firmly trapped within his hammering breast. He made himself turn away, dismissing her.

A moment later the bell jangled and the door shut.

He found himself by the window.

"Mr. Merrick. Now about that watch crystal…"

Rhys pressed his hand to the cold damp of the glass. She seemed so small now, a dark patch against the winking, rain-slicked buildings.

A boy shot out of nowhere and pulled at her skirts. He held out a bedraggled and muddy flower. Clearly some discard from a rubbish heap. Rhys winced, but Mrs. Weston seemed to have no qualms about touching the lad, who must have found every puddle in the street. She bent, brushed his reddish-colored hair, and spoke to him. He pointed down the street gesturing wildly. Mrs. Weston opened her reticule and gave him a coin Rhys knew she could ill afford. The boy snatched it, thrust the flower at her, and dashed off with a whoop.

This woman, with her one shilling, put all his ducal philanthropy to shame. But all logical thoughts of pence and pounds dissolved when she tipped her face up to the feeble sunlight and lifted her veil.

"Mr. Merrick, the crystal? Or perhaps something else strikes your fancy?"

Rhys tried to blot out the shopkeeper's voice, but the moment was gone. She had already lowered her veil and was moving off in the direction of Fleet Street.

"Yes," Rhys said softly. He turned away from the window. "Yes, I have found something I want."

## Chapter Two

*Two weeks later*

Olivia Weston dared another peek above her. Two very lethal-looking swords dangled a good twenty-five feet above her head. If one had an active imagination, one could imagine those swords slipping their confines and summarily slicing the head from one's body.

She shifted slightly on her bench—its own instrument of torture—but she would not be cowed into moving. If there *had* been another spot to move to.

When faced with Roydan House, she had very nearly turned around. A veritable colossus. And the man who lived within, a Goliath. That would make her David, holding a bill instead of a slingshot. She snorted. Not the most formidable of weapons. Still, in her heated anger, she had almost knocked at the mansion's front door before remembering her current status, and scurrying around to the servant's entrance.

Was she addlepated? If his mistress hadn't paid, what made Olivia think she had a chance with His Grace, the sixth Duke of Roydan?

Still, surely his secretary, Mr. Wilcove, could spare her a moment?

He had to. Her dearest Eglantine was counting on her.

Olivia had left Egg back at their shop shivering

under three shawls next to a nonexistent fire. Egg had been attempting to string a row of minuscule jet beads before her next fit of coughing. She had not been successful and beads had skittered everywhere. But instead of a curse worthy of a dockside worker, there had been only dead and empty silence. In that moment, it was as if all their woes had been poured through a sieve and distilled into Egg's hopeless eyes.

Olivia squeezed her own lids shut, wanting to block out the next image, Eglantine slowly sinking to her hands and knees to carefully gather each and every bead—

"By Saint Anne, we *will* be satisfied!" Olivia opened her eyes to find the glaring gap in a stringent chevron of swords that marched up the walls. The hole irritated her—like a dropped stitch in a row of knitting. *Where was that foil?* But the four full suits of armor, Sir Mutton, Sir Haggis, Sir Dunce-a-lot and, last but not least, Sir Portly—she had named them all in the last hour—gave up no secrets.

*Drat, Daria Battersby and her bobbling breasts.*

"Dear Rhys and I had a little falling out, is all," the woman had said just yesterday. "I am quite sure Roydan will settle this little matter in a trice. You must come back, and we will discuss a few other sundries." Then she had launched into an excruciating and detailed account of Mrs. Peebles's gout, involving the need for specially made slippers. Olivia shuddered.

"Sundries, my eye," she said to Sir Mutton who stood nearest her bench.

If only she and Eglantine had known the anxiety this overfed peacock of a duke's mistress would cause them, they would have waltzed her right back out of the shop and barred the door. Instead, firewood had been sacrificed for silks and bread for Belgian lace. Then Wes's beloved watch—she missed its familiar weight in her left pocket. And finally, just three days ago, her mother's paisley shawl. She scrubbed the back of her hand over her eyes. Silly to get so upset over a bit of wool.

Suddenly her imagination had the missing sword in her hand, and she was *en garde* with the author of her misery, the buxom Mrs. Battersby.

*Take that!* Creating a mental series of feints and parries, Olivia had the woman huffing and puffing in no time.

*Slice*—one sleeve gaped. *Slash*—the other soon followed. Now the poor lady's bodice lay gaping, her bosom a tad less buoyant now.

Next, Olivia dispatched her turban and the plumes that sprouted from the disastrous piece of millinery. On second thought, that would be doing the woman a service. Olivia mentally plopped it back on her head. Backward.

In short order Olivia reduced the duke's mistress to a quivering mass of flesh, clad only in her bedraggled turban and jewels.

"Please, I beg you, Mrs. Weston, have pity," the phantom Mrs. B. panted. "You see the shape I am in; I desperately need your skills to conceal my flabby folds with your magical undergarments." Olivia hesitated in her delicious torture. *Flabby? Magical?* Well, it was only the truth and, after all, Olivia's daydream. "I will pay you twice what I owe," Battersby continued. Olivia tickled the woman's chins with the tip of the foil. "Have mercy," Mrs. B. cried, "and you shall have whatever you wish!" *This was getting better.* "You shall have my jewels"—*tickle*—"my carriages"—*tickle, tickle*—"my servants"—an out-and-out *poke*—"even my house in town!" And when Olivia still did not relent—"And the duke. Yes, I give you the duke as well!" She ended on her knees, her turbaned head bowed in supplication.

*The duke? Really?*

As a girl she had dreamed of being a duchess. But before she had the good lady rising and "Your Gracing" her, Olivia remembered Egg saying something about this duke being known as...the Monk.

At the time she had listened with only half an ear, but the story somehow involved a very public men's club, the famous courtesan Harriette Wilson clad only in an ermine cloak and diamonds, and the duke's words, "Madam, you seemed to have dropped something."

Apparently the papers had a romp with the tale, the culmination being a garish cartoon by Gillray depicting Mrs. Wilson and the duke entitled, "The Monk." The name, Egg said, had stuck with the duke all this time.

The image of a sober old codger in an ancient bagwig tottering on his creaking knees in prayer flashed through her mind.

Hmm...perhaps she would forgo being Duchess of Roydan at present. Instead, she decided to put Mrs. B. out of her misery. Olivia rose from her bench, happy to stretch her cramped limbs and nearly numb posterior, and prepared to execute her *coup de grâce.*

\*\*\*\*

The foil went flying.

Rhys watched the sword as it sailed end over end,

16

looping high into the library's vaulted ceiling. The blade, threatening to unman a dozen or so innocent, frolicking cherubs, descended with a clattering *smack* on the top of his huge desk.

Light as the sword was, it scattered papers, priceless pieces of his Tompion watch, various tools, and yes, the inkwell, which teetered for a second, as if testing his tolerance, before tumbling to the Aubusson carpet.

Rhys wanted to curse. But he never cursed—at least out loud. Not even when he was quite alone.

"Damn!" The word slipped out. By God, what was happening to him? He never lost the grip of number forty-seven. The foil was a particular favorite, the balance so perfect for his height and bearing.

Rhys took a steadying breath and crossed the room to pick up the now half-empty inkwell. *Crunch.* He froze. No doubt that was, or had been, part of the escapement of his priceless watch.

He pressed his lips together.

Using his handkerchief, he carefully righted the inkwell, avoiding the spreading ink now marring the cream and red carpet. He brushed his hands over the fine wool nap to retrieve—please God—all his clock works. Lastly, he shuffled the various papers into a heap, hesitating when he recognized his Uncle Bertram's letter. He need not actually read the letter. He knew very well what it contained, for this was the third he had received in as many days. He threw it on the desk where it landed next to the beautiful, heart-shaped watch case.

Thank God the case still sat squarely in the middle of the mess, as if it were a sun to all the orbiting chaos surrounding it. He brushed his fingers over the scrollwork feeling the depression where the enamel had worn away.

*Mrs. Weston.*

Why did he have this insane feeling he had let the real treasure go?

There was a scratch on the door.

"What?" The question exploded from his lips, the pain of a headache flaring.

Wilcove entered and bowed.

"Your Grace, my deepest apologies for the interruption—"

Seeing his secretary brought Rhys back to his present woes. "Have my solicitors made any headway with breaking the codicil?"

"As to that, nothing new has been discovered, Your Grace, but Messieurs Fink and Ponzer continue to persevere."

Rhys flung his uncle's letter aside and began sorting clock pieces.

Wilcove continued, "I can report we have found the proposed beneficiary's brother, the Reverend Rodger Gooden of Hammersmith. But I am afraid the trail goes cold from there. The reverend was never on the best of terms with his sister and has not heard from her in over six years. The last correspondence was from the Indies."

"I want a man sent immediately to investigate."

"Yes, Your Grace. I have anticipated you and thought to send Mr. Wadmond."

One year—well, less than one year now—to marry and start "producing." Bloody codicil. As if he didn't have enough to plague him, now he must take on a wife? Still, he could not ignore his father's last jab. Dee Gooden would never have Valmere, his mother's estate. Even if it meant paying her thousands.

But he had to find her first.

"Is that all?" Rhys asked. *By God, the balance wheel was missing!* He looked on the floor, lifting his feet.

"Not quite, Your Grace, another matter has come up that unfortunately requires your attention."

*Nothing.* "What is it?" Rhys said riffling through the waste bin next to his desk.

"It is not an 'it,' Your Grace, it is a 'she.'"

Rhys's gaze locked with Wilcove's. "It is not Mrs. Battersby again?"

"Not precisely, Your Grace."

Rhys kept his voice steady and well-modulated as he put the waste bin down. "What is *she? Precisely?*" Wilcove was an excellent secretary, but the man had a tendency to be a bit too literal even for Rhys's own considered standard.

"She is a tradesperson, Your Grace. A dressmaker."

Rhys waited, and then raised an eyebrow ever so slightly. Wilcove, used to reading volumes in the mere quiver of Rhys's nostril, rushed on.

"Your pardon, this dressmaker claims to have a rather large outstanding bill"—he produced a paper— "for several gowns, five to be exact, and some other incidentals, which Mrs. Battersby seems to have commissioned."

Rhys's headache pounded. "It was my understanding we settled everything of that sort weeks ago."

Thursday—his birthday—when he had broken it off with Daria Battersby. Her settlement had been more than generous, but not content, she had dared to breach his house, bursting into this very room.

"So you need to marry some milksop miss and sire a brat or two," she had lisped. "La, *that* need have nothing to do with us." The desperate look on her face had put him on guard. "I know what you need, some new diversion…" And then she had sunk to her knees, her hands on the buttons of his falls—

"Your Grace?"

Rhys snapped his head back to Wilcove, adding a crescendo to the pain throbbing at his temples.

His secretary continued, "I tried to impart to the woman in three separate letters that Mrs. Battersby no longer enjoys your protection. I was loath to bring such a trivial matter to your attention, but the woman is rather tenacious. And you did wish to be apprised of any new complications involving Mrs. Battersby."

"I see." Rhys's gaze strayed to his uncle's letter. He seemed to be surrounded by tenacious people these days. "I presume that is the bill?"

"It is, Your Grace." Wilcove placed it in his outstretched hand.

Ridiculous what ladies spent on fripperies these days. Clearly this dressmaker had padded the bill knowing his position. And sure enough, it was dated just after he had broken their contract. Wilcove's feet shifted ever so slightly.

*Damn Daria!* She had always been a grasping woman, but now she went too far. He had made no pretense of loving her. In truth, he had chosen her for the very fact that it would be impossible for him to love her. Hell, he did not even *like* her a good deal of the time.

Several Sevres figurines and his great grandmother's Venetian mirror had been sacrificed to her tirade that day. Daria's "pleasing mistress" mask had shattered right along with them. Thank God his clepsydra water clock had not been within her reach.

Daria would have to be checked and, by God, he would start with this dressmaker.

"Send her away."

"Very good, Your Grace. I will deal with this Mrs. Weston." He bowed and left the room.

Rhys pinched the bridge of his nose, sighed, ripped open his uncle's letter, and began to read.

Uncle Bert wanted to move things along. He proposed a young woman to fulfill the role of duchess, a Miss Arabella Campbell.

Arabella Campbell…Somehow attaching a name to the woman made the prospect all too real. He tossed the letter aside.

*But where was his bloody, infernal balance wheel?*

He wrenched the chair out from beneath his desk and seized a lit taper. Dropping to his knees he crawled under the massive piece of furniture.

Not one speck of lint, never mind a fingernail-sized golden wheel. He grabbed his foil, using its thin blade to swipe under the desk—

Wait, *Weston?*

The candle tipped and Rhys jerked as hot wax burned a painful trail down the inside of his wrist, just as his head connected with the underside of the desk.

Mrs. Weston. *Good God, could it be?*

\*\*\*\*

21

Olivia shook out her numb limbs, sighted the knight-errant Sir Haggis—who kindly stood in for Daria Battersby—and advanced.

However, her sally was spoilt by the heel of her boot catching the recently mended tear in her best petticoat. When she righted herself, instead of impaling her foe, she faced a thoroughly alive flesh and blood man with a whip-like foil. One poised to pierce her very heart.

She shut her eyes, sucked in a huge draft of air, and prepared for death.

Nothing happened.

A musky scent filled her nose, and her heart thudded—both responses proving she was very much alive.

She dared to open an eye. This man was no fancy, hatched from her overactive imagination.

*Good Lord, she should have eaten.* Blackness engulfed her vision. and the floor rose to meet her just as an arm of hard muscle and bone snaked around her backside pulling her right up against his broad chest. Her eyelids popped open. Flashes of light skittered across her vision, but they in no way diminished the impact of his eyes. Brittle chips of the clearest amber imprisoned her just as surely as his arm. The same eyes that had invaded her dreams these past two weeks.

"Mr. Merrick?"

## Chapter Three

"Mrs. Weston."

Oh, God's teeth, his voice was still the deepest burnt umber. As if the bright sharpness of his eyes had melted, leaking sweet, rich honey down into his throat.

But why was plain Mr. Merrick brandishing a sword in the Duke of Roydan's hall?

She opened her mouth, but nothing came out. She tried again. Heavens, she must look like a gawping fish. On the third try she managed a breathy, "Sir—I mean, Mr. Merrick. I mean—"

His arm abruptly dropped, and he took several steps backward.

*Lord, the man was beautiful. Her dreams had not done him justice.* But then she had been so very tired and hungry that day at Crups, it was a wonder he made any impression.

He was dressed more soberly and finely now, but his plain attire did nothing to diminish huge shoulders, a shaded jawline, lips that would have a sculptor salivating, and an impressive blade of a nose. And that was just the top third of him. His powerful legs were planted wide, his arms long and loose, yet ready, at his sides, the foil held so lightly in his right hand. And then, of course, those eyes...

Foil be hanged, his eyes were his real weapons. Even the long black lashes framing the icy gold did nothing to soften the cold that seeped forth. The eyes of a hunter. She felt—devoured.

That's when it came to her.

"Tiger." Blast, the word slipped out before she could quash the impression. She swallowed, her mouth like paper.

He blinked, frowned, and finally raised an eyebrow, skewering her with the same look he had unleashed on her at Crups when she dared to thank him.

A cough penetrated her wretched brain. She turned toward the sound. Sir Haggis had suddenly acquired a rotund, gnome-like page.

"Your Grace, I beg your pardon. I was dispatching Mr. Wadmond and only just came to remove Mrs. Weston," said the little man.

*Your Grace?* She looked to Mr. Merrick for confirmation, but only saw his lips pull into a straight line.

*Was this man the duke? This Adonis? No, surely not. He might not be Mr. Merrick, but he was most definitely no Monk.*

"Never mind, Wilcove. I will deal with her myself." He turned to her. "Mrs. Weston, if you will give me a moment…" His eyes turned warmer, softer, making him seem almost vulnerable. Likely just a trick of light, for in the next moment they shuttered, his teeth clamped shut, and his jawline jumped in concert. Turning abruptly, he strode to the wall of swords and thrust the foil back home. "Send her to me in five minutes." And he left the room.

Olivia collapsed on the bench.

Well, thank God one mystery was solved and symmetry restored. She would not be kept up this night thinking of *where* that foil had got to. She swallowed a bubble of laughter, glancing at Wilcove. Which reminded her...

Ignoring the little man, she heaved herself up on shaky legs, and crossed to Sir Haggis, who was thoroughly intact, from his plumed helmet to his chainmail sabatons. But sure enough, directly behind the knight, was a hairline crack about four feet high and half as wide. An old priest's door. That she missed it in her endless waiting was a testament to the joiner's expertise.

But Wilcove was speaking.

"Madam, if you will please to follow me." He gestured to the larger door to his left. Just as she turned from Sir Haggis, his visor flashed in a kind of wink. Olivia bit her lip. She was about to meet a duke—well, about to meet him properly. Adjusting and smoothing her crushed skirts, she nodded, and in what she hoped was her most regal stance, followed the secretary.

\*\*\*\*

Rhys stared at the name signed to the bottom of the dressmaker's bill.

*Mrs. Olivia Weston. Olivia...lovely.*

He had just managed to tug his cravat back into some reasonable fall and scrape his fingers through his hair when the knock came. Well, it would be over in a moment and his curiosity would be satisfied; this *modiste* would become all too mortal and his heart could stop its racing. Ready, steady— "Come," he said pulling at his cuffs and schooling his face into its most ducal expression. At the last instant, he plucked the heart-shaped case from his desk and shoved it in his pocket.

"Mrs. Olivia Weston, Your Grace." And the door clicked shut behind Wilcove.

His entire speech dried up in a heartbeat and lay like chalk upon his tongue. While his body, once again, rang like a soundly struck tuning fork, every nerve frizzled and too alive. He did not like the feeling.

Mrs. Weston seemed to be in a similar state, her mouth forming a perfect O.

He was trying to refute the notion of instant attraction when she laughed. Well, to be precise, it was more like one barking yelp. But the sound served to snap him back to reality. His vision narrowed on her now—thank God—firmly shut mouth. No one, not even a considerably more than indifferently pretty person, laughed at him. Most especially not a tradesperson. And decidedly not a woman.

"Madam? You find something amusing?"

She opened her mouth, then shut it and sank into an elegant curtsey.

As she rose, a shaft of sunlight pierced the gloom of late morning, bathing her neck. Dust motes drifted at the light's edges like demonic sprites, setting the stage to play havoc with his senses. Except he did not believe in sprites, demonic or otherwise. She swallowed. *How could a neck be that long? That white? What would that skin feel like against his lips? Taste like—*

"Pardon, Your Grace—water?" She made a show of clearing her throat, her hand waving through the beam of sun, making the sprites dance about.

He gestured to a small table and watched her profile as she selected a glass and poured the water.

Scrolling through a catalogue of Mrs. Weston's attributes, he frantically tried to fix on what about her person had put him in this state: lightish eyes—possibly green—dark, almost black hair, alabaster skin, that neck, graceful but not lush curves, an elegant bearing. But these he had seen a hundred times in a hundred other merely beautiful women. These were nothing compared to her—*what was the word?*

Bloody hell, he could not even think. This woman, this Mrs. Weston assaulted his senses. He had not had such a visceral response to a woman—well, ever. And he had seen her what...? Only at Crup's shop for possibly ten minutes and now for maybe the space of two?

Mrs. Weston set her glass down.

"I sometimes use my surname in order to remain anonymous." He thrust the words up like a shield, daring her to respond. She didn't.

Already a soft hint of her spicy scent wafted toward him. "I see you are not wearing your paisley shawl."

She moved her hands to touch her arms but dropped them abruptly. "No." She shook her head. "I mean, no, Your Grace."

"Did Mr. Crup prevail then?"

"Mr. Crup?" She frowned, and then her forehead cleared. "Oh, no. No, he did not."

"Ah," he said. She fidgeted with the edge of her sleeve. He would be content to watch her for hours. She frowned again, and her lips pursed ever so slightly. He was staring. "I am glad you still have it. You seemed very partial to it," he finished rather lamely. Well, at least he would not need to subject himself to Crup's yapping again. He had already been back to the shop, twice.

"I did not say I still had it, Your Grace. I only told you I did not sell it to Mr. Crup." She let her sleeve alone and clasped her hands in front of her. "He did not appreciate its value. I was able to find someone who did."

A dozen or so questions shuffled through his mind but only one slid out.

"Is there a Mr. Weston?"

"Pardon, Your Grace?"

"I assume the watch you sold is your husband's?"

She looked as if she would not make him an answer, but in the end his title must have won out over her need for privacy.

"Yes, it was."

"Won't he be sorry to lose such a prize?" His voice sounded sharp even to his ears.

"No, Your Grace, he will not. He is dead."

"Ah." Relief, absurd pleasure, and then guilt flooded through him. Afraid it might show, he nodded once and shifted a paper on his desk. She was waiting for him to speak again. Instead he sat.

His breeches felt inordinately tight. He glanced down at his lap and immediately pulled himself under cover. Clearly not having a woman in over a month was playing havoc with him.

"Mrs. Weston,"—his voice only slightly high— "my man informs me you feel you are owed compensation for gowns which a Mrs. Battersby ordered from you some weeks back. I have the bill here." His voice sped up. He took a breath.

"It is rather excessive for five gowns and various other odds and ends, but I understand they were needed immediately?" He did not pause for an answer. If he

28

did, he would have to look at her again, and he didn't think he could manage it without leaping over the desk to ascertain if her skin could possibly be as soft as it looked. "Do not accept any further trade from Mrs. Daria Battersby on my behalf. That—connection—ended some time ago."

He had to get out of this room. But he had a slight, or rather a stiff, problem…

He pressed his fingernail into the red and swollen wax burn on his wrist. Pain flashed, but unfortunately had no effect on his cock stand.

Lurching out of the chair, he grabbed the nearest sheet of paper from his desk and used it as a shield in front of his falls. He limped across the room and jerked at the bell pull. Thank God, Wilcove appeared a mere second later. "Wilcove, issue Mrs. Weston a draft for the specified funds. And show her out."

For the second time in a day, Wilcove's eyes widened, and his lips pursed ever so slightly before his face slid back to dead calm.

Rhys risked a look at her. Surely it would be safe now that he had his escape route.

It was a mistake. His throat constricted painfully, and panic bloomed in his gut. Suddenly he wanted to take his words back. He did not want Olivia Weston to disappear from his life a second time. He wanted her somehow tied to him. To need him.

"Your Grace, I cannot thank—"

He held up his hand as much to repel her as to stop her words. He needed to get out before he did something ridiculous—*more* ridiculous. He turned, crossed to the door on the opposite side of the room, pulled it open, and slipped into blessed solitude.

29

He pressed his back and arms against the door as if she had the power to seep through wood, to overwhelm him again.

*Green. Her eyes were most defiantly green.*

He needed a drink.

Rhys fumbled for the brandy, splashing some into a glass. He tossed it back, hoping to wash the woman out of his heated body. His eyes watered and throat burned, but he took another and then one more for good measure.

As he contemplated a fourth he saw, clenched in his other hand, the paper he had used as a shield. It was his uncle's letter.

He set down his glass and cracked the door, painfully aware he was behaving like a schoolboy. Good, she was gone.

He strode to his desk, swept the mess that was his life to one side, and began to answer Uncle Bertram's letter.

Yes, by God, he would be, "quite happy," the nib of the quill caught and ink spattered. Rhys bore down harder, "to meet Miss Arabella Campbell."

Chapter Four

A tiger—

Olivia squeezed her eyelids shut. *Idiot.* The worn leather seat of the carriage provided no comfort. She shifted pulling at her sleeve and then skirts. Her meticulous tailoring felt more like an ill-fitting sack whose seams puckered and twisted, the fabric chafing against her suddenly sensitive body.

For the third time, she drew open the strings of her reticule and pulled out the duke's draft, scanning the miraculous number written there. But the unsettled feeling remained.

Perhaps she should not have taken the cab? Admittedly an indulgence. She was contemplating knocking to have the driver stop when a bottle in an apothecary's shop window flared, catching a fragment of sun.

His eyes—very like the color of his eyes. Like nothing she had ever seen in a mere mortal.

Hmm…Possibly equal parts of sienna and umber, then a dab of blue-black and orange chrome yellow…or perhaps French ochre? Then a quantity of white lead. It had been so long since she had even thought of painting. Her fingers twisted in the strings of her purse, so eager to capture the exact hue.

*You find something amusing?* A shiver slid down her neck to her spine, taking a wicked detour straight to her breasts. She covered them with her arms, mashing them to submission.

"Three bob, Miss."

It was the driver. Good heavens, the Duke of Roydan was stalking her as surely as a tiger, even in the privacy of her hired carriage. She shook herself. "Ridiculous! I will never see him again," and she handed the driver his fare.

"Oh, if I had a penny for every time I heard them words—well I wouldn't be driving this here hack." He pulled at his cap, clucked to his horses, and moved off.

*Barmy bugger.* Olivia pushed into the shop.

It appeared no one was about.

"Egglet!" A rustle came from the back. She headed toward the sound. Eglantine was rising from the small pallet tucked against the far wall near the stove.

"Oh, lovey, you're back?" Egg pasted on a bright smile. Too bright.

"Where is Hazel? Oh, dearest, you are not well and have let the fire go out again." Olivia crossed to their small stack of precious firewood—Egg's lungs could never tolerate the dust and soot of coal. "Let me get you a cup with a bit of something."

"No, no, now settle yourself. I sent Hazel home as there was not much to do, and I must have dozed. My bones are not meant for this lumpy old cot," Egg said, rubbing her shoulder and smoothing her ruffled hair. "But enough about me, you must tell me the news. Were you successful?"

Olivia's deliciously teasing scenario, involving knights in shining armor, gnomes, and secret doors, missing swords and monks, dissolved as she saw the worry in her friend's eyes. Instead Olivia pulled out the draft and held it before Egg's nose.

"Feast your eyes on this, lovey," she said in her best cockney accent.

"Cor, blimey," Egg mimicked, "ain't you the cat's cream!" She took the draft from Olivia's outstretched hand. Egg's jaw dropped open like a nutcracker on Christmas, her gaze meeting Olivia's.

"Yes, love; it's the whole lot of it." The women had resigned themselves to only partial payment for the bill, if indeed they were to get any of it.

"You must tell me everything. Did you actually see the duke himself? Is he the Monk everyone claims him to be?"

A *monk?*

Olivia hesitated. "No, he does not inspire *heavenly* thoughts."

"Go on. Tell me everything." But Egg had begun to cough, her small frame racked with heavy rolling hacks.

Olivia made herself go numb. She waited silently, willing herself to remain calm. Egg hated for a fuss to be made over her "little spells."

"Here now, you are dead on your feet from worry and exhaustion." Olivia handed Egg some cold tea. "There is time enough for talk and celebrating later after you've had a good long rest."

"But, Olive—"

Olivia narrowed her gaze and cocked her head. Her friend sighed and squeezed Olivia's hand. "Very well, I suppose you are right and not to be gainsaid. I will be a good egg and take myself up for a quick nap. But I expect to be ready for the full details this evening."

"I promise to rival the great actress Mrs. Siddons with my telling, but only if you rest."

Olivia stood by the narrow window waiting for Egg's wheezes to settle into soft snores.

Across the narrow alley, a stray breeze hit a broken window pane, fluttering the dingy black-gray curtain behind. The gray flashed a moment of brilliant blue—the inner protected fold of the curtain—like a bit of open sky against relentless gloom. The curtain was not dull from sunlight; there was none that could penetrate the tight confines of the alley. It was colored with the black soot that rolled down window panes, settled on sills, and penetrated curtains. And lungs.

Suddenly the window was thrust open and a chamber pot emptied. Somewhere inside, a child cried out and the window slammed shut.

Olivia turned to now-sleeping Egg. She gently pulled the old coverlet up under her dear one's chin.

Eglantine was just on the far side of fifty now and was at last beginning to look it. She had always been sweetly rounded—her Egg, as she had christened her long ago—but now she looked gaunt, her skin loose and gray. Olivia could not bear the thought of life without Eglantine Wiggins. This frail woman was Olivia's home. No matter where they had lived, an army tent or lovely rooms in Saint Germaine, Egg had been her rock—sharing grief over the loss of their husbands and then Olivia's child...

Ah, dear Jamie.

Olivia blinked and swallowed hard. She had hoped they would be able to make a good living in London and eventually put down some roots in the country. But now, looking at Egg, she saw that was impossible.

Olivia sank to her knees beside the bed and whispered to her sleeping friend, "By God, Egglet, I will get you out of this foul city if it is the last thing I do."

****

"Oooof!" Daria Battersby clenched her teeth, her hands twisting in the sheets.

"Ah, you like a bit of rough play, do you, my plump partridge?"

*Plump Partridge?* She turned her head aside as much from Lord Acton's sour breath as from his words.

Daria's newest "beau" settled in again to pull and grunt over her breasts, his mouth too wet, his hands like a cold, flaccid pudding.

Her gaze drifted to the familiar painting on the wall next to her bed. A pink-cheeked girl of several decades ago was being pushed on a swing by a young gentleman. Her mouth was open in laughter, her limbs fully extended as she leaned back into his attentive eyes. Daria could not make out the girl's subtler expressions any longer, no matter how hard she squinted. But there was no need; she knew the bliss and easy confidence reflected in the young woman's face.

She used to be that girl. Why, men had clamored for just a *smile* from her. She could have had anyone. Indeed, puritanical, mad King George had even given her the eye once or twice.

But she had only wanted one man. The man who had wanted nothing to do with her, the one they called the Monk, Rhys Merrick, the Duke of Roydan. And, by Jove, she had got him. So what if she knew he had taken her mostly out of revenge, so what if he was cold and withdrawn. *She* had succeeded where no other woman had.

Yet she did not live in a fairy world. She was a

35

practical business woman. She needed to be careful after Roydan. She could not afford the gossip of another jilt. Not at her age. She would be…dear God, thirty-five this July, a perilous age for a woman of her profession. Every assignation must be dissected and analyzed. She needed to choose her new protector wisely.

"My dear," Acton wheezed, "my stays, could you loosen them just a trifle? I know you are eager as I for 'wee' Charlie to find his snug little bed."

Daria squeezed her eyes shut. "Oh my, sir, you are a card. You well know there is naught that's *wee* about dearest delectable Charlie," she whispered in his grotty ear as she jerked at the tapes of his stays.

"Heh-heh." His belly spilled forth, pooling over her as a sigh hissed from between his fleshy lips.

Daria reached down between her legs. *Sweet Jezebel.* She was dry. Dry as a bone. She felt for the edge of the table next to her bed and homed in on the small pot near the lamp. She had much rather minister to the old sot with her mouth and have it done with. But his lordship seemed to prefer the old-fashioned way. She quickly slathered the salve on her quim.

"Ah, it looks as if young Charles might need a little coaxing to find his way," the old man said, shifting his considerable weight off her and back on the bed. "Do you think you could persuade him, my duck? He sometimes can be quite naughty."

Daria bit her lip and wrapped her hand around his miserable pizzle. *Hell, it would be a very long afternoon.*

*Damn Roydan for submitting her to these has-beens!* She felt the beginnings of tears. Disastrous. She never cried. Tears, she had learnt at a very tender age, lead to nothing. All that messy emotion left you exposed, like a gutted fish. Daria Battersby would not go down without a fight. Actions were what were needed now—*Not* Actons! *Plump partridge, indeed.*

"Out!"

"What, my duck?"

"I said out!"

His lordship blinked. She pushed at his bulging belly and heaved him off. "Wee Charlie must find another place to rest his thoroughly limp head."

By Jupiter, she would make that superior Monk beg to have her back.

Chapter Five

Rhys hadn't needed to bestir himself by traveling to the Campbells in Dorset; the possibility of having an alliance with the great house of Roydan had brought the family scurrying from their country rustication and into the throng of the London season.

He stood in the doorway of the Campbell's blue and gold withdrawing room as the butler announced him. All conversation stopped except for one poor man who must be hard of hearing. His partner gave him a swift elbow and after a shocked "I say!" he turned to see the commotion—or rather the absence of commotion.

"Your Grace." An extremely tall woman sailed across the room towing a girl behind her. "I am Lady Campbell. We are so delighted you could join us."

Rhys bowed. "Lady Campbell."

"May I present my daughter, Arabella?"

The girl stepped around her mother's skirts and Rhys's first impression was the absurdity of this mother attached to this child. Rhys bowed and the girl performed her curtsey. As she rose, her plumed headdress brushed his nose. Rhys guessed the feathers were worn to make her appear at least a reasonable height. But other than her short stature and perhaps a rather silly gown, all ruffles and yards of fussy lace—definitely overkill on such a lush figure—Rhys conceded the Campbell's only child was near perfect. Her eyes were bright china blue, her complexion flawless, her hair blonde, and when she smiled, a dimple appeared in her left cheek.

Rhys was used to astonished admiration from the female sex. He was not a vain man, but he knew, at least initially, his physical person inspired sighs and once even a swoon from the female population. However, he did not detect a flicker of interest from this girl beyond a tepid smile.

It might not be such a bad match. At least one of the perks of being a duke was that he was not required to do a lot of silly wooing. Rhys held no illusions of marital bliss and devoted companionship. He needed an heir and, he supposed, a spare to fulfill his duty. The girl certainly looked healthy enough, and though they did not seem to inspire lust in each other, they might rub on well enough. Perhaps they could get right on to the business of contracts?

Why then did he feel so bloody empty?

"I believe this is your first season, Miss Campbell?" he said, when they were finally seated next to each other in the dining room. He tried to concentrate on the girl through the beginnings of a sick headache.

"It is, Your Grace." She met his eyes square on with nary a giggle.

"And only just seventeen, Your Grace." His headache flared in his left temple. The mother. Again. Rhys pushed aside the turtle soup and turned politely to his hostess who fluttered her eyelashes. *Was the woman attempting to flirt with him?* "How I remember my own come out not so many years ago. And now, to have a full grown daughter..." She dribbled off, no doubt waiting for his gushing reply as to the impossibility of having an offspring so old.

He turned back to the daughter. "And do you have a favorite place in London?"

"The British Museum," she said decisively. "But unfortunately I have been only once. I am far too occupied with dressmakers these days."

Well, they had one thing in common.

"Arabella is to make her curtsey soon." Rhys tried to ignore the harpy, but her daughter merely sighed and applied herself to her soup. Years of breeding won out, and he turned once again to her ladyship. "Too soon by half," she continued. "We have engaged Madame Broussard for the gown. She came highly recommended by Lady Hepplewhit..."

Lady Campbell continued to fill his ear instead of her mouth.

He shifted, feeling for his watch under his napkin, as the footmen removed the soup. Rhys flipped it open. His death's-head case—how fitting for this dinner—the domed ivory skull hinged open to reveal the watch's face.

Presently, the Tompion Heart's works were still strewn helter-skelter about his desk. He had made a total hash of his carefully ordered plan of reassembly. And to make matters worse, he had still not found the balance wheel that had fallen to the floor when *she* invaded his life.

Mrs. Weston. Seamstress. *Modiste. Mantua-maker.* Devil.

He snapped the watch shut. Two minutes since the last time he'd checked.

*He had no other appointment.*

Rhys resisted the urge to squeeze the bridge of his nose and instead took another sip of wine. A sea of nodding heads and smiling faces looked eagerly up from their dinners.

Why did he feel so separate from these people?

A plain, rather toothy girl, seated below the salt, gave Rhys a cow-eyed look and tittered. He considered the effort of raising an eyebrow, but Lady Campbell was there before him. At her slight cough, the chit darted her gaze to her hostess and then ducked her head to contemplate her partridge and extreme folly.

"My dear Roydan, won't you try the aspic?" Her ladyship signaled to the footman who brought the dish between them. "It is an old family recipe. I am sure I have been asked, I know not how many times, to divulge the ingredients. However, I have never faltered in my resolve that it should stay within the *family*." She gave him a covert look. When he did not partake, she took it upon herself to delve out a portion.

The mess lay quivering on his plate. The pink, glistening flesh pocked with whitish globs. Very much like Daria Battersby's thighs.

"But I will give you a hint, it contains—"

Bile rose and Rhys gestured for more wine catching Uncle Bert's gaze in the process.

"Lady Campbell," Bert said, "I must ask what the spice is in the ragout of beef?" The woman thankfully turned to poor Uncle Bert.

Rhys took another swig of wine. Mercifully, Olivia Weston's image easily replaced Daria's. The dressmaker was nestled quite close to the forefront of his brain, like a brand. And if he was totally forthright, and he always tried to be, it was branded a good deal lower as well. *Damn it!*

His plan of yesterday had been a complete, unmitigated disaster.

He would drive by her shop. He would wait there until he saw her again. And then, upon seeing her, he would see she was nothing special, that there was nothing there to keep him tossing on the rack every night plagued by the notion he was missing a vital part of himself. She would be reduced to a mere seamstress. A seamstress well past her first flush of youth. He would be able to get on with things—his life, his marriage, and subsequent progeny. And most of all, Valmere would be saved.

But there he sat, huddled in his carriage like a besotted fool, drooling and breathless. Over a nobody!

And she had not been alone. She was with a man. A rather well-looking man, if one's tastes tended to red-headed dandies.

Rhys's teeth met and ground. Mrs. Weston might be a widow, but it did not necessarily follow she was also lonely.

He could still see her laughing. A doubled-over, arms-hugging-sides kind of laugh. The sound was brilliant sunshine, shattering the dullness surrounding her. She'd pushed the man in a teasing manner and deftly ducked as he tried to push back. Rhys yearned to be in that bright space of light—to be the one bathed in her joy, her animation.

He pressed his temple, willing logic to vanquish his rioting thoughts.

"Well, ladies," Lady Campbell said, "I think we should leave these men to their port and talk of politics while we have our tea. If you will excuse us, gentlemen?" Footmen scrambled to assist the company. "You will not be too long, my lord?" she said to her husband. It was by no means a question.

Rhys returned to his seat and reached for the rounded bowl of the goblet that had been set in front of him. He declined the cigar.

What he wouldn't give for a nice pipe with his old steward Mac, a good stout ale, and a well-aged peat fire. He took a swallow, hoping it would settle his stomach. It didn't.

Dash it all, his watch case was open again. Closing his fist around it, he shifted in his seat and stretched his cramped legs. Heavy cigar smoke and talk of prison hulks wafted around him, both threatening to send him to the nearest chamber pot.

*Thirteen minutes past eleven...*

What was *she* doing now? Was she with the ginger-haired man? Was she laughing again? Teasing him? Kissing him? Tugging off his coat, her hands raking through his hair? Hair now turned from red to dark black—*his* hair, *his* lips...

Rhys was jerked from his reverie by the scraping of a chair and the servants bustling to assist the gentlemen.

"Shall we go in to the ladies, Roydan?" Lord Campbell's face disappeared in the haze of smoke as he rose and stubbed out the nub of his cigar. The other gentlemen, following his cue, began to rise as well.

Rhys must have stood, along with everyone else. Lord Campbell, his expectant face wreathed in smoke, made Rhys's stomach roil as sweat beaded his upper lip, his collar and cravat strangling him.

*Damn it, he should never have paid Olivia Weston.* Stupidly, he had given her the money in trade for some bloody peace. Ha! Far easier to make his clock work without a bloody balance wheel. Instead he had lost her, lost his money; hell, he didn't even have the gowns he'd spent a small fortune on.

He needed air. Rhys could not face what awaited him in the drawing room—the ladies and the nauseating small talk that went with tea and courtship. It was too soon. It was all happening too soon.

He wanted to see *her*. His need speared through the haze like a window thrust open to the cool fresh wind. The pounding in his head stopped. Rhys had sudden clarity, but more importantly, he had another plan.

"Your pardon, Lord Campbell, gentlemen. I am afraid I must excuse myself. I am not feeling well."

Lord Campbell's expectant face crumpled. "Should I have a doctor called in, Roydan? Perhaps you only need some air or to lie down for a moment?" He started to signal to a nearby footman.

"No, no, I do not wish to disturb you or your guests. I am sure all I need is a quiet night of rest in my own bed."

Uncle Bert moved to him. "You do look a bit pale, Roydan. I will see you home and rejoin the party."

"No, Uncle. I insist you stay. It is nothing." Rhys turned to Campbell. "If you will have my carriage called, I will be on my way." His lordship looked rather pale himself. "Lord Campbell, will you please make my apologies to her ladyship and to Miss Campbell? It has been a delightful evening."

He made his bows and strode out of the room, with perhaps a shade too much vigor, remembering Uncle Bert's frown and pursed lips. Well, it could not be helped.

By God, he already felt lighter.

****

The shop bell jangled. Olivia jerked up. "Blast!" A perfect pearl of red oozed from her finger. She quickly stuck it in her mouth and sucked. Heavens, if any blood had gotten on the bodice, she would—well, she would start over, of course.

She squinted to see the clock—was it after eleven? Plague take it, Egg should be fast asleep, not risking her health to come and fetch Olivia to bed. There was nothing for it; Olivia would have to take Egg's scolding.

"Yes, I know I am late, but you should not have come." In truth, she was happy to be rescued from the infuriating scrap of silk and lace that simply refused to lie properly. She took a moment of pleasure as she jabbed pins into the dress. "Give me a moment to tidy up," she called out, suddenly realizing she was bone tired, her eyes gravelly and burning. "You cannot know how eager I am to be in bed."

Utter silence.

Olivia froze in the midst of throwing a cover over the dress.

"Egglet?"

Nothing.

She dumped the cover on the table and moved to the door, grabbing a lamp and the heavy fire poker that stood propped by the entryway. Surely Egg had turned the sign to Closed and locked the shop door in the vestibule before going above stairs? They would have a laugh when Olivia appeared ready to brain her dearest friend. Still, Olivia braced herself and walked through the doorway.

It was not Eglantine.

It was a *he*. And he was huge, his shadow looming over a good half of the shop's ceiling. *He* was His Grace, the Duke of Roydan. She barely registered the sound of the poker as it struck the floor with a resounding *thunk*.

"I collect you were expecting someone else."

Chapter Six

His voice curled around her.

Olivia blinked and remembered to breathe. "Your Grace—" And then her brain, along with her voice, failed her. A pity her eyes didn't fail her as well, so extraordinary was the picture before her. This man, this *personage*, in her shop, so casually removing his gloves and hat, as if it were some drawing room in Mayfair in the middle of the day, instead of a dim shop tucked in an obscure corner of Cheapside well after eleven of the clock.

"Your Grace," she tried again, "this is most unexpected." He did not deign to answer. Well, to be fair, it was not strictly a question. She tried again. "Isn't it rather late, Your Grace?"

"Is it? I hadn't noticed." He frowned, absently smoothing his gloves as he glanced about the shop, clearly irritated at something. He paced between a set of gilt chairs and the large cutting table, stopped, turned with military precision, and barked, "I assume you were expecting your lover?"

"I beg your pardon?"

"Your lover, madam."

*Lover? What the dev*—oh God, the "eager to be in bed" when she had thought he was Egg. She fought the creeping blush that was no doubt staining her hot cheeks, but lost the battle. He stood there like some sort of poised tiger—*Blast!*

The audacity of this man. He was waiting for her to give him an answer to her *private* affairs? Olivia drew herself up. She owed this man nothing. She was just about to tell him so when she thought of the bill he had settled—the monies that had saved the shop. *His* funds.

She took a breath and set the lamp down. "No, Your Grace. I have no lover. I had assumed you were my partner, Mrs. Eglantine Wiggins, returning for me."

He stopped twisting his gloves, and his shoulders dropped the barest fraction. He turned away from her.

She watched his reflection in the darkened front window as he carefully smoothed and laid his mauled gloves in his beaver hat and then placed the articles with infinite care on the small table nestled between twin chairs. He lightly brushed the satinwood scroll at the table's edge with his long, now bare fingers as he slowly straightened.

"Ah," he finally said, still facing the window.

"Yes, Your Grace."

A pause.

"Egglet? An unfortunate name."

"Yes, I suppose, Your Grace." An impatient edge had crept into her voice. Well what could the man possibly want? And at this time of night?

Their reflected eyes caught in the window. One square pane held the picture of her pale face cast in a frown, while another showed his portrait of utter calm. She tried to smooth her brow to match his.

"I have come for the gowns," he said.

Her frown slipped back into place, now even deeper. "The gowns?"

He turned, still implacable. "Yes, Mrs. Weston, the

gowns I purchased from you five days ago."

"But, Your Grace, they are no longer here." She swallowed against the lump in her throat. "I thought you understood they are with Mrs. Battersby."

"I understand no such thing. I purchased the gowns—five to be exact—and a number of other female fripperies. Those I will forgive, but the gowns, I must have. I have come to claim them."

"Your Grace, I do not know what to say." *Surely he would be reasonable?* "The gowns were delivered to Mrs. Battersby more than a month ago. You cannot expect me to retrieve them at this point." She tried to make her words not sound like a question.

Oh God, he was going to demand his money back, and it was almost entirely gone. Used to pay debts, buy tea and candles, fabric and notions.

*Damn the man!* She prided herself on her calmness under fire. She was simply overtired, that was all. She must think. She must say the right combination of words so he would pick up his hat and gloves and leave and never return.

He fished his watch out of his waistcoat but never looked at it. "I see."

He *saw*…? Oh, thank goodness. He understood and she had her reprieve. He would take himself off now.

But he did not. He lowered himself, folding all six and more feet, into the nearest of the gilt chairs. He looked absurd. Like a giant come to play in a nest of gnomes. His fingers absently found and stroked the bloody table again. Her nipples tightened. And though his molten gaze never left hers, she would swear he knew exactly what was happening under her bodice.

"It would appear you have a problem, madam."

Olivia pulled herself up, hoping to restore her equilibrium, and took her firmest tone. "Your Grace, I am unable to return your funds. They are long spent."

"Mrs. Weston, I do not require the funds." He waved his hand dismissively. "What I require are the gowns. I paid for them, is it not right and just I possess them?"

"For that I am very much afraid you will have to apply to Mrs. Battersby, Your Grace. Now if you'll be—"

"Nay, madam, I apply to you," he said looking directly into her eyes.

Her mind raced, conjuring dire scenarios. The Marshalsea prison. The duke blacklisting her. Being tossed out of their lodgings, their possessions sold for a mere pittance. Or worse, flung into the street to be snatched up by street urchins and she and Egg left to beg.

In the midst of her tragedy, the duke dramatically raised one eyebrow. He, no doubt, used that considerable weapon to silence all his numerous minions. Well, she would not be so cowed.

"Have you nothing else to compensate me with?" he asked, as if he were mentioning the weather.

Olivia's whirring mind stopped dead. Ah...*now* we have it. Her vision narrowed. The bloody cheek of the man.

"Surely you have something you can barter with, Mrs. Weston?" he continued, paying not the slightest attention to her most lethal stare.

Two could play this game. "I am a dressmaker, Your Grace. I make and sell dresses. That is the full extent of my commerce."

He steepled his large, square hands under his chin, his longest finger resting lightly against his lips. *Lord, he had beautiful lips.* Their perfection infuriated her. What was worse, the man seemed to have no notion of the havoc his innocent gesture wreaked within her body. Why could his lips not be thin and bloodless as dry biscuits? She found herself licking her own. Did he not even mean to reply?

"Then I suppose you must make me a gown or two." He raised his eyebrow again as he stroked his bottom lip.

*What?* She dragged her gaze from his mouth; had she heard him properly? This was utter nonsense, "Your Grace, I am unable to comprehend your request."

He stopped stroking—praise God—and raised his eyebrow a fraction higher, if possible.

"You cannot be serious?"

"I believe I must be, since you claim to have no other talents with which to recompense me," he said, with not even a hint of a smile.

To her horror she blushed, again. *Damned infernal ape.* By God, she would checkmate him yet.

"Very well, Your Grace, I have several gowns on hand I use as models. You may have those. I will send them to you in the morning. Now, it is very late, and I'm quite sure you have more pressing things to occupy your time, so I will bid you good night, sir."

"You are in error, madam." He shifted slightly in the small chair. "I have nothing pressing. I will see the gowns now, Mrs. Weston."

"*Now,* Your Grace?"

"Yes, unless I am keeping you from a paramour?"

"As I said before, I have no lover. It is simply that

it is late, and no doubt Mrs. Wiggins will be worrying by now."

"I'm sure a few moments longer will not be amiss." However, he must have seen she was very near the end of her rope. "Very well, I will see *one* of the gowns tonight. After all, I want to be sure of the quality of garment I have purchased."

This man was insufferable.

"As you wish, Your Grace." Olivia turned to leave the room.

"And Mrs. Weston"—his voice plunged to an impossible low—"I wish to see the gown on."

She turned to face him then, sure she would see a smirk on his face, but she was disappointed.

"You will model it for me."

The man was dead serious. At this point she would do anything—well, almost anything—to get him out of her shop. She turned without a word and pushed through the curtained door.

*Saint Anne, give me strength.*

She clenched her shaking hands and took a gulp of air as if she had been held under water.

What to choose? The black cherry tiffany would have to do. It was the most circumspect of the dresses available. The wafer-thin silk leapt to her skin like a magnet, clinging to her fingers, showing every knuckle and sinew. She shook it off, and the silk crackled as if alive.

Heat gathered in her body. Well, and why not. She was certainly entitled to some anger. However this heat didn't feel like anger. Her traitorous body felt so *alive,* so *primed.* Not only were her breasts so sensitive she wanted to claw them, her tiredness seemed to have evaporated into thin air. By God, she could run to Richmond. And back.

She peeled down her bodice, and then her chemise. She wore no stays. Her fingers grazed her ruched nipples, and her insides performed a flip.

"Damnation!" Skirts and petticoats dropped to the floor.

"Do you need assistance, Mrs. Weston?"

She froze in the middle of her pooled skirts, ready to snatch them up should he dare to breech the back room. The muscles in her thighs clenched along with her jaw. Sure enough she saw the tips of his evening shoes just under the curtain. "No, Your Grace." Lud, she was as skittish as a chicken on Sunday.

His spotless pumps finally disappeared, and she expelled her pent up breath in a rush.

As the tiffany slid down over her breasts, past her belly and hips, over her thighs to brush her ankles, she knew it was perfect. It was made for her—for her body.

She ran her finger over the ribbon that wove cunningly through a channel in the bodice, and then formed small loops to hold on the tiny sleeves, continuing to the back of the gown where it plunged well below the middle of the back and tied in a bow, its ends fluttering almost to the floor. This one ribbon held the dress in place. She had spent hours engineering the whole thing to drop with one deft pull.

Olivia jerked at the ribbon forcing it into a less than ideal bow.

She did not spare a moment to glance in the mirror. If she had, she likely would not have gone through the door at all. A hairpin pinged to the floor; at the same time she felt a long looping curl graze her shoulder. She shoved it aside, jerked her skirts up to retrieve the pin, and then stopped.

By God, she would not take the time or effort to cater to *him*. The duke would have to take her as he found her. She threw back her hair and marched out of the workroom.

He was examining a sketch on the cutting table when he turned toward her. He stood utterly still, gaping like a great hulking lummox. The paper fluttered to the floor.

Olivia clenched her teeth. Not only was her physical person on display, but her livelihood and way of life as well. So be it. She resolutely kept her arms at her sides.

What did he expect? Yards of ribbons, ruffles and bows? The demimonde was her niche. And rather than sell herself on her back she chose instead to clothe the women who did.

She raised her chin. "As you see, Your Grace, there is nothing inferior here. I am quite proud of my workmanship, and this design in particular is a favorite of the gentlemen.

"The gentlemen?" The gape collapsed into a scowl.

"Yes. And the ladies as well—my patronesses. In Paris I was quite sought after. I'm sure I will have the same following here in London, as soon as I can properly circulate."

"Circulate?"

Was he addlepated? He seemed capable of only one-word rejoinders.

"Yes." She tried speaking to him as if he were a small child incapable of comprehension. "Mrs. Battersby was a great coup for our shop. But now she has lost your protection, Mrs. Wiggins and I will simply have to begin anew. Now, Your Grace, will you take the gown?"

Reason told her only a few seconds could have passed as they stood, his gaze locked to hers in a stalemate, but it seemed interminable.

Finally his jaw twitched.

"Could you move, please?" Was it her imagination, or was his voice higher than usual? Then what he actually said registered.

"*Move?*"

"Yes. Could you move across the room? I find to judge a garment, or anything properly, one must see it in motion." Her face must have reflected horror, for he hastened on, "You would not expect me to buy a horse simply by looking at its lines would you, Mrs. Weston? I would wish to see it run as well. I'm sure you understand."

*Blast him and his bloody horses.* She strode forward, happy to vent some of her anger in movement; however, she realized a split second too late there was nowhere *to* move. The receiving room was not large and was mostly taken up with the cutting table. The only area with any appreciable room was at the far end of the shop where the huge paneled mirrors stood. He was standing directly in the path that would be her best direction. Consequently, she found herself almost flush up against him.

She knew he was tall. Any fool could see the man was at least two or more inches over six feet, but from this vantage point—directly beneath him—he was so *very* tall. She could smell the starch of his shirt mixed with a faint whiff of smoke and possibly brandy. She

slid her gaze over the shirt and waistcoat to his cravat—
a conservatively tied Oriental—to the firm, slightly
cleft chin, moving on to the lips, very swiftly past
those, and finally resting on his eyes. Pure molten gold.
Yes, exactly like those of the Burmese tiger she had
seen at a menagerie in Paris. His bearing was just as
predatory.

"It would appear, sir, in order for me to *move*, as
you require, you will have to bestir yourself as well."

She thought she saw one side of his mouth shift
ever so slightly upward into what might be the merest
twitch of a smile. She could not be one hundred percent
sure because, to do so, she would have to look at his
lips. The duke shifted his weight and made a small bow.
Her shoulder brushed the superfine of his midnight blue
jacket as she hurriedly squeezed past him.

She strode almost to the mirrors before wheeling
around and giving him what she hoped was an
accusatory look.

"Well, Your Grace. I hope you are satisfied."

"Satisfied, Mrs. Weston?" He raised that infernal
eyebrow. "Oh no, madam, I am very far from satisfied.
However, I am hopeful I will be, in the not so distant
future." Again his gaze raked over her. "Yes, I do live
in hope." He turned and began to gather his things.
"You may send this gown to me in the morning."

"But won't you want the young woman to come in
for a fitting?"

The duke stopped in the middle of donning his left
glove. He looked at her as if she was being deliberately
obtuse or worse, coy, and once more raised that bloody
eyebrow. She chose to ignore his rapier-like weapon.

"Your Grace, this gown is deceptive in its

simplicity. It looks uncomplicated, but in fact it requires, at the very least, one fitting to assure it hangs properly. I will not send out a gown that does not fit perfectly. You must understand I have my reputation to think of."

Hot brandy eyes seared hers. "Madam, believe me, I am very cognizant of your reputation. As a *modiste* you need not fear," he said as he slowly drew on his left glove and flexed his fingers. "I assure you the gown will fit like this glove."

With that, he turned and opened the door.

"I will be back for the next gown tomorrow. Shall we say at the same time?"

He clearly did not need or require an answer. Olivia's mouth dropped open as the shop door closed, its jangle of bells mocking her frayed nerves.

Oh God, it was not over. Not nearly over. In fact, it seemed the Duke of Roydan had just begun.

Chapter Seven

As the shop door shut behind Rhys, the blessed night air hit his heated cheeks, and he sucked the cold into his body.

The possibility she might be waiting for a lover had thrown him off stride and nearly had him abandoning his whole plan. He could still hear her voice ringing from the back room—"so eager to be in bed."

James, his footman, jumped down from his perch, but Rhys waved the coach on. The idea of being cooped up in a carriage with his thoughts set his teeth on edge.

*Blistering Hell, who was this Lothario who had taken over his body?*

He was not one of these mercurial dandies who could shape themselves and their behavior to the company and situation. He had no seductive and suggestive rhetoric. He was himself, always.

A thought, like a fist to his gut, stopped him dead.

*By God, had he aped his sire?*

It could not be. He was so vigilant. But still, as he took one step and then another, he could not shake the feeling, as if he had put on an ill-fitting and gaudy suit of clothes.

James pulled his forelock as the horses and carriage passed by. Rhys stared at the matched pair's glossy and rippling flanks.

*Dear Heavens, he had asked her to move.* Heat

flooded his body in another rush, and he tugged at his cravat. Likely a blast sent up from his father in Hell.

The image of Mrs. Weston, framed in that curtained doorway, had slammed into him as soundly as John Jackson's left hook when the man was dead sober. But as she had pushed past him, striding down the long, narrow hall, she had proved to be a true thoroughbred. Yes, this was a horse he would buy in a heartbeat.

If possible, the gown had been more fetching from the rear, revealing a good bit of Olivia Weston's back and backside, held up by very long legs. He had never seen fabric that appeared to be liquid, as if the dress had been poured over her body. What a contrast plump little Arabella Campbell was in her fussy dress and feathers. This gown's only ornament, a silk bow tied just below a sweet, heart-shaped birthmark more than halfway down her milk-white back.

Rhys clenched his hands, fingers still aching to pull that delicate ribbon.

He sucked in another draft of air. And when he asked her for *other* compensation—Rhys winced. That he had actually uttered those words without collapsing was a minor miracle.

She had pokered up immediately. He suspected she would. She was no loose woman. Indeed, he would have been disappointed if she hadn't been offended. He *was* offensive.

As the Duke of Roydan, he simply ordered exactly what was needed and it was done with no question or fuss. His deepest wants, he simply denied. Easy as well. Oh, but if only he could say, "Mrs. Weston, I require you to lie beneath me, utterly naked while I push into your pretty, sweet—" His cock jumped like a dog for a bone.

"You cankerous pimp!" The shout came from just above him. Brakes ground, horses screamed, and black iron hooves slashed the air mere inches from his head. Rhys threw himself back and away.

His hip cracked painfully against the paving stones of the road. Horse breath blew hard in Rhys's face as its huge head bobbed. Its hooves clattered, scrambling to gain footing. Rhys instinctively held up his hand. "Easy now. Easy," he breathed. Images and sounds clicked one after another building a picture for his muzzy brain. He had nearly been trampled to death.

"Bloody beetle-head!" The hack's driver spit the words at Rhys. "Would serve you right to have your head bashed in. Full of nothing but air by the looks of you. Wandering in the bloody street as if you owned the world."

The coach door flung open. A pink-slippered foot and white-stockinged ankle thrust out of the doorway only to be jerked back inside, punctuated by a delighted squeal. A shot of mingled laughter foamed over the driver's curses as the coach rocked.

"All right. Out you go," said the driver. "This rig ain't no bawdy house."

More laughter and then a man jumped out and reached up to swing his paramour down. The couple appeared oblivious to Rhys and his near death. The man only paused in his ardent lovemaking to carelessly flip a coin at the driver who dove to catch the silver causing the horses to jerk in their traces. Rhys vaguely heard the driver yell another epithet. Whether it was meant for Rhys or in response to the man's form of payment was unclear. Still muttering, the cabbie moved his fractious horses up the lane.

Rhys took stock of his pounding heart and his torn and bleeding palms. He jerked off his ruined gloves and tossed them aside. They lay pale and otherworldly against the filth of the street. He flicked a bit of moldering potato peel from his breeches and picked himself up, testing his legs. He stumbled toward his hat, which had rolled a good twenty feet down the street.

The couple entered an alleyway just in front of him. Rhys should move on. It was patently clear the woman wanted this encounter.

But he did not move. Instead he retreated to a shadowed alcove.

It was over quickly. Truly, there had not been much to see, just a tug of her skirts and then the pumping of hips, a heavy grunt and clothes hastily righted and smoothed.

As they passed his hiding place, their arms clasped about each other, Rhys pushed farther back into the shadows. However, just as he thought he was safe, the woman looked back, tipped her head, and made a soft clicking sound with her tongue. Then she smiled right into his eyes.

Rhys remained frozen to the wall until their footsteps and soft laughter faded and then died.

He waited ten more seconds and snapped his head back. Cracking pain shot through his skull to his teeth and jaw. He pressed his raw palms to the wall and raked them over the coarse and tearing brick. But the pain did no good; it could not blot out his vulgar spying, or deny the heavy throbbing of his cock.

He had tried to dam up his natural urges. Tried to divert that raging river into smaller, more manageable streams—streams of intellect, exercise and duty. But this new need terrified him.

This desire was not in response to a common street woman. He had—or used to have—Daria for that. If only it were just a physical craving. But it wasn't. Olivia Weston drew him as no other woman had. Her tenacity, her loyalty, her sense of fair play, her biting humor, the way she impatiently brushed the hair from her face…

By God, it was as if a carefully tended dam, built up over many years, had suddenly burst and his enormous need of this woman rushed out to drown him.

Rhys pushed himself away from the wall, and brushed off his hat. *Lock and Company*. He ran his finger over the label. A gentleman's hat, the very height of civilization. He carefully settled it squarely on his head. He would put this Mrs. Olivia Weston behind him. He would govern himself and be honorable in his pursuit of Arabella Campbell. His title demanded it of him, and his father could continue to roast in Hell where he belonged.

****

He was late. Nearly gone midnight. Not that the duke had set a specific time and not that Olivia was expecting him. After all he was a duke. Dukes did not have time for mere *modistes*. She was really relieved. She was—

*Was that a noise in the street?* Foolish girl. She moved to snuff the lamp.

The jangling bells sent her heart almost out of her chest and the lamp to the floor. Jesus, Mary, and Joseph, he was here. So be it.

But this time she was ready. Ready for his height

and breadth. Ready for his deep, liquid voice. Even ready for his eyes—well almost—but, nonetheless, she must face him. Squaring her shoulders, she parted the curtain and walked though.

Her mouth dried up, her heart skipped several beats, her breasts tightened under her severe bodice, and the man hadn't even turned around. Yes, things were going swimmingly.

She cleared her throat.

He was putting a basket on the small table near the shop's front door. He seemed in no hurry and finally turned toward her.

She focused on his chin. "Your Grace, I have taken the liberty of modeling the second dress to save us both valuable time. As you can see it is extremely fine workmanship, if I do say so myself." She took a much needed breath. "Now if you would excuse me, I will remove myself to the back room and pack it up for you." Olivia turned to go.

"Mrs. Weston?"

"Yes, Your Grace?" she barely glanced in the duke's direction.

"Do you take me for a fool?"

"Why no, Your Grace."

"Excellent. I am happy to hear it."

"I will not be but a moment." She took another step, her only thought, escape.

"Mrs. Weston."

Damn. She turned back again. "Yes, Your Grace?"

"I believe that is a day gown suitable for walking or perhaps riding in a carriage?"

"Why, yes, you are correct." She resumed her exit to freedom. "I will only be a moment."

"Mrs. Weston."

She stopped again and jerked the curtain to the back room open. The sound of its rings clattering together lent a certain satisfaction to her mood.

"While I will grant you the—stitching—seems very fine, that is not the gown I bought."

"I do beg your pardon, but how would you know specifically what was ordered?"

"True, I am unaware of the exact specifics, but I know that gown is unsatisfactory."

"Unsatisfactory?"

"You are very keen, Mrs. Weston. Unsatisfactory is precisely what I said." How he managed this rejoinder without the slightest hint of sarcasm, she would never know.

However, it did not stop her from using a liberal dose. "And, pray tell me, Your Grace, what precisely is so unsatisfactory?"

"Well, madam, the simple fact it is a carriage dress."

"Ah-h-h." So that way goes the game. "Do none of your *ladies* ride in carriages?"

His one brow lifted and then he frowned as if the subject deserved his careful consideration.

"Well, as to that, I have no...*lady* at present, but if I were to acquire one, I would suppose she would ride in many carriages and perhaps a phaeton or curricle as well."

Was there not one ounce of humor in the infernal man? His gaze was steady, downright somber. But somehow his manner of regard made her think the words coming out of his mouth had absolutely nothing to do with his actual thoughts.

"Is this the kind of gown you are known for?" he asked, interrupting her thoughts.

This was most definitely not going as planned. She remained mute.

"No," he settled into one of the minuscule chairs. "I thought not. This is not remotely like the gown I saw last evening. I paid for a Weston—well several to be precise—and I expect to have a Weston creation. If I may peruse the back of the shop"—he rose. "I am sure I will find just the gown I require."

This was too much. "Your Grace, I am afraid that is not possible. I have nothing else near finished."

But she was talking to his exquisite back.

She hurried after him.

The duke immediately went to the gowns and began riffling through them.

"Your Grace, this is highly improper."

She might have been an insistent fly for as much attention as he gave her. He was probably the sort who could read, as well as comprehend, in the midst of a herd of wild elephants. He paused over the sheer black model with midnight tulle and indigo spangles, cocking his head as his gaze raked over it and then over her. He hung it over a nearby chair.

She tried again.

"Your Grace, I must insist you return to the front room. I will attend you there."

He spared her a brief glance but continued on his quest.

As he fingered a peach chiffon, his gaze trolled around the room and then caught on the draped dress stand in the far corner. *Damn and Blast!* He must have the sight of a homing bird. The room was quite dim and the form was nearly hidden behind a high table littered with paper patterns and rolls of fabric.

Sure enough, he abandoned the chiffon and crossed to the form, but she was there before him, heading him off.

"Your Grace, this is unfinished—just a rough mockup of something I am working on. It is nothing that would interest you."

Her words seemed to spur him on. He deftly stepped around her and lifted the muslin sheet from the stand.

His breath caught.

His gaze never left the gown as he slowly removed his glove. His fingers hovered and then brushed the edge of the delicate sleeve. The touch was one of reverence, as if the lace would dissolve under his all too human touch.

Olivia could not help a thrill of pride watching him, seeing her work through his eyes.

"Yes," she thought she heard him murmur.

"Yes, I will have this gown," he said louder and with more control. "Unfinished, though it is." He pierced her with his amber gaze.

She pressed her lips together. Oh, how to deal with this man?

"Your Grace, it is quite imposs—"

He moved through the curtained doorway and to the basket he had brought. He produced a bottle of wine and two crystal glasses and began pouring, oblivious to her stammering protests.

"Mrs. Weston." He offered her a glass. "You possess an extraordinary talent."

"That is quite beside the point, Your Grace. What I

have been trying to convey to you is that gown is not available. Not to you. Not to anyone."

He raised a ducal eyebrow along with the glass of wine.

"That particular creation is for my own personal wardrobe," she answered him as if the mere raising of his eyebrow was a reasonable rejoinder.

He stopped drinking. "You said you did not have a lover."

"Whether I do or do not...which I do not"—for some reason it seemed important he know that—"does not signify." She continued, "If you must know, I need it for my business."

He paused and carefully lowered his wine glass to the table.

"Your business, madam?"

"Oh, blast you. I need it to generate custom."

His gaze narrowed. "Could you elaborate?"

"To solicit ladies, and sometimes gentlemen." Still his eyes seared her. "To order gowns." Why did he fluster her so? "I act as a kind of model for my creations. And I need this particular gown for Mrs. Parkington's mask this next Thursday."

She raised the glass that had somehow appeared in her hand and gulped the wine down in a neat swig and then thrust it back at him.

"Mrs. Weston, I wish you had said so in the beginning." He took the crystal, his fingers lightly brushing hers, causing her heart to jump ridiculously. "It is a simple matter. We shall attend the mask together." And he blithely refilled the goblet.

Oh no, this was by no means the direction she wanted to take. "I thank you for your kind invitation, but no." She clasped her fingers, hoping by squeezing the blood from them they would cease to tingle from his touch. She only succeeded in mashing Wes's ring into her knuckle while the tingle continued along with the pain. "Your Grace, I believe our business is concluded. If you would be so kind as to leave, I would be most obliged."

"But I have not been obliged, Mrs. Weston, and there's the rub." He gestured to the other chair, offering her wine. She ignored both. He shrugged and settled into his chair again with the wine next to him. "I do not wish to appear vain, madam, but I dare say your *custom* would benefit greatly with a duke as your escort."

Well, he did have her there. Still she tried to parry his logic with her own. "I owe you a few gowns, Your Grace, not my time. That, I am thankful, is still my own to dispense with as I please."

He took a long swallow, set down his glass. "If you will attend Mrs. Parkington's mask with me, then I would be willing to forgive the other three gowns." He stood and offered the wine again.

*What to do?* She could not think. She took several steps away from him, but his gaze, real as a touch, enveloped her. She mentally shook him off. *Think.* It would be quite a coup to enter the ballroom with the Monk. She was sure to garner instant attention.

He held out her glass, very much like a snake with a shiny red apple. Heavens, he was an amazing looking man. But to spend a whole evening with him? A shiver ran through her, settling in her loins. No, it simply would not do. She was just about to tell him so when she thought of Egg.

Right. There was no choosing really. Women in

their situation did not have the luxury of choice.

She took the offered glass, making sure her eyes never left his.

"Very well, Your Grace, it seems we have a bargain. I will see you Thursday." The wine flooded her mouth. It tasted of earth and currants. So decadent and expensive. She deposited the glass on the cutting table behind her, walked to the front door, opened it, and left the shop without a backward glance.

Rhys listened to the tread of her feet as she made her way from the outer vestibule up the steps to her apartments above. Did he imagine a door softly closing? A whisper of skirts falling to the floor?

He expelled the breath he had been holding and replaced it with a deep draft of wine.

He had told himself he wasn't coming. He had made sure to fill his day—the morning, with estate business, and most of the rest at the House of Lords, trying to make those stodgy oafs see reason. He had dined at White's with his uncle, who had not-so-subtly rebuked him for his manners of last evening, and then he had spent the last three hours walking the streets determined not to find himself at Hamley Place.

It had not worked.

He had given himself another chance. And strangely, he was not sorry.

Rhys poured the rest of the wine and looked around. It appeared he would be left to close up.

He walked into the workroom, ostensibly to extinguish the light, but he was once again drawn to the dress. It shimmered, almost alive, in the soft light. He knew instinctively it was not so much the gown itself—which was extraordinary, as if a fairy had blown a golden-blonde cobweb over the form—no, it was more the notion of the woman in the gown that took his breath. For his mind had already taken that leap and forged the two together.

She would be exquisite. The lace had been dyed to exactly match the color of her skin. The effect being— save the golden shimmer—she would appear quite naked.

**** 

"Are you sure you don't want me to come with you?" Egg said from her chair by the stove. "I dare say I could come up with some ensemble. Do you recall my Queen Bess?"

Olivia had said nothing to Egg about the duke's late night visits and that he would be her escort this evening.

"No, and please do not resurrect that atrocity. Good Lord, we need a patron not an arrest. Besides, we have gone over this before. I will be quite well on my own." Olivia pulled the golden gown off of its stand.

"If only Jeb was available to escort you, I would feel much better." Egg rose to help slide the gown over Olivia's elaborate coiffure.

"Egglet, please—" The gown covered her face, cutting off the impatience in her voice. Lud, her nerves were strung tight as a young lady at her come out ball. But Olivia was no green girl, and this mask a far cry from any *ton* event. She emerged from the lace to take her friend's hand. "You will wear yourself out with your needless worries," she said as much for herself as for Eglantine. "After all, I am no young miss."

"Well, you are *my* 'young miss'." Egg gently tucked a stray curl back into Olivia's chignon. "And I cannot—nay I *will* not—give up the privilege of mothering you, just a bit."

Olivia ducked her head and Egg's familiar rough-tipped fingers cupped her cheek. She hated keeping things from her friend, but Eglantine's endless questions would be far worse. So Olivia stood placidly while Egg continued to fuss and coo over her chick.

"I wonder what he is like?" Egg said, wetting her fingers to smooth the delinquent curl.

Olivia wrinkled her nose. "Who?"

"Why our dear Monk." She waggled her eyebrows.

*Oh not again.* Egg had been next door to visit their landlady, Isabelle Harton, this morning. Ever since Mrs. Harton had found out about Olivia's visit to the Duke of Roydan, she had been filling Egg's ears with all kinds of gossip.

"Very strict habits." Egg shook her head dropping her voice dramatically. "Probably in reaction to his father, Isabelle says."

"His father?" The words were out before Olivia could stop herself.

Egg made a face like a prune. "Apparently a Miss Virginia Newton was never quite the same after her dealings with the old duke. Isabelle says it is rumored, years later, the poor girl lifted her skirts, in broad daylight, and pissed on his grave."

"Good heavens. As bad as that?"

"Worse. Isabelle says—"

Olivia held up her hand.

"Very well, Miss Squeamish, I will spare your delicate sensibilities."

Egg motioned Olivia to turn as she inspected the back of the gown. "Anyhow, Daria Battersby became obsessed with the new duke. Her fixation was likely the reason the Earl of Benchley rigged the whole White's incident in the first place. You see Benchley was Battersby's protector at the time and fiercely jealous."

Olivia made no comment; however, her silence did not deter Eglantine.

"But Isabelle maintains it was the Gillray print with Harriette Wilson that finally pushed the duke to the brink. Evidently it hung in the front of Hannah Humphrey's shop for months." Egg, getting into the spirit of things, took up a length of dark wool and a ruler. "There he was, in full monk's robes complete with sackcloth and ashes, flagellating himself while Harriette Wilson flashed teeth and diamonds." She flailed the ruler about her shoulders with relish.

"You could go nowhere without encountering some reference to a monk," Egg continued. "So the duke set out to find the best whore the city could offer. And, surprise, she just happened to be Daria Battersby." She took a hasty breath. "Egad, do you know the pie he'd been eating for his dinner that night at White's is still known today as Monk's Pie? I will be sure to order it next time I dine out."

"Enough of 'Isabelle says' and your dinner." Egg's breath was coming too fast and too shallow. "What of me?" Olivia said removing her hands from her hips and dipping into a curtsey. "Will I do?"

Egg humphed, clearly disappointed with her audience, and dropped the cloth and ruler on the cutting table. She stepped back, casting a critical eye over Olivia. "Do?" Egg's face split into a smile. "Those bacon-faced tarts will be falling arse over tit when they get a look at you." She touched the scrap of lace at the shoulder of the dress. "I cannot imagine why you would even think of wearing the black tulle instead of this beauty."

"So you have said only a thousand times." Olivia had dearly wanted to defy the duke by wearing the other gown. "Now here is your tea"—Olivia handed her the warm pot—"and your silly book."

"Ah yes, *The Italian* by Mrs. Radcliffe. Do you know it was modeled after *The Monk* by Matthew Lewis? I am reading it as an homage to our own dear monk who has provided the means for us to live these past weeks. Now if only I had some of his delicious pie." Egg giggled.

*Little did she know their dear duke was providing more than funds these days.*

"Do not stay up too late reading that drivel." Olivia pulled Egg's shawl a bit more snugly around her. "You will be no earthly good to me if you are not rested. I need you ready for all the work we are going to have when I knock those jades for six with our newest creation," she said, opening the shop door for Egg. "We will not have a moment to call our own. We will be so *à la mode!*"

"Well in that case I'd better hurry and find out if Ellena will be kidnapped and taken to the house by the sea." Egg blew her a kiss and took her book and pot of tea up the stairs.

Finally, blessed quiet.

Olivia stood before the great three-paneled mirror situated in the far corner of the shop. The women reflected back looked nothing like the woman inside; they appeared serene, even confident. They laughed. All three consummate actresses, brilliant at shielding the quivering mass of jelly that lay beneath the glittering gold gown and creamy white skin.

Olivia turned to see the back of the dress; the actresses turned as well, graceful as swans. It fit like a second skin, the pink of her birthmark peeping from beneath the lowest line of the gown. The mirrored ladies smiled; it was perfect.

God's teeth, the great Duke of Roydan—the Monk—was escorting her to a demimonde mask. It was too incredible. They were sure to make a stir, for everyone would know him, even wearing a mask.

The women in the mirror flinched. *Surely no one would recognize her?* After all, over twelve years had passed since she had been in England. And in London…

Olivia closed her eyes, feeling hot shame engulf her.

Her step-mama's words still rang in her head. *Open your eyes, Edgar, she is a beauty—not conventional, but if we spend a little blunt to fire her off, we might be able to get some rich, old nob to take her.*

Still, Olivia was to have her dream, a proper come out.

She had spent hours unearthing, sketching, and re-making her mother's old court dress, complete with five foot train and ostrich plumes. And despite the circumstances, she had felt very much like a queen herself when she had made her curtsey before Queen Charlotte. Then the balls and the musical evenings and the rides in Hyde Park…and Lord Ivo Daughtry.

She had thought him her angel, complete with a halo of golden curls. And clasped in his arms she had forgotten her fright at being quite alone with him, only wanting his kiss. Besides, he would surely sink to his knee afterward and ask her to be his.

Such an innocent dream—a fairytale.

The *ton* had called her ruined. *Ruined.* What an odd word to associate with a human being, as if she was broken and no longer useful, something to be thrown away. Ivo Daughtry had certainly thrown her away.

Expelling a deep breath, she purged all those poisonous memories. Mrs. Adolphus Weston had eventually risen out of those ashes and reclaimed her life. Now, Olivia Weston, dressmaker, would do the same.

She smoothed the gown over her waist and down over her hip bones—bones still too prominent. What was the time? Perhaps she should go above stairs to check on Egg?

"Whoa," a voice called from the street.

He had arrived.

****

"Is there nothing to be done?" Daria twisted in an attempt to see the back of her gown. "It fit perfectly last week when we tried."

"Once again, madam."

Daria sucked in a deep breath, pulling in her stomach as Foster jerked at the stays. Daria heard the snap even as her belly filled the now-gaping corset. Foster frowned at the dangling cord.

"Oh, hell!" Daria ripped the lacing out of the maid's hand and flung it at the fire.

"Madam, if I may—"

Daria shot her a deadly look. "Well, speak up, woman. We do not have all day."

"I believe the red crêpe is a bit more…forgiving,"

she offered. "Shall we try that?"

"Hell's harpies!" Daria gestured for a handkerchief and mopped her brow. "I suppose we must at this point. I cannot keep Lord Morton waiting much longer."

There was a time when she could have let her beaux cool their heels for hours while she primped and fussed over her toilette, but times had changed. Oh how had she had sunk so low as to be hurrying for the Lord Mortons of this world?

In the end, after much squeezing and fluffing and tacking a bit of tulle here and there, Daria critically surveyed the final product. Yes, she thought, yes, by God, she would do quite well. In the right light, her face was quite good, and her breasts, when properly supported, were still magnificent. The Weston chit was really rather brilliant. Too bad she could no longer mine that particular vein…But never mind that. When she had Roydan back, she would be ordering more things before the season was in full swing.

"Foster," she said, taking her outrageous mask of feathers from the maid. "You may tell his lordship I am ready."

Chapter Eight

As she and the duke entered the lower hall at Madame Parkington's, Olivia ceased to wonder how merry ol' England would compare to the wild delights of Les Halles.

The footman wore a bejeweled turban, a cropped vest of delicious persimmon velvet—exposing an expanse of rippling muscle—billowing bloomers, and a huge curving sword. Olivia would have sworn he had been imported straight from the Kasbah.

"May I teck yer cloak, madam?" Well, Persia, by way of Scotland perhaps.

As she surrendered the wrap the Scotsman gasped, or perhaps it had been the duke? Hum, his face betrayed nothing.

The entire stairway was draped in silks to resemble a long tent, the lower portion swathed in saffron. But as they ascended, Olivia had the feeling of leaving the bright sunlight, entering a sunset of oranges and reds, and finally being swallowed in the deepest indigo of night. Huge footmen, all dressed as Mamluks, waved enormous plumed fans from the sides of the stairway. The farther she and the duke ascended, the sparer the attendants' costumes. Good gracious, their silk pantaloons were now nearly transparent. She was sure the last poor fellow would be quite naked except for a well-placed palm frond.

"Well, Your Grace, what do you make of the place?" It was the first time she had addressed him since entering his carriage.

He spared her a look before studying first one side of the stairway and then the other. As if that was not enough, he turned back to the entrance, now far below them, and spent a long moment looking at something. She looked as well but could not begin to imagine what had so thoroughly captured his attention. Finally he turned back to her. "Mrs. Parkington seems to take prodigious care in creating a most authentic setting. I am quite convinced the footman who greeted us is carrying nothing less than a twelfth century cutlass...possibly even from the Abbasid era. An extraordinary"—his masked eyes found hers— "specimen," he finished, with not even a glimmer of a smile.

Impossible. She was about to turn away, giving up the idea the man possessed any scrap of humor, when she noticed his ears. Were they just a shade too red? Perhaps he was human after all...

They reached the top of the stairway and stepped onto a small dais. Every inch of the ballroom ceiling, and a good deal of the walls, was swathed in deep purple silk. Tiny mirrored stars had been fixed into the canopy, and colossal jewel-toned lanterns, the size of small carriages, hung from the peaks of the tent, casting a kaleidoscope of shifting color across the silk.

But just as impressive as Madam Parkington's décor were her guests; a river of colorful couples, whirling upon the polished marble floor and eddying around the perimeters of the room, served as a mirror image to the glory above.

Then, like a child's wind-up toy, the dancers slowed, stuttered, and finally stopped. The music followed suit, hiccupping as the players one by one stopped their bows, flutes, and horns. Olivia looked about her, trying to determine the cause. The company gasped, as if all the air had suddenly been sucked out of the room, and their masked eyes homed in on…her and the duke.

Olivia turned to Roydan, sure at last this scene would move him. She was correct, it did.

He drew her forward, down the few steps, and into the frozen crowd. A wide, deferential path formed. Moses could not have looked more commanding when he parted the Red Sea. Now the room was dead silent, no one dared even a whisper.

Then someone did move. A large woman in an absurd, red, frizzled wig and a huge ruff rivaled only by her more enormous bosom, puffed up to Olivia and the duke. It would seem Queen Bess had made an appearance after all. Olivia suppressed a smile. This frizzled and frazzled woman must be their hostess, Madam Parkington. The poor woman was decidedly overwhelmed and only just remembered her curtsey, which she executed with surprising grace, given the largeness of her person and her extreme agitation.

"Your Grace, I never hoped…I mean to say…I am most humbled and gratified you have chosen my poor affair for your evening's entertainment."

The duke looked at her for a long moment, perhaps, Olivia thought, deciding whether to even deign to even speak with his hostess.

Some unseen scale tipped in her favor—maybe it was her twelfth century cutlass? "Madam"—he gave a brief bow—"I see I shall have to work harder on my disguise at your next affair."

Madam was about to go into further raptures, but the duke gave a nod to the orchestra and the music immediately commenced. He reclaimed Olivia's arm and moved past their hostess and into the throng.

Olivia had a difficult time not gaping along with the rest of the guests. She knew they would cause a stir but never dreamed the ball would stop dead.

*What would it be like to be the mistress of this man?* The thought slipped by her vigilant fortress like a songbird from its cage. She stole a look. Ramrod-straight, yet he possessed a kind of ready grace, as if at the slightest provocation he could spring into action. Lud, she had seen it firsthand in his hall when he'd nearly impaled her. Now she imagined him not as a warrior, but moving as a lover...

*Steady, feet on the ground.* This line of thought was hardly useful. She was here to work. Besides, the duke barely seemed interested. Indeed she was rather shocked by his extreme reserve thus far. Not that she expected him to leap on her, but the man who had entered her shop spouting all kinds of innuendo, seemed to have vanished.

Anger flared, settling deep between her shoulder blades. He was so bloody calm. How could he be so, when her heart was thumping along with the orchestra's scotch reel?

She took a stab at him. "I suppose you are used to being thoroughly admired wherever you go."

"And why would you imagine that, Mrs. Weston?" He raised an eyebrow without a trace of reciprocal anger.

*Humph.* Really, she could not treat his answer with any credence. It was abundantly clear he was the most exalted person in the room. And he knew it. He must. So she remained silent.

"Actually, I have never attended a mask...of this sort."

Again, she should not believe him. After all most men his age—he must be at least thirty—would have delved into the seamier world outside Almack's and their various clubs. But she did believe him. Perhaps he was a bit of a monk.

Her gaze followed his, trying to see the ball through his eyes. Her first impression of sheer opulence narrowed as she watched him focus on specific vignettes; just to their right, a corpulent woman, in the far too scanty gown of a milkmaid, sat on a huge silver platter surrounded by fruit. Her companion roughly pulled her breasts free, spilling his champagne onto their heavy globes as he bent to lap at them.

She looked back to him. The duke's sober black dress and simple mask—his only nod to whimsy—stood out like a cool drink of water in a sea of heavy and cloying port wine. Was he repulsed? His head was tilted back, focused on the starry canopy.

"I wonder at the logistics of hoisting those lanterns. They must weigh over forty-five stone." He adjusted his mask and turned to her. "Would you care for champagne?"

"Definitely, Your Grace. I am parched." Good heavens, he was a surprise.

As he turned away to get the wine, she scanned the room again, this time trolling for a perspective patroness. She dismissed the milkmaid. The woman was too far in her cups to be worth the effort to convince her of her need for Olivia's talents. But bless Isabelle Harton, she had been right; the mask was a crush. Everyone who was anyone was there—painters, opera singers, actresses, writers, mistresses—all the fringes of society.

Olivia noted she was garnering as many looks as the duke. Good. She hoped to spend a sufficient amount of time in the ladies' retiring room as well as in the ballroom. In Paris, she found she could speak more freely with the "ladies" without the gentlemen interfering. Rather a tricky bog, luring men with her person, but not alienating the women who might want her wares.

An icy chill shot up Olivia's back to settle at her nape. She tried to shake it off, but the feeling of unease gripped her and spread, as if a cold shadow loomed over her. Sure she would encounter something horrible, she ducked her head and wheeled to confront the evil presence.

There was nothing. Silly. She was about to turn back, when a man, leaning casually against one of the huge posts that held up the canopied tent, raised his glass in a salute to her. He wore a heavy, ornate mask of a satyr with huge horns and a ruff of curling fur about his shoulders. His gaze slid over her body, making her feel soiled, as if his hands were on her. She imagined dirty and over-long nails and spider-like fingers. The feeling was so very familiar. Did she *know* this man?

He made a slight bow. She could not see clearly, but she was sure a slow smile curved behind his grotesque mask.

She shivered.

"Mrs. Weston, are you chilled?"

She pulled her gaze away. It was the duke with her champagne. "No, I thank you. I am well." She took the proffered flute and gulped. Bubbles rushed her mouth and tickled her nose. Lord, this was nonsense. She was no newcomer to this sort of entertainment and the crudeness that went with it. She could well handle a salacious glance or two. After all, hadn't she come here to gain attention? She took another sip and turned back to confront the leering man, but he had vanished.

Daria had been brushing a crumb from her skirts when the crowd hushed. She looked up to find the source, and her mouth dropped open along with all the others. It was a good thing she had managed to swallow her canapé in one deft bite, or it might have fallen right out of her mouth and been lost in her décolletage.

How dare he attend this ball. And how dare he attend it with some skinny *chit!* Daria promptly closed her mouth and raised her quizzing glass as Mrs. Parkington pushed her way through the crush, veritably mowing down her guests in her haste to greet Roydan.

There it was, the nauseating fawning and groveling. Daria used to lap it up on the rare occasions when Roydan took her out. But seeing it lavished on some drab who had the audacity to poach *her* man, now turned her stomach.

Marie Antoinette's hair shifted, blocking Daria's view. She charged forward and elbowed the hair and the woman attached out of her way. And for a brief space all was clear. The neck came into focus first—the long gracefulness of it and the particular tilt of the head. Very well, she was a beauty. Then she saw the gown.

*Hell's Harpy*, it was Olivia Weston. Her *dressmaker.*

The huge room became suffocating in a matter of seconds. Daria flushed, turning what she knew to be a deep and highly unflattering shade of red especially given she was wearing the blasted color. She heaved in a great gulp of air. Lord Morton looked at her in alarm, muttered something about getting her some punch, and rushed off.

"Well, my dear Daria, if one has to be supplanted, at least his betrothed is quite a stunner."

Daria peeled her eyes from the couple to see Eveline Barton at her elbow. *Oh Lord, not her.* The woman had always wanted Roydan. No doubt she was here to crow over Daria's ousting.

Daria forced what she hoped was a reasonable laugh. "Betrothed? By no means, Eveline, you mistake the matter entirely. *She* most certainly is *not* Roydan's betrothed." She pried open her fan and furiously applied it to her overheated cheeks and bosom. *Was no one else having vapors?*

"Oh, but I understood that is why he had to forego *your* pleasures, my dear, because he was to choose a bride?"

Daria stopped fanning herself. She would like nothing better than to brain the woman with it. "Yes, well obviously, he is here to look for me." Daria laughed again, but didn't like its desperate edge and stopped. "You see the woman on his arm is merely my dressmaker." The sneer fell from Barton's face. "I have been rather put out with Rhys of late. He is, no doubt, vexed and taking his revenge like a schoolboy. I suppose I must have pity on him."

"Your dressmaker? Well, Daria, you certainly have held your peace. Her gown is stunning. So deceptively simple, yet so very…shocking." She turned and looked Daria up and down. "Is yours one of her creations as well?"

Daria stood a bit taller and tried to suck in her belly, hoping her color had somewhat receded. "Why yes, it is."

"I must say, my dear, it takes a good stone off you, if you'll pardon my saying so. I have not seen you looking so well in an age."

"Thank you, I'm sure." Daria lifted her chin. "I would be happy to give you her direction." *Over my dead body.*

"Oh, that would be most excellent." Barton clapped her hands in girlish glee. Daria snorted. "As you have no doubt heard, I am off to the continent with Lord Danvers in two weeks' time and a few new gowns, especially of this kind, would not go amiss."

"Danvers? Is he still creaking along? I thought he was quite dead!"

Barton instantly raised her fan at a full tilt. "No, he is quite well, thank you, *quite* well, if you catch my meaning." She slapped the fan against her gloved palm a bit too firmly, Daria thought. "Now I had better not keep you. I am sure Roydan is on pins and needles…waiting to reclaim you."

"Mrs. Weston, would you do me the honor of dancing with me?"

It had been so very long—a lifetime ago—since Olivia had danced. "Oh…yes." Her voice sounded soft and ghostly in her ears. "Yes, Your Grace," she said more firmly, "I would very much like to dance."

Olivia adored dancing. She had practiced for hours in the dusty ballroom at Stokesly Hall, her old home. There was no dancing master, not even a pianoforte. It had long been sold. But she could sing to herself as she moved about the room.

In her imagination she was never subjected to the "obligatory dance." The one where a gentleman must solicit a wallflower or relative, or perhaps the highest-ranking woman, and spend a half-hour's time marking out the appropriate steps and conversing with the appropriate small talk of weather and the latest watered-down gossip. No, in her fantasy world, the dance would be that rare encounter where magic happened. Her partner always tall and handsome and the dance could only be the waltz.

Of course it had been forbidden. Even now it was considered rather scandalous in the ballrooms of the *ton*. Certainly it was never attempted in the country. But here in the lower circles, it was all the rage. And Mrs. Parkington's mask was no exception.

She was sure the duke, as well as half the room, could hear her heart galloping wildly in her breast as they made their way to the center of the room. But passing politely nodding couples, she knew she must appear as serene as her three-mirrored actresses back at the shop.

He held out his hand; she hesitated and then slipped hers into its warm curve. His long fingers enfolded hers so completely. A tingling quiver snaked from her elaborate hair, down over her breasts, taking a fluttering loop at her belly and knees, and finally rushing on to her toes, which curled tightly within her slippered feet. And though they wore gloves, and though he did not betray an ounce of emotion, she knew he had experienced the same feeling.

He brought his other hand to rest lightly on the small of her back, just below where the gown met her skin. The sudden warmth made her want to press back into that heat. She swallowed. She lifted her left hand to find his right shoulder, completing their connection. His muscle flexed beneath her fingers. His coat needed no padding.

Then it was time. She looked straight into his eyes.

She shouldn't have. She should have gazed over his shoulder at the other assembling couples, or perhaps at his chin, but she didn't. She met his eyes square on.

*Dear Saint Anne, she was in deep.*

He shifted the hand at her waist, his thumb softly grazing her bare skin. Such a small gesture but it felt as shocking and decadent as if he had bent her back on her heels and kissed her for all to see. His jaw tightened, and his thumb settled in its new position, the pressure now stronger. Instinctively, she curled her own thumb more tightly around his hand.

Surely she was allowed this bit of sin? Surely she was allowed to forget herself in his arms and pretend he was her love, if only for these brief minutes?

And so, she pretended.

Bubbles of small talk popped around them, but it did not touch their world—their cocoon. Then the music began and she smiled.

There were no false starts, no mismatched steps and murmured apologies. Their heights were well matched and their long limbs graceful, but their synergy was beyond mere symmetry and grace of movement. They were *one*. They moved as one. It was as if the air between them was a tangible thing with mass and weight. As they moved, it moved with them, pressing into each of their bodies, merely an extension of their oneness. For this moment, as they glided in looping circles around the ballroom to the strains of Vivaldi, time stopped.

There was no need to squint to make out the horror before her. Daria had been secretly tracking the couple since they arrived, but now she watched helplessly as Roydan escorted Olivia Weston out onto the dance floor.

"No-o-o-o!" *She could not have said that out loud, could she?* She glanced around; sure everyone was looking at her, tittering behind their fans, or worse, looking at her with pity. She should not have bothered. Absolutely no one was remotely interested in her. Her gaze went back to the couple just as Roydan took the chit in his arms. But this was all wrong. Roydan never danced! In all the years Daria had been in his company, she had never danced with him or *seen* him dance a single step.

It would be a waltz, of course.

Something snapped. Startled by the sound, Daria looked to Lord Morton, who had finally arrived with her punch. Following his lordship's eyes, she looked down at the mangled fan in her hand. She hastily thrust it into the nearby potted palm, and the punch soon followed. Snatching the arm of the still-gaping earl, Daria made her way onto the crowded floor.

She smiled her best smile as she pushed the earl around the floor. Damn, why had she grabbed Morton to dance with? He was a veritable clod and deaf as a post to boot. She laughed as they clumped passed the duke and Mrs. Weston.

"Very funny, your lordship," Daria tittered.

"What's the joke, my poppet?" said Lord Morton loudly. But Daria's eyes were already fixed on the striking couple, who had just sailed effortlessly by.

How dare he flaunt his new dalliance in front of her? How dare he step so far outside his normal habits for a mere dressmaker? Just wait till she got her hands on the chit. And by God, she would. She just needed a diversion to split them up. Even as she thought this, the dance was ending and she could see Mrs. Weston making her way to the ladies' retiring room with Eveline Barton right on her heels. Good, at least Barton was good for something. Now she would have a few moments alone with Roydan.

She just caught him disappearing onto the terrace. She dumped the earl on Prudence Radcliff and hurried to follow the duke.

\*\*\*\*

What Olivia needed was some air, but then the duke would have escorted her out of doors, and what she needed even more than air was to be *away* from him. Especially after the half hour they had just spent together on the dance floor. Especially after being held in his arms, with his eyes boring into hers. Especially after feeling light as air as he guided her so beautifully among the other dancers. She had seen and felt no one but him. He had surrounded her in his private world— the world of only his arms, his eyes, his smell, his breath, his grace. God, it had been sheer bliss.

And a mistake. The pretending. She had let her guard slip, and joy had found its way inside, if only for a moment.

89

But this duke would only use her body for a time and then reject her. And a life of superficial decadence was not one she wanted. She had rejected it time and time again. As much as she hated to admit it, she felt a bit sorry for Daria Battersby who was the man's latest discard. Well, Olivia would not be another.

She pushed her way past a leering Caesar and down a short hallway to safety.

****

Daria found him taking the air on the terrace. His long body canted over the balustrade, arms locked under wide shoulders while he surveyed the shallow back garden. Heavens, he was still as magnificent as the first time she had seen him.

She had been shopping in an alley off Petticoat Lane. In the middle of intense bargaining over a particularly lovely—and naughty—ivory snuff box, she dropped the bauble and immediately crossed the narrow street.

It was a bookseller's shop. A place she would never have entered of her own volition. Yet she ended up spending almost a full half-hour's time thumbing through dusty volumes, desperately trying to gain his attention. Nothing had worked. In the end, the only thing she had to show for her efforts were thoroughly ruined gloves and a volume by some atrocious Greek—*in* Greek, no less.

But he had touched it, his beautiful hands skimming over the pages. She had caressed those same pages back in the privacy of her boudoir, imagining those hands on her body, and she vowed she would have him. She had worked on him for months with nary a glimmer of interest on his part, and then, quite suddenly, his man of affairs arrived to present her with contracts.

At first Roydan had been insatiable, coming to her sometimes three times a day. She was used to lavish compliments on her lovemaking skills and proudly possessed an extensive repertoire, but he never wanted anything more than standard fare and even that was hurried. Afterward, she had always felt she had dirtied him somehow.

She kept telling herself she just needed time and she would make him love her—need her—but in nearly five years his emotions never entered the boudoir. Not once. In the end she had been happy enough to have Thursday evening come and go and the business done for that week.

Still she had given him her best years. She was not going to surrender him now to some halfpenny seamstress! Daria felt the familiar frown between her brows and quickly smoothed them. Adjusting her bosom, she pinched her cheeks and prepared for battle.

"Rhys, darling." His head snapped up and he slowly straightened, his back a massive black wall. She was taking a great risk. He did not like for her to call him by his given name, and even less endearments, but desperate times, she reasoned, called for desperate measures. She would not go so far as to touch him, however. She had, after all, spent at least one evening of every week with him and had learned a thing or two about the man. "You cannot be serious."

He turned to her. "Mrs. Battersby."

She made a moue. "Rhys, surely you can do better than that. You can't still be angry at me for ordering a few silly gowns, can you? It is very hard of you. To subject me to seeing you flaunt that *dressmaker* is too cruel. I am sure in your man's mind you thought you were doing just the thing to get back at me. Very well, I am cowed, and I own you have struck a chord—especially *waltzing* with the girl. But let us put the past behind, my dear, and we shall say no more of it."

"Mrs. Battersby," he said in his lowest bass. *Oh dear, this was not a good sign.* "I am attempting to do just that." He executed an almost nonexistent bow. "I wish you good evening."

****

Olivia had not found peace in the retiring room, but she had found a client. Mrs. Eveline Barton was very insistent about having seven or so gowns made up posthaste. The lady would come to the shop tomorrow afternoon to see some models and sketches.

A tall man stepped into her path. It was the Satyr-man.

"Madam," he said in a slightly lisping yet deep voice. "I wonder if I might have the honor of the next dance?"

As his words slid over her, the fine hairs on her arms stood on end and inexplicable adrenaline rushed through her.

"You may not," said the duke, who materialized behind her. He must have been waiting for her just to the other side of a bank of schefflera and orchids. Her cold hand was immediately enveloped in his warm one, his touch thoroughly shocking. He clearly meant to lay claim to her—to warn the other man off. But his hand, its firm heat pressing her own, felt not so much like a savior, but very much like a lover's touch.

The Satyr-man, obviously angry, bowed stiffly.

"Another time, perhaps." Then he disappeared into the milling crowd.

"What do you think you are doing?" she jerked her hand out of his, turning her unsettled feeling into reliable anger. His touch was too warm and too *right*. "You are most officious, sir. You do not own me. How am I supposed to generate custom if I am never to mingle with anyone?"

"That, Mrs. Weston is certainly not my affair," he said, in his haughtiest tone. "It is my understanding you agreed to this outing in recompense for settling an outstanding bill. A rather large bill, if I am not mistaken. Now if you wish to renege, I would be very happy to negotiate another settlement."

Olivia glared at him through her mask. *Oooh*, he was infuriating. But the evening was not a complete loss; she did have the Barton order, which was quite handsome.

"No, there will be no other negotiating. I will play by your rules, at least for this evening."

"Very well then, let us depart. I have had quite enough of this entertainment," and he whisked her toward the entryway.

Daria watched them disappear into the tunnel draped in midnight silk. She had truly lost him. Her heyday was dead gone, and all that remained were the Lord Mortons and Actons of this world.

"Mrs. Battersby?"

Daria turned to the masculine voice. A rather well-looking man, from what she could see, stood before her, tall and slender, wearing a mask of a Satyr. He made a deferential bow.

"Sir? Do I know you?" She noted the cut of his

coat and his linen—not in the first stare of fashion, but fine enough. His boots were worn, but perhaps that was part of his costume. He wore no jewelry.

"No, madam, but I know you. You are the famous Daria Battersby, the toast of the demimonde."

*Sweet Jezebel, if he had some blunt, he might be a ripe one.* Oh, if she only had her fan. It was always such a useful prop when preparing to flirt. Still, she rested her hand on her décolletage in lieu of the fan. The gesture met with success as the man's gaze dipped. "La, sir, you are too generous."

"Not so, my dear Mrs. Battersby, but I would like to be." He caught her hand and raised it to his lips.

Better and better. "You have me at a disadvantage, sir." She playfully pulled her hand away and laid a finger to her lips. "I know you only by your huge horns and beard, Monsieur Satyr, but I do not see your pipe, sir." She tsked. "Perhaps you have hidden it away and only blow upon it for a select few?"

He smiled, his teeth very white against the dark of his mask and beard. "Oh, I assure you I have a pipe, my dear nymph, but my preference would be for you to make music upon it."

Enough dallying, it was time to see if the man had the goods—and it had nothing to do with the size of his pipe.

"Before I lose my heart, I would know who is tugging at its strings."

His mouth twisted and then flattened. "Never mind your heart, dear lady. I think we are both more interested in other things?" He paused and smiled. "I happened to be on the terrace while you were having your *tête-à-tête* with Roydan."

Daria felt as if she had been doused with freezing water. "How dare you, sir." She must get away. She turned and saw Morton waving to her, his mask cocked at a ridiculous angle, his chins waggling beneath, but she could not hear him through the roaring in her ears.

"Don't you want your precious monk back?" The man's words snapped as surely as a trap. Daria whipped around as if to protect herself, preparing for his killing blow. He smiled. "I believe we may be of some service to one another...in more ways than one."

Chapter Nine

Rhys stared out the window of his carriage, knowing she was only an arm's length away. It might as well be a mile. He had nothing to hold her to him now. The silly sham of the gowns was spent and the mask over as well. He must let her go. He was an honorable man, or at least he had been.

He risked a look. She was wedged in her corner of the carriage, her head turned to the window.

God, he wanted her. His honor was nothing against her. His bloody honor had crumbled the moment he took her in his arms and she smiled at him. Just thinking of that smile had his heart knocking against his chest. What a fool. No doubt she used that surefire weapon to slay hundreds of unsuspecting gentlemen, leaving a trail gasping in her wake. But in his heart it had felt like that smile, that gift, had only been for him.

He willed her to turn her head, to look at him, and then he might be able to speak. But her gaze remained fixed. He finally looked away and back out into the night.

With nothing but blackness to occupy him, he tried to think of his future with Arabella Campbell, but his mind would not comply. Instead, he calculated the damage to his morals if he took a mistress while preparing for marriage.

Certainly the Campbells presented no impediment

to his lust. The old man himself had made it perfectly clear that he expected Rhys to have his dalliances. The family was so thrilled with the possibility of having the Duke of Roydan for a son-in-law, Rhys could have an entire harem living under his roof and Lord Campbell would not bat an eyelash—or his daughter, for that matter.

Rhys closed his eyes.

The carriage lurched, dipping wildly. Rhys's shoulder and head banged sharply against the coach wall. The horses shrieked and his coachman let out a "Bloody hell!" from somewhere above. But the pain from his head was nothing to finding the woman of his dreams in his arms.

He did not think.

He kissed her.

The frantic knock at the coach door had him fumbling for the latch to keep the world out. But already her soft lips were pulling away. More pounding from outside and a hard tug on the door.

"Your Grace! Are you and madam well?" The world had crashed in.

Rhys let her go, and she pushed back into her corner. He looked away, pressing the back of his hand against his lips. His breath came fast. *Oh, God, what had he done?* Damn it, she was too close, he needed to be away and *out*. He fumbled for the latch and heaved himself out of the coach.

Rhys spent a full ten minutes outside discussing every minute detail of possible damage to the coach, his servants, and the horses until he could no longer delay the inevitable. He could not very well ride atop the carriage with James—*could he?*

Ridiculous. Yes, he had become quite ridiculous. His footman was standing there with the door open waiting for him to proceed. Rhys pulled himself in, rapped the ceiling, and they were once again moving.

Five—now six—streetlamps illuminated her profile and then died away to dusky gloom. He waited for the seventh, each time hoping to see in her face a glimmer of want to justify the enormous need that engulfed his body. Nothing. Eight. And nine. How much time had passed? Still, her profile hung, like a frozen Madonna, within the coach's window frame. Why could he not speak? It seemed a Herculean task, the silence so deafening, it was do or die. Very much like hurling himself off a cliff. Now ten.

He jumped.

"I am tired of subterfuge." His voice sounded harsh and overly loud. He took a breath and began slower and with, he hoped, more control. "Artifice is not in my nature, but I find I am out of sorts when I am in your presence. I apologize. It is very—unsettling—to me." He took another breath. "I thought this feeling would simply go away if I did not see you. In my experience, it always has." He swallowed. "It did not. Then I thought if I *saw* you again it would go away, but it did not. It *does* not. I have tried to pave an honorable way toward marriage, but I find I cannot escape you. You fill my every moment, and it confounds me. So be it. I can no longer struggle against such a force. I—"

"You want me only because I am not available to you." Her words came in a quiet rush. "I imagine you are very used to getting what you want almost before you think it, much less ask for it. I have frustrated you, and you cannot stand it. That is the only reason you stubbornly pursue me." She met his eyes now. "I am an ordinary dressmaker. Someone you would never stoop to notice." He opened his mouth to speak but she held up her hand to stay him. "Yet because I thrust myself under your nose, demanding payment and then vexing you, you have set me up as a challenge to your male pride." Her eyes closed. "I wish you would let it go." She took a breath and opened them. "I wish you would let *me* go. I am sure you could find far better amusement in no time at all."

"If you would allow me to finish." It was imperative he get this crass business part behind them. "I do not offer you a mere dalliance, madam, I would have you as my mistress." There, it was out.

One look at her face told him his tack was all wrong, yet he knew no other way of being. Surely she would see beyond his meaningless words and know how much he wanted her, needed her. He plowed on, "I am planning to marry soon, you should know that, but it will not affect our relationship and contract." The neat and tidy words fell from his mouth, so at odds with his rioting emotions. "You will have *carte blanche*—a house, gowns, jewels, a carriage and horses, a generous allowance and, should we part company, you will have a stipend for life."

She stared stiffly in front of her.

Did she not mean to even favor him with an answer? Unprepared for the possibility of refusal, he was unsure how to go forward.

Finally she spoke, her words barely above a whisper. "I wish to go home."

A bitter rawness filled his chest. "You make me no answer?"

She looked at him then. He almost wished she hadn't. "Trust me; you will not like my answer."

"On the contrary, I am most anxious to hear what you have to say." He heard the words as they left his mouth, but they were a lie. He wanted to stop her answer with his hands, with his mouth.

"Ah, you are used to being answered. You are used to having your way in things. But I assure you, you *will not have me*." The ribbon snapped on her golden mask, and she threw it aside. "No doubt, I am insanely foolish to refuse your most generous offer, but it is much too costly for me. Oh yes, I'm sure I would be draped in silks and jewels and have servants galore, but I would not have myself, you see. I would be just one more thing for you to own. No, I thank you; be assured your entire dukedom could not buy my freedom."

Was his offer so abhorrent? His person?

The image of his father swelled like a hideous phantom.

She did not want him.

The pain and humiliation of this realization would have knocked him sideways if he had allowed it, but he did not. Instead he gave her his most freezing look, his shield now firmly in place.

"Ah, I see. My deepest apologies. I will trouble you no further." He looked away, dismissing her.

As if on cue, the coach pulled to a stop and the door opened. She slid past him. He dug his fingers into his thighs and pressed his tongue painfully against his teeth. A mist of fine rain dampened his face as his footman lowered the steps and assisted Mrs. Weston out of the carriage. She murmured something. But before she could turn, Rhys pulled the door shut and rapped on the roof. The coach lurched forward.

Olivia's hand shook trying to fit the key in the door. *Blasted rain!* It had turned from gentle to an outright downpour in a matter of seconds, now running down her forehead, into her eyes and down her cheeks. Finally, the lock clicked, and she pushed into the dank vestibule pausing only to slam the door home. She rushed up the narrow set of stairs while working at the frog closures of her soggy cloak. Her foot caught in its hem, and she yanked the heavy wool to her knees. At the top of the stairs, her breath roaring in her ears, she ripped the cape off as if it were the cause of her distress and kicked at the mangled heap.

*Why? Why was she so furious?*

Stepping over the cloak, Olivia laid her hand and then ear against the door listening for any rustlings or coughs from within the next room. All was quiet. Thank goodness. She was in no mood to face Egg.

Picking up her cloak from the floor, she moved into the main room.

*The dinner had been hideous.*

The man had absolutely no skills at conversation, much less wooing. He had been extremely polite, almost to the point of absurdity. As if he had practiced his words like a piece to be recited, and even he couldn't quite believe what he was saying. But as stilted pleasantries fell from his lips, his eyes, often shuttered and remote, were telling a different story.

She had glimpsed sorrow, even despair.

And lust. Yes, his head and heart were most defiantly at odds with each other; strict denial paired with intense hunger. Banal gibberish underscored with white hot lust. She knew it to be lust because she felt the same tug and fullness in her own body.

She had tried to ignore these baser feelings and draw him out, to divine *anything* that might prove fertile ground for a mental connection. But there was nothing there to divine. Oh, he made an ineffectual pass at speaking of his work in the Lords, and possibly there was a bit of passion when he spoke of his estates and his horse, but not one of these topics included an actual person. But why should she even care? She would never have to see him again. She should be thrilled.

She kicked off her slippers and then rubbed the small of her back as she laid her cloak over a chair, fingering a ruined clasp.

And why had she been so indignant at his offer? She was no priggish miss. She knew the way of the world and all the signs that made it a man's dominion. She knew as a mere female her space within that sphere was narrow and confined. And, as a woman nearing her twenty-ninth birthday, with no real family or connections, her own personal realm was infinitely smaller still.

Lud, what had she expected from the man? And a duke no less? Did she expect marriage? This last thought brought her over the edge into hysterical laughter. She found herself on the floor, tasting tears.

They had *danced*. They had waltzed to Vivaldi. He had held her within his arms and, heaven help her, it had been magic. The world had opened up wide, and they were the only two figures within that freeing space. *She* had opened.

Punishing herself, she pushed to expose the emotion that lay under her sorrow, welcoming the stab of humiliation. She had made herself vulnerable, had let herself yearn and want. The realization brought clarity to her weeping, and now released, she heaved her sadness in great gulping sobs at the embers smoldering in the cooling grate.

Finally calm, she stood and quietly removed the gold gown and found her wrapper where Egg must have thoughtfully left it.

She touched her mouth where his lips had been, finding where her teeth had cut into the inner flesh, and welcomed the sting. His kiss was certainly not that of a consummate lover, far from it. It was elemental and raw, almost sloppy, teeth and lips banging and bruising. But, oh, what he lacked in finesse he more than made up with...*want*. Like a starving child who had suddenly been given heavenly bread and treacle. The kiss had been that of a starved man. It made her both want to cry and to fill him till he was bursting, to give him that which he so craved. What he desired. *Herself.* And if she were honest, what she desired as well.

She would never willingly be his mistress, never be his on contractual terms. Being bought and paid for was loathsome but to be with him, to *fill* him...

Olivia pulled pins from her hair. What would he look like? Would he be hairless? Or would he have a mat of fine black hair trailing down to an arrow over his flat stomach ending in a nest of dark at his cock?

Absently, she smoothed the placket opening of her wrapper feeling the soft, worn cotton. How big would he be? She gasped as her fingers brushed her nipple. How would his testicles fill her hands? Would they be loose and flowing or would they be drawn up tight and hard with need? She squeezed her breast. And what would he smell like—his particular musk? Would it be sweet or earthy? Would he cry out with his release, or would he be mute?

Her hands had found her own secret place. It had been so long since she had touched herself, but she was wet and ready. She moved one of her hands up again to her breast—the barest touch—and then plunged her longest finger into her waiting flesh and convulsed around skin and bone.

Dear God, she wanted him.

\*\*\*\*

It was truly raining now.

James was stammering his eighth apology as Rhys descended from the coach.

"It is finished," Rhys said, almost to himself. Then, in a firmer tone, "See to that wheel and give an extra measure to the cattle." He brushed aside the proffered umbrella and made his way into the house.

Yes, it was finished. He would not have his heart's desire. Well, it wasn't as if he was unused to the feeling. Yet, with this woman, it was so hard to bear.

Tinsley was at the bedchamber door. Rhys submitted to the valet's ministrations, raising the appropriate arm or leg. It was a ritual they knew as well as breathing.

Quiet and efficient, Tinsley finished quickly and left with a brief, "Goodnight, Your Grace."

Long after the valet had left the chamber, Rhys lay in bed and stared into the deep blue silk canopy. The ribbon from her mask slid over and over between his fingers. He felt an enormous pressure behind his eyelids—as if his eyeballs were too big for their sockets—and then the sensation of wetness. The wet slid slowly across his cheeks and rolled into his ears.

Chapter Ten

"Foster!" Daria shouted as she thrust her dripping ice into her maid's waiting hands.

"May I dispose of it, madam?" Foster whined.

Daria stopped in the process of drawing on her gloves.

"Oh, bother." She turned back, gesturing for the sweet. "No, no, *you* hold it." The cream threatened to ooze over its paper cone onto Foster gloves as Daria savored a last lapping bite, and then she dismissed the maid and cone at once.

"Madam—"

Daria held up her hand to silence the woman and then paused, torn between another bite and her business ahead. "Enough. I have had enough." She stepped away from the carriage.

"But, madam—" Foster shifted the dripping cone.

"Confound it, woman, I have no need of you. Wait in the carriage."

The maid, her face pinched, gave up and switched the dripping cone to her other hand.

Daria turned away, barely registering the sound of a splat followed by a "Bloody hell" from somewhere behind her. She jerked on her last glove, adjusted her tippet, and pushed into Weston's shop ready for battle.

"I vow I have never seen such a rig," Weston exclaimed when Daria stepped through the door. "I tell you it housed an entire three-tiered birdcage complete with finches singing 'Ode to Thee.'" Weston had piled a wad of netting atop her head and was swanning about the shop, tweeting and flapping like a bird as her partner, Wiggins, doubled over with laughter.

The women had not even heard the bell. Daria cleared her throat. "I presume you must be describing old lady Fitzhugh's latest coiffure?"

"Mrs. Battersby," the older woman stammered, glancing sideways at her partner, who, still swathed in netting, was wiping the tears from her eyes.

"Oh, Mrs. Battersby, I do beg your pardon." Weston began unwinding the yards of netting from her head. "I am afraid you caught us in a moment of levity."

"Think nothing of it," Daria said, drawn to the beautiful length of sarcenet draping the large cutting table. "Fitz is as ridiculous as she is old. Several years ago, she painted her entire body black—and I do mean entire—and dressed herself as a page from East Africa. And as if that was not enough, she had a footman lower the chandelier and he hoisted her—" Daria stopped. "Never mind." She abandoned the fabric. "Suffice to say she has become quite tame of late." She turned her full attention to the younger woman, who had successfully removed the netting and was just managing to pat her hair into some semblance of order. Her mussed beauty set Daria's teeth on edge.

"So, Mrs. Weston, it would appear you have been quite busy in these last few weeks."

"Busy?" Weston's brows rose and then settled. "Oh, yes. We are busy now. Mrs. Wiggins and I have just received a most generous order."

"Yes, Eveline Barton." Daria waved her hand.

The two women exchanged a surprised look.

"You know very well, I am not talking of Barton or her dresses. I am speaking of Roydan. The Duke of Roydan."

"The duke? I am not sure I comprehend." Weston glanced at her partner, and Daria caught Wiggins's look of confusion and surprise. Ah, so Weston was keeping the Roydan affair to herself. Daria filed this tidbit away. Possibly something she could mine later.

"Oh, please, there is no need to be missish with me, Mrs. Weston. You know all too well how *busy* you have been and with whom."

The woman had the good sense to remain silent.

"Now, let us set about how we—"

"Excuse me, madam, but I don't think we have anything to discuss."

*Insufferable chit.* "I see." Daria's eyes narrowed. "We will play it your way." Adopting her most regal attitude, she looked about and lowered herself into the nearest of a pair of chairs, her performance only slightly hindered by the fact that the chair was obviously made for a child and not a reasonably sized person. Now settled, she turned her entire attention to the woman standing before her. In her experience this usually reduced an inferior to a quivering mass; however, it seemed less than effective in Weston's case. No matter.

Daria cleared her throat. "If I must spell it out, I refer to your appearance with Roydan at Mrs. Parkington's mask last evening." Weston seemed genuinely surprised, and her partner, totally shocked. "You have certainly changed your spots, Miss Butter-wouldn't-melt-in-your-mouth. Well, I give you full marks for seeing an opportunity and taking it."

Weston squared her shoulders. "Madam, I do not begin to know to what you are referring."

"Come now," Daria chided. "You saw an opening and you took it. You slipped right in shall we say."

"Now listen here, Mrs. Battersby!" Wiggins started forward.

"No, Egg. Let her finish."

"You are wise, Mrs. Weston. Yes, I think it is best we get this all settled as soon as may be. Don't you agree, Mrs. Wiggins? It is loathsome to have secrets among friends, is it not?" Satisfied the older woman got the message, she gave her attention back to Weston.

"I would hate for you to get your hopes up for naught." Daria looked the younger woman and down. "Oh la, what a joke! You are not even his type. As slim as a willow with no bosom to speak of. I could hardly credit it when I saw you arrive at the mask with my dear Rhys. It is obvious he chose Parkington's mask, knowing I would be in attendance. I am very much afraid you were only a pawn in his scheme to make me jealous, my dear Mrs. Weston. Poor Roydan, he was never much for an apology."

Weston shared a speaking look with her partner. "Mrs. Battersby, I am sorry to contradict you, but it was I who wanted to attend Mrs. Parkington's affair. Your 'Dear Rhys' begged *me* to have him as my escort."

Daria itched to pop the obnoxious woman on her pert nose, but realized it would be difficult to rise with any real grace and abandoned the idea. Instead, she held her place, looking as much down her nose as possible, which was rather difficult being situated so much lower than Weston. "Do you take me for a fool? The duke does not beg anyone to do anything. And he never allows the use of his Christian name—excepting by myself of course," she added hastily. "I can see you know nothing of him and his ways." A wicked thought occurred to her. "I collect you have not even shared his bed yet, have you?" Sweet Jezebel, the woman actually blushed. "No, I can see you have not."

"Mrs. Battersby, I will have to ask you to remove yourself now, as we are expecting a *paying* customer."

"I had hoped we could be civil about this, Weston. But I see that will not be the case. How dare you presume to poach on *my* territory? You who are *no one*? You may deceive the duke with your games and eye flutterings, but you will *not* deceive me! I have put down ten times the likes of you, and I will again. You mark my words."

"My *dear* Mrs. Battersby, I would not dream of interfering in your conjugal bliss. By all means take him," Weston paused and with a nasty smile continued, "if you can."

Daria felt the beginnings of what felt, shockingly, like defeat. Livid, she hefted herself out of her chair.

"Oh you think you are so clever, but let me give you a word to the wise. Roydan is not called the Monk for nothing. Believe me, I have used my *considerable* prowess to inspire him to, shall we say, greater heights, but to no avail. He is, quite simply, a dullard in the boudoir. I told him so last evening when he cornered me to beg me to come back to him."

The woman only smiled wider.

Daria felt very much like a small child who had just had the head of her favorite doll snapped off by an evil playfellow.

How had this interview got away from her? And why the devil did they keep the room so bloody warm? She had allowed this woman to rile her when she was here to set the hook. His lordship was very specific in his instructions, and she had made a hash of it with her jealousy.

Daria resisted the urge to swipe her upper lip. "Believe it or not Weston, I came as a friend. I, like you, have been disappointed with life's trials once or twice in my life. I know what it is to make your way in an unfair world, and I wanted to extend an opportunity to you."

"An opportunity?"

"Well, an invitation really, to the Dillingham ball." She drew a card out of her reticule and placed it on the cutting table. "I happen to know her ladyship personally, and though she is newly raised from her humble beginnings, she still has the taste of an actress. She would be the perfect patroness for your shop." Weston's gaze went to the card.

"Well," Daria continued, "I will not keep you. You obviously have much to do."

Daria moved swiftly to the shop door. Weston did not know with whom she was dealing. But she would, oh yes, she would.

"Oh madam—" Wiggins ran after her.

Daria turned with slow dignity.

"Yes, woman?"

"I do beg your pardon…"

Daria cast her most magnanimous look at Weston and turned back to Mrs. Wiggins. "It is not for *you* to apologize, Wiggins. But we women must stick together and let bygones be bygones."

"No, Mrs. Battersby, I only meant to mention you seem to have some residual food crusted to your— chins."

Daria's hand shot halfway to her mouth before she recovered her composure. Wiggins raised a small hand mirror to Daria's face along with a handkerchief.

Looking in the mirror Daria saw, as plain as the nose on her face, a large blob of dried whitish cream on her chin. Her mind flashed back to Foster and her nattering. Drat.

She darted a look at Weston but saw only studied composure. Daria calmly took the proffered handkerchief, dabbed at the mess, folded it neatly and handed it carefully back to Wiggins. Turning, she waited for the woman to open the door, and walked through it without a backward glance, but not before she heard the eruption of laughter.

****

Rhys's tears were appalling to him in the light of day. He had not cried in…well since his mother's death twenty-four years ago.

Last night he had listened to the rain mixed with the ticking of his clocks, but the sounds had not soothed him. Ironically his bed hangings looked very much like the purple and blue tent he had danced under just hours before. In an effort to blot out that image, he had concentrated on finding all the constellations picked out in diamonds.

His eyes moved to his favorite, Orion the hunter with his jeweled belt and mighty sword. Orion would slay all the dragons and fiends of the night—well, that is what his mother had told him as a child. But the Great Hunter had failed miserably last night. He could not even vanquish one dark-haired, green-eyed witch.

Rhys had marked out three and then four and finally five bongs from the French portico clock on the mantel. He would have sworn he had never slept at all, but he could not recall hearing the next six so he must have fallen asleep.

The sun was out in full force now—the light clear and radiant as it often was after a long hard rain. Even the puddles had dried to only the barest sheen.

His body felt tight and pent up like a sneeze that would not come. He needed exercise.

Rhys was just on his way out when Safley announced Uncle Bertram.

"I hope I'm not disturbing you, Roydan." His uncle stood inside the doorway.

"No, not at all, sir."

In spite of his answer, Rhys was disturbed. He did not want this conversation.

"Safley, will you see to some ale?" he said as he walked to his desk and shoved the morning papers under a pile of letters.

"If it's all the same to you, Roydan, I'd rather have something a bit stronger," his uncle said sheepishly. Rhys squeezed his teeth together. If his uncle had need of fortification at this time in the day, it did not bode well for their upcoming conversation.

"Very well, Uncle. Safley, you may leave us. I will pour."

"Your Grace." He bowed and the heavy door closed behind him.

"A very good man your Safley. He has been with you a long while now, I believe."

Rhys raised an eyebrow. "Sir, he has been with me

since I attained the title over seven years ago. I believe you recommended him to the position."

"Ah, yes. Quite right." Uncle Bert coughed. "I have never steered you wrong, my boy, have I?"

Rhys handed his uncle a brandy. "No, sir, you have always had my best interest at heart."

"I try, my boy. I try." Uncle Bert looked distracted. He took a large swallow, nodded appreciatively, and settled himself into a wing chair next to the fire. Rhys sat as well.

"Well, I will not condescend to you by beating around the bush." He cleared his throat. "Campbell is wondering if the girl has put you off somehow."

Rhys pressed his tongue on the hard ridge just behind his teeth.

"Perhaps she is too plump?" his uncle offered.

Rhys took his first sip, savoring the slow burn. "She is most attractive, sir."

His uncle visibly relaxed into his chair and took another mouthful of brandy. "Yes, she is a sweet young thing, isn't she? I like a bit of flesh on a girl myself. Gives a man something to hold on to, don't you know."

*Christ.* Rhys had to stop himself from lurching out of his chair and pacing the room.

Uncle Bert took another taste, shifted forward in his chair and then back again.

"So my boy, what *is* the holdup? You certainly don't want to lead the family on, do you? You must know all the papers have marked how attentive you have been to Miss Arabella."

Yes, Rhys knew only too well what the papers had been saying. Yet another cartoon by that damned Gillray, *The Monk Meets his Match*, depicting Rhys ripping off his monk's robes to reveal a timid Arabella beneath. Still another with him kneeling at the altar, again in monk's robes, with a diminutive Arabella perched on an altar holding out the collection plate and desperately trying to remove his halo, to replace it with a pair of horns.

This last was too much. *Damned infernal rags. Can't they ever let a man in peace?* The *broadsheets* and their ilk could poke fun at him all they liked, but he drew the line at their involving the Campbells as mercenaries, and particularly, Miss Arabella as a wanton. He had not even bothered to read this morning's papers.

There was no point in prevaricating. He must go forward or retreat entirely. And why retreat? There was no other eligible woman he wanted. Arabella Campbell would do just as well as any. True, she did not seem overly keen for the marriage, but that would mean there would be no unrealistic expectations for love and happiness.

"You are quite right, Uncle. The papers have been odious." He desperately wanted this conversation to be over. "I promise to speak with Lord Campbell within the week." Even as he spoke the words, he felt the heaviness of his title crashing down on him.

His uncle, watching him keenly, finally spoke. "Listen lad, if the girl doesn't suit, we will find another. No sense in shackling yourself to a chit who does nothing to…inspire you. I am only offering Arabella Campbell because she has impeccable bloodlines, seems reasonably intelligent, and is, to my mind, quite fetching. But there is still time to retreat. I just caution you, your oar is in, and you must decide to set sail or no, and soon. I know you would not want to dishonor the girl or her family."

"No, Uncle, you have done right in coming. I am out of sorts lately."

"Anything I can help with, dear boy?"

Could he confide his uncertainty to his uncle who was his only real family? Could he unburden his heart? But how could he open his heart to Uncle Bert, when he did not know his own feelings. *Uncle, I am in lust? I am unable to put a mere dressmaker out of my mind? And she doesn't even want me?*

The whole notion was preposterous. He shook his head as much to himself as for his uncle.

"No, Uncle Bert." He tried to smile. "Unless you would like to switch roles with me, sir?"

Bertram laughed. But Rhys must have let a bit of his despair slip past his smile because his uncle stopped abruptly, leaned forward, and looked him squarely in the eyes. "I am sorry I was not about when you were young, lad." Then he looked away, saving Rhys from having to do so, and took a slow sip of brandy. "I knew what your father was. True, he and I were separated by almost fifteen years, but I heard the stories. We had a few dramas of our own." Uncle Bertram's lips tightened, and his gaze tracked to the portrait hanging above them.

Rhys glanced at the painting as well, but he need not have. He knew it in all its agonizing detail—the surly expression, and the beginning signs of dissipation that already marred the subject's face.

The old duke had had an insatiable appetite for all the vices. He had been a spendthrift, a debaucher of women, a miserly landlord, a cheat, and a fraud. But perhaps his worst sin was his indifference to anything not solely for his pleasure. Rhys had never, or almost never, come within the old duke's field of vision, but when he had—

Rhys turned away from the picture. He had thought about exiling the thing to the attics but instead he used it as a constant reminder of what he *would not* be.

His uncle cleared his throat. "And then, after your mother's death…well, you went off to school and I went into the army." Bertram smiled ruefully. "Being the spare is not always easy either, my boy. Though, in answer to your question, no, I am very happy being simply Lord Bertram, thank you." He laughed. "Why do you think I am so anxious to get you married and producing?" Bertram rose and filled his glass then gestured with the bottle to Rhys who shook his head. "And now we have to deal with this damned codicil to Ian's will." Bertram snorted. "Ian's solicitors were a bunch of lazy, drunken, opium-eating sots. Too bad the firm's new owners are such a thorough lot, else those files would have remained buried for decades. Well, lad, 'tis a folly to cry for shed milk. We must go forward.

"Perhaps it will be for the best in the end—a blessing in disguise?" His uncle's eyes softened as he spoke and Rhys wanted to look away. "I would like to see you happy, lad. You are due for some happiness."

Rhys tried to answer his uncle's smile, and though he felt his lips twitch upward, he knew it was more of a grimace. *Happiness?* He was not even sure what it was anymore. The feeling had eroded to almost nothing. A vague shadow lurking at the edges of his heart. Duty, responsibility, and now lust…those he knew well. But happiness…

"Be easy, Uncle, I will speak to Lord Campbell soon." Rhys shifted, and then stood. "If there is nothing else? I have had Sid saddled and waiting, but I shall have him untacked if you need me further?"

"No, no, my boy." His uncle rose and set his glass on a side table. "You mustn't keep that fine beast waiting. I'll warrant there is no better animal this side of the channel."

\*\*\*\*

Thoroughly soaked and winded, Rhys pulled Sid up. They had just done a bruising run through St. James's Park when the rain had come—sudden darkness, and then sheets of water accompanied with blinding lightning and rolling thunder. Everyone on the street had dashed into doorways and tea shops to watch the drama from relative safety. Within a minute the streets were empty.

He raised his face to the cold, lashing wet. The weather and the emptiness suited his mood but apparently not Sid's. The beast threw his head and worried his bit. "Hush, boy." Rhys patted the horse's steaming neck. Sid liked to put on a bit of a show.

Uncle Bert's little speech had thrown Rhys. He knew his uncle cared for him, but the real anguish in his uncle's eyes, especially when he was talking about wanting Rhys to be happy made Rhys shift in his saddle.

Digging his heels into Sid, he headed for the Horse Guards. He gravitated to this particular corner of London more times than he could count.

Rhys had actually thought to go into the Guards like his uncle. The idea of rules and strict discipline suited him, and he thought he would have made a good officer.

When his father had heard, he was apoplectic. He had barged into Rhys's rooms at the Albany. The only time he saw his sire was when the old duke needed money. All he had to do was threaten to sell Valmere, and Rhys would give him the blunt. It was their old song and dance. But this visit was different. His father looked worse than usual.

"By God, I will take care to bankrupt every last estate and see you ruined!" he had said. "You are worthless except as my heir, and you think to take yourself off to tangle with old Boney and get yourself killed?" Rhys could still see him staggering around the room, spittle spewing from his mouth. "*I* still have a healthy appetite. I am not done. I chose poorly twice now, but perhaps Dee Gooden might be just the ticket. How would you like her for your dearest step-mama? You were once very…fond of her. And when she whelps then you may go to the devil for all I care. I'll wager that miserable little pickle between your legs has probably dried up by now for lack of use." His father's pupils were mere pin pricks; he had been so fuddled on opium. "By Jove, I would swear you weren't mine if I had a hope of getting away with it."

Well, in the end his sire had had the last laugh; just as Rhys was preparing to go to France, the old duke had the temerity to die. Rhys had almost gone anyway, but with the estates and farms in shambles, he'd had no choice. Duty called, and it had been his rudder ever since.

Sid tossed his head, wanting to be out of the wet. "All right, old boy, let us see if we can find you a treat."

The men's daily exercises must have been called off because of the rain. He dismounted and made his way into the stables, leading a snuffling Sid.

It was strangely quiet inside. Usually on a rainy day, the men were jammed into the barracks polishing and grooming, trading insults and dares. He saw a stable boy and called to him asking for Colonel Barret. The young man recognized Rhys immediately, pulling his forelock and bowing.

"Your Grace, the colonel took most of the regiment and their families on a picnic to Richmond." When Rhys made no comment, the boy shyly offered, "It was his young wife's idea, Your Grace. I expect they are all huddled in the Fife and Drum just about now." The lad smiled, ducking his head.

"Ah, I had forgotten the colonel was lately married." Rhys felt an unexpected swell in his throat and swallowed it like foul medicine. "I shall make use of a stall to dry off my mount."

The lad jumped into action. "Pardon, Your Grace, here I am blabbing while you are soaked through. Please come and sit. I'll get a blanket, put on a pot, and then see to your mount. I will be only a moment."

"No, I thank you, I am well enough. I will see to the horse myself, but a mug of ale would not go amiss."

"Of course, Your Grace. Right away." And the boy-man ran off.

Rhys sighed. Why did he always seem to come off demanding when he really wanted to be amiable?

Rhys walked Sid to a nearby empty stall, untacked the horse, found a bit of toweling, and methodically rubbed down the animal. Sid nickered and bobbed his huge head against Rhys's shoulder.

He had a great respect for horses, and this one in particular. Sid was very nearly Rhys's best friend. Rather pathetic, but how could one quibble with such a loyal, trusted comrade? Sid just happened to be a horse. Well, there were worse things in life.

Rhys closed his eyes—wet horse and Sid's own particular dander mixed with all the familiar smells of a barn, seasoned hay, oats, leather, linseed oil, and earthy sweat. The patter of rain *tat-tatted* on the roof above them, becoming a kind of meditative music to work by. He smoothed his hands over the horse—he need not open his eyes, he knew every line of the beast from Sid's soft velvet nose to his rough silk tail.

But his father's image would not be laid to rest. Rhys stiffened, and Sid jerked his head.

He was seven years old.

His father had arrived at Valmere out of the blue as usual. But that morning he strode into the stables as if he had never been away, demanding to see the progress his son was making in the saddle.

Rhys could be found hanging about the barn most days. He had loved all its many treasures—the loft, full of magical, winking fairy dust, the shoot that would become his slide, landing with a whoosh in a pile of new-mown hay. Old Mac's room with its warm stove and ancient rocker sitting on a bright rag rug. The rug had replaced the old threadbare one that had finally worn through to the wood floor. Mac had gone red right up to his whiskers when Mrs. Cotton had thrust the rug at him last Christmas muttering something about "auld men and their auld worn-out things." The room held the smells of tobacco and coffee, of tallow and peat— smells that had seeped into the very walls.

But the barn's most amazing riches, hidden behind towering walls, were the horses themselves. And the very last stall, tucked right next to Mac's room, held the most splendid treasure of all; it was home to Jolly, Rhys's Welsh pony.

That day Rhys had brought Jolly out of his stall for his father's inspection. He dared a shy smile, so proud of his beautiful pony. His father might find fault with Rhys, but anyone could see Jolly was perfect in every way.

The duke made a slow circle around Jolly and then stopped directly in front of Rhys. "Is this a joke?"

Confused, Rhys looked to Mac but then seeing his father's mistake turned to him and said, "No, sir, his name is *Jolly*, sir."

But his father was speaking again. "By God, when I was your age I was riding a sixteen-hand hunter, not some *toy*. You will remember you are the son of a duke." Rhys stupidly had the urge to cover Jolly's ears as hot tears washed his eyes.

"Mackenzie, I will not be humiliated on my own estate. See that the boy gets a proper mount for the morrow. Till then, I suppose this nag will have to do." He turned to Rhys. "Well, don't stand there gaping, tack the thing up."

Rhys's fingers slipped on the bridle's throat lash and Mac had to come to help tighten the girth. The whole process took twice as long as usual. The only sound was his father's crop snapping against his booted calf. The sound stopped suddenly. Rhys looked up from lowering a stirrup and just caught sight of the horse and rider as they pounded out of the paddock.

Rhys heaved up into the saddle and fumbled for the

stirrups. Mac squeezed his thigh, "Steady, lad," he said, winking. And Rhys had raced off to find his father.

The duke had gone into the northern park and had jumped the stile that separated two fields. He stopped and turned back to watch Rhys. There was no mistaking the challenge. Rhys's breath caught, fear squeezing deep within him. There was no choice, he must go. He clucked to Jolly, and the pony, ever game and trusting, surged forward.

"Lean over his withers, lad." He could hear Mac's voice in his head, but all his practice was for naught in the face of his frowning sire. Fear and a desperate wanting to please took hold instead of calm reason. He went into the jump unbalanced, too far back in his saddle, his reins too long. He squeezed his eyes shut and waited for the worst. He felt the pony lift, and they flew through the air.

It was over in a moment.

*Thunk!* Rhys's eyes snapped open as he grabbed the pommel. They had done it! The earth was again solid and sure beneath them. He immediately sought his father's face; sure their performance would earn some glimmer of praise.

His father rode right up to Rhys, looked directly into his eyes and said, "No son of mine will ever make such a sloppy show. See that you do better on the next." And he wheeled his great black and galloped to the next field.

Rhys dashed at his tears with the back of his hand, ashamed. He was no baby. He *would* prove himself. He dug his heels hard into the pony. When Jolly stumbled Rhys used his crop.

His father was headed neck or nothing for the

hornbeam hedge at the far edge of the field. He looked back, and Rhys thought he could detect a smile on his father's face. The hedge was clearly the next challenge. But surely his father would veer at the last moment. Surely he did not expect Rhys to take a jump that high? Mac had never let him jump anything half so tall. Rhys watched in panic and awe as his sire and the black sailed over the hedge.

"Sir, I don't—"

But his father was gone. Rhys pressed Jolly forward; the pony tossed his head and snorted. Rhys knew he should not take the jump. But he knew just as surely, he must.

The hedge loomed before them, impossibly high at twenty yards away. Now at only ten, it was monstrous. He leaned into Jolly, shortened his reins, and squeezed his thighs. *Come on, boy.*

Rhys heard a click and jerked.

"I've brought your ale, Your Grace."

Rhys could not speak or move. His forehead pressed against Sid's flank; his hands clenched the towel.

"Your Grace?"

"Leave it," Rhys managed to wring out.

The boy hesitated, clearly unsure how to proceed. Finally, "I'll just put it here on the shelf, shall I?"

Rhys heard the click again as the stall door closed.

He could still see Jolly's rolling, pain-filled eyes.

He had held the pony's head, crooning nonsense to the poor beast. He tasted the bitter tang of blood in his mouth, felt the earth shudder as his father rode up and dismounted, heard his own screams as his father pulled him from his beloved pony. And finally he heard the

123

click of the pistol as his father cocked the gun and shot Jolly right between his eyes.

But the sight Rhys could not live with was the look of utter trust in the pony's soft, brown eyes, even in the face of Rhys's betrayal.

Chapter Eleven

Olivia desperately needed to concentrate.

The half-finished sketch of an evening costume stared back at her, daring her to continue. She looked down at the pencil stub, took a deep breath, and willed her fingers to relax.

She had staved off Egg's questions for the moment, but she knew they were bound to come sooner than later. And when they did she needed a story. A good story. Egg could sift out one tiny falsehood in a bucket brimming with truth.

Olivia glanced down. *How had ruffles got on the hemline?* Hideous. She scrubbed it out.

But really Daria Battersby was the outside of enough. How dared she flounce into the shop drawing battle lines? Heavens, she could have "dear Rhys" for all Olivia cared.

"Bother." She scrubbed out the battleaxe, which had miraculously appeared, buried in the gown's bodice.

Well, one thing was dead certain; she would never have to lay eyes on him again. After all, they did not move in the same circles. Not even remotely. She would never have to see that cursed eyebrow raise, as if to say, "You are nothing." She would never have to sit across a dining table, receiving scowling looks and enduring tedious conversation. She would never have to ponder how his voice could be so wonderfully low, yet so melodic. She would never have the urge to rumple his pristine linen or dislodge a curl from his head or actually see him sweat. But most importantly, she would never have to suffer being clasped to his body, twirling dizzily around a glittering ballroom to the sounds of Vivaldi. Yes, she was *very* glad. *Mightily* glad.

Unfortunately, not *seeing* him did not necessarily translate into not *thinking* about him.

She pressed pencil to paper. At first a few tentative marks, and then, gaining momentum, her whole body took over. She lifted off the high stool as her hand flew across the page, filling the paper with sweeping lines, jarring dashes, and cross-hatched shadings. She stopped only when her fingers cramped painfully.

Olivia stared at her creation, and it stared boldly back. Gone was any notion of a dress. Oh the gown was there, but no longer the focus. The dress was merely a container for the woman inside. And that woman was herself. But—*not*—herself. This woman's head was thrust back, her eyelids hooded and lazy, her mouth a mysterious smile. She lay cradled in the arms of a man.

Rude as the drawing was, and only in black and white, she knew the man's eyes to be pure gold. His mask lay discarded on the floor, while hers dangled from the tips of her fingers, only a breath away from joining his.

She did not know how long she stared at the picture, but her heart had now slowed, her breath was steadier, and her bottom had found the edge of the stool.

Olivia slowly spread her fingers over the image

and squeezed. The woman's waist collapsed backward like a broken doll, as the man's legs buckled, distorted and useless; his wide shoulders warped, and then bowed like an old man. She flung the wadded ball to the floor, her pencil skittering along the table and rolling to join the drawing. Then she laughed. It was all so hilariously comical...absolutely...hilarious.

*Damn it! Concentrate.* She reached for another bit of paper to begin again. It was the broadsheet from this morning. Well, it would do for a rough sketch. She retrieved her pencil from under the stove, and sat, ready to seize on the first brilliant impulse.

Magic. She needed a bit of mag—*Monk?* She stared at the paper. "*Monk?*"

*What?* She looked closer. "The Masked Monk?"

Olivia banged her forehead on the table along with her fists. "Ahhhhh!" Was there no escaping the man?

There was even a picture. It was quite crude, even grotesque, but spot on. How the artist cranked this out so quickly was nothing short of miraculous. Anyone with half a brain could see it was the duke—his tall, muscular figure towering over the minuscule dancers surrounding them, his shoulders wider than Prinny's girth. The caricaturist had got Roydan's nose just right, a blade of a beak arching out from his tiny black mask, dark curling hair, slightly shadowed jaw. And then his lips. They were beautifully drawn, as if the artist could not bear to distort their perfection. She would agree and could add they were softly firm, with a trace of sweet sauternes—

She abandoned the duke and her gaze raked over the woman pictured. Would this Michelangelo capture some tell-tale feature of herself? No, the mask hid all.

Olivia's breath emptied in a rush of relief.

She read the blurb three times.

*"The world has surely gone topsy-turvy. Could our beloved Monk be turning in his cowl and halo for a mask? Madam Parkington had to pick her teeth up off the floor as the D of R made his way into her Persian Mecca last evening. This would have been enough in itself, but it seems our Monk has traded in his old 'Bat' for a new confection. Mouths were agape as our Monk waltzed—yes, waltzed— with this stunning creature. Her costume was the sheerest spun gold and her mask the Sun. Surely underneath she must be a Nun? But perhaps our dear duke is changing his 'habits'?"*

"Ha!" Really, these rags were too much. She could not help feeling just the tiniest sense of pride at the mention of the stunning creature in her golden gown.

Her laughter dribbled away, and her thoughts drifted along the well-traveled path of the previous evening. Only now, all the awkward and annoying bits were gone—which left her with only a handful of memories, but those moments were so—so *potent*.

*Why* was she so attracted to this silent, impossible man? She did not even *like* him. She ripped the paper in half. And then again. It was not enough, not nearly enough. She grabbed an armful of old papers and threw them in the air. As they fell she heaved them up again, stomping and twisting her foot and then her whole body, to grind them into the floor. Still not enough. She began ripping them to pieces. Yes! This was more like it. It felt good to exercise her cramped muscles, to do something *big*, something *destructive*.

"What on earth are you about?"

*Oh dear*. It was Egg. Olivia stopped mid-throw. Scraps of newsprint floated like gray feathers around her body. She plucked a stray bit from her left shoulder, smoothing it onto the drawing table by her side. "Just exorcising a few demons."

Olivia waited for Egg's quip. It did not come. All Olivia got was a tired half smile. Egg moved into the room to lean heavily on the cutting table. A lump rose from Olivia's belly and lodged squarely in her throat. She swallowed hard, trying to force it down so she could speak. It remained fixed, threatening to choke her. Egg was too pale and drawn, her breathing too shallow. Olivia knew better than to call attention to the fact. Egg would only push herself to act livelier and tire herself even more.

Olivia swallowed again. Finally the lump moved down. "Well, now that I've got that out of my system, I say we deserve some tea." After all they were English; tea would cure just about anything, wouldn't it?

"If you will recall, my dear," Egg said, stopping for more breath, "I am just returning from the last rest you insisted I take." Egg frowned. "You will make yourself sick as well, and then where will we be?"

Lud, she must look a proper mess if Egg saw fit to comment on her state. Olivia scraped her hand through her hair, jamming a loose pin back in place, and scrubbed at her eyes hoping to erase the signs of having wept most of the night. Her body ached, not only with exhaustion but with a tightly curled yearning she could not seem to squelch no matter how tightly she had laced her corset that morning. If Egg were to cut the strings,

Olivia felt quite sure she would collapse in a heap and be buried in her sea of paper.

The very last thing she wanted to do was to go back to that bloody sketch, but it was more important to restore some sense of normalcy in front of Egg who had quite enough to deal with just managing to breathe. "I will stay and finish this drawing, but you must sit by the stove and I will fetch you the bit of beading that needs doing. Then we shall both have a well-deserved cup."

"Very well, but I insist you tell me about the ball and more especially about the Monk. You have not been very forthcoming, and I believe I deserve my share of the entertainment."

Well, at least this was more like her old Egglet. There seemed no avoiding the conversation. The duke must be dealt with and then she would not talk of him ever again. Or think of him. Or even dream of him. She crossed the room to help Egg to the chair by the stove and retrieved the beading. Egg smiled as she began the tedious work of stringing tiny seed pearls.

"Isabelle says he is extremely handsome if you like the harsh, austere sort," Egg said, her tone wheedling. "I only saw the old Gillray caricatures, and it is quite difficult to judge a man who is depicted on his knees using a knife and fork to fend off a highflyer baring her breasts. And then there was the one with the two-headed elephant. My dear," Egg said loudly, "you are not even listening."

"What? Oh, I assure you, I heard every word—breasts, elephants, and all. He was only a means to an end. Now we must forget about the duke. The whole encounter will be our little secret." She did not dare look at Egg. Instead she plunged on, "And look what he brought us? I believe Eveline Barton used to be touted as one of the finest dancers at the Paris Opera. Though to be fair, she never danced some of the more demanding roles. But still, she is a good beginning.

"I dare say we will have to turn orders away soon." She knew she was rattling on, and what's more she knew Egg knew. One look at her friend's face, and she would see the smirk. So Olivia did not bother to look.

She was saved by the arrival of Hazel and Jeb.

"Look here! Have you seen the papers today?" Hazel thrust the paper under Olivia's nose.

*Damn.*

\*\*\*\*

A bee droned in one ear, Lady Campbell in the other. Rhys adjusted his hat, trying to situate its short brim to block as much of the sun as possible. He was sure the adjustment made him appear quite rakish, but at this point in the afternoon he frankly did not care. A slow roll of perspiration inched its way down the back of his neck and into his wilting linen. One would think it was full summer instead of early May.

They were attending Lady Sutton's Venetian Breakfast. Lady Campbell popped up from her seat no less than a dozen times with some excuse to leave her daughter with Rhys so they might have a *tête-à-tête*. But then her resolve would fail and propriety would win over. She would flutter about and eventually plop herself back down, continuing as dutiful chaperon.

Rhys would have found it mildly amusing, but for the fact that every time the good woman rose, he was obliged to do the same. In this heat the exercise was becoming tedious. He was thankful when the old Dowager Countess of Havermear trundled by and complimented Lady Campbell on attending the "young people." Since then her ladyship had ceased her popping, but unfortunately her yammering increased two-fold.

Rhys spent precious energy waving away the insistent bee. If only he could do the same with Lady Campbell. Well, at least he was not called upon to actually respond. A nod every so often was all the lady seemed to require. Miss Arabella, even less attentive to her mamma, twirled her parasol and looked about the garden. Their lack of participation in the conversation had absolutely no effect on her ladyship's prattling. Rhys had just resolved to make his excuses when—

"—looking forward to the Asherton's musical this evening."

In that second, the bee and heat ceased to exist.

"It is said Mrs. Pembly is not to be rivaled for her rendition of Mozart's Queen of the Night," Lady Campbell said, and loaded a cream puff into her mouth.

*Damn.* He had forgotten he agreed to accompany the Campbells this evening to Lady Asherton's musical.

Rhys sat straighter. "I do beg your pardon, Lady Campbell"—who became so startled he had actually spoken that she almost dropped her puff. Rhys pressed on—"I must have neglected to mention, I took the liberty of sending our regrets to the Ashertons." The half-eaten cream puff dropped onto her plate. "We are now engaged at the Dillinghams this evening." Rhys flicked a nonexistent piece of lint from his breeches.

"Oh…Well…Yes, of course, Your Grace, whatever you deem best." She glanced at her daughter as did Rhys, but no help there. Miss Campbell was busy dealing with the errant bee. "I am sure you know all the best entertainments."

It was clearly meant as a question, but one Rhys chose not to answer. He congratulated himself on smoothly diverting their plans for the evening and prepared to take his leave.

But no, it was too much to hope for, as a frown creased her ladyship's brow. "Dillingham, you say?" A frozen smile hung on her face. "I don't believe I know the family."

Rhys flicked another imaginary bit of dust from his sleeve. "Lord and Lady Milton Dillingham? They are quite new to town. I thought Miss Campbell would find a mask amusing."

"A mask?" Lady Campbell's smile slipped just a fraction.

Well, he could not blame her. Being a vigilant mother, she was no doubt mentally scrolling through Debrett's for any Dillinghams. Rhys could see the precise moment when her ladyship connected Milton Dillingham with Nan Houser, former actress, who was now Lady Dillingham. Her smile shattered. He imagined it falling onto the plate with her half-eaten cream puff.

"You are fond of a mask, Your Grace?" Miss Campbell having dispatched the bee, was all attention. Did he detect a slight challenge in her voice?

Obviously Lady Campbell heard it as such and swooped in. "Oh, my dear, how marvelous! I don't believe we have ever attended a mask. I suppose they are *de rigueur* these days?" Lady Campbell shifted to the very edge of her seat. Rhys feared she would launch herself into her daughter's lap if she proved recalcitrant. "Arabella, we must put our heads together to find you something marvelous to wear." Suddenly the delights of Mrs. Pembly's aria were nothing compared to a mask. "Perhaps we could coordinate a costume with the duke. Apollo and Daphne? Or perhaps Antony and Cleopatra?" But even Lady Campbell seemed to see the absurdness of her fair, plump daughter as Queen of the Nile. "Well, I dare say we will think of something enchanting."

"I believe the principal activity at a mask is dancing?" said Miss Campbell. It appeared she was not going to back down.

Lady Campbell prepared to launch, but one look from Rhys sent her back in her seat.

The girl rose. Rhys followed suit. "Do you dance then, Your Grace?" Ah, a standoff. "I have heard rumors." Miss Campbell cocked her head to look up at him. "But as yet, have seen no evidence."

As they were standing not two feet from each other, she had to tip her head back quite far to meet his eyes. The motion pointed up the fact that they would look simply ludicrous on the dance floor, for she would fit precisely—under his armpit. Her lips quirked to the side. By God she was picturing the very same image.

A hit! *Cheeky girl.* He could not help giving her credit for challenging him. Had she read the Parkington blurb?

He was saved from a rejoinder by her thoroughly frazzled mamma. "Arabella, dearest, you know the duke does not dance."

Well, he supposed there was no getting out of it. It was his penance for ditching poor Lady Asherton, who would no doubt be devastated at the loss of her duke. "I would be most happy to stand up with you, Miss

Arabella." He gave her a slight bow.

Did the chit just give him an approximation of a "humph?" *Amazing.*

"Oh, how delightful, my dear. We are so honored, Your Grace." Her ladyship fairly danced herself as she fluttered around the pair. "For my part I have always loved the cotillion—so elegant. I should dearly love to see the two of you perform a cotillion."

"Not a waltz, Mamma? I hear they are all the rage at these kinds of entertainments."

By God, she *was* toying with him. He could not help having some genuine admiration for this young girl.

Why could he not fasten on Arabella Campbell with any degree of lust? She was uncommonly pretty, and he found himself appreciating her wit and intelligence, but that was where it ended. And it was not enough. Try as he might, he could not force his mind into accepting lush curves, blonde hair, and a cherubic face when he yearned for black silk, full lips, and a willowy figure.

Here he was, crying for the moon when he had the sun in the palm of his hand. He hated that his mind had been so thoroughly poisoned by a dressmaker; that he would toss aside his morals so cheaply. He hated the disruption to his life and his plans. He hated that in the deepest, most secret spaces in his heart, he dared to call her…Olivia. Just Olivia…

But there was a chance he would see her tonight. This ball was just the sort of affair she could gain entrance to—the fringes of society. There would be a lot of social climbers attending, particularly later in the evening.

Lady Campbell's shriek pierced his ear. "The waltz? Surely you jest, Arabella!"

He fell back to earth.

"You most certainly will not attempt that dreadful dance. I hope, Your Grace, the Dillinghams will not support such lewd shows. I cannot imagine *you* would condone such behavior, Your Grace, given your reputation as the Mon—I-I meant to say…Well, it is…unseemly. I vow—"

But Rhys ceased to listen and her daughter resumed her seat and went back to twirling her parasol. Lady Campbell also sat. Unfortunately, she neglected to remember her plate with the cream puff.

Rhys sighed and rose to call a footman. He would ask to call on Lord Campbell on the morrow. Then it would be done. But until then, he still had this one last night. He just might see her one last time…See his Olivia.

\*\*\*\*

"Where will you go, Mrs. Egg?" asked Jeb as he pasted together the long boxes that would hold the Barton gowns.

Olivia carefully finished pinning a tiny feather to the long line that rimmed the gown's bodice, just in time to catch the small smile on Egg's face. It was a lovely sight to see these days.

They had worked feverishly for eight straight days, only leaving the shop to go above stairs to sleep. But the finish line lay just ahead. Olivia stretched her fingers. The tips were raw. She blew gently on them.

Egg paused in her work pleating the front placket on the green percale. "We haven't decided as yet, but it must be somewhere quite picturesque as I have promised Olivia a scene worthy of her talents as a painter." She gave Olivia a softly maternal look over the tops of her spectacles. Olivia shook her head, smiling, and went back to her feathers. "I should like the sea myself. I have always been partial to the wild sea cliffs, but I dare say that will be for another time. We must stay closer to home at present."

Hazel, who was busy ironing, chimed in, "Oooo, I would be quite terrified of the sea. I have heard tales of great sea monsters gulping a body up in one tidy bite. And I should be terrified of being sucked beneath those black waves. No, give me a quiet cottage, perhaps by a lake at the very most, and I should be quite content."

"You've no taste for adventure, Hazel, old girl," said Jeb, abandoning his box and coming up behind her. "I would bet ready money you've not been beyond Hampstead Heath. But woe betide the beastie that threatens my girl." He took up a ruler and brandished it as if it were the lightest of foils. Advancing on Hazel, he whipped his "sword" about her touching her arm, her belly, her shoulder. Hazel stood with her hands over her eyes her smile spreading beneath. "Don't you know I would wrestle the poor monster till it gave up and skulked back into the depths from whence it came?"

Olivia and Egg exchanged a smile.

"Lord, do you hear him go on! Now get away with you, you great red-headed beastie," she said, wielding her iron, "before I clout you." But Jeb, ever light on his feet, simply danced away, laughing.

They all settled back into their jobs.

Ah, to live in the country and to be able to paint all day long. Egg knew her so well. Yes, it would be heaven. She had not even thought of her painting in such a long time. To capture a seascape, those ever-changing waves, and instead of a sea monster, a body within those waves, flashing in the bright sun as he pulled through the foamy curls. His body fairly waltzing along the surf—

She stopped her sewing and looked up. Three pairs of eyes were staring at her, the mouths below cast in various states of mirth.

"What? What is the bloody secret? Don't tell me I was humming again, because I know quite well, I was not."

They all exchanged looks and blithely went back to their tasks.

"Oh, bother. It means nothing. I assure you, I have put that masked ball and the duke quite behind me." No one said a word. "It is only that I have not danced in such a *very* long time. And Egg, you *know* Vivaldi is a particular favorite of mine." Olivia dared them to make another peep—which of course they hadn't in the first place—made a peep, that is. The fact infuriated her all the more.

Egg innocently asked Jeb to come and thread her needle and went back to her pleating. Hazel ironed, and after helping Egg, Jeb went back to his boxes.

One row of feathers completed. She blew again on her fingertips, laid the tape measure against the fabric, and carefully made a mark with chalk. Now on to the next.

"*Ta, dah, dah, dah dumph, da, dumph, da dumph.*" Olivia heard a soft, slightly off key, soprano and jerked up. *Oh bother!* She flung down her measuring tape and stormed out to the music of her friend's laughter.

*Blast the man!* It was almost worse now he stayed

away. Every tall, elegant gentleman had her heart frantically beating. Every handsome black carriage she passed had her marking the crest. Indeed, there had been one carriage in particular she could not fail to recognize. It had to be his, though it bore no markings. By Saint Anne, it was there across the street right now. She had a mind to go over and have it out with him.

She had resolved to do just that when Jeb ran out of the shop.

"Miss Olivia, it's Mrs. Egg, she can't catch her breath."

****

In the end, they had not called for a doctor.

"How will we go on our holiday with no funds?" Egg said, fighting for every breath. "A doctor? Pooh!" Which was really a cough disguised as a "pooh."

"Hush, now, dear. You must save your breath to breathe."

"He would be sure to leave us with nothing, Olive. I will *not* let a trifling cough spoil our lovely plans."

Egg pierced Olivia with her most formidable look. "You and Jeb will go to the Dillinghams. I will be well enough here with Hazel. And we *will* go to the country at week's end." When Egg was mulish, there was no use arguing with the woman. "Now off with you before I get really ornery."

Chapter Twelve

*What was he doing here?*
The newly minted Lady Dillingham and her lord were not the sort of *ton* Olivia would ever put the great Duke of Roydan amongst. And this mask was decidedly not an event he should be escorting his almost betrothed—well, she supposed the lady was his *almost* betrothed, for as yet, she had seen nothing in the papers. She squeezed her eyes shut at the memory of combing the pages for the announcement. *Fool.*

Busy ushering Arabella Campbell—it *must* be her—into his carriage, he should not have seen her. He was turned away. But for some impossible reason, he chose that precise moment to turn and their gazes locked. Even though she was masked, even though there were no less than half a dozen carriages between them, and it was full dark with only carriage lamps and a few torches to light the way for the guests, there was not one shred of doubt in her mind he knew exactly who she was. It was as if some unseen magnet drew them together.

Well at least they were leaving and even better, Arabella Campbell was only partway in the carriage. The duke could not very well abandon her midstream else the poor woman would find herself in a heap on the cobblestones. Even in her panic, Olivia could not help relishing the image. Still, she had to move quickly. She could not face him again. Using the few precious seconds, she dashed up the stairs, thrust her wrap at the waiting footman, and inquired the direction of the ladies' retiring room.

"She's not quite feeling the thing, you know," she heard Jeb say to the footman.

Garish, masked figures jumped out of her path as she barreled down the hall to safety. She pushed open the door and immediately felt suffocated in a sea of over-powdered, over-perfumed, and over-loud females all vying for the limited space before the mirrors. She turned right around and went through the next available door shutting it firmly behind her.

\*\*\*\*

*Where was she?*

He had scanned the ballroom three times already. Having given a description of Mrs. Weston and her mask to a maid, he now lurked around the ladies' retiring room, waiting. Several ladies exited, each making it all too clear they would be available should he have a need. He wished he could disappear into the woodwork. Finally the maid returned, shaking her head.

Mrs. Weston had disappeared into thin air. Meanwhile, Miss Campbell and her parents were waiting in the carriage for his return. He had muttered something about losing a watch fob before dashing off. No doubt his huge landau was causing all sorts of upheaval and congestion as it sat in the drive. He gave one more look about the ballroom—nothing. Damn, he must leave. His prospective in-laws would be wondering at his sanity at this point.

\*\*\*\*

"Ahhhhh!" screamed the white blob in front of

Olivia.

"Pardon me," Olivia said, blinking. The blob quickly focused into a mob-cap and the woman beneath into a maid.

Olivia limped out of the closet with as much dignity as she could muster, unfolded herself, and gingerly rolled her neck. She looked back at her prison. That particular door had been a hideous mistake. She plucked her mask from the handle of a broom, pulled out a few broken feathers and used them to fan her hot, damp cheeks. "Do you happen to know the time?" she said as if ladies hiding in closets were an ordinary occurrence.

The gaping maid was too busy poking in the closet to mark Olivia. "But where is the gentleman?"

Olivia started to point out how ludicrous the notion was of sharing the space with a *cat*, much less a full grown man.

Instead she handed the maid her broken feathers and sailed—well maybe not *sailed,* her muscles were not working quite properly as yet—but that was the image she hoped to project as she started down the hallway.

"I'm not daft, you know," the young woman mumbled. "It's just he asked me to have a peek in the ladies' room for you more than a half hour ago. Your pardon but I never imagined a lady'd be holed up in there."

Olivia snapped to a halt. Jeb would not have been worried about her whereabouts; it must have been the duke. *Had he actually followed her?* Her stomach did a little traitorous flip. *Was he still here?* No matter, she would rather face the Devil himself than hide any longer.

"Cor, you look a sight," Jeb said petulantly as she pulled him away from a game of faro. And a very good thing too. The boy had no business playing with these young blades.

"Never mind, is he gone?"

"Saw him leave in his fancy rig five turns ago." He seemed to want to say more, but one freezing look silenced him. Satisfied, she pulled him away, and they went to work.

"Ain't you minus a few plumes there, Miss O?" Jeb asked not quite innocently as they joined hands in a waltz.

"Enough out of you, you cheeky bugger. Just try to not step on my toes, if you please. I have been mangled quite enough this evening." Jeb smirked; Olivia knew all too well he was the lightest, most graceful dancer at the mask. And possibly all of London. He whirled her in a brilliantly sweeping arch, just to make sure she didn't forget it.

\*\*\*\*

Rhys checked his watch—just gone three twenty-three. Would she still be here? He turned to ascend the steps to the ballroom. *Drat*, he had forgotten his mask. A side table held a few discards. He picked up a huge horned mask; it was a satyr complete with furled ruff. It would do as well as any and best of all, it would cover his head completely. He was bending to put it on when another mask caught his eye. He dropped the satyr and pulled on the second.

The ballroom was even more crowded now. The riff-raff had begun to arrive, and the evening was heating up. Rhys hung on the fringe, methodically combing through the couples as they spun by, hoping to see the shape of her long white neck or the particular curve of her back.

When Rhys was a young man, his uncle Bert had prodded him to attend *ton* events. "You need a bit of polish and confidence, is all." It had been agony. He had been so terribly shy—convinced anyone who approached him only did so because of his title. He had been certain the young ladies would see how defective he was and laugh behind their fans. It was then he discovered how well his ducal mask could serve him— a raise of his chin or better still, his eyebrow, would send those London misses scurrying for the safety of their mammas. And at two-and-thirty years, that mask was now second nature.

*There!* He saw the man's red hair first, and then her as they made a neat turn. His throat closed painfully, and he dug his nails into his palms through the leather of his gloves.

She was liquid air. Her gown, like blue sky and shifting clouds, seemed to bear her up as she drifted across the floor. Then she tilted her head up to her partner and smiled at him. White-hot jealousy hit him full on.

It was the same smile she had given him.

The bells around his head jangled, and he realized he was halfway out onto the floor. Even in his frenzy, the irony of wearing a fool's cap complete with jingling bells was not lost on him. He just managed to stop himself from shouting her name, reaching for her, as she sailed by.

Couples eddied around him muttering complaints, but he remained frozen to the floor. He could not move toward her, yet he could not move back to the shadows either. He had no reason where she was concerned. *For fools rush in...*

Masked figures were stopping to gawk at him. *She* would stop soon as well. She would see his utter foolishness and laugh, or worse, pity him. That, he could not bear. Anything but her pity. He turned and fled.

\*\*\*\*

"What do you make of that gent in the fool's cap? Foxed as a pickle, I'd say," Jeb said as he led her off the floor. Olivia had no time for idle chatter. They were attracting a good deal of attention, and a throng of gentlemen began to surround her.

"Your pardon, madam, are you engaged for the next set?"

"Look here, Crowley, I was here first."

"Perhaps we should let the lady decide?" This from yet a third gentleman.

Several other gentlemen hanging on the periphery were jockeying for a better position. As the pushing and posturing ratcheted up, Olivia knew from experience there would soon be a scene. It was one of the risks of her profession, when a gentleman was told *no*, but interpreted it as *yes*. A dead bore and very provoking. Jeb, however, seemed to love this part of the game. He embraced his role of protector as a true knight of old. Olivia heaved a sigh. She swore he exacerbated the trouble just to be able to drop a few of these danglers.

She had managed to avoid an out-and-out brawl but had no Lady Dillingham for her trouble.

Now on their way home, she leaned back into the squabs and closed her aching eyelids, hoping her actions would signal Jeb to leave off his ranting.

"Miss O, I wish you had let me give him a basting." Jeb's voice filled the confined space inside the carriage, pressing into her head. Plague take it, even her hair hurt. "I would have been more than happy to rearrange that cove's smug face. Sure he had some fancy moves, but I reckon he was all mouth and no trousers. I could have shown him how a chap from Cheapside delivers the goods."

Silence was apparently too much to hope for. She could feel his weight bouncing and shifting—too keyed up to register anything outside the parameters of his ego and a good fight.

Toeing off her slipper, she gingerly flexed her squashed toes. Jeb's tirade faded into the background as the steady *thump, thump* of her head took over. Oh to be home, take down her hair, and put up her feet.

Someone was tapping her. She opened one eyelid.

"Miss O, would you mind if I jumped out here? Some nobs were jawing about a match at The Penny Oyster. I thought, if you didn't need me anymore, I would pop off for a quick look about."

Olivia closed her eyelid, nodded, and waved him off.

A rap on the roof and the carriage pulled to a halt. The door opened and slammed—Olivia winced—shut. At the last minute, she shouted out the window "Be careful!" But the hackney was already moving.

As she watched him lope away, she smiled. He was a gem…Well, more like a bantam red rooster with his brood, forever strutting and fretting about his "ladies." Especially Hazel. She and Egg had a small wager going as to when Jeb would declare himself.

Wes had taken him from a raw recruit to a ready soldier.

Memories rushed through her like a fresh, cold stream. His and Jeb's red heads bowed together over a chess board or a lecture on the importance of cleaning a gun. Then all too soon, both of them were gone. One to fight in Cadiz, the other, to a grave outside of Morocco.

But oh, the look on Jeb's face when she and Eglantine had knocked on number fourteen Hamley Place. Poor Egg had been crushed to within an inch of her life, and they all had to dash the tears from their eyes as Jeb introduced them to his aunt.

They had been a family ever since.

Yet, as the carriage rocked her in a steady rhythm, her thoughts spiraled toward the melancholy. She was lonely—not *alone*, but lonely. Unfinished? Yes, that was the word. Like a quilt, mended in some areas, well-worn in others, but essentially unfinished—gaping areas with not an ounce of color or pattern, and no hope of filling the dead, white space that stretched before her, making up the other half of her years.

Lord, now she was becoming maudlin. She had no time for wallowing in self-pity. She blinked to clear her eyes, but realized her tears were from more than just emotion. She smelled smoke.

*Smoke?* The driver was turning onto Hamley Place. Her stomach pitched. She reached instinctively for the door latch, fumbling, she could not make it work. Then the door sprang open, slamming back against the coach.

Her world narrowed into action, the sounds around her isolated and unreal, as if coming from very far away, only a background to the roaring in her head. The slap of her slippers as her feet hit the cobblestones, the pain registering as just a sensation as she staggered to keep her balance. Her ribs heaving up against her corset. The driver yelling something she could not distinguish as she pounded toward smoke and chaos.

*Please God, not Egg! Please God, I don't want more! This family—this life is enough! It's enough! Please God, not my Egglet—*

\*\*\*\*

Rhys struck out, blindly groping for an extra pillow to muffle the incessant hammering inexplicably going on somewhere in the mansion. The hammering continued, only now it was housed deep within his aching brain as well. Still not content, some fiend was throwing gravelly, hot sand behind his eyelids and making his mouth into cotton wool.

*What the bloody blazes.*

Reaching for another pillow, he connected with something solid. It was Tinsley. Rhys risked another look, only cracking one lid this time. Sure enough his valet was rubbing his nose and attempting to speak.

"Your Grace, I would not have disturbed you, but Monsieur Angelo is expected in twelve minutes."

Rhys turned his head slowly and deliberately. It did no good; his head felt like a small, crowded room where at least ten blacksmiths with anvils had taken up residence.

He ran his tongue over his teeth. They had grown fur sometime in the night. "What...time...is it?" Tinsley recoiled, his hand covering his now doubly assaulted nose. Rhys's own eyes watered a bit from the stench of Scotch whiskey.

"It is nearly nine now, Your Grace."

Rhys was sorely tempted to take up a pistol and

shoot his valet and then himself. But Monsieur Angelo's time was not to be trifled with, not even for a duke. Besides he desperately needed the release of a good bout; after all, this was his betrothal day.

"Get me up and into a cold bath. Slowly, man."

\*\*\*\*

For the second time in as many weeks, Olivia was back in the ducal mansion facing the various instruments of skill and death. However, this reception was nothing like her previous visit. She had not a moment to ascertain any missing weaponry before immediately being ushered into a blue withdrawing room, greeted in the most solicitous manner by Mr. Wilcove himself, and offered tea while His Grace was being found.

After pacing the length of the room several times, she just had convinced herself to sit when the chamber door opened and the duke appeared.

"Mrs. Weston, this is most unexpected. I—"

"I will do it. I will become your mistress."

Silence.

His eyebrows—both of them—disappeared into his hair which was...disheveled? His coat did not lay flat as if it had been hastily donned and his cravat, while fresh, was carelessly tied. He had not even shaved? My God, was he actually sweating? He looked almost...human.

All these thoughts crammed into Olivia's head in one instant. She must have caught him in the midst of some vigorous exercise.

He retrieved a handkerchief from a pocket and hastily mopped his brow.

Oh God, had he come from a new lover's bed?

This was unbearable. The burn of a blush flooded her face and she turned away, humiliated.

But she had nowhere to go.

Ironically, the fire had been a small one, or so the turncock of the fire brigade had said, but to Olivia's mind, it might as well have burnt the whole building to the ground. All their hard work had been utterly lost. The damage from the smoke alone had permeated every swath of silk, every length of muslin, every ribbon and lace—everything. The Barton gowns, which had been carefully packed in silver tissue and boxes, had been trampled and drenched into a filthy pulp.

But that was nothing. Nothing to seeing Egg's torn and blistered hands. Her cracked and bleeding lips, swollen to twice their size. Nothing to the black mucus she had retched, causing her throat to swell till Olivia wanted to run from the room. Nothing to her red, running eyes that tried to speak for her because she couldn't...

Olivia's silly pride had utterly dissolved as she watched black, churning smoke pour out of the upper rooms, praying her Eglantine would come out alive. Yes, she would sell her soul to the Devil if need be. But, as it was, it would be to a gorgeous, wealthy duke.

Squaring her body, she lifted her chin, despite her burning cheeks. "I will be your mistress. That is, if the position is still available."

"Yes," he almost shouted. "Yes, Mrs. Weston," he said again, now quieter, "it is most assuredly available."

"Good. Well..." *How did one do this?* "I have some requirements."

"I am all attention, madam. Shall we sit? Has tea been ordered?" He moved toward the bell pull—

"You misunderstand; I have not a moment to spare. It is Egg—Mrs. Wiggins, my business part—There was a fire—"

The duke started. "A fire?"

But Olivia held up her hand. "Please, I—She is very ill. I cannot lose a moment. I must have a proper doctor—" She broke off in a sob. He moved toward her, and then abruptly stopped and turned to the door. He opened it and shouted for his butler and for a carriage to be readied posthaste.

He turned back into the room, hesitant, as if he was unsure what to do for her. He started to hand her his handkerchief, but seeing it was damp with sweat, thrust it back in his pocket.

He seemed about to speak when his butler appeared.

"Safley, send for Dr. Asher immediately," the duke said. "He is to present himself as soon as may be at—where is Mrs. Wiggins at present?"

"Our neighbor, Mrs. Isabelle Harton, at number fourteen—"

The duke turned back to Safley. "Yes, number fourteen, Hamley Place. Mrs. Weston and I will leave now and meet the doctor there. Make haste, man."

The butler bowed and left the room. A small commotion could be heard through the door as various servants were dispatched.

Olivia found her own handkerchief, blew her nose, and took a breath.

"You see, she was laughing and she could not catch—" Olivia pressed her knuckles against her mouth. "She is the only family I have. I cannot lose her."

"Rest assured, madam, all will be well. Dr. Asher is my own physician and you will not find a more learned man in his field."

She met his eyes—warm brandy.

"I want to be with her. I must be, till she is better. I want to nurse her. I trust you will give me that time, that consideration, before I take up my—other duties."

"When we determine what is best for Mrs. Wiggins and when she is on surer ground, it is likely she will need to go to the country. I will send you and her, along with Wilcove and Dr. Asher, to one of my country estates. There Mrs. Wiggins will receive every attention and yes, you will be there to supervise every detail of her recovery. You will be hindered by no one, not by me or anyone. You have my word."

"Yes, I thank you. May we go now? I have left her with our young seamstress, and I am most anxious to be at her side."

"Of course, madam."

He sprang to the door. He seemed relieved to finally have something concrete to do as he spoke with Safley. She stood transfixed, watching him manage everything. He beckoned to her, and she moved toward him.

Egg would be well.

And she would be his.

Chapter Thirteen

That very afternoon the duke moved Olivia and Egg to a small house on Bennett Street, not far from Bedford Square.

She and Egg were like two small rocks in the midst of a whirling stream of activity; everything happened around them. They had been given lovely bedchambers with a connecting door, meals had been delivered at all hours of the day and night—mostly left untouched—and Dr. Asher had been at least twice a day to check on his patient.

The duke's people had even combed through the burned shop and apartment above for any item that could be salvaged. Unfortunately, those items had filled one small trunk, but they had included a silver-backed brush and hand mirror that had belonged to Egg's mother, Olivia's miniature of Wes, and the tiny violin he had bought for their child. The instrument had been only slightly scorched, but the bow was ruined, snapped under a large boot. These precious keepsakes were now lying next to the women's respective beds. The rest of the things had been packed up and stored in an unused bedchamber.

"I assure you, Mrs. Weston," said Doctor Asher when he came to examine Egg a week into their stay, "I am quite certain His Grace is very sensible of your gratitude, but I am even more certain he would be

153

uncomfortable with too much praise. Besides"—he chuckled—"you would have to catch him. He is scarcely within these walls and when he is, he only dashes about issuing orders and looking quite grave."

\*\*\*\*

A soft knock jerked Olivia to her feet, her book slipping from her lap to land with a *thud* on the carpet.

"Madam." It was Albert, the footman. "His Grace wonders if you might spare a moment to meet him in the drawing room."

Her heart bumped in her chest; she would see him. *Would he keep his promise? Did she want him too?* Suddenly the thought of being held in his strong arms, cradled against his chest, seemed like bliss.

"Yes," she said, too strongly. She ducked her head and put a hand to her hair. "I will be only a minute." Albert bowed and left.

She ran to the small vanity, fumbling for stray pins in her rumpled hair, and sat.

Worse than she expected. Dark circles shadowed her too-large eyes. Her lips were chapped, her skin too pale except for, dear God, a red spot just to the right of her nose. Hideous. She shut her eyelids against the threatening fullness. She had imagined being so calm, so composed when she met him again. She shook her head, opened her eyes, and met the enemy reflected in the mirror. Then she attacked.

Upon entering the drawing room, her heart seemed to drop several inches in her breast, and her stomach heaved up in sympathy. Even from across the room, she could see a difference in him. It was not evident in his manner of dress, which was still soberly impeccable; it was more in his eyes—an almost haunted look. A table between them was the only thing that saved her from rushing to his side and making a fool of herself. She caught its edge and her wits as well. He looked so very tired.

But the duke was not alone. He had been in deep conversation with an unknown gentleman. They had abruptly broken off their talk when she had entered.

"Ah, Mrs. Weston. May I present Sir Richard Ford?" Olivia dragged her gaze from the duke. The man wore a telltale red waist coat signaling him as a Robin Red Breast, the mounted division of Bow Street. "Sir Richard is head of the Runners."

The tea tray had barely arrived when Sir Richard launched into a barrage of questions. Questions she had already answered on a half dozen other occasions. Yes, Egg had sworn she had doused the fire. No, their neighbor—yes, Isabelle Harton—could not say for absolute certain whether the person she had seen leaving the building was male or female. Yes, it had been a long, dark cloak with a hood. No, Hazel could not produce the paper that had called her away. No, she could think of no one who would want to do them harm.

She felt like a mouse among falcons, as they circled about her.

Finally, worn down, she blurted, "There was a black carriage that sometimes seemed to be following me." Her gaze flicked to the duke.

He halted, shock on his face. Olivia looked away but irritation pricked her feelings of guilt. After all, *she* had no reason to feel awkward. She pressed on. "It stopped just down the street from our shop on several occasions."

"And you have no idea who it might have belonged to, Mrs. Weston?" Sir Richard, followed her sight line till his gaze rested on the duke as well. She hesitated.

"Mrs. Weston," the duke said, "you must tell us anything you deem pertinent."

"Very well." She sat up straighter. "Actually, I thought it might have belonged to you, Your Grace."

He gave a start but recovered quickly.

"When did you begin to notice this carriage, Mrs. Weston?" said Sir Richard.

"Shortly after the Parkington Ball—about seven days ago." She looked at the duke.

His frown cleared, and his shoulders dropped. "I assure you, it was not mine."

Sir Richard did not pursue the line of questioning, and after a few more questions, he took his leave.

"Why did you not mention this carriage before, Mrs. Weston?" The duke's question came on the heels of the door closing. "Were there no distinguishing details? No outriders? No special livery?" He was like a teakettle at full boil—with the lid firmly in place.

"I did not think any of it would signify as I thought the carriage yours."

A strange look came over his face. He looked...guilty.

There was a knock at the door.

"Come," he said, moving to the door.

"Your Grace," Albert said, bowing deeply, "this just came by special post."

Roydan took the note and popped the seal, scanned it, and then crushed it within his hand. He turned to her, hiding the note behind his back like a naughty school boy. He seemed...lost, unsure, as if he wanted to say more. But after a moment of awkward silence, he bowed briefly, "Your pardon, madam, I must leave you."

She curtsied, giving up any notion of thanks.

Olivia watched from the window, hidden behind the heavy brocade curtain, as he mounted his horse. Just as she thought to lose him in the dusky gloom, a watchman lit the street lamp. In the sudden island of light, she thought she saw him turn back to the house—to her window. Instinctively she drew back, her heart knocking against her ribs. She waited a moment and then pressed her face to the glass. But he had disappeared into the rising fog.

What went on behind that ducal facade? He was so very reserved, and from an outsider's vantage point, he appeared almost disdainful but she was finding that characterization would be wrong. It would be too hasty. *Could he be...shy?* No, that was not quite right. She grappled to find the right word—untried? Yes, somehow almost—virginal. It seemed impossible for a man of his years and a duke as well, but deep in her heart she knew it was true. And that truth might very well slay her.

****

"My dear Rhys, I am so glad you came to call."

Rhys took in Daria's dangling curls, peignoir, and a feathered slipper that hung from one of her stockinged feet. She had arranged herself artfully on a chaise, the light falling dramatically over half her face and décolletage. She had lost some flesh in the last weeks, looking more like the Daria of old—the pink shades on the lamps no doubt helped the illusion. Daria was always clever at setting the perfect scene.

Jess Russell

"I do not have time for your games, Daria." He
went to the window and jerked open the heavy curtains.
"What is this about Dee Gooden? What have you to do
with her?"

She blinked, turning away from the light. "Me?
Nothing."

"Then you waste my time." He made for the door.

"For any other man I would say she must be some
trollop who is making trouble, but we both know your
very limited palate when it comes to the fair sex, don't
we?" He gripped the doorknob, and her voice sped up.
"Contrary to what you may think, I do not spend my
days, or nights for that matter, wondering how muddled
your life has become. I have much better ways of
employing my time."

Enough. Rhys pulled the door open, hoping the
action would get Daria to come to the point. It worked.

"I know nothing of this woman, but I do have a
friend who used to know her very well and may have
some information as to her whereabouts."

Rhys shut the door and turned back to her. "Who is
this friend?" No one knew of his father's codicil
involving Dee Gooden and Valmere excepting his
solicitors and a few of his most circumspect servants.
Was someone leaking information about his private
life?

If only he could find Gooden and pay her off. He
was sure she did not want an old estate by the sea.
Money had always been her Achilles heel. Rhys
planned to take full advantage of that flaw, but first she
must be found.

Daria reached for a bottle on the table next to her
and poured a glass. "Ah, no, my dear duke, it does not

158

work that way. You do not hold the reins in this particular race. You will get no answers until we see some gold."

He would be very happy to shell out, to the king himself, if he could be assured of Dee Gooden disappearing, and quickly. He did not want her hanging about making more trouble in his life. He must play this carefully; else Daria would bleed him dry. "Then *we* have a problem." He shrugged his shoulders. "I do not pay for promises. If your information leads my men to her, then you will be paid. And handsomely. You have my word, and I have never been false with you, Daria. Whatever anger you harbor against me, you know I have always been totally honest in our dealings."

"But I need the money now!" She sat up and crossed her arms against her chest like a child who had been denied a sweet.

"You can't have gone through your quarterly allowance? It is impossible. It is not even mid May."

"I do not have to answer to you." She tossed back the rest of her drink, but her bravado was marred by the wince as she lowered her arm. "It is only that I have some new expenses."

"More like a new paramour who is bleeding you dry. You will get no money from me without results." He turned and left.

\*\*\*\*

Olivia had left Egg sleeping and was retiring to her room, when she tripped on the plush carpet. She gasped and groped for the doorknob behind her, either to steady herself or to escape, she was not sure which.

Stacked on her bed was a mountain of silver-and-pink-striped boxes.

It was beginning.

The idea frightened and drew her at the same time.

After what seemed an eternity, she relaxed her hold on the knob and finally let go altogether. She took a tentative step, as if she were approaching a beautiful but wild animal. She reached out, brushing her fingers over the topmost package; the package that stood out from the rest by its plain brown wrapping. The one tied with an incongruous ribbon she knew cost a small fortune. The one that scared her more than the mountain of smooth, perfect boxes beneath it.

The ribbon, embroidered with primroses, felt heavy and cool, like cream in her hand. She pulled and the stiff paper released, to open like a flower.

She brought a small chair right up to the bed, sat, and wept.

A long while later, when she'd wiped her eyes and blown her nose, she gingerly lifted her mother's paisley shawl from its paper and swathed herself in its familiar soft warmth.

Not so familiar. It smelled of him.

For the next hour she went through every box and parcel. There were chemises, stockings, slippers, boots, bonnets, fans, and even a parasol.

When she finished, her bed, and every available surface, held a stunning palette of color and texture. She turned slowly, memorizing the nubby wools, the wefted shimmer of the damasks, the plush sheen of a sable muff, the intricate cloisonné of forget-me-nots above the ivory handle of the parasol, the lilting goose biots crowning a riding hat. It was all too much. Too impossibly beautiful. She sank to the floor under the weight of its beauty, digging her fingers into the carpet.

Methodically, she reached for one of the boxes that littered the floor, and then for the nearest gown, a glistening dress in shell pink embroidered in green.

She could not do it. It was the green embroidery that stopped her. She was positive it matched the exact color of her eyes.

Well, the duke had a swarm of eager servants. A maid, or three, would pack it all up. She could leave the room and not even have to look.

Rising she went to the bell, but her hand fell limply to her side. She *wanted* this. Yes, it was all too much, and she should send it back, but she could not. It had been so very long since she had had anything she had not made herself or, she laughed ruefully, re-made.

She moved back to the bed and traced a particularly beautiful bit of openwork on a chemise. He must have paid a small fortune for this wisp of fine gauze and Venetian lace; the workmanship was so exquisite. Had he picked these out himself? Had he pored over finely drawn plates of Ackermann's latest offerings? Had he imagined her in these gowns? No, surely not. Yet she wanted to believe he had done just that.

She sank onto the bed, finery spilled out all around her. Drowning her.

Later, as she unwrapped and bathed Egg's hands, taking one finger at a time, Olivia began her own particular rosary of penance. Living in Paris so long, she knew the Catholic custom. She should not have left Egg alone the night of the fire. Another finger, she should have made sure Hazel had arrived before going off. Yet another, she should have called in the doctor despite Egg's protestations. Another, she should not have been so preoccupied with her own silly fears—

An entirely new horror hit her as she began the thumb. The duke must have reimbursed Eveline Barton for her lost wardrobe as well as providing Olivia with a whole new one. Oh Lord, how much more could she be in his debt?

"Are you meant to wring my hands like that, Olive?"

Olivia gasped and dropped Egg's hands as if they were burning.

"Oh, Egglet! I am sorry...I..." And then she burst into tears.

**\*\*\*\***

The footman's sharp rap on the small door in the front of the traveling carriage startled Olivia. It slid open. "We are approaching the grounds, madam. You said to be sure and wake you."

"Yes," she whispered. "Thank you, Albert." Sleep was never a possibility. Her face had been pressed to the window for the last hour or more.

As they neared the massive iron gates, Olivia lowered the window and leaned her head out. The drive was long and meandering, going on as far as she could see. They traversed woods and parkland for some time before finally coming to a fork in the road. They took the smaller road to the right, and as the coach turned, she saw the house, Valmere, in the distance. It was situated on the precipice of a hill, a lush wild valley spreading below. She could not hear the sea, but she smelled its sharp tang. It must lie on the other side of the mansion. She only had an impression of a sprawling hodgepodge of gray stone and windows before the house was hidden from view by a copse of lime trees.

After a time, they turned again. An avenue of pollarded plane trees made a kind of lacy tunnel as the carriage entered the drive. She held out her arm as if she might capture a bit of the shifting light. Then her breath caught. The trees had opened wide to frame the dower house beyond.

*How could he know? How did he know what bliss looked like?* Those images only lived tucked in a secret corner of her heart. How could he possibly divine those private pictures?

The house's hard edges were softened by ivy and climbing roses. Huge mullioned windows broke up its facade and would spill light into every room, and multiple chimneys would warm the deepest corners. To the left, a small walled garden huddled under the shade of a spreading lime tree, and a white gazebo, crowned in wisteria, peeped between the slats of an arched gate. And to complete the picture, a barn cat, sunning itself in the portico, looked up and flicked its tail.

"Egg, dear," she whispered to her sleeping friend, "we are here. We are...home."

Chapter Fourteen

Lord Bertram Merrick looked as if he liked a good mystery. Olivia and Egg were a mystery, and his lordship seemed bent on solving it.

"I must say I was shocked when I received the note from my nephew informing me you and Lady Wiggins would be taking up residence in the dower house for the foreseeable future. I understand Lady Wiggins is a very distant cousin?" Olivia nodded. "And where is her family's estate? I could not make it out. My nephew must have been in quite a rush as the ink spattered dreadfully."

"Guernsey, Lord Bertram." *Guernsey?* "Lady Wiggins's estate is in Guernsey." And why had she said it twice? As if saying would make it so?

Lord Bertram's eyebrows rose. "You don't say. How singular." Olivia valiantly held his gaze, her smile fixed in place by sheer will. "The duke tried to dissuade me from coming to the estate this year," his lordship continued. "Citing renovations and repairs." Again Olivia remained mute. What was there to say? "Though, thus far, I have yet to see a speck of dust let alone an actual restoration."

"Lord Bertram." They were coming through the garden gate. "I am very sorry, Lady Wiggins is not yet well enough to enjoy company. She will be truly vexed when I tell her of your coming to call." Only a moment or two more and he would be at his horse and on his way. "But Dr. Asher has insisted that she keep very quiet. I am not sure when she will be able to receive company."

"My dear Mrs. Weston, I too am sorry to be deprived of making her acquaintance. But, in the meantime, I thoroughly enjoyed talking to you. I hope you will feel free to make use of the estate as much as you like."

"Oh, thank you, Lord Bertram. But I doubt my duties to Lady Wiggins will allow me to stray very far." The older man raised his eyebrows, and Olivia could imagine his mind racing to fit her and Egg into some plausible slot. Judging by the appreciative look in his eyes, *mistress* was clearly near the top of his list. Heat crept up over her collar bones, neck, and then undoubtedly stained her cheeks. What was worse, she could see he approved of the duke's choice.

"The property is…most dramatic," she soldiered on. "I must say I was wonderfully surprised. I fully expected formal gardens with acres of box hedges and regimental columns of precisely groomed trees, not a leaf or petal daring to be out of place." She ducked her head, wishing the earth might gape open and swallow her. "But perhaps the duke does not spend a great deal of time at this particular estate," she said hopefully, "and prefers to use his resources elsewhere?"

Lord Bertram smiled and shook his head. "My dear, there is no end to Roydan's resources. And Valmere is actually the favorite of his properties, though it is one of the most minor, if one could call this wild splendor *minor*."

"I had thought"—Olivia hesitated, picking a bit of

grass from her skirts—"Lady Wiggins and I would be quite alone here. Indeed I was much surprised by your visit, sir."

Lord Bertram grinned. Though he did not look very like his nephew, Olivia imagined how that luminous smile might look on the great Duke of Roydan. "Yes, I gathered my nephew had not told you I would be in residence. Likely he hoped you and Lady Wiggins would escape my notice, but I simply could not let that happen. Not when such charming company is so close to hand."

Olivia smiled back but pressed further. "I don't suppose His Grace will be joining you at such a minor estate?"

"On the contrary," Lord Bertram looked as if he was rather enjoying her fishing expedition. "Though he would never neglect his other estates, especially Beckham Abbey, he usually spends a good deal of the summer months here at Valmere." He hesitated a moment before continuing, as if he were not sure how much information to dole out. "You see it was his mother's property—one of them. She brought a substantial dowry to my brother, but this was her very favorite. She adored the sea, and she lived here with my nephew for much of the year."

"But I understood from the du—Mr. Wilcove, we would not see much of His Grace."

"Well, that may be. Roydan can be rather capricious." The snort came in a rush out of Olivia's nose before she could stop it. Her reaction earned another laugh from Lord Bertram. "My nephew is an onion, my dear; there are many layers beneath his papery shell." Olivia wanted more, but the duke's uncle apparently decided to leave her dangling on that little hook.

They had come to his horse, and as Lord Bertram turned to mount, he stopped. "I confess I was very intrigued when Roydan wrote to tell me of you and Lady Wiggins coming. My nephew does not often have guests here at Valmere—well, actually, truth to tell, he *never* has guests at this particular estate." He looked at her from beneath his wiry brows, but she steadfastly ignored his opening. "You can imagine how my curiosity was piqued. I hope you will forgive my interest?"

"Oh, of course, Lord Bertram. I hope you will call again sometime." She stepped back, already retreating to the safety of the house.

"Thank you, Mrs. Weston." He bowed from his horse. "You may count on it. I will, I hope, see you and your mistress say, next week? Till then, I wish you a good morning."

He clucked to his mount and tipped his hat, looking very much like a dog with a good juicy bone.

****

Rhys had James drive him almost all the way to Valmere, a distance of two days' travel, only to order him back again. A week later he had Tinsley pack his trunks again, but then would not give the order to leave. The trunks sat stacked and ready against the walls of his dressing room for the better part of a week.

Rhys pushed into the chamber only to collide with his valet. "Damnation, Tinsley! Why must you always be underfoot?" The man weighed no more than a rag doll as Rhys set him on his feet. "Have I injured you?"

"Not at all, Your Grace."

After making a thorough appraisal of the valet, Rhys noticed his trunks looked as if they might have exploded. "What are you about, Tinsley?" More items of clothing lay over a boot bench and several chairs.

"Your Grace, I am very much afraid your hunter green will never be quite the same. Please, I must ask you to let me release it, if only to shake out its creases for a moment or two."

"It cannot be. We are leaving this instant."

"But, Your Grace." Tinsley retrieved a glove from the floor and brushed it before handing it to Rhys. "What of your appointment with Mr. Cruthers?"

"Cruthers?"

It was very unlike Rhys to forget an appointment let alone the man himself.

"Yes, Your Grace. If you recall, we scheduled a fitting for your new suit of evening clothes."

*Oh, blast.* Poor Tinsley had finally got him to try a new tailor and actually order new clothes, and he had forgotten. Rhys was torn for a moment, but only a moment. He needed to resolve this situation with his dressmaker before he could meet his tailor.

"It can't be helped, Tinsley. We will reschedule."

His valet's usual poker-straight bearing slumped a fraction. "Yes, Your Grace. We will reschedule."

The whole entourage was out the Old North Road and headed to Norfolk in no more than an hour.

As the miles slipped by and London receded into the past, Rhys felt a heaviness slough away from him. His lawyers peeled away at mile thirty along with the news from Mr. Wadmond that nothing had been found in the Indies, and the search for Dee Gooden continued. Daria Battersby and her "friend" had not been in contact and were cast off back at the Pig's Gate Tavern nearly fifty miles ago. The Campbells lay twelve miles back and finally Miss Arabella in the last six.

He knocked on the carriage roof signaling his coachman to stop. His outriders were already bringing Sid alongside. They knew his habits well. He always took this last stretch on horseback.

Only the gentle creak of his saddle, the sharp smell of turned earth, and the sky, blue and clear enough that linnets could be heard singing to each other from the edges of the woodlands, filled Rhys's senses. The surrounding hills rimmed with lupin and foxglove had begun to bloom as the English summer found its way north. Their tall and waving plumes always gave him a feeling of hope.

All would be well. Uncle Bert's letters told of Mrs.—or Lady Wiggins's steady recovery. Mrs. Weston would now be ready to take up her duties. Lord, *take up her duties*. What a dry, soulless way of describing the myriad of fantasies Rhys had stored in his brain.

The fantasies were part of the reason for his prolonged delay in coming to Valmere. He had lived with them for weeks now. Sometimes changing the color of her gown, or how her hair would fall, or the shape of her mouth as he drove into her sweet center…

Olivia Weston was like a gorgeously wrapped package he was afraid to open. What would be inside for him? Would he feel disappointed and empty, or once opened, would he be insatiable? Weren't fantasies better than nothing?

Well, it was high time to find out. Enough of playing the role of Hamlet. To bed or not to bed. His mind "sicklied o'er with the pale cast of thought."

Good God, how dramatic he had become.

He had not seen her since that day with Sir Richard. He'd been busy with his lawyers and the investigation, such as it was. Then the added annoyance of dealing with Daria—the furtive messages and clandestine meetings, which led to nothing. Finally organizing the dower house for the ladies' arrival, and going over the daily reports from Dr. Asher. But in truth he had been afraid to see her. Afraid she would see his terrible need of her. So it was easier to stay away. But now, with Mrs. Wiggins recovering, she would be expecting him.

*God, if only she would want him just a little.* Hope seeped into that tender void that lay quietly waiting between the steady rails of his oh-so-rational behavior.

Rhys squeezed his thighs harder into Sid's now heaving sides, rocking to urge the horse even faster. He closed his eyes—utter trust—man and animal moving in perfect concert. Only sounds and motion. Only thundering hooves and wind pressing his eyelids, the flash of bright orange and then dusky green as he passed the oaks that intermittently lined the byway. They would be coming to the gates soon. He knew this stretch of road like he knew his name. Instinctively, he eased Sid to a canter. They were on the stone bridge now; Rhys heard the clop of hooves up the gentle rise and then down as it spanned Foggit Creek. Now a space of bright as the forest gave way to the fields just outside the estate's parklands.

He registered a startled, "Good evening, Your Grace" as he tore through the gates, the keeper's words trailing to nothing in the wind. He leaned over Sid, whispering nonsense for encouragement. "Yes, my beauty. That's it, love." Words he had only uttered in his mind and would never be able to say to Olivia Weston...*Olivia.*

He pulled up on Sid and opened his eyes. He was dead in the center of the road where the lane to the dower house led off to the right. Reality struck him full force. The object of his dreams was no more than one and a half miles away. He could be there in about four minutes, maybe sooner.

Sid pawed the ground eager to be moving. Rhys's vision narrowed as he pictured her—Olivia—in the walled gardens of the dower cottage in one of the frocks he had chosen for her—maybe the dark green one with the square-cut décolletage. He would ride right up and vault the wall. Surprised, she would drop the roses she had been collecting as he pulled her into his arms. Her fingers would spear into his hair and caress his face—

A slow trickle of sweat ran down his temple and into his collar. His boots were dull with road dust. He ran his tongue over his teeth, feeling the grit of travel. He released a rein and felt the slight stubble on his cheeks. She would surely cringe from him, disgusted.

Very likely she would not want him, but he would not give her such a blatant reason for rejecting his person. When he came to her, he would at least be clean.

He took one last look down the avenue of trees and then sharply reined left, back toward the mansion.

As he rounded the last gentle curve in the lane, a gibbous moon, hanging low over the house, began to illuminate the dusky sky. His eyes ran over the familiar sedge-gray stone. A window in the south tower winked as it caught the sun's last light. He was home.

"Took you long enough, lad." Uncle Bert came striding from the house to greet Rhys as he handed Sid's reins to his young groom.

"Give him an extra measure, Matthew. He has worked hard. And mind his right front fetlock, it may need a wrap." The boy looked up hopefully. Rhys had the unreasonable urge to smooth the hair away from the boy's face. He clasped his hands behind him. "Tomorrow we will continue your study of linear functions." The boy grinned and led Sid away with an extra bounce in his step. Matthew reminded Rhys of himself when he was young, always keen to solve some mathematical dilemma.

Rhys turned to his uncle, who immediately clapped him on both shoulders. Uncle Bert was usually not so exuberant; well, no doubt he mostly took his cue from Rhys's own reserved manner. He extricated himself and got a good look at Bertram. The man was positively glowing.

"Uncle, you are looking well. I do believe you have lost a good stone or two."

"Exercise, my boy, exercise. Nothing like a good brisk walk and some gardening to get the old blood flowing."

*Gardening?*

"But where have you been?" Bert continued, "I expected you weeks ago. You have been very close-mouthed about the Campbell girl. Is she why you remained in town?"

Rhys scrubbed his hands through his hair and rolled his neck. Ah, yes, the Campbell girl. He had been hoping she'd stay lying along the road with his other cares. But apparently she would not.

****

Olivia released her breath in a *hiss* and pressed her eyelids shut, but a moment later her gaze was once again tracking the moonlight as it spilled in from the casement. Long, soft patterns of light bathed the walls and ceiling. She snorted. Better to have lightning and crashing thunder. That would have suited her mood far better.

Her gaze shot back to the window. Her thoughts seeped through the fragile pane to the picture she knew so completely—the felt of new-mown grass surrounded by a ruffled hedge of blue hydrangea, the statue of Apollo beyond, who kept watch over a few straggling apple trees, and then the canopied road. The road *he* would come to her by. *But when?*

Blackness again. She pressed her teeth against her bottom lip. But the dark only served to focus her mind on his face, his body.

She flopped on her back and willed herself to let go. Wes had taught her an eastern technique of relaxing, to start at her very center and imagine a snake slowly uncoiling, creating space for more breath, air, peace. She focused on the spot just below her belly and took a long, even breath through her nose. And then a longer release, the air spilling over her lips in a slow hush dispelling the duke's image.

She imagined her snake. He was silky black with a sheen of deepest aubergine. His lithe, powerful body lay in a tight coil. Then, with each breath, like a spool of silk, he unraveled in a slow undulating spiral, liquid, endless as he spread to fill her belly and chest, eddying into crevices that had long lay dormant and empty. At last, he completely filled her, causing a heavy pulsing low in her womb.

The snake lifted his head and his tongue flicked just as his eyes opened. They were pure amber.

She flipped in her bed and shoved a pillow up against her belly, then lower.

She flung the pillow. Almost too late, she remembered her newest painting. Legs tangling in the bedclothes, she lunged to catch the canvas, snatching it just before it crashed to the floor. The easel did not fare as well, and it went down with a *smack*.

Olivia froze; did the noise wake Eglantine? No. The only sound was the *skritch* of a branch at the window.

The painting safely back in its place, Olivia turned to attack the sheets and jammed her toe into the steps that led to her high bed. "Owww!" She wrenched the linen from around her legs and heaved it onto the mattress.

God's teeth, could one hasty, fumbled kiss weeks ago be the cause of all this turmoil within her body? How many men, with more expertise, had tried to persuade her into a dalliance and failed? *Why this man?*

She could *not* get back in that bed.

She hobbled over to the window seat and tucked herself up, the pane felt blessedly cool against her forehead as she pressed forward toward the darkness beyond. Toward the empty road.

Wasn't all going as they wished? Olivia asked the waxing gibbous moon. In the two short weeks since arriving at the estate, Egg was remarkably improved. She had even enjoyed a walk in the garden today with Lord Bertram, now a faithful visitor. And just yesterday, Dr. Asher proclaimed her bandages were to come off in the next couple of days.

And Olivia was painting. The attics had revealed a treasure of old canvases, brushes, paper, and crayons. But best of all, vials and vials of oil paints. Just the smell alone could send her into ecstasy, and with a bit of linseed oil, they had become living jewels.

She shoved her legs up under her, staring out at the moonlit park. It was all Roydan's fault. Daria Battersby had been one of the most sought after courtesans in the kingdom. She must have been doing something very right for the duke to have employed her for nearly five *years*. Most mistresses didn't last five weeks. How would Olivia measure up? It had been a very long time for her—years in fact. Over four years, if one were counting.

"Enough!" Olivia said to her ghostly reflection. This line of thinking would get her nowhere. Her beautiful room was too large, too lonely, the bed too empty and cold. She went to check on Eglantine.

Propped high on pillows, Egg lay with her mouth open and her eyes shut, but no soft snores. She was awake.

"Egg?"

"Do you imagine I could sleep through all of that racket? It put me in mind of young Bobby Tuttle. You remember, the company's goatherd? The fool lost track of his charges, and they nearly knocked the tent down around our ears?"

"How could I forget? I lost my favorite chemise and several paintbrushes to one of those fellows." Olivia laughed, shaking her head. "I am sorry to disturb you. Do you need anything?"

"No, nothing. And I am up now. Come, I miss our cozy chats." Egg moved over and patted a place for Olivia. Olivia lay down as she had on so many nights in so many cramped rooms.

Despite Egg saying she was for a chat, they both remained silent. The light curtain shifted and billowed in the breeze.

"Do you still miss Herbert?" Olivia finally broke the silence.

"Ah," was all Egg said for a long while. "Sometimes I think of what would have been. If he would have eventually lost *all* his hair." Egg giggled. "If we would have had our farm and grown lavender like we'd planned. If we'd have had a child...But it's been so very long for me. Truth to tell, I can hardly call to mind his face anymore." She paused. "His voice and the smell of him are more clear to me...isn't that funny?"

Silence filled the room.

"Wes never wanted to marry," Olivia whispered. "I don't know if I ever told you that."

Egg turned to her. "You're wrong, Wes loved you dearly."

"Oh, he came to love me, I have no doubt. But his true love was an Indian girl. Her parents forbade them to marry, and then she died. Wes never told me how. And I never asked."

Olivia's nose prickled, and her eyes filled. "I forced his hand with my terrible predicament. I wish I had had somewhere else to go." A hot puff of sad laughter escaped her. "Egg, you should have seen his face when I arrived in Portsmouth without a chaperon or even a maid. Wes immediately asked for leave to take me home, no matter the scandal. But when I told him...what had happened...Well, as you can imagine, he wanted to go back and kill Biden. Thank God I stopped him from that folly. Besides, I nearly killed Lord Biden myself." Tears slid steadily over her cheeks and she laughed. "Bless his soft heart, Wes would not let me be dishonored. We were married a week later in Calais. But he did it out of duty. He never would have chosen it."

The old memories stiffened her body—horrid red-brown smears on white thighs, the chipped blue and white bowl where she was told to clean herself, the glass of half-drunk sherry, the snapping of the sheet as her stepmother, yanked it from beneath her; then her words, "Just for insurance. He can never claim I bilked him. And wear the rose gown, you need color. Lord Biden is partial to pink." And finally the sharp taste of bile in her mouth.

She still could not abide the taste of sherry.

She sniffed and swiped her arm along her nose. "Wes was so very patient with me—never touched me for months. I didn't deserve him. I wanted so much to give him everything. But I could not..."

Egg's bandaged hand touched hers. "I did not know him long, but I do know you made him so very happy." Egg's voice was matter of fact, trying to draw off some of the heavy memories. "You must know he adored you." Egg laughed. "When Colonel Parton took that ball in the leg, he said he could not imagine a lovelier more devoted wife or a more thoroughly smitten husband. 'I don't know how Major Weston landed that fine gem of a lady,' the Colonel said, 'but I'd bet ready money it wasn't his looks that did it.' The

Colonel was always a bit of a scamp. I do believe he was half in love with you, Olive."

Indeed Colonel Parton had offered for her just after Wes's death. But she had never told Egg. Besides, Olivia never wanted to be rescued by another man. If she married again, she wanted a man who came to her free and clear.

Well, she had got herself into yet another situation where a man had swooped in to save her. It seemed to be her destiny.

She kissed Egg's bandaged hand. Dear Egg always seemed to say the right things. They talked a bit more about the war and Paris. The silences got longer till Egg's only answer was a gentle snore. Olivia tucked Egg's hands under the covers and slipped out of the room.

Back in her own bed she shifted her pillow.

Wes would never have approved of her celibate state. He had always wanted her to know the fullness of physical love, how to take as well as give.

And oh, she wanted to take and give now. This monkish duke frayed the edges of her reason, slipping under her resolve to press on her most secret places.

*When would he come to her? How would they begin? What would it be like to lay with him?*

She pushed the pillow hard up between her legs again, pressing the other end to her breasts. Her hand slipped from her belly to thread in the nest of hair between her legs. A soft moan escaped her lips.

God help her, she knew she would get no sleep this night. She might as well paint.

## Chapter Fifteen

The duke would come today. He and his uncle had called yesterday, but Olivia had managed to be out. It would be utter rudeness, not to mention cowardly, to be missing again. Consequently, by the time they were announced by Mrs. Fields, the ladies' housekeeper, Olivia was in a state. Her face must have frozen in some approximation of a smile, because as she greeted Lord Bertram, he smiled back. Now if she could only remember to breathe.

She turned to the duke. Her gaze slid over his beautiful hunter-green riding coat, with its boutonnière of stephanotis, and the fine linen of his shirt, its collar points laying just so against his freshly shaved cheeks. His mouth was pulled into a rigid line, as if he were clamping his teeth together. She could not meet his eyes. It was enough to *feel* his gaze as it raked over her, taking in her sprigged muslin gown of the palest daffodil. One of the gowns he had bought her.

She had yet to thank him for the shawl or for retrieving the few items saved from the fire or for any of the kindnesses he had shown. And why should she? After all, it was done with one end in mind. She smoothed her damp hands over her yellow skirts. Heavens, she might as well have been wearing nothing, she felt so exposed.

She and Egg sat, and the men followed suit.

Everyone smiled at each other, except the duke of course, and then, silence.

Finally someone mentioned Lady Wiggins's continued health and the duke contributed a rejoinder—she heard his low rumble—but honestly she could not attend. She was too busy adjusting her skirts and the lumpy pillow behind her.

The tea tray arrived and she practically leapt on it, anything to occupy her.

"Oh—yes, dear. Why don't you do the honors?" Egg pulled away from the tea service.

It was so very hard to hear over the pounding in her head, which now had taken over her poor heart as well. She was sure everyone could hear it.

Somehow she managed to pour without spilling a drop.

"Milk, Your Grace?" *Was that her voice?* The pounding became huge African drums, like the ones she had seen and heard while living in Morocco with Wes. But the duke's response was lost in the pulsing beat. She took a quick peek at Egg and Lord Bertram, but neither was looking at her. She took a guess and added a splash of milk.

Spoons tinkled against china cups, in sharp counterpoint to the primitive thrum in her head. Not to be overshadowed by piddling spoons, the drums beat louder still.

"Do you take sugar, Your Grace?" she told herself that when he answered she would be able to meet his eyes with utter calm. But the pounding went on, and her imagination, not satisfied with sound, added scantily clad, gyrating dancers. She only managed to get to his lips, which was a good thing because she read the 'no' very clearly. Otherwise she might have dumped four or five lumps in his tea, and then they would all know she was barmy.

She handed him the cup, being absolutely careful not to graze his fingers. Not a drop spilled, as she imagined flailing, naked arms, along with pumping hips and buttocks. A frenzy of erotic motion. Considering the uproar in her head, she was quite pleased with her performance. She even tried a smile and to attend to the conversation.

"—weather has been unseasonably warm, Roydan," remarked Lord Bertram. "We have begun to resurrect your grandmamma's old rose garden."

Now would be a safe moment to look at him, when she was sure he was busy translating Bertram's "we" to include only his uncle and Egg and not necessarily herself. But like a coward, she only sipped her tea, keeping her eyes on the rose-patterned cup.

*Drat!*

She cleared her throat, and all eyes locked on her. Lord Bertram and Egg looked at her encouragingly, like a child who might actually participate in an adult conversation. They were even nodding, as if they turned a skipping rope and she was desperately trying to jump in. *Thwap. Thwap. Thwap*. She jumped.

"I believe I encountered a flock of cormorants near the northernmost cliffs yesterday."

Their gazes locked and tangled.

His eyes were still deep gold. Still set off by thick black lashes. And still made her feel as if he were starving. But how had she thought they were ever cold? Indeed they seemed to warm her from head to toes.

"They are no doubt tending their nests," he

answered. Then he took a long sip of his tea, his eyes never leaving hers. He returned his cup to its saucer and balanced it on his knee. "A pity you missed their courtship. It is quite a show. The males wave their long necks about, preening and posing, while the females bend theirs right over their backs." Now she was quite hot. Surely he must feel the heat as well, though he looked completely unflustered. "The eggs are incubated by both parents for about a month," he continued. "A shag is quite fervent about the care of—"

*A shag?* Oh, good Lord, cormorants were sometimes called shags. Could he be teasing her? She ducked her head and reached for a biscuit. The hot flush rushed to flood her neck and chest—and lower. *Dear God, females bending over backward?*

She swallowed, pushing the dry biscuit past her tightening throat. Very well, she would ride this out, and she anted up.

"I have never had the pleasure of seeing them bend over backward, Your Grace, but I have seen them holding their wings thus." Olivia spread her arms out wide. "I believe that is their way of not letting the other birds come too close."

He raised an eyebrow, along with the stakes. "Now you mention it, Mrs. Weston, you remind me a bit of the bird, long neck, black glossy feathers, green eyes…"

Her neck was surely flaming red at this point. She gripped her tea cup. "I cannot tell Your Grace, is that meant to be a compliment?"

But it seemed the game was over as he made no rejoinder, and the conversation moved on. It irked her to think he might have won.

The gentlemen left a short while later, but not before she and Egg had been invited to the mansion for dinner the next evening.

"Mrs. Weston," said the duke, "have you been to the house yet?"

"No, Your Grace, I have not had that pleasure."

"Ah, well, I hope you will find it to your liking. It is a jumble of styles as my relatives sought to make their mark on the place, and I dare say I am prejudiced, but I think it one of the most picturesque of my holdings."

She made no comment except for a curtsey and a "Goodbye."

\*\*\*\*

Later in the garden, Egg sipped her tea while Olivia attempted to paint a portrait of the cat, Temperance, who, Olivia finally concluded, did not deserve her name.

"The duke looked remarkably well this afternoon, did he not?" said Egg.

"He did not appear any different than usual." Olivia did not like the direction she supposed Egg to be taking.

"He is extremely polite. Well, that is to say he is polite when he actually speaks. And his *eyes*...One cannot but look at his...stillness and think there is great depth there. And perhaps sorrow..." Egg's voice trailed off again till Olivia thought the conversation might be finished. "But"—No, too much to hope for—"it is possible I am reading far too much into our host's character." Egg adjusted her spectacles down her nose. "You, my dear, must have a much clearer picture, having spent an entire evening with the man?" She looked to Olivia, who was suddenly very intent on mixing the perfect shade of blue for Miss Temperance's left ear. Egg went on despite Olivia ignoring her friend, "But his uncle is all ease and charm. Do you know he has insisted on taking part in our little vegetable patch as well as the rose garden? The man actually donned garden gloves and dug the whole of the north end. I must say it was astonishing."

Olivia took a chance to peep up from her cat's ear to see her friend staring out at nothing, a wistful look on her soft, round face. Olivia almost abandoned Temperance's portrait right then in order to capture that look on Egg's face. But in the next moment, Egg set down her tea cup and cleared her throat.

"My dear, I have not mentioned this before"—oh dear, this was decidedly not a good sign—"I suppose I did not want to think too much about it myself, but *why* is the duke taking such an interest in our plight? He barely *knows* us. I have wracked my brain, and I cannot think why he would embroil himself in our troubles."

"I dare say he is rich enough to spare one small corner on his many vast estates." Her voice sounded surly even to her own ears.

"I do not mean to sound ungracious, far from it, but his character, as I've observed, does not seem to lean toward charity to those with whom he has so little connection."

Olivia shifted her brush and took up a rag to clean it. She was not adept at lying to Egg. "I suspect it may come from a misplaced sense of responsibility. He was not at all certain Daria Battersby did not have something to do with the fire at our shop." Olivia eluded Egg's raised eyebrows by teasing Temperance with the end of her brush.

"Oh, I cannot believe she would be so evil! Granted she is vain and jealous, but I cannot see her stooping to arson. Is the duke so sure?"

Olivia abandoned the cat to fetch her cup of tea. "No, Egg," she said, perceiving that she had started her own particular fire with her tale, "by no means is he certain. I dare say his suspicion was only part of what brought him to act in our case. Mostly, I think it was because I was so desperate and that he could well afford to give us aid."

"Ah," Egg said, and then folded her arms across her body.

Olivia took a swallow of stone-cold tea.

\*\*\*\*

Olivia was fully prepared for her next meeting with the duke. As she and Egg climbed out of the carriage, Olivia banished all thoughts of drums, dancers, and large glossy birds.

Close up, the house was less imposing than the great sprawling mass one saw from the turn to the dower house. However, the closer view in no way diminished its beauty. It became instead like a patchwork quilt—a square of Jacobean, a bit of newer Georgian, a long wing of Tudor, crowned with medieval towers and Gothic chimney pieces. Somehow all were harmonious, linked by ivies and the patina of time and sea winds on the native rock. It was not a house of symmetry, but it felt alive and warm.

Olivia thought she saw a face in an upper window as she scanned the facade, but it disappeared in the next moment. She joined Egg at the door and they entered.

The duke had invited some of the local gentry, and

Olivia was quite pleased with her performance. Indeed the whole party's manners were stellar; the most correct remarks were made on a variety of civilized topics, the weather being one of the chief subjects—wasn't it always. Another fulsome conversation was focused on Egg's recovery and Lady Bainbridge's roses. Though, to be fair, the talk of roses was mostly a monologue, Lady Bainbridge never missing the opportunity to hold forth. The syllabub was exclaimed over, the roast pork had been done to a turn, according to Mrs. Hargett. Olivia sighed. How obliging of the dear lady, for if you missed the remark the first or even second time, you were sure to get it on the third and even fourth.

The only glitch in the dinner service, if it could even be called such, was perpetrated by a mere footman, who had inadvertently filled her wine glass with actual wine, instead of the watered down stuff the ladies usually were served. At this point in the evening she would have been very happy to drink it and a least half a bottle more; anything to alleviate the tedious conversation rankling her frazzled nerves. But before she got the glass to her lips, she heard a cough to her left and the butler was there with a replacement. Olivia looked to see the duke's reaction; he merely raised an eyebrow.

Thank goodness Egg, who was doing a remarkable job serving as hostess, rose and asked the ladies to please remove to the drawing room for tea.

Olivia sipped her tea and listened with half an ear to the various stages of blight attacking a rose variety called Flossy. A few stray tea leaves swirled in her Limoges cup and finally settled. A pity her nerves could not follow suit.

The gentlemen soon joined the ladies and her cup rattled in its saucer, once again disturbing the tea leaves. Her stomach not only swirled but performed a small flip. This was the portion of the evening that would afford the duke an opportunity to speak with her in relative privacy. As he entered, he spoke briefly to a footman who promptly opened the French doors to admit a breeze—she hoped—for the room was suddenly very stuffy.

Perhaps the duke was setting the stage to ask her to step out into the garden? Or would he corner her next to the tea tray and propose an assignation for the following day? Or perhaps, she should lay her neck back to signal her readiness, and he would leap over the chaise lounge and claim her?

A short bark of laughter escaped her mouth, which she immediately covered with her hand.

Her timing was most unfortunate, for as she glanced around, the rest of the company was looking decidedly grave. She managed to catch Reverend Hargett's last few words, "poor unfortunate orphans," before he petered out, pursed his already tight lips, and added a sniff for good measure.

*Oh bother!* She had been doing so well. But, honestly, *when* would he make his bloody move?

The answer was, he did not.

With Mrs. Hargett's final homage to the roast—"to a turn"—ringing in her ears, she wondered, as she and Egg rode home in the ducal carriage, if the duke even noticed her beyond the wine incident and her outburst of laughter? Which she now recalled had earned her a second raised eyebrow. Other than those instances, he had hardly looked at her, much less proposed an affair.

Well, perhaps he would send a note tomorrow.

He did not.

It was almost two weeks since the duke had taken up residence at Valmere. And though he had come to tea twice since, and she and Egg had dined again at the mansion, nothing had happened. Surely he would declare his intentions within the next few days.

He did not.

\*\*\*\*

As he broke the seal and opened yet another letter from Daria, a folded paper dropped out. "The enclosed note holds irrefutable proof of my friend's close connection with Mrs. Gooden," wrote Daria. Rhys picked up the neat square. It was obviously much older. He turned it over. No address. He opened it and smoothed it on his desk.

The hand was distinctive, childish but with many curlicues and needless flourishes. It was her writing. He had seen it only once before, in a note she had written him thirteen years ago. He closed his eyes and leaned back in the chair, the memories spinning out like the line on a fishing reel....

*Meet me at the boat house at five.*

*Dee*

He had been home from Oxford a whole week before he saw her.

Mac had expressed some concern about the fences at the northernmost edge of the property and had asked Rhys to inspect them. This was their old pattern, Rhys would report back, and the older man would call for tea and a pipe and they would have a chat about things, or more likely just sit by the fire.

Cantering Anthos over the last little rise, Rhys

pulled up. Sure enough, the fences were immaculate, nary a rotting post or broken rail. He was turning to head back for the tea and Mac's company when he saw a lone figure walking along the ridge of cliff toward the sea.

It was a woman. He could see the long shape of her gown and the curve of her bonnet. He would have ridden away, though he was curious, but she called to him. Still, he hesitated. Could he pretend he hadn't heard? He was shy of women. But she might be in some distress, and being polite, he cantered to her, dismounted, and walked the ten or so yards to make his bow and inquire if she needed his assistance.

As he approached, he saw she was young and a beauty. At ten paces he could safely say she was the most beautiful woman he had ever seen.

"Good afternoon, my lord," said the woman. He blinked and just remembered to bow. She laughed at his dumbness. "You are likely wondering who this forward lady is, speaking to you with no formal introduction and in a blustery wilderness no less."

He was still getting over the music of her laugh. He swallowed. Bowing again. Preparing to speak.

She laughed again.

"If you'll forgive me for being so bold and dominating the conversation," she said with a flashing dimple, "I am newly come to the area. I am staying in the cottage beyond the rise here." She cocked her head prettily. "'Twas the old Barker place, I believe."

Another pause and another opportunity for Rhys to get his wits together.

He licked his lips. "Yes, it has stood empty for some time now. I wonder how you heard of it." The words formed in his mind, but never got beyond his wet lips. Instead he bowed. Again. *Stupid clod.*

"I collect you must be the young lord home for his summer holiday?"

Grasping at anything, he found his voice. "Yes. Yes, Miss, I am Rhys"—he gulped—"I mean, I am, Marquess of Beckham, ah, Lord Beckham. Yes..."

She made a curtsey. Dark ringlets bobbed and bounced off her pink cheeks. And though her gown was rather demure, he spied the beginning of a magnificent cleavage.

His mouth turned to cotton.

"What a pleasure to meet you, Lord Beckham. But I must correct you; I am no Miss. I am a Missus. Mrs. Gooden if you please, my lord." Another smaller curtsey and another—God help him—flash of décolletage.

"Ahhh...." he managed. "Mrs..." He felt as if he had been soundly punched in the stomach.

"However, I am a widow. My dear husband passed away more than two years ago." This said under long, upswept lashes.

"Ahhh..." he said again. And hope bloomed.

Over the next few days he endeavored to "accidentally" meet up with Mrs. Gooden as often as humanly possible. She would come out and, bless her, pretend surprise. Then they would walk. She chattered away, remarking on the weather, a current fashion, the week's sermon—he made a note to attend church—and he would measure his steps to fit her tiny ones, head bowed in rapt attention.

He rarely commented, but she did not seem to mind his brevity. Indeed she did not seem to look to him for any meaningful response but rambled on, seemingly happy to listen to her own lilting voice.

It was a very good thing she took no notice of his silence, because Rhys would have been hard-pressed to repeat any of her conversation. His mind so fully occupied with her smell, her tiny white hands, her lashes against her cheek, her breasts pushing against the muslin of her day gown, her slippers peeping out from beneath that gown, her legs swishing inside that gown, thighs brushing...There was not an ounce of room for actual comprehension of language. Not when her lips were so interesting in themselves. *God, her lips*...He stumbled. She caught his arm to steady him.

"Your p-p-ardon, madam."

"Oh! Must I be a madam? It sounds as if I am ancient." She stopped, lashes dipping. "You must call me Dee, at least when we are out of company."

Rhys froze.

"Please?" She lifted her chin, as if she were waiting for something.

By God, he must make a *move!* He plunged toward her waiting lips and found utter sweetness—ripe, cool berries mixed with hot honeyed—*tongue?*

She made a small sound—or maybe it was him? He pulled away suddenly, unsure, trying to quell his ardor.

Then a miracle. Her hands came to rest on his shoulders.

*She wanted him?* He tentatively put his arms about her. She was so small and soft, like a bird. He did not want to crush her. She pulled him closer, her lips moving beneath his, soft and coaxing. He began to follow her lead, and where she led was pure heaven.

How they parted, how he got back on his horse—

which had become just a horse now and not his beloved Anthos—how he got home, he did not know. He even forgot to call in on Mac. Hours later, the old man had to seek him out.

That had been four days ago, and as he lay on the rocky beach, his forehead pressing against the sand, all he could think of was that excruciatingly potent kiss. And when could it possibly be repeated. She had been away for three days now. Where she had gone he did not know. *When* she would be back was the question pulsing in his mind with each incoming wave.

He had finally got an answer to his prayers in the form of a note—

*Meet me at the boat house at five.*

*Dee*

The paper had curled as a red ridge of ember ate at those nine words. But as he had flung the charred bits into the wind thirteen years ago, he had known they would ever be burned on his heart.

He made himself sit straight and look down at this newest letter.

It was a love letter. Dated January 24 but had no year and no salutation beyond, "My Dearest Lord and Master" and signed simply, "Your Dove, Dee." Clearly this new friend of Daria's had had a very intimate connection with Dee Gooden. How else would he have a letter this personal? But was this just an old love? Did he have any idea of where she might be now?

Rhys would have to take the chance. He rang for Shields.

"Have my carriage prepared posthaste. I leave for London within the hour."

\*\*\*\*

Sweat tricked down Olivia's back, finding the channel between her shoulder blades. The heavy basket bumped against her thigh, catching at her skirts, as sand filled her half-boots.

Her heart felt nearly as heavy as her boots. The duke had been called away suddenly, and no one knew when he might return.

The picnic was Egg's idea. Olivia had suggested several lovely spots along the way, but Egg seemed to have a very specific place in mind. Sure enough, when they rounded the next cove, there was Lord Bertram with a fishing pole, not doing much fishing. Exclamations of surprise and delight caught a rare breeze, and Bertram hurried to meet them. Egg ignored Olivia's withering look and smiled, innocently turning to Lord Bertram.

They settled on a low, flat rock to share their picnic.

"Well, ladies." Bertram got up to brush a few crumbs from his coat. "I believe after Cook's Bath buns I am very much in need of a walk. Do I have any takers?"

Olivia was sorely tempted to jump up and declare she would love a walk above all else, but she was not so cruel. Egg was already rising with the help of a beaming Bertram.

Olivia dutifully played her role. "Lady Wiggins, would you mind terribly if I stayed behind? After so much food and wine I find I am more desirous of a nap than a stroll."

Olivia settled back onto her elbows, sheltered somewhat from the sun by an overhanging rock, and watched the surf. A flash of white caught her gaze farther down the cove. It was a man. She sat up. It was the duke.

He appeared to be shucking off his boots, stockings, coat, and cravat. Then he strode into the sea as if going into battle.

The spray spattered his breeches and the fine batiste of his shirt. Cupping handfuls of water, he doused his face and neck. The water ran down his chest and back in little rivulets causing his shirt to stick to him.

Olivia had seen him dancing, sipping tea, dining— always the most civilized of social situations. Always hemmed in by a room or a carriage. And always fully attired.

He plunged into the water, diving under a huge curling wave that seemed to swallow him. She waited breathlessly to see his dark head and the white of his shirt. Then, there he was, surging out of the water, like Neptune come to life, but instead of cold white marble, he was warm bronze and rippling flesh and sinew. The clear victor against the sea's endless flexing muscle. He cut across the waves with long pulling strokes.

Now almost directly in front of her, he was too close. She pushed back into the shelter of the rock and willed him not to look her way.

A sea bird cawed high above drawing attention to itself. The duke, emerging from the water, turned and looked up. His Adam's apple slid up and down his throat, and the corded tendons in his neck stood out as his arm rose to shade his eyes.

Gentlemen were always covered to their chins in fine linen, their valets taking prodigious care and pride in executing the perfect knot or fall. Such a shame to cover that fine, strong column and the bit of chest exposed below.

She had never lain with a man she truly lusted after. Oh, she had flirted and even dabbled in Paris, but when it came to the crux of the matter she always begged off. No man had ever been enough to pull her over that precipice into such intimacy.

Wes had been her only lover—excepting that terrible first time—and though she had learned to love his body and what it did to her, she had not been particularly attracted to it. He had been stocky and hirsute, muscles thick and compacted into his boxy frame and his skin often red with sunburn and covered in freckles. Beauty and the beast, he had called them.

But this man before her was the exact opposite, lithe and rangy, with wide, sculpted shoulders tapering to a narrow waist, and the most delectable posterior. She tilted her head in order to get the best view as she sank her teeth into a smooth ripe plum. Her toes curled in her boots and a gust of wind cooled her cheeks. That same wind caught the brim of her bonnet, its bright yellow ribbons fluttering as it flew into the sky before being dashed to ground and then dancing briefly over the sand to snag on a fallen branch.

He turned, startled.

Oh dear. He charged out of the water and right up to her, his breath coming like a bellows, his glorious Adam's apple working in his throat. She did not know whether to fling herself at him or retreat, when his gaze flicked to her mouth. Only then did she feel the plum juice wet on her lips and running down her chin. Dear God, she had the terrible urge to lick.

"It was not a whale, Eglantine. There is no shame

in being short-sighted. It was most certainly a large black boulder."

The duke jerked toward the sound as if he were a fish on a hook. Shocked herself, she sat up and guiltily swiped at her lips with the back of her hand.

With some effort, the duke pushed himself away, his hands spearing through his hair, as he spun around churning up the sand. He nearly trampled Lord Bertram's fishing rod. Instead, he seized it, and Olivia was sure he would have broken it to pieces, except Egg and Bertram were upon them.

"Oh, Your—Roydan—you are back." Egg was trying to act as if a soaking wet, barefoot duke, who seemed to be in the throes of some tortured emotion, was not in the least out of the ordinary. She turned to her companion for help, but Lord Bertram was strangely mute. Egg, ever the savior, turned back and continued, "Well, it is good you are here. You may settle our dispute. Will you please tell this silly man that the North Sea must contain at least one or two whales? I simply will not be budged in this matter."

The poor man desperately tried to find his footing, looking from his uncle to Egg and then back again. In the end he did not even attempt an answer. Instead he tried to don his coat, but it was simply too tight, or his body too wet. He could not gather the rest of his cast-off items quickly enough. He balled the whole mess up and shoved it under his arm. His valet would no doubt have vapors.

"You must excuse me, Lady Wiggins." He bobbed his head to her but made no eye contact. "I have just returned. I did not realize—the time. That is—I must leave you now." He made a curt bow and strode off toward the direction of the house, but on his way, he passed Olivia's bonnet. He stopped, squared his shoulders, turned back, retrieved the bonnet from the branch, marched back and presented it to her with a formal bow.

Then they all three watched till his figure disappeared behind the rocks. Egg met Olivia's gaze and hooked her arm through Lord Bertram's. "And I am not short-sighted," she said to his lordship as she towed him toward the far rocks.

Olivia waited a full seven waves before she devoured the rest of the plum and hurled the pit into the sea.

## Chapter Sixteen

Rhys refilled his pipe, first pressing the tobacco into the bowl with the pad of his thumb, and then reached for a bit of straw to light it. He pulled in air, igniting the leaves, and sat back, hoping the familiar comfort of his old steward's room would settle his nerves.

He closed his eyes, willing himself to dispel the vivid images lapping the shores of his brain—her mouth sinking into that plum, the juice running down...

He had taken himself off to the next cove and plunged his hot body into the water using fistfuls of sand to scrub his thighs and arms. But when he'd emerged, his cock still bobbed heavy and hard against his belly. He ended up wearing himself out by swimming, and—in the other way as well.

Rhys shifted in his chair.

The London trip had been a waste of his time and money. Daria's friend had been "called away," but Daria had instructions for Rhys to go to a bawdy house in Seven Dials, where he would find Dee Gooden or at least news of her. It was the beginning of a long string of "Oh, that bitch? She was here a while back, but I had to throw her out. She weren't clean, you see. Too many blokes complained." The next establishment said nearly the same, only adding that she seemed to have a need for laudanum as well as drink. At the last place, he had missed Gooden by only a few days. As he was leaving, a bawd pushed her gray pockmarked breasts up to him and smiled through black and broken teeth. "Two bits for a toss, gov?" She couldn't have more than thirty years but looked to be at least sixty. He almost felt sorry for Dee Gooden. Almost.

Mac sat in his old rocker to Rhys's left, and Toby lay between them on the well-worn rag rug, his huge head between his paws. The old dog occasionally slapped his tail and lifted his head for a scratch. One or other of the men would comply, and then he'd settle back into a snuffling snore.

"The young miss is a fair lass."

Rhys stopped his rocking and just as quickly resumed it. Mac always had a tendency to read his mind.

"Young miss?" He knew very well who Mac was referring to but played dumb just the same. "Are you referring to *Mrs.* Weston, by any chance?"

His old friend only looked steadily at Rhys and continued to puff on his pipe, his lack of words conveying more than a whole sermon.

Rhys drew on his own pipe. A long moment passed. But their companionable silence was over.

"I am *not* in love. You, of all people, know I do not believe in love. Indeed, I do not even think I am capable of it."

Again, all Rhys got for his protestation was another sage look and an exhaled puff.

"I will admit to being in *lust*. Yes, that I will own." A shard of ember popped, landing on the edge of the rug. He nudged the coal with his boot and tamped it out. "It has quite overtaken me, but I assure you it will

199

*not* end as it did years ago." Toby stared up, and Rhys realized his voice had risen. He slowed his rocking. "You may trust me on that. I have learned a thing or two since my raw youth. I am in complete control of this particular situation. Indeed, all I have to do is say the word, and she is mine."

The old man waited a moment, stubbed out his pipe, and rose, but as he left the room Rhys felt Mac's light touch on the back of his head.

Rhys did not stir himself but sat smoking and staring into the hearth's dying embers as those painful memories surrounded him...

*Meet me at the boat house at five.*

*Dee.*

He had arrived at the boathouse at two that afternoon, nearly insane with want and anxiety.

Dee came in breathless and laughing, sorry to be late. He began to kiss her, his pent-up passion spilling out of every pore. He was quite sure he would drown soon.

She laughed again and pushed him aside. "Not yet, silly boy."

He felt the hot blush of confusion, but deferred to her experience. He splashed the wine he had brought into two goblets and prayed his hands would stop shaking.

He met her by the window. "To love," she said, taking a small sip.

He tried to kiss her again, but again, she pushed him away, this time with some anger. Stretched to his limits, he gulped his wine. Nothing was going as he had planned. She seemed somehow different, and he did not know how to approach her.

Suddenly as if some phantom clock had chimed, she threw herself at him and began to pull her bodice down, free her breasts, and open his falls all at the same time. Rhys was shocked but so hungry for her he was quickly consumed.

"Well, well, what have we here?"

It took Rhys a moment to comprehend this terrible intrusion. Only Dee pulling away made his mind connect to the voice so like his own. Dear God, it was his father.

Dee broke from him, and Rhys turned to shield her. But she pushed him aside and did not even attempt to cover herself. Then she smiled.

*Smiled?* Rhys, with his breeches around his ankles, did not know where to look, at his father and the four burly footmen who stood flanking him, or at his lover who was looking like a cat with a dish of cream.

"Dee, I see you have been busy, my dove," drawled the duke.

*Dee? He called her Dee?* Nothing made sense. As if he had stepped from a beautiful dream into a hideous nightmare.

She made a moue and walked slowly to the duke. "I have been lonely. Surely you would not begrudge me a bit of dalliance, Ian?"

*Ian?*

"I could not deny you anything, my dove," said his father. "I only wonder at your choice of plaything. Why would you choose to sully yourself with this oafish pup? He is nothing."

Dee looked back at Rhys. "Oafish pup? Really?" She laughed. "Hmm...Do you mind, my love"—she shot him a wicked smile—"if I have a look? Who knows? I may even like the son better."

The duke let out a low laugh and gestured to the footmen. "By all means, remove his clothes. The lady wants to see what she missed."

Finally all the pieces clicked into place, and Rhys erupted like a madman. A scream tore through him and he lurched for his father. The footmen were upon him in a moment. Three held him fast as the fourth smashed a fist into his mouth.

"Enough," said the duke. "There will be time enough for that later. We must let the lady look her fill first."

Dee began a slow circle around Rhys. "Ooooh, he is a tall, awkward lad. And skinny as a scarecrow, all arms and legs." She looked up at his face. Rhys jerked his chin up, his breath coming hot and fast in his nostrils. "A scarecrow with spots." He felt his neck and face flush. She noted her effect on him and cocked her head. "But his eyes alone are enough to set him above the rest of the male population." Her mouth thinned and she narrowed her eyes. "Why *is* it men always seemed to have the lashes we women crave? It is truly vexing!" Dee shook her head, moving on. "But what a set of shoulders, Yes, with a few years—and stone—he might do well enough."

Heat fired his face and neck, and his scalp burned as a footman's fist tightened in his hair.

"But why ever would I want the son," Dee said, turning back to the duke, "when I have the finished version right here before me to confirm my opinions? Is he not a near copy of you, my love?" She moved to the duke's side, and deftly opened the older man's falls. Rhys clenched his teeth to stop from screaming.

"Oh," Dee crooned. Then she turned to Rhys, homing in on his now thoroughly limp member. "But now I see something *very* different." Rhys would not look, but he could not miss his father's hand as he pushed Dee's head down. "Yes, my love," she said from between the duke's legs, "I believe in the final analysis, he is quite paltry next to you."

The fist in his hair loosened, and the footmen relaxed their grips slightly, their attention riveted on the kneeling woman.

Rhys ran.

Pain shot through his knees to his chin. He had forgotten his breeches still lay round his feet. He spat blood and gritty sand as laughter rang above him.

"Not so fast, my son." His father's boot nudged Rhys's bleeding face. "I don't care for interruptions. Your behavior calls for some form of punishment, don't you agree? We can't have you poaching on a man's property without some consequences, can we?" At the duke's order, the footmen yanked Rhys to his feet. "Obviously I have been far too lenient in your upbringing. Tie him to that chair." And then he walked to a cot-like bed against the far wall, Dee giggling after him.

Rhys had been wrong. The real nightmare was only beginning.

His father took Rhys's "love" on the bed like a dog, all the while looking straight at Rhys, who would not give his father the satisfaction of looking away.

When his father lay satiated, like some sort of pasha, the woman—she had ceased to be Dee—offered him a glass of the wine Rhys had brought. The duke merely flicked his finger when he wanted a sip.

"How did you like that, my boy? Quite an education for your poor mind, I am sure."

Rhys could hardly feel his body much less his numb mind.

"What? No thanks? Oh, Dee, I am not sure he has learned his lesson. What can we do to make this a truly enduring tutorial?" The duke rose and stood in front of Rhys. "Ah, I know, my dove, come." He crooked his finger at the woman. "Come and see if you can raise this poor—what was the word you used—ah, yes, paltry thing from the dead."

Rhys spit in his father's face.

The strike came in an instant, but it had been worth it to see a glimpse of his father's rage. Rhys was nearly senseless by the time his father was finished with him, his eyes almost completely swollen shut and his lips torn and bleeding. Still, he would not look away.

His father laughed. "All right, lads, now it's time to see if there's any life in the boy. I'll give you ten guineas he can't get it up for Miss Dee here. What say you?"

And the bets were on.

To Rhys extreme humiliation, the fifth Duke of Roydan lost his bet. As the woman lowered her head and took him in her mouth, Rhys's cock began to stir...

The fire was nearly all ashes now. Just as the old boathouse had been reduced to ashes as soon as Rhys had attained the title.

He heard a soft whining and then a wet nose pushed into his fisted hand. Rhys slowly opened his fingers, and Toby's tongue licked them once and then again. Rhys buried his face in the dog's furry neck and stroked his long velvet ears. The dog thumped his tail and nudged Rhys again. Rhys sat up, slowly sloughing off the terrible memories, replacing them with the familiar sights and smells of Mac's home. He stood, feeling suddenly as ancient as Mac. "Come, Toby, old boy. It's time we both got some relief."

Chapter Seventeen

"It will be a small party again," Egg assured Olivia. "Just ourselves, Lord Bertram, the Hargetts, Squire and Mrs. Winslow, Lady Bainbridge and her son, Percy, who is lately home from Oxford. That is nine...I am forgetting someone...Oh, good heavens, of course, the duke—Roydan, as I must remember to call him." She laughed and shook her head. "Dear Olive, it is not always easy to remember I am Lady Wiggins now."

What a contrast the two women presented—Egg practically skipping about Olivia's bedchamber, chattering like a magpie, while Olivia slumped at her dressing table applying a bit of rouge to her too-pale lips and cheeks. Her mood was foul, and her mind thoroughly tired of trying to guess Rhys Merrick's next move—or lack of movement.

She glared at the mulish face in the mirror and rose to take a final look at her gown. Well, at least it was not one of *his*.

She had worn it to the Dillingham mask so it had escaped the fire, only a scorch and a few small burns marred the sheer cerulean organza overskirt. Easily mended. Tonight she had paired it with a golden-pink petticoat. The gown had always been a favorite and reminded her of a sunset over the Seine—that opalescent light that happens at dusk.

Egg came up behind her. "Ah, I remember this

beauty. Wasn't it for the Comte d' Orsay's going away ball?" Olivia nodded. "But you have re-made it, how clever you are. One would swear it had never seen Napoleon or a breath of fire and smoke."

Olivia, now more confident, gathered her shawl. "Shall we deign to grace these mere mortals with our glorious persons?"

The guests were already assembled in the drawing room when Olivia and Egg arrived. The duke, in conversation with Lady Bainbridge, immediately excused himself and went to greet his final guests.

"Lady Wiggins, I trust your health continues to improve?"

"You are all kindness, Roydan. I have only the slightest tenderness in my hands now, and my lungs have never been better. The sea air at Valmere has done me wonders. I only wish I could bottle it and take it away with me when I go."

"I am gratified to hear it, my lady. But you have only just arrived. You must not think of leaving us."

"I am flattered you think our stay has been so brief. Indeed I had begun to think, with my health so improved, Mrs. Weston and I should be moving on and not tax your generous hospitality. After all, we have been in the dower house nearly six weeks."

"Nonsense!" Lord Bertram had appeared to stand at Egg's elbow. "I will not hear any more of this silly talk of leaving." He smiled at her. "Roydan, surely you would not be easy with our fair ladies departing any time soon?"

"No, Uncle, at least not until I have patented my sea-air elixir," the duke said with utter seriousness. "And I am quite sure that will take several years, perhaps even a lifetime."

Olivia's stomach pulled itself into a neat french knot.

"That is a lovely gown, Mrs. Weston," he said, turning to her, his gaze like a brand.

"It is old, Your Grace. Indeed, I believe you have seen it before?" Her question hung in the air between them.

"I'm sure I would remember if I had," he said finally.

It was no admission, yet he did not precisely lie either. She employed his own weapon, raising her eyebrow.

"I thank you for consenting to be one of our small party," was all he said.

"Your Grace," she murmured dipping into a brief curtsey. But he had moved off to join Reverend Hargett.

Olivia preferred to be a spectator for most of the evening. She noted the various conversations that swirled about her but took no part.

The dinner done, they were all gathered together again, when the conversation turned to painting.

"I believe your mother, the late duchess, was painted by Mr. Reynolds, was she not, Your Grace?" the Reverend offered.

"Yes, it was her wedding gift to the duke."

"Mrs. Weston," the Reverend continued, "I understand you are fond of painting. Do you admire the works of Mr. Reynolds?"

"I would imagine there is no one who could doubt Mr. Reynolds was one of the great masters of our time, Mr. Hargett. Yes, I admire his work very much, though

I have not seen as much as I would like."

"I would be pleased to show you the portrait now if you wish, Mrs. Weston." The duke rose, his steely face showing no pleasure whatsoever.

"Oh, I did not mean to beg a viewing, Your Grace."

"I should very much like to see it myself," Percy Bainbridge bounced up from his seat next to his mother. He found himself face-to-face with the piercing eyes of the duke. "But now I recall"—he peeled his eyes from the duke to settle on the next available person—"I particularly wanted to hear your thoughts, Reverend Hargett, on the merits of gas lighting, and so I will forgo the pleasures of Mr. Reynolds for the time being." And he scurried to join the Reverend.

"Madam, will you come?"

She hesitated. *Was this a challenge?* Lord knew she was mightily tired of this frustration and inertia.

"Yes, thank you. I will come," she said issuing her own challenge. But he either missed the dare, or more likely, chose to ignore it.

He led her through a maze of halls and passageways. They finally came to a huge set of double doors. He opened one side, and they entered a great hall. It must have been one hundred feet long and half as wide. She looked above to a ceiling made mostly of glass. In the daylight it would allow the portraits to be viewed at their best advantage. But now, only feeble moonlight and stars shone through, casting rows of venerable Merricks into shadowed ghosts. He gestured her forward, holding a candelabra to light their way.

The paintings were arranged chronologically. The first subjects wore huge ruffs and collars, enormous coats and jeweled stomachers. Next were sitters with powdered wigs dressed in lavish brocades.

She and the duke proceeded slowly down the hall. The candlelight momentarily brought to life the sitters' white, solemn faces before dying back to blackness. She stopped at a portrait of a rather youngish man who bore a striking resemblance to the present duke. She glanced back at him, but he made no comment and they continued on.

At last they came to the end of the hall. If she thought the portrait of the earlier young man resembled the duke, this portrait was him incarnate. It must be his sire, the fifth Duke of Roydan. The resemblance was uncanny. If it hadn't been for a slightly different era in clothing, she would have sworn it was the man standing just behind her.

She turned to that man now.

He merely looked at her and moved on to the painting next to it, the Reynolds. His mother. He used a candle to light the tapers on either side of the work, and then blew it out and set the candelabra down. She thought she heard him take a deep breath but when she looked over at him there was no way of divining any emotion, his gaze was fixed on the portrait.

"I did not know you painted," he said.

"There are many things you do not know about me, Your Grace." It was churlish of her, but she was not in the best of moods. She gave her full attention to the portrait. The Duchess had not been a beauty, but Olivia's heart turned over as she gazed into the young woman's eyes.

They remained quiet for a long while.

"She looks wistful—expectant," Olivia whispered.

"As I said it was painted as a wedding gift to my father. She hardly knew him—then."

Silence.

She stepped back in order to view both portraits at once, trying to see where a little child might fit into these people's lives. The woman, so very young, almost a girl really, and the man, maybe as much as twenty years older, and already a bit jaded looking. She did not think there was much room for one small boy between an immature young wife and a man who looked as if he could devour her in one bite.

He coughed and she was brought back to the here and now.

"Shall we return to the others?" He gestured for her to precede him.

Silly to think the sight of his mother might miraculously cause this man to expose the emotional workings of his mind—of his heart. Disappointed, she took one last look at the young woman, hoping her soft brown eyes might shed some light on the grown man who stood behind her. But Georgiana Roydan, like her son, was giving up no secrets today. Olivia turned to go, and the duke extinguished the candles, leaving them to walk in the moon and starlight.

Their steps echoed on the parquet floor. Halfway down the hall, she risked a glance at him. He seemed far away from her, as if he were somewhere out there with the stars, a million miles away.

Every measured step back to the party ratcheted up her nerves and frustration. What did this man want from her? He drew her away from the other guests and then had nothing to say to her and more importantly, nothing to *do*. She was here to be his mistress, yet he made no move. He did not even touch her if he could avoid it. Just now, when any other gentleman would have offered her his arm, he remained aloof, hands clasped firmly behind his back. She had had enough. They were nearly at the double doors. It was past time to get the rules straight.

"This is intolerable." The words squeezed between her lips. He turned to her astonished. Yes, by God, she was angry.

His eyebrow rose.

"You do not even *touch* me!"

He stared at her dumbly. "You wish to be touched?"

That got her moving. She whirled around, skirts flying, her breath spewing her exasperation.

"God, anything but this blind uncertainty. It is driving me to distraction!" She stopped her ranting to look at him. He looked—fascinated? She charged up to him again.

"I won't have it anymore." She jabbed a finger at his chest. "You have more than fulfilled your part of the bargain. You see for yourself Egg—Lady—Mrs. Wiggins—is nearly recovered and is, in fact, thriving. She has had every attention and care. I cannot begin to tell you what that means to me, but what of *my* part of the bargain? I do not understand you. You are either playing the obsequious courtier to a young maiden or the standoffish autocrat. I assure you, I am no maid, and the fact that you happen to be a duke does not overly impress me. Please, I beg you, put me out of my misery and let us begin!"

He stood before her like a veritable clodpoll. Had he even heard her words?

"Begin—"

And then she kissed him.

More like launched herself at him. She wrapped her arms around his neck, her fingers tangling in his hair. Her lips found his—*eye?* Well, he was very tall, but apparently not that tall. To be fair it was rather dark. And she *had* squeezed her eyes shut before she launched herself. However, she quickly rectified her misfire, as her lips skated over his nose to find and settle on his. She clamped onto them and thrust her tongue home.

Slowly—dear God, too slowly—it dawned on her that, in the throes of mauling him, she never felt a reciprocal thrust, never even felt his arms take hold of her. Mortified, she started to pull away when she felt them.

Bless you, Saint Anne. She deepened the kiss…but, no…*was he pushing her away? Was he grabbing her arms to hold her, or was he setting her away from him?* In her befuddled haze of lust she could not be sure.

Light hit her face and shot across the floor from the doorway. The hall door stood wide open.

His arms dropped as if she were on fire. It took a moment longer for her to comprehend the full horror of the situation, but it came crashing down soon enough. She released him and feverishly smoothed her skirts. As if performing an odd minuet, they took a step away from each other and then spun as one to see who the intruder was. *Please not the Reverend or Lady Bainbridge*

"Ah, pardon, Your Grace, Mrs. Weston." Percy Bainbridge stood in the doorway, his candelabra

wavering as he shifted from one foot to another. "I—
Lady Wiggins is feeling tired and we thought to give
her a ride in our carriage."

"Yes, thank you, Mr. Bainbridge." Olivia's over-
loud voice echoed in the cavernous room. "We have
stayed too long. Let us go now. Your Grace." She gave
a bare nod and flew across the room and out the door to
be left alone with her utter humiliation. Poor Percy
joined her a moment later. The boy clearly had no
reference for catching a companion and a duke in the
throes of making love. Olivia rejected the idea of
making a comment to ease his embarrassment. Frankly
she could think of none and instead practically ran
down the hall toward what she hoped was the right
direction out.

After only two wrong turns, they joined the others
already assembled in the front hall. She reached for her
shawl as if it were a life raft, immediately swaddling
herself in its folds. Egg gave her a concerned look and
asked if she was feeling well. She murmured something
about it being overly warm in the gallery.

Egg raised an eyebrow.

Olivia turned, avoiding the question in her friend's
eyes. Right, it was *hot* and she was huddled inside her
wrap as if she were freezing. *Idiot!*

The duke came only a few moments later to give
his goodbyes to his guests. He actually tried to take her
hand. She could not look at him. Hiding her hands in
her shawl, she gave him a curtsey, murmured some
pleasantry of thanks and moved to the waiting carriage.

She had much sooner have walked out in the cool
night air but did not want to draw attention to her
discomfort. She managed to keep up a reasonable

chatter on the carriage ride home, suffering through Lady Bainbridge's litany of advice on the proper way to preserve strawberries. At least Percy was not staring at her as if she were a Jezebel. That in itself was cause for thanks.

Egg was merciful as well and let her go upstairs with only a kiss and a wish of a good night.

She was finally alone.

*He did not want her.*

It had never occurred to her before. But the thought, once formed, began to make hideous sense.

That was why he did not pursue her. That was why he did not touch her. That was why he had gently pushed her away when she threw herself at him. The facts crashed over her like waves drowning her hopes.

Hopes.

Drawing her pillow over her head she tried to blot out the feeling of loss. But her clattering mind was not so generous. It replayed the scene over and over again with alarming accuracy. Oh how he must pity her.

The clock in the hall bonged four times.

Perhaps she could pack her things and disappear?

\*\*\*\*

*The woman's face was a frozen crust of white lead paint, rouge, and patches. If she moved one muscle the shell would surely crack off. She peered through an intricate web of golden filigree attached to the neck of her gown. Olivia supposed it was the collar of the dress, but it looked more like a cage.*

*As the woman labored down a long stretch of beach, her voluminous brocade skirts dragged behind, snagging on sea-bracken and turning dark as they soaked up salt water.*

215

*She turned toward the water. The dress ballooned up around her waist as she waded into the surf. Muddy white and pink dripped down her cheeks and from her neck to stain the bodice of her gown. Olivia wanted to shout to her to stop, but nothing came out of her mouth. The water now slapped against the lady's breasts.*

*The paint had nearly melted away, enough so that Olivia saw the face of the woman clearly. It was she. And she was about to drown.*

*That golden cage now surrounded her. Olivia clawed at the neck of the dress trying free herself from its prison of sure death.*

*Salt water filled her mouth. She lifted her nose and eyes. Suddenly, a huge winged-serpent reared out of the water, its black beak piercing the waves, its enormous body causing the waters around it to swell and dip. Olivia slid into a trough as a massive wave formed in front of her, but instead of submerging her, it lifted her to its crest, and deposited her on the beast's broad back.*

*She looked around her. Glistening and scaly sinew had miraculously become a ship. She could see no captain, no crew. Olivia grabbed the rail as the vessel turned sharply and made for an island in the distance. The ship flew through the black waters. Now only a few hundred yards away from the island, it seemed to increase in speed. Sweet Saint Anne, the island looked to be solid rock. Olivia wound herself into the tarred lines.*

*The vessel smashed onto the shore, its timbers shattering. The great canvas sails billowed, tore themselves from the broken masts, and wrapped around her, lifting her up to hurl her onto a narrow stretch of sand.*

*Stunned, Olivia watched as the wreckage trembled and miraculously began to reassemble, not as a ship, but as a huge, ornate picture frame. The sails rose inexplicably in the windless air and knitted together to form the canvas within. Finally a flock of birds, cormorants, hidden behind the rocks, took flight and swarmed over the canvas and then vanished.*

*Olivia stared at the enormous painting. The subjects were various men, women, dogs, horses, and even a child. And they all were staring directly at her. They all had one face. The face of the duke.*

*Something was pushing her to enter the picture. To become one with it...*

"Olive."

Olivia buried her head into something soft, but the pressure continued.

"My dear, I hate to disturb you."

Olivia blinked. "Egg?"

"I am sorry to wake you, love, but a note has come for you. I thought it might be of some importance. It is from the duke."

"The duke?" She sat up, struggling to sort her dream from real life.

"Yes, my dear. A footman is waiting below for a reply." Egg handed her the folded paper.

Olivia looked at Egg, still not comprehending. The letter in her hands felt real enough, the address, "Mrs. Weston" in a bold but elegant hand. *His hand?* She flipped the note over. A dark red seal of a griffin. The Roydan seal.

As Egg crossed the room to pour a glass of water from a stand by the dressing table, Olivia cracked the wax and opened the paper.

Would she please meet him at Sea Cottage at five in the afternoon? It was signed simply, Roydan.

What did this mean? Why had he been so brief? She had much rather he left his rejection as it was. She could not bear him explaining his change of heart in person.

She read the note again hoping it might offer some miraculous insight into its author.

"Olivia?"

"Yes." She managed a small smile.

"May I give the footman a reply?"

"Oh, a reply—Yes." She traced the ridges of the letter's seal.

"Is that your reply, dear? Yes?"

"What?"

"I said, is your reply *yes*?"

"Yes. That is my reply."

"Very well, dear, I will go and tell the footman." Soft lips bussed Olivia's forehead. "Imagine, Albert has been waiting since seven this morning. The poor boy is like to float away with all the tea I've given him." And the door closed softly behind her.

****

Rhys had arrived at the cottage too early. It was not even half past four.

As soon as his footman had returned with her affirmative reply, Rhys knew he would somehow muck things up. Now he had too much time.

Why had he said five o'clock? It was an endless time to wait. God, he'd thought he would go out of his mind just waiting for her answer. When questioned, Albert had said Mrs. Weston was still abed and Lady

Wiggins had finally had to rouse her.

So *she* had no trouble sleeping. He'd tossed and turned all night, been up at five this morning, written thirteen notes and summarily cast thirteen notes into the fire. Finally, he had scrawled the most commonplace missive ever conceived, sealed it up, and sent it on its way before he was tempted to compose another.

But she had said yes.

He glanced around the tiny cottage. Shortly after her answer he had several of his most circumspect servants out to clean the place. He had been there to supervise everything. Fresh linens had been fitted on the bed, which had been brought in to replace the old bedstead, a small privacy screen stood in a corner, new curtains hung in the freshly washed windows, a fire was laid and wood stacked, new beeswax candles replaced the old tallow stubs, and a large basket loaded with cheese, bread, fruit, cakes, and wine now sat atop the large deal table across from the stone fireplace.

Two cushioned chairs had been brought in as well as a small chaise. A Turkish carpet in warm reds and browns now replaced the rushes that had covered the floor. Rhys did not know much about décor but he could see her in this room, and that was enough to please him.

He had rushed home to bathe and change his clothes. Then he pared his nails and cleaned his teeth, and changed his clothes again. He was so woefully ignorant as to how to conduct an affair, much less one with a woman he desperately wanted.

Thinking the gray coat too solemn, Rhys had been about to change when the door opened.

Tinsley.

Rhys looked down at the total chaos at his feet. He stood in a flotilla of linen, superfine, buckskin, and boots. A twang of guilt plucked at his nerves, but instead of an apology, he gave the valet a raised eyebrow. However, the gesture was wasted on the fellow who was already moving to restore the room to rights.

"If you'll pardon my saying so, Your Grace, that sedge-green you have chosen has always been a particular favorite of mine." And he continued methodically clearing up as if Rhys's behavior was an everyday occurrence and not the wildly out of character exhibit they both knew it to be.

Stepping over a particularly fine pair of Hessians, Rhys went to clean his teeth for a third time.

He now paced the cottage floor from window to window—precisely eleven steps. He halted mid-stride. Dee Gooden's face flooded his brain before he could stop the image. This would *not* be like all those years ago when he had so feverishly waited for a woman.

Rhys swiped his hand over his face and then thumbed open the case to his watch. Disgusted with his nerves and sabotaging thoughts, he jerked the fob from his waistcoat and flung the watch into a drawer.

*Perhaps she would not come at all? Perhaps she has changed her mind?*

He wrenched open the door and strode through the garden gate. Shielding his eyes against the sun, he looked to the west, the direction she would most likely come.

Nothing.

He sought the familiar shape of his watch but only found the silk of his waistcoat. *Dolt.* Should he go in and fetch it? He felt almost naked without it.

But it was too late. A flock of geese had risen up from beyond the ridge as if to herald her arrival. She appeared like a mirage out of the midst of them, leading her horse. The birds wheeled and cawed in protest, their grazing disturbed. But she seemed relaxed and unflappable, a counterpoint to their cacophony.

She had come.

He could not make out her expression; the sun was too bright. He was desperate to gauge her mood. Did she want him?

As she drew nearer, she lowered her gaze, her lips drawn tight as if steeling herself for battle instead of love. Not a hint of softness...or desire. Steadfastly avoiding the question in his eyes. He reached out for her, but she had already moved past.

He tied her horse, Opalina, next to Sid and caught up with her in time to hold open the gate. She passed through, careful not to brush his body, and walked directly through the open cottage door.

*She had come.* His brain kept repeating the amazing refrain. He was strung so tight he feared mere breath would break him. He had waited so long. He could wait no longer.

****

The cottage had been transformed, no longer the rough place she had used once or twice to shelter from the wind and rain.

A primrose-colored curtain filtered the fading sunlight to a soft, ripe peach, flushing the room with warmth. The light caught the deep ruby of the wine, in its crystal decanter, flashing a spangled prism on the wall behind. The rough table held a feast of more color and texture, glossy plums, pebbled raspberries, crusty bread, chalk-white cheese. They all spilled out of a rush basket and onto a faded paisley cloth. The whole scene reminded her of a Vermeer painting she had seen once in Paris, so lush, so seductive.

She turned toward the bed. Oh, yes, it became abundantly clear this was a well-orchestrated seduction. Silken pillows lay mounded against the bed's headboard, and a tasseled throw, in a deep Pomona velvet threaded with gold, covered the bed. He had transformed it into a haven. A lover's nest.

She heard the door softly close and even as she turned to him, her mouth still open in awe, his hands and lips were upon her.

*Oh yes. Yes.* Her body, so prepared for humiliation, cast off her doubt and shame in a heartbeat to embrace his want.

His hands were all over her, in her hair, over her cheeks, down her shoulders and the small of her back, finding her derriere and dragging her center up and into his hard need. He pulled at her skirt, ruching it up and up over her knees, thighs, and waist. Pulling it in bunches to her back.

His other hand was busy in his falls, wrenching at unaccommodating buttons. Her hands came to join his to help free him. At last he sprang loose. His breath, a rush of sweet cloves, against her cheek and nose as his hot length pressed into her damp curls. She gasped.

She wanted to look, to see him, but his mouth covered hers. His knees bent as his hands found her bottom again. Briefly, she felt the hot tip of his cock before he plunged into her wetness.

*Oh, heavens, yes.* She had no idea whether she said

the words out loud. If she did his only response was to shift her, hiking her higher. Her legs closed and locked around his waist as he drove into her heat again and again, his strokes long and hard.

She came before he did. She threw her head back, her center so tight against his pumping cock, and shattered. Ah, it had been so very long.

Then she watched him as he drove toward completion and release. He was not long in coming. A low moan came from his very depths, sounding almost painful in her ears. He shuddered and she felt his seed pump into her. Oh, what a sight! His face so fierce, so beautiful.

He buried his face in her neck. His body, utterly still after such vigor, seemed frozen to her. She felt wetness on her neck. Olivia wanted to turn to him, to see if he was well, but at the same time, she sensed his need for quiet and stillness. Finally she touched his hair and tried to speak. But he would not allow it. Her movement seemed to bring him out of his trance, and he gently shifted her, his penis, just beginning to soften, slipped out. He carried her to the bed, laying her gently down, and before she could open her mouth to speak, he disappeared out the door and into the fading sunlight.

\*\*\*\*

Rhys found himself out in the small yard behind the cottage facing the sea. He took a deep breath, his arms wrapped tightly around his shaking body.

It had been real.

*Oh, God, he was alive.*

He had waited for the emptiness. His face pressed against her neck and shoulder, he had waited for the loneliness to fill his body, to slam into him with a visceral force, to remind him of the deadness that lay deep within him. He had prepared himself for the feeling, but it had not come. By God, he was alive, filled.

He dashed the tears that still ran down his cheeks and swiped at his running nose. He had had to leave her to digest this incredible feeling. This wonderful fullness. What must she think of him?

He had never wanted to kiss a woman before. It was too intimate, too personal. But, God, he could not get enough of her. He could not get enough of her ripe, firm lips, the taste of her tongue and inner flesh of her cheeks, of the edge of her teeth against his own lips and tongue. *He wanted her again.*

Rhys returned to find her fully dressed, sitting primly on the edge of one of the stuffed arm chairs. Disappointment pricked like a hard and unexpected frost. He had hoped she would want to repeat the act, at least once more. She watched the dying embers, her hands lying softly curled in her lap. He noted her hair was down, or nearly. Only a few pins held what was left of her chignon. It was glorious. His cock jumped inside his breeches.

"Your pardon, I cannot stay away. I want you. I want you all the time. I cannot think of anything else but having you, of filling you. I apologize. I have lost all control."

She looked away. Her teeth caught her bottom lip. She didn't seem to be listening to him. But she must understand he was not usually like this. He *could* be in control. He would try to contain himself for her. But his words died on his lips, as she slowly rose and began to take down the rest of her hair.

This time it was slower—but not by much.

Rhys concentrated on the most mundane of things, gathering his shirt, his smalls, his breeches, as if the act of dressing would restore normalcy to his careening emotions. He could not look at her, not yet. It was too soon, too fresh. If he did, he would very likely leap on her again, God help her. He was like a green boy.

How he got home, he did not know. He recalled they had been very polite with each other, very considered and politic. She had veered off shortly after they set out, and he had made himself not stop to look after her. He made himself go forward. He could see the house before him, yet he did not want to go home.

Sid jerked to a halt. Startled, Rhys looked down. His hands were twisted in the too short reins.

"Dolt! Can you not keep more than one thing in your brain at a time?" Sid threw his head as if to concur.

They had not made another plan. He was so bloody ignorant. When would he see her again? Touch her again? Be alive again?

Chapter Eighteen

Apparently the duke did not normally attend the village church. Lady Bainbridge had told Eglantine that Reverend Hargett overlooked this fact due to His Grace's considerable charitable contributions over the years. The last being a brand new roof and church steeple to replace the crumbling one erected at least seventy years ago which, at the time, was only meant to be temporary.

So when a hush fell over the entire congregation and all heads turned to fix on this exalted person making his way up the aisle, Olivia had no need to turn her gaze with all the others.

Even the fly hovering in the window above the altar began to buzz with anticipation. When the duke settled, Olivia was situated squarely behind his very large shoulders.

For her, the service ended at that moment. If someone had quizzed her about Reverend Hargett's sermon, or the hymns she had only mouthed, she could recount nothing. It was not so much *seeing* him, for aside from the extraordinary width of his shoulders encased in a coat of the finest coffee-colored wool, the slight curl of his hair as it brushed the coat's collar, and his left, perfectly shaped ear, there was not much to see. But it was everything. She could observe him, unobserved. She could smell him, but best of all, she could hear him.

It was another reason she only mouthed the words to one of her favorite hymns. Egg looked at her—Olivia loved to sing—but since she would not meet her friend's gaze, Olivia could only guess at the bemused surprise on Egg's face. She turned back to her hymnal.

Who could sing when the Duke of Roydan was singing?

She'd never imagined him singing. His voice was a lovely bass, deep and resonant. He even sang a bit of harmony. Olivia stood utterly still, as if any movement might make him stop. She had lain with the man, yet she knew almost nothing of him. What other secrets did he hold?

"Come along, my dear." Egg touched her sleeve. "You are very distracted this morn."

The duke moved down the aisle followed by Lord Bertram and Sir Everett and Lady Bainbridge. Olivia and Egg followed.

In the vestibule Reverend Hargett was already addressing His Grace. "Such a fine day and so pleased to have you amongst us this morning. We are most honored."

Roydan gave a brief nod and seemed ready to move on but Lady Bainbridge, who apparently could not pass up an opportunity to hold forth with the duke, stopped him.

"Your Grace," the lady called, "I could not help but overhear our dear reverend's remark of the delightful weather we are having. It would be a shame to squander such a gift from God and take our dinner indoors would it not?" She did not pause for his answer. "I have a great notion to have a picnic. My dear Lady Wiggins, what do you think? Is it not the best plan?"

"It is as fine a day as I have seen, Lady Bainbridge," agreed Egg.

"So Roydan, it seems the rest of our day, and I dare say our peace, has been overtaken by the ladies," said Sir Everett with a chuckle.

"Your pardon, Lady Bainbridge, Lady Wiggins, but I am very much afraid I will have to forego the pleasure of a picnic as I am promised to Mrs. Weston." The duke's gaze bored into hers. "I believe we are to see the Norman abbey this afternoon."

Out of the corner of her eye, Olivia saw Egg's mouth pop open to refute the plan. But then just as quickly it clapped shut.

All gazes now fixed on Olivia. "Yes," she said, looking at everyone but the duke.

However the company's uniform silence seemed to require more of an answer. She cleared her throat. "Yes, His Grace has been most kind to offer to show me the ruins. I have heard they are not to be missed."

Lady Bainbridge, clearly disappointed with her thwarted outing, said, "Oh, yes, indeed, they are truly epic." Then her face brightened. "Perhaps we should all go?"

"Lady Bainbridge, I hope you will forgive me, but I do not think I am quite up for so long a trek." It was Egg, bless her heart.

"Oh, but of course, Lady Wiggins, how thoughtless of me. We will let the young people scamper about those crumbling ruins, and we civilized folk will proceed with the picnic."

There was a flurry of agreement and arranging of carriages, and times, and everything that accompanies an impromptu outing. While this was taking place, the duke found a moment to speak with Olivia.

"I will call for you at the dower house at three o'clock?"

"No," she said, almost cutting him off. He started to speak, but she continued, "I will meet you *there.* At *two* o'clock, Your Grace."

He nodded. "As you wish. I am solely at your pleasure, Mrs. Weston." She thought she saw a hint of a smile.

"Your Grace," Lady Bainbridge called, "since you have declined to join our feasting in favor of other pursuits, I must insist you give us your opinion of the best spot for our afternoon."

Olivia was quite certain His Grace would choose a direction as far away from Sea Cottage as humanly possible.

\*\*\*\*

He tied Sid next to her mount, his hands fumbling to make a loop with the reins. By God, she had arrived before him.

Her hair was already partly loose and flowing down her back, tied with a dark red ribbon. He drank her in as she turned at the sound of the cottage door closing behind him.

Like an arrow from a long-stretched bow, he was so ready to be inside her warmth. To feel that fullness again. To make sure he was not dreaming that incredible feeling.

He began to open his falls even as he moved to her. She, likewise, raised her skirts. They met, mouths clashing, hands tearing at stubborn buttons and yards of gauzy fabric. She grabbed the length of his cock, her hands so cool against his hot flesh, and guided him into her wet center.

He sank into her sweetness. The tension in his face releasing, eyes closed to blackness, every part of him centered on their joining. His mouth found her mouth, then her cheeks, ears, and the soft, downy hairs at her temples. He returned again to her mouth as if she was breathing for the both of them—she was his air—his life. And finally, blessed relief.

He wanted her again right away. It frightened him, the power she had over him. Like nothing he had experienced before, his control in tatters. Yet he could not, would not deny himself this woman. This joy.

They made it to the edge of the bed this time. He pushed her legs up to loop over his shoulders and watched her come—the bliss cracking sharply over her. Only then did he allow himself to explode, spilling into her core. As she received his seed, he held her firmly. He did not want it to dribble down her legs to be dabbed away like some mess. He *wanted* a part of him to take root within her, for him to be a part of this beautiful woman.

After a time, she rose and went to the basin next to the fireplace. Taking up a bit of linen toweling, she dipped it into the water and then wrung it out, the trickle of water in the basin, like music. She turned and walked to him bending to wash his penis. He should have stopped her, but could not. She was so gentle, so careful and attentive. He stood there like a dumb beast, hands dangling by his sides, watching her, feeling her.

She smiled at him then. It was the first time she had ever truly smiled at him. Well, there had been that time when they had waltzed at the Parkington mask, but half her face had been covered. He clenched his jaw.

Her smile was an aria soaring to an impossibly high note of such depth and clarity he almost could not stand its brilliance. *This smile was for him.* That he could possibly deserve this gift was impossible. But he was selfish and starved enough to pretend he was worthy. He wanted to be worthy of that smile. Of her.

"Would you like wine? Or perhaps some bread and cheese?" she said, as if blinding him with her considerable light was an everyday occurrence in his world. She deposited the wet linen next to the bowl and then moved to the table that held a basket of food. He instinctively reached out for her retreating figure. He clenched his hand, and then dropped it to his side.

"Some wine, yes." He began to put himself to rights. It was not easy because his damn cock was already at half mast. *Stupid.*

She made a kind of picnic on a blanket that she lay before the fire. They ate and drank in silence. He wondered if she was thinking the same thing as he; what a different sort of picnic they were experiencing than the one proposed by Lady Bainbridge.

"I did not know you sang."

Apparently her thoughts were not of comparisons and picnics. He shifted and sat up straighter. "There are many things you do not know about me." Did she recall she had said the very same thing to him not two days ago in regard to her painting?

"Touché."

Ah, she did remember.

They remained silent, but it was not stiff and uncomfortable; they were simply quiet.

When they finished she gathered the odd bits of

food together in a napkin and moved them to the table and began to tidy the cottage.

He watched her from the blanket in awe of her littlest movement. The way she frowned slightly as she brushed crumbs from the table into her hand and tossed them in the fire. How she grasped the poker and prodded a log that threatened to roll out onto the hearth, and then used a small broom to sweep up the ash. So tidy…so sweet. Her bum…so utterly perfect.

He drained the wine in his glass and licked his lips. Rhys had not seen the female body completely unclothed for a long time. It must be years now.

Daria, for the past two or more years, insisted on wearing a corset of some sort and often a peignoir as well when they met. It was always some cunning contraption likely fashioned to minimize her growing waistline and shore up her sagging curves. She might as well have left them off and been comfortable. It had been ages since her body held any interest for him.

Thursday would come and they would simply lie down, he on top of her. She would then make the appropriate sounds of pleasure, which for the last few years had become less and less, and he would plunge inside her, pumping with fierce precision and then, at the last moment, he would pull himself out to spill in his waiting hand.

And then he would wait for the emptiness. And it always came, always.

He had once thought of replacing Daria, but he supposed he had got complacent as well. Why risk another woman who would likely produce the same feeling? Besides, no other woman had caught his fancy, though plenty had tried.

"Some more wine, Your Grace?" She was holding out the flagon.

Rhys jerked out of his memories.

*Your Grace?*

*After what they had done? After what she had done to him?* Did she not see he was laid open and totally exposed to her? *Your Grace?*

He wanted to be more than a bloody title. He wanted to be more than a rutting beast. This woman made him want *more* but he didn't know *how*…how to make her *see*…*To see him. To see him as…Rhys.*

Oh God, what a fool he was. Simply because *he* had been transformed did not mean she was on a similar path. Clearly she was not. What a stupid clod. He should take his leave. He had had his pleasure. God knows he did not want to frighten her with his enormous need of her.

A muscle jerked in his jaw line. Olivia was used to reading all kinds of men, having spent much of her adult life following the drum, surrounded by scores of Wes's fellow soldiers. She knew bravado and swagger. Certainly knew hurt and grief and the myriad of ways men dealt with these unwelcome emotions. She sensed his disquiet and more importantly his readiness for flight.

She did not want him to go.

Finally he answered, "Wine is not what I want." He rose from the blanket to take the decanter from her and set it on the nearby table, but then he seemed at a loss as to what to do next. He stood mutely, staring at the table.

"Tell me what you want."

His shoulders twitched, but he said nothing.

She finally said, "Tell me—what you need."

His shoulders bunched. A long moment passed, and she sighed. He would not answer.

"I want to have you again and then again after that," he finally barked, whirling around to face her.

He might as well have slapped her. "Ah, the 'duke' speaks."

Rhys felt as if he'd entered a game and did not know the rules; only that he wanted to win. He would not stay to suffer her rejection. He was at the door when she called his name. Not Your Grace, not even Roydan, but—

"Rhys," she repeated. "Rhys, what do *you* want?"

He could feel her just behind him.

If he'd been standing on the precipice of some cliff he could not have felt more danger than the act of answering her simple question. "I want—" His vision narrowed. *What he wanted? To have his heart's desire? To have—her?* He strained toward that thought like a muscle that had been long unused.

"I want—what I want is to look at you," he whispered. Then he turned to her, his voice stronger. "I want to look at your body."

She smiled.

"Yes, Rhys, I would like that as well."

She reached for him. His huge hand encompassed hers, and she pulled him gently back into the room.

"Would you put another log on the fire while I undress?"

"No."

She turned at the sharpness in his voice.

"I meant I would like to undress you, if I may?" he amended. "Will you wait till I return?"

234

She nodded. He dashed out the door, afraid if he was too long she would have a chance to change her mind.

When he returned she was pulling all of the pillows off the bed and chairs, heaping them on the rug before the fire, making a kind of bower for them.

He settled the logs into the hearth, wiped his hands on a napkin, and turned to her.

Rhys had never undressed a woman before. It was impossible, yet true. He looked at this woman standing before him, and he wanted it to last forever. Slowly, like a boy coaxing his first bird to sit in his hand, he touched the ribbon in her hair, pulled it, and watched it snake across her neck and shoulder to be discarded on the floor.

Next came the few pins holding up the rest of her hair. He spent an infinite amount of time just caressing the locks that settled around her shoulders, back, and breasts. How could hair be liquid silk? He was fascinated to see how it flowed endlessly over his hands, occasionally catching on a rough callus, but then slipping free to lick his wrists and forearms. His thumb inadvertently brushed her nipple. She gasped. Had he done something wrong? One look at her face told him she was…well.

Seeing her ardor nearly undid him, but he steadied himself. This woman was not performing. She wanted him. *Him.* It was a heady feeling to sense the power he had over her.

He turned her to begin undoing the tiny covered buttons at her back. She held her hands loosely over her belly, her head bowed. He slowly peeled the gown open like an unexpected gift.

She wore no stays. He slid the fabric off her shoulders, stepping back to see the full beauty of her. The gown had gathered at her elbows, and when she released her arms, the dress floated to the floor.

She stood between him and the fire, her body clearly outlined within the cotton batiste of her chemise. He could not take his gaze off her. She turned to him.

The chemise was not merely an undergarment but a beautiful creation of tucks, pleating, and open work. He knew this because he had labored over this particular item in Madame Louaneau's salon, imagining Olivia in it. He also knew that the neck would be released with one pull of a ribbon. He did so.

He could have stood there forever looking at this woman; she was so exquisite, so perfect in every detail. But he wanted to be inside her even more. He began undressing. She lay down to watch him. He was more than a bit uncomfortable with the idea of undressing *for* her, but she seemed to want it, and he could deny her nothing. When he was naked he went to join her on the pillows, but she stopped him.

"Rhys, you are beautiful, so very beautiful. Come to me."

He had never experienced a joining like this—a loving like this. Somehow she had made this makeshift bower a haven for him—a place to trust, to lay down his guard. They had looked into each other's eyes as he began, at first tentatively, to explore her wonders. But he was happy to be in her hands and follow her lead.

She had ended up on top of him, setting the pace to a slow undulating canter instead of his forceful gallop. She seemed to sense his coming release and would back off just enough to make it last and last. Finally it was too much for her and she rode him hard, her hands tangled in his hair. She bucked and cried out. He watched in pleasure and awe, and then spilled himself into her.

Rhys awoke slowly. He must have fallen asleep. He had never done that before. He had *always* taken himself off after the act.

She was still sleeping, nestled into the crook of his shoulder, her leg thrown over his. Just the sight of her beautiful white leg, so casually draped over his own— he was not sure he could stand this fullness. He might burst out of his skin. Then her toes flicked and then flexed; finally her whole body undulated in a stretch, burrowing into his. If only this moment could last forever. He would happily smash every one of his precious clocks and every time piece in the world if only he could stay within this moment.

But her eyelashes tickled him and her breath fluttered the fine hairs on his chest. She was awake. She would pull away soon. She would get up and get dressed and possibly make small talk, and then she would leave him.

He panicked.

"I will have the contracts drawn up today or tomorrow morning at the very latest. You will want for nothing."

Even before he finished speaking, she stiffened in his arms. Cold replaced the warm heat of her body as she pushed herself away from him and quickly got to her feet. It was all he could do not to grab her back to him.

"As you wish, Your Grace." And she began

dressing, not once looking at him.

He saw the moment falling to shattered pieces but could do nothing. Even a great clod like him should have known better, but he was so new at this, his feeling muscles as flaccid as a newborn. One thought hammered within his thick head; he could not lose her.

Suddenly he was eight years old. The doctor had said he must go, his mother needed rest and would see him in the morning, but as the huge door closed he knew it was a lie, and he would never see her again. He had wailed, clawing at the door to be let back in, somehow thinking if he could get back inside her chamber he could save her.

The door had burst open. His father. The brass knob split open Rhys's cheek, blood mixing with tears. Rhys tried to squeeze past his sire, but the duke jerked him back and threw him into the body of the footman who had come to see to the clamor.

"Get rid of him," the duke barked. And the door banged shut again.

Rhys would always remember the finality of that door slamming. He rubbed the small scar on his cheek below his left eye. He never saw his mother again.

Olivia. His Olivia was moving. Rhys could not let this door close. He lunged up out of the nest of blankets, but did not know where to go or what words to say to bind her to him. *If there were a child...?*

"I have not been careful. You may be with child." She did not even pause in her dressing. Instead his words seemed to spur her on. "I will, of course, provide for any children there may be." He could not stop himself. Everything he was saying was driving her further and further away from him. Yet he did not know how to make her look at him, how to make her *see* him.

She was finished dressing now. "There won't be any children." She finally looked straight at him. "I am barren."

And the door closed.

Chapter Nineteen

The contract never came.

He never came either. They managed to avoid each other without much fuss. She threw herself into her painting, but still the days dragged by and the nights were even longer.

"Bert, you are making an absolute muddle of that rose bush." Egg waved her pruning shears at poor Lord Bertram as she charged in to save the day—or, more aptly, the bush. "You must be sure to count the leaves and cut at every cluster of five."

"Eglantine, do be still or you will end in pricking your hands. Here let me come 'round you." His lordship situated himself directly behind Egg, his hands covering hers, his head bent to her ear. He whispered something and Egg giggled. Oh, what a sight, to see her dear Egglet actually giggle again.

Olivia was very much *de trop*. She gathered her sketch pad and crayons and slipped out of the garden.

Besides she was so weary of scuttling about the house and gardens like some scared rabbit, afraid to run into him, or, if she was honest, to miss any communication.

Would she agree to a contract if one ever presented itself? Did she have a choice? Had a few couplings shattered her resolve so thoroughly? Was she that weak? It was ridiculous. He was an arrogant lummox who did not know the first thing about the needs of a woman, emotionally *or* physically. She should be happy he was done with her and, hopefully, he would consider her contract with him already fulfilled.

But still...

She missed him. She could not seem to blot out his look of wonder as he touched her breast or traced the curve of her lower lip. Or the shock on his face when she had captured that thumb with her teeth and sucked it into her mouth.

She pushed through the garden's far gate, heading to the old track that led to the home farm.

Sweat rolled past her temple as a light wind played on the club sedge and wild grasses. They shifted from yellow ochre to sienna and then back. She had been out for hours with nothing to show for it. Perhaps she would actually get out her things and sketch.

"You're a right un' with those paints, ain't ye, Miss?"

Olivia glanced about her and instantly recognized Mr. Mackenzie, the old steward. *Oh! Where had he come from?* She could see nothing but low-lying fields with woods in the far distance. She must have been too engrossed in her thoughts to have seen him approach.

Mac could be found hanging about the stables and kitchen garden, but she had never had occasion to actually speak with him. His old dog stood next to him. The animal was half blind with one ear missing. They were a fitting pair.

She was about to introduce herself but stopped. He seemed to know who she was.

"The duchess was a fair painter, too," he continued, gesturing to her pad and chalks. "Not so much big, grand pictures like yours, no, she painted birds and flowers and such."

*He had seen her paintings?*

He began to move off.

"Mr. Mackenzie? Mac!" She caught up with him. "May I walk with you?"

Olivia had the feeling he was taking her measure. It suddenly seemed very important he approve of her. She must have passed muster because he nodded slowly and continued walking.

As they fell into step, the old dog looped around their legs, looking for attention. Bending, she ruffled his good ear. Timid about breaking the silence she waited, taking her cue from the old man.

"The duchess loved the small creatures of the earth you see, the ones no one paid much mind to." He stopped again and gave her a long searching look. She stood up straighter. His mouth did not smile but his eyes did. "She would take the young master about with her and show him the tiniest bit of flower or bug. She would go all barmy for a good bug. The young master used to bring them to her by the scores."

Mac let out a rusty laugh. "One time I remember he found the biggest auld bullfrog you ever would want to see. Near as big as ol' Tobe's head here." The dog instantly perked up at the sound of his name. "The duchess was like to scream in fright at the beastie, but she soon calmed herself and even took the thing into her hands exclaiming over it as if it were true treasure." Mac shook his shaggy head and sniffed. "That did it. He then brought her all manner of creatures large and small. The ol' hognose snake for her birthday was something Mrs. Cotton will never forget."

"He loved her very much," Olivia said, hoping to draw more out of him.

"Oh, aye." His two words said everything.

They began walking again, her thoughts consumed with the image of a dark, reed-thin boy, all arms and legs, gamboling after his young mother.

After a while the steward continued, "He almost went to pieces when she died." Mac squinted, suddenly interested in something in the far distance. "The old duke sent the lad packing off to school as soon as the duchess was set in the ground."

"Oh!" She stopped, shocked. "How old was he?"

"Just eight years. The duke had wanted to send him off at six, but the duchess would have none of it, you see. She couldn't bear to part with him. It caused a good row or two betwixt them. She did not often cross the duke, but on this, she held firm."

Her own mother had died when Olivia was nine. She knew that feeling of helpless, inconsolable loss. She could not imagine losing her home and all that was familiar at the same time.

"And what of his father?"

The old man shook his head. "Ah, that is another story for another time, young miss, for it is a sad tale, to be sure."

They had made it as far as the tree line where the woods began. Suddenly Toby's head bobbed up; he stiffened and sniffed.

"Ah-ha," Mac crowed. "He's an old un, ol' Tobe, but he's still got a good strong nose on him. Don't you, ol' feller?" He gave the dog an affectionate scratch. "Well, we best be off. He don't get much entertainment these days and it looks as if he'd like a go at yon rabbit." And tipping his cap, he disappeared into the woods.

As Olivia watched the pair, she could not help but feel old Mac had given her a precious gift, a window into Rhys's mind.

*Rhys.*

He was no longer the duke or even Roydan. Picturing him and his young mother, their heads bent together over a hideous frog, somehow he slipped some unseen barrier to become simply Rhys once again.

The picture made her think of her own mother. So many times they had bent over a bit of sewing or a drawing, the tinkling of her old music box a background to their work. After her mother died, Olivia had practically worn the thing out winding it over and over till Nanny Jean threatened to put it in the attics. Olivia had promised she would not play it again, she would just hold it. Instead Nanny had put it on a very high shelf, far above Olivia's reach. "There, I'll not trust you to open the thing. You can be content to look at it from there."

Olivia sat below the shelf, a magical spot, marked out with fairy rocks she had found in the woods. She would say her magic prayer and, in her mind, the lid would open. The beautiful family would spring into a loving circle, all holding hands—a blonde mother, a handsome and dark father, and between them, two perfect children, a boy and a girl.

It was almost better that way. There in her enchanted spot, the music went on and on forever, never winding down to stutter and stop in the middle of a phrase. The beautiful family never dropped hands, teetering to collapse into a broken heap. She might even imagine the little girl, who was blonde like her mama, to have dark black hair, like herself. She remembered asking her mamma one birthday if she could please have hair the color of the sun? Her mother had stooped and smoothed Olivia's hair. "Ah, but I would miss my sweet moon with her midnight hair and eyes like sparkling stars."

Her tender, quiet mother...She was gone by Olivia's next birthday.

She had wanted to be that kind of mother. To have a child who did not have to grieve a mother's death and a broken family. A child with bright red hair instead of blonde...

Wes...

He'd been gone four years now. At times it seemed like a lifetime ago and then, in a heartbeat, it would be so fresh—*my goodness, I will be twenty-nine in September.* She rested her hand on the hollow bowl of her belly.

It was her fault. The problem was she never had regular courses. She could go for months without bleeding. By the time it was clear she was increasing, the doctor had guessed she was nearly five months along, too far along to make the journey to Gibraltar.

Wes had been training new recruits for guerilla warfare at their posting in Daidatz, near Tangier. They were in no real danger, she had argued. Still, he had not been easy, but Olivia was implacable. She would not be away from him now that they were finally to have their heart's desire. Worn down, Wes gave up arguing and began preparing to be a father.

Never shy about how much he wanted her and how much he enjoyed her body, but now, with her increasing, he *adored* her rounded belly. He often laid his head next to it, whispering secrets to the child within. She batted at his head complaining of being left out. "I am merely the vessel for your true love." But then he would prove so well how wrong she was.

One rainy day he came home early, dripping wet, his hands behind his back. She rushed to him, thinking him hurt. "By God, woman, stop your fussing. I am attempting to surprise you," he ordered her to close her eyes and hold out her hands. The memory of that slippery, feather-light wood—the miniature violin, the very one saved from the shop fire.

Insisting he get out of his wet things, she watched as Wes capered about their bedchamber in only his smalls, brandishing the tiny bow like a conductor's baton. She laughed and called him an ass. Braying and kicking his heels, he had picked up the tiny instrument and sawed away at it. "Now this, my love, is the sound of an ass." Oh what a racket, but she had loved every second of it.

He vowed their child would not be a soldier, must look exactly like its mother, and finally, would have music in its life.

Those two blissful months, imagining, planning, and arguing over the sex and various names. Olivia wanted Adolphus, after Wes whose Christian name was Adolphus James. But Wes said, "Over my dead body."

*Oh, God.* Olivia squeezed her eyes tighter, but those memories, once started, would not stop.

Colonel Parton had come with the news and caught her when she collapsed. He had stayed with her for the entire day, assigning a nurse to remain by her side for as long as it took her to recover and deliver the baby.

Eglantine Wiggins had had been that nurse.

Jeb had come to visit her too. She remembered asking him what day it was. Was it Tuesday? He said no ma'am, it was Sunday. But Jeb was wrong. He had to be wrong. Wes was supposed to be back on Tuesday. Then her head would start shaking and terrible noises would come. She tried to stop her ears against those hideous, wailing sounds, but they kept coming and coming. She had begged Jeb to please stop those piteous cries.

It had been friendly fire. The men were at their exercises and a musket that should not have been loaded had mysteriously been charged. The young recruit had sworn he had not known. The poor lad had hanged himself three days later, although Olivia only heard of his death months afterward.

Thank God for Eglantine. She had finally persuaded Olivia to eat, if not for herself, then for the baby.

Olivia had been standing by the window when her waters broke. "No-o-o!" She sank to the floor furiously mopping up the wet with her wrapper. It was too soon. She still had at least seven weeks left in her confinement.

Her breasts had been painfully swollen with milk that would not be needed. But her belly had shrunk so fast. Eventually her breasts gave up and shrunk back as well. She felt flat and so very empty, like a pasteboard cutout lying in that bed.

She had awoken; it was dusk. Where had the day gone? But she heard voices in the other room. The doctor was speaking quietly to Egg, something about an infection due to the haste in delivering the baby. She needed complete quiet if she was to recover. Egg had murmured something Olivia could not follow, and then after a long pause the doctor said, "No, she will have no more children." There was more talk, but Olivia had stopped listening.

James Adolphus Weston—little Jamie—was gone and buried in the earth next to his father before she ever had a chance to see him, to hold him, to have him clasp her finger in his tiny fist. She desperately wanted to ask Egg if his hair had been red, but she couldn't bear it.

The months that followed were still a blur. Egg had been her savior and her only reason for living. She simply had not let Olivia give up. She'd willed her to live, and eventually Olivia did.

To have a friend who was a woman was sheer joy for Olivia. She had never had a close female friend, being always surrounded by men and the Army life. It had been a long, hard road, but she and Egg had survived. And they would continue to survive though their next step was so uncertain. *Oh, where would they call home after Valmere? How could Egg leave her Bert?*

And how could Olivia let go of her own terrible fantasy? *Standing in their cove, arms about each other's waists, feet and legs bare as the water foams over their toes. He bends to whisper something in her ear and she turns to kiss his mouth. Then a sound, a cry. They turn as one, and laughingly run to a blanket where a bassinet sits. He gently lifts the edge of a blanket, bordered in the palest blue, and scoops their son into his arms. Then he looks at her, his eyes shining with love.*

Olivia squeezed her eyes shut again. The tears

slipped out anyway.

A mourning dove called, beautiful and plaintive. A moment later its mate echoed back in clear, round chords.

****

Had it only been a week? Despite his lawyers badgering him with daily communications of wills, and cases of So-and-so vs. Such-or-other, yet another message from Daria wanting money for information, his tenants plaguing him with drainage problems and too much sun or too little rain, and Uncle Bert admonishing him for leaving the Campbell girl hanging, Rhys was never busy enough to be able to put Olivia out of his mind for more than five minutes, if that.

He tethered Sid in a shelter of an outcropping of rock and strode up to the promontory hoping to find some peace.

Each time he came to the estate, he prepared himself to see the cliff bare and the old watchman gone. But as he rounded the top of the rocky path, his breath caught. There it was, lowering out of the mist, like an ancient king rising above its rude domain, daring the spring to come and touch his battered and broken crown.

As a boy he had lain beneath the tree's weathered arms and dreamt of castles and crusaders, of King Arthur and dragons, and of huge sea vessels with towering masts.

The sight never failed to calm him. Not being a particularly religious man, he supposed it would be like seeing a holy relic to a priest. He reverently touched its chapped bark, his eyelids closed. His talisman.

How was he to get past this woman? How was he to snuff out this flame that gave him such life? Such hope?

The old tree's response was only a faint moan. He was pathetic, looking to trees for answers when he hardly knew the questions.

Really it was a simple matter. He should just ride over and take the blasted woman. After all they had made a bargain. Two encounters were not nearly enough payment for his investment.

Investment? More like entrapment. Envelopment. Enlivenment. *In love…?*

The thought slid under his skin, making him shiver. Preposterous. She might as well be on the moon, their stations were so unbreachable. And what would be gained? Was he to finally open his heart to a woman who held no future for him other than something transient and sordid? And it would eventually become sordid. He must take a wife, and it could not be Olivia Weston. As it stood, the codicil was still firmly in place. He must marry and soon.

His men had combed every bawdy house in London and beyond, but Dee Gooden was nowhere to be found. Maybe she was dead? He had almost rather find her, pay her off, and know it to be done than wonder if she might suddenly appear to threaten his peace. He could not lose Valmere. His memories, good and bad were steeped in these cliffs. His mother was buried here.

He had been to his mother's grave this morning hoping for a sign. But unless you counted one scared rabbit skittering past the headstone and a tattered butterfly lighting for a moment on his shoulder, there was no enlightenment from his half-hour's time.

Someone had laid yellow roses at the stone's base. Mac, he guessed, or perhaps Mrs. Cotton. He added his own somewhat crushed heather and sweet william, and flicked at a nonexistent weed.

Why did she have to die and leave him so very lonely? Surely he would not be so inflexible and cold if she had been there to guide him. Other people seemed capable of love, why not he? Why should he be denied that staple of life?

Rhys glanced at the tiny headstone next to hers. Christopher Ryan Addison George Merrick—such a long name for such a short life. Christopher had flowers as well, but Rhys had no heather for him.

Rhys rolled his head back, looking up into the huge arms of the tree, the prickle of nostalgia sharp in his nose. The oak's gnarled fingers held a few bright new leaves as if they were offering them up to God. Proof of the life it still held within its ancient roots. He concentrated on one small leaf as it shuddered and winked in the light. *How could it last against the winds that lashed this bluff? How could such a fragile wisp hold on?*

Rhys turned out to the fetch of open sea. It was a bloody leaf, for God's sake. He hated the helplessness that accompanied such maudlin thoughts. He hated the feelings that seeped beneath the wall he had so carefully constructed. This fortress had been impregnable to messy emotions and passions that would, from time to time, hurl themselves at his battlements. But it could not withstand Olivia's laughter, her smile, the tiny scar that he loved to trace on her left thigh…Why could he not simply take what he wanted? His father always had. Had he tamped down his father's vices so much he was now incapable of satisfying any of his baser requirements?

But that was the problem; he did not just want his *itch* scratched. The idea of Olivia simply servicing him because of some contract, where every detail and eventuality had been laid out and witnessed by his solicitor, made his stomach roil.

But what else was available to him with this woman?

He must marry.

She was unsuitable.

Those two rules were as fixed and timeless as the old tree. His back against the tree, he wrapped his arms behind him around the trunk, his exposed wrists pressing painfully into its bark. *What did he want?* He wanted...He wanted her to...he squeezed tighter...to love him.

Shards of heavy bark broke off in his hands and he let his arms fall. The thought escaped the dark recesses of his brain, and like Pandora's famed box, once open, he knew instinctively, he could never recapture it.

*Love. He loved her.*

He closed his eyes, as if blotting out the world would make him safe in his precious dream. Yes, if she could love him just a little...

He supposed to gain her love required trust and openness, vulnerability. Concepts he had so little experience with. Nevertheless, his mind strained toward the ideas. He *wanted* these things in his life. *But how?*

It was no use. He was defective. His heart was the problem, everything out of order and garbled, so his mind had to take up the slack. He was like one of his clocks, handsome enough, but too tightly wound, too measured and in control. He was a thing—a machine. There was no use pretending.

The thunder brought him back to earth as the wind came up sharply. A curtain of heavy rain pelted the slick waves into dimpled pewter, the winds pushing it to claim more and more territory till it finally lashed at him on the rock. He held his hands out to the wet and looked up at his tiny leaf, so bright against the darkening sky, so strong in its ability to bend with the wind and endure the pounding rain. A flash of lightning and a frightened neigh. Sid.

Seeing a puddle steadily filling a depression in the rock, he realized it had been raining for some time now. What a fool. Here he was in the bloody rain, risking poor Sid and his boots no less, when he should be tupping the woman he desperately wanted.

Rhys mounted and headed to the dower house.

He had not seen her sheltering against the base of the far cliff. Her blue-gray gown must have made her chameleon-like against the rock face. He had been pressed against the old tree for what seemed an eternity, like a figurehead braving the blast.

She had stood transfixed as well; sure that if she moved a fraction he would glance down and catch her spying, breaking the spell. Nature finally broke it for them in the form of snapping thunder. She heard the whinny of a horse. And he was gone.

In a frenzy, she began to dash down charcoal marks on the white pages held between her shaking hands. The marks became the old tree, the ragged cliff, and the man. She ripped a page to unearth a blank one. More marks shaping his harsh and tortured profile, the hands, huge and square, gripping the tree, the wind blowing the many capes of his coat about his body. More blank sheets and more marks.

Her hands, now cold and raw, could hardly hold the chalk, but she was loath to quit. She stared up at the cliff, still seeing him there so fresh in her mind. But the rain had found her, blowing into her meager shelter. She had stayed too long. No matter, the image of him was indelible on her mind. In her heart. She had no need of studies and renderings. She knew the painting. It already existed fully realized in her soul.

\*\*\*\*

Rhys managed to race across the parterre and get to the stables as the worst of the storm hit. It was going to be a wild one. He had been bent on going to her, ready to hash out some sort of agreement, when the storm really broke. Sid was never good with thunder and worse with lightning. So Rhys deferred his own needs, choosing to stay in the stables to soothe the poor beast. He would change out of his wet clothes and order the carriage as soon as the storm abated, and then they would resolve this mess—his mess.

Sipping his warmed ale, he weighed the risks of removing his soaked boots. Would he ever get them back on?

The stable door swung wide admitting a strong wind and a soaking footman.

"Have a care, Albert," Rhys whispered as Sid wheeled at the sound of the door crashing back on its hinges.

"Pardon, Your Grace," the young man gasped, holding his side with one hand and swiping the running powder from his wig with the other. "I am sent to tell you Lady Wiggins is at the house now, Your Grace, and in such a state."

Rhys tossed the rest of his ale and hung the mug on a hook. He called to a groom to take over with Sid.

"What is the matter? Is it her lungs? Has Dr. Asher been called?" He thrust his arms into his cloak and rushed to the door.

"No, Your Grace, her ladyship is well. It is her companion, sir, Mrs. Weston."

Rhys stopped dead.

Albert gulped. "Lady Wiggins says she has been out all day and has not come home. She fears Mrs. Weston is out in the storm."

Rhys need hear no more. Heedless of Sid's nerves, he shouted for a horse to be saddled posthaste and then sprinted past Albert into the deluge and the house.

****

She should have left long ago but the sky, the mercurial sky, kept her riveted to the cove.

What a show. First brightest cerulean blue, and then churning into more turquoise and then into an impossible green-yellow, like an old bruise that hung above the black roiling sea. She rolled up her drawings of Rhys and tucked them beneath her arm. She gripped the nub of charcoal, the damp chalk disintegrating in her fingers as she pushed herself to capture the drama being played out before her.

*Oh, if she only had some color!* She turned to the cliff face, seeking the niche where she had stored her precious paints, but they might as well have been in Timbuktu. By the time she got there and back, the sky would have moved on to a whole new spectacle. Instead she scrawled "viridian, mars yellow, venetian red" in

255

the paper's margin, hoping the notes would be enough.

She stopped only when the charcoal was reduced to the size of a pea. The rest ran in a mess down her arm. She flung it away and rolled her drawings up with the others, sheltering them against her body. She felt so alive, so vital. She took one last look at the boiling brew above her and turned for shore.

How was it possible the sea had risen so fast? Feeling the cold water lapping at her ankles, she jerked the hair from her eyes, willing herself not to panic. Good God, the storm was right on top of her. As if to mock her, lightning pierced the back hurling clouds and a bare moment later, thunder boomed in answer. She almost lost her balance as the freezing water surged up to her calves.

Gasping, she tried to take stock of her situation. The rocks, which had served as stepping stones to the beach earlier in the day, were hidden with sloshing water, and like capricious children, only revealed themselves when it was far too late.

She used her free hand to wrench her twisted skirts from around her legs and held them high as she blindly felt for the next rock.

She made it but just barely. On the third rock, she was not so lucky; her ankle twisted and she slipped. She flung one arm out to catch herself, the other still clutching her precious drawings.

Water soaked the bottom edges of the paper and the charcoal images began to shift, running in muddy streaks down the wilted pages. A particularly strong gust of wind ripped most of them out of her arms. Her mouth opened in a silent cry, her arms reaching to capture at least one. But it was hopeless. With a crazed laugh, she tossed the rest up into the wind and surf. They rode the churning foam and then disintegrated into nothing.

****

"She went out this morning early, about six or so." Mrs. Wiggins wrung her still-reddened hands. "Mrs. Fields said Amy gave her some bread and cheese about then."

She took a few steps toward the window and then turned back to his uncle. "The morning was so fine. Was it not, Bertram? I never thought...Last evening when she proposed her plan, I told her to have a care, for old Mac had said it was sure to storm today. She only laughed and said she could brave a little water and not to fuss."

Rhys pulled out his watch. It was half-four now and with the storm, almost full dark.

"Lady Wiggins, did she say where she was going?" Rhys tried to make his voice sound calm.

The woman shook her head. "Only that she wanted to catch the sunrise. Oh, but that has been ages ago. I had been to Mrs. Hargett and only got home myself as the first drops of rain began to fall." She began crying in earnest now. "Oh why did not I come home sooner?"

"Now, now, Eglantine, you could not know and must not upset yourself unduly. Roydan will find her." He softly stroked her hand. "Be assured, she will be safe and within your sight in no time."

Rhys's brain clicked into military mode. There was no room for emotion—only action.

"Your Grace." It was Shields. "Mrs. Weston's horse has just returned to the stables." But before he could ask, the butler shook his head. "No, Mrs. Weston was not with Opalina. The head groom said it's likely the mare was frightened in the storm. The reins are broken."

"I want every man available, mounted and ready to move out as soon as may be." He turned to Shields. "Bring my pistols and plenty of powder. We will need rope as well and as many lanterns as you can find. When the storm finally abates, there will be almost no moon." He turned again to Mrs. Wiggins. "Madam, you must have Dr. Asher at the ready." The woman looked as if she might faint at any moment. Rhys caught her hands. "She will need you strong and ready when I bring her home. And I assure you, madam, I will."

"Let us move out!" He said shoving the pistols from Shields into his pockets. "We have not a moment to spare."

Rhys pulled his hat down low, pushed through the door, and out into the storm.

****

The problem was she could not swim.

Yes, she was chilled to the bone, yes, she was terrified of the thunder and the lightning, but mostly, she was petrified of drowning.

The water was over her knees and rising steadily. Her ankle, even half numb with cold, throbbed as if it had a heart of its own. She lifted it out of the water, her skirts dragging against her, just as a huge wave rolled through the inlet. Scrambling to save herself she thrust her leg back down into the brine, but her ankle collapsed under her weight, and she plunged below the waves.

Rhys spent the next hour combing the coast, but the light was almost nonexistent in the gloom and driving rain. He had set up a signal with his men, if anyone found her, to fire off three consecutive shots. Thus far, he had heard nothing. But with the competing thunder, it was impossible to distinguish nature from man.

He began to doubt the wisdom of attempting to scale the cliff side. It had seemed the most prudent plan when he stood on the lower bluff trying to get a better vantage point of the cove below.

Rain lashed his face, and his hat lifted off his head. It skittered along the face of the cliff only to be dashed back against the black streaming rock and then plummeted into darkness. His hair plastered against his cheek, he jerked his head, needing to see his next hold in the rock.

His foot slipped and his arms tore with pain, stretched beyond human capacity, or nearly. His hands bit into the crag as he fought for purchase. Pieces of shale fell away, and his knee scraped against the jagged rock. He would not be able to support himself much longer. Scrambling, his foot connected with a narrow shelf nearly up to his waist. He began to move on.

Lurching up out of the water, Olivia gasped for air, her ankle screaming in pain. Her burning lungs sucked in mist-soaked air as an incoming wave tore at her, threatening to crash her into the huge rocks. But even as she fought, she felt the dreadful pull below. The undertow.

Her head rang as it cracked against a rock, her teeth smashing together, the salt in her mouth mixing with the tangy iron of blood. She must hold on or be sucked under.

Her fingers slid over slimy rock as seaweed snaked

by her mouth and wrapped round her neck. There was nothing to hang on to. Her lungs were burning again, panic seeping into every pore.

*Oh Saint Anne, how could she keep fighting this terrible pull?*

She couldn't. She had no more strength, and she let her body go lax. Ghostly pale, her dress floated up around her, a final shroud. Her mind disconnected from her body, as if she were merely a spectator in her own death.

But, no, something was pulling her back. Her numb mind tried to focus. Then she saw. It was her gown. Miraculously it had wrapped itself around the boulder, snagging on something.

Praying it would hold, and using her last bit of energy, she reached up and grabbed the thin fabric pulling herself back into the dress, even as the cloth shredded.

Blessed air rushed into her lungs as she scrambled onto the top of the rock. Dear God, she was safe.

Her gown, still clinging to the rock, seemed to wave an eerie farewell, before it disappeared into the black water.

But her victory was short-lived. The water continued to rise at a furious pace. The rock would be submerged all too soon. She could not stay, but she could not attempt to swim either, certainly not in these turbulent waters. Olivia raised her face to the weeping sky finding a miraculous star amid the storm clouds.

The thunder cracked three times in succession directly overhead, but there was no lightning. The storm must be moving off, but even so, it was too little too late. She shivered, lay down on the rock, and closed her eyes.

The water lapping her ankles should have terrified her—it had risen that high—but she only stared as it crept up her laces, now to the edge of her stocking. Death would not be long now.

About to close her eyes for the last time, she saw her star had moved closer, and an angel stood beside it. Rhys. Her angel was Rhys. He would take her to heaven. He called to her. Yes, yes, she would come, but she was so weary. And so cold. Surely one should not feel so cold in death? When she opened her eyes again, her angel was gone; only the light remained. *No!* But no sound came from her lips. She did not want to die alone. Please, God, let him come back to comfort her in her last hour.

Then he appeared. He was there right beside her. He was speaking to her. *Could angels speak?* She could not make out his words, but words did not matter. She only comprehended his arms coming around her, sweeping her off the rock and into the swirling waters. She did not care as long as she was in his arms. Safe. So safe.

The small beach was suddenly crowded with men. *Where had they all come from?* And Rhys seemed very much alive as he shouted orders to the men around him. Someone wrapped her in blankets and hoisted her onto a horse. Warm arms encircled her. His arms. She remembered some of the ride home, mostly the warmth and the smell of him—salt and leather and the faintest hint of gunpowder. The rest didn't matter.

\*\*\*\*

The bed was too big. It made her look so small, so very fragile. Rhys stood in the shadows of the rose bedchamber at Valmere watching Dr. Asher work over her. Her wet black hair was the only contrast to her pale face and the stark white of the linen sheets. Dr. Asher had given her some laudanum, and she slept. Her head was being cleaned and bandaged—another bit of white to cover most of her hair. Her hands were next and then the cover was pulled back and her gown lifted to reveal her left hip. Rhys started forward. The bruise was already black as pitch and huge against her white skin. He reached for her.

Mrs. Wiggins's gaze found his. Reality crashed in, and stayed his hand. He should not be there watching these private ministrations. He had no right to this intimacy. But she was his *Olivia*. They did not understand; she was *his*.

Someone was at the door. Tinsley.

Yes, he did need a bath, and no, he would be no good to Mrs. Weston with a horrid ague. Besides he could do with a brandy—or five—yet another reason to take himself off. With one last look he left the room.

He had almost given up hope when he saw her there in the cove.

His light had caught a flash of white. He had passed the lantern back along the cove and saw what must be her face lifted, almost as if she was looking straight at him on the cliff. What if he had not taken the time to make a second pass?

*Oh, dear God, thank you.*

As he sank back in his bath, three words rolled over and over in his head. *She was safe. She was safe.* She was *home*.

\*\*\*\*

He stayed away. Why would he not come to her? It

had been four days already. She was almost fully recovered except for some tenderness in her ankle and a small lump on her head. The bruises would be weeks to fade but were not painful.

The hall stretched ahead, deserted. She should not be prowling about outside his study, but she was so tired of being cooped up in her beautiful room with its view of the sea. And when she had quizzed Dr. Asher, he assured her the duke would be gone all day. The knob felt hard and cool in her hand; she turned it and pushed the door open.

The study appeared large and airy despite its walls being filled with shelves containing all manner of things, books among them. A mix of sweet tobacco, wood smoke, old books and something else—oil?— hung in the air. It was so clearly *his* room, and she an intruder. But once there, she could not resist.

Angled in the corner of the room nearest to her stood a small harpsichord; stacks of handwritten music littered its top. She lifted a sheet. It looked to be his writing. She tried to pick out the tune in her head, but she was never good at sight reading and could not risk the noise to actually play. Besides, there was so much to see. She moved on, trailing her fingers along books on engineering and new farming methods. Books on mathematics, the Pythagorean Theorem, Newton's works, Descartes, and Aristotle's *Poetics*.

A series of bird's nests filled an entire shelf. Each one impossibly ephemeral yet so perfectly engineered. Bits of straw and horse hair, threaded with sea grasses, and what looked like butterfly wings and the down of some bird. She imagined him finding one, his strong fingers brushing the grass searching for eggs or bits of broken shell. And then, oh so carefully, wrapping the nest in his handkerchief, and putting it in his pocket. There were also bits of rusted metal—maybe old coins or buttons?—a tarnished spoon and several odd-shaped rocks with what looked to be the impressions of tiny sea creatures within them.

His huge desk dominated the room. Less like a desk and more like the kind of table where she used to cut fabric. In the middle of it stood a large magnifying glass fixed to a stand. She drew nearer. Tiny tools lay neat as surgical instruments in a handsome leather case. She imagined his large hands wielding those tools—so careful and precise. Nearby was a tray covered with a silk-velvet cloth. She glanced to the door and, satisfied no one was coming, lifted a corner. Shiny gears and wheels, springs and cogs lay in neat rows. Each had a number next to it attached to the bottom of the tray with a pin. The smell of oil was strong. She bent closer to touch the largest gear.

"It is the works of a rare, late seventeenth-century Tompion pocket watch with a cylinder escapement."

Olivia jerked, covering her mouth with her hand.

"Or will be when I uncover its mysteries," he finished.

"Oh." She bit her bottom lip. "I am afraid you have caught me snooping." Her voice trailed off. She would not "Your Grace" him, yet she could not possibly call him Rhys either. He was dressed for riding. His buff breeches and slate blue jacket reminded her of sand and sea. She drank him in, in great gulping draughts.

He frowned. "You are a guest in my home. You may go wherever you wish."

The image of his bed chamber skittered across her

brain and hotness spread over her cheeks. She ducked her head, and randomly pointed to a small S-shaped piece in the tray. "And what is this for?" Too late she realized he would have to cross the room and come to her side to see properly.

He did so and leaned over, his jacket brushing her arm. The urge to pull away was huge, but she made herself stay fixed.

"Ah, that is the cock."

She flinched away from him, an utter coward. *Dear Lord, he could not be serious?* She risked a look at him. He was, very serious.

"The cock is vital. It attaches to the movement plate and the pivot wheel."

"I see." She saw absolutely nothing other than his liquid gold eyes. "Well, I will not disturb you. No doubt you have much to accomplish."

"No, please do not leave on my account. I only came to fetch something." He paused as if he wanted to say more.

"I have no wish to be in your way."

An odd look came over his face. "You are not in my way. I will only be a moment." He went to a cupboard below a row of shelves and pulled out an object about seven inches high made of various metal parts. He held it next to his side, almost hiding it. "It is only a toy for our young groom."

Olivia drew closer.

He hesitated and then held it out as if it were a trifle. "It is meant to be a penguin—a flightless bird that lives in the arctic wastelands."

Olivia touched its shiny crown. "He is beautiful."

He frowned again. "It is an automaton," he said, as

if he could not equate science with a thing of beauty. "Made up of old clockworks and scraps of metal. Something I do in my leisure time. I have promised this fellow to young Mathew, our stable boy who is keen on automation."

"What a lovely gift. It must take infinite patience to create such a thing." She smiled shyly, and he frowned. "Will you show me how he works?"

Silently he crossed to the desk and carefully moved the tray and some papers aside. She stood across the desk from him. He turned the bird's head, and the crown sprang open. Ahhh, she thought, but she must have said it out loud because he looked over at her. A small key in the shape of a fish was revealed, which he removed and set into the toy's now-open beak. *So clever.* He carefully turned it three or four times.

Olivia held her breath as if she were waiting for an actual birth. Miraculously, the little bird stuttered a step and then two and three and onward across the desk while its beak opened and shut and stubby wings flapped.

"Oh," she breathed, her gaze finding his. "I am—"

He ducked his head. "Yes, it required some patience."

"Your Mathew is a lucky little boy."

The duke straightened, his lips pulling tight. "No, not so lucky..." but he did not elaborate.

"Well," she said breaking the lingering silence, "I believe I will go rest now. If you will excuse me?"

"Mrs. Weston?" She stopped halfway to the door. *Ah, we are back to Mrs. Weston.* "I trust you are improved?" He took a step toward her. "Are you well?"

His words spoke of something much deeper than

her mere physical health.

"Yes." She tried to smile. "I am quite recovered. Indeed, I do not see how I could avoid it as I have had every attention possible. Keep this up, sir, and I will never want to leave you." Oh, had she really said that? The flush sweeping over her assured her that she had.

His face remained unfathomable, but his eyes looked so…yearning.

"What I mean to say is," she pushed through her embarrassment, "I do not know how to thank you. It seems you are destined to rescue me."

She ventured a small laugh, hoping to lighten the atmosphere. But his face suddenly contorted, as if a damn had burst. His words came out in a fierce rush.

"Confound it woman, how can you laugh? Do you not perceive how close you were to death? To be out all day with no word to anyone? How could you not anticipate the coming storm and get yourself to safety?"

Astonished by his outburst, Olivia swallowed. "Your Grace, I am heartily sorry to have caused such trouble and worry. Believe me; Egg has raked me over the coals a dozen or more times already. I am very sensible now of my extreme folly. I sometimes tend to get caught up in a moment, in trying to capture that moment with paint." She gestured toward the window as if it would aid in her explanation. "The light, with the coming storm, was like nothing I had ever seen and the way into the cove was very passable at the time. I say this not by way of an excuse, but only as an explanation," she finished trying to defray some of the heavy emotion that still poured off of him.

"Why did you not swim to shore? I know that particular cove and, if attempted early enough, one can easily swim to the safety of the beach."

"Yes, I could see that. It is easy enough if one knows how to swim."

His head jerked up like a shot. He took a slow step toward her. "Am I to understand you do not swim?"

"I do not, Your Grace." She met his eyes squarely.

This last set him pacing about the room. She watched him in some awe. He seemed very angry.

Suddenly he stopped and faced her. "You will learn to swim as soon as may be."

She raised an eyebrow. "And who shall be my teacher?"

He raised his own eyebrow, accepting the challenge. "Why, myself, of course." And with that, he left the chamber.

## Chapter Twenty

Olivia felt light as a feather.

His fingertips miraculously suspended her body as she lay on her back in the soft, shushing water. Her ears lay just beneath the surface, muting the world around her, the sun, heavy and pressing on her eyelids, so warm. Her small cocoon-like world utterly peaceful.

Well, except for her rioting heart.

She dared a squinted look, sure he could see her heart leaping about beneath the wet linen of her bathing costume. He was frowning furiously down at her. Not that she was surprised. This had been his demeanor from the outset of her lesson. She felt like a naughty child who had thoroughly displeased her parent.

When they first entered the waters, her dignity had taken quite a hit; she clung to him like a tenacious sea creature. But he had firmly peeled her arms off as soon as he waded into the small pool that lay within the cove.

It had taken her a long while to trust him with her body, but once that had been achieved, she surprised herself with her progress, treading water, head above the waves, feet kicking and arms pushing back and forth.

"Now flatten out your body, like this." She swirled around in the lapping waves to see his demonstration. "And reach your arm long, cupping your hand to pull the water back toward you."

As his arms cut deftly through the sea with such grace and economy, her own stilled. He was so beautiful. She could watch him forever.

Foamy brine closed over her nose and eyes.

But before she could begin to panic strong hands gripped her arm, and he fished her up like a sack of oysters. "Blast you, pay attention!" She pressed her laughter between her lips. "Now reach."

He stood in the middle of the pool, frowning and barking directions. She did not care. She loved it. As she reached one arm out before her, cupping the water as he had shown her, she felt so utterly free. By Saint Anne, she was swimming.

Olivia caught glimpses of him as his eyes and body tracked her progress. She loved how vigilant he was. Never letting her stray too far from his reach. Her muscles screamed but she wanted so much to please him. Remembering an old tale from her childhood where mermaids and mermen swam beneath the waves, she became bold and dove under. The earthly world disappeared to give way to the muted, tranquil sea world. She became a mermaid.

Once again, vise-like arms gripped her body, heaving her up out of the water.

She came up laughing. But his panicked face made her heart constrict in sweet pain.

"I am well," she assured him, resting her hand on his cheek. "Truly, Rhys, I am—"

He kissed her.

She pulled back to see the question in his eyes and kissed him back.

Lips still locked, he scooped her up into his arms. His heart beat heavily next to her breast as he cradled her to him. She felt the pumping of his powerful legs against her bottom, and the rigid rising of his penis against her hip as they made their way to shore. Olivia nestled in deeper and he groaned.

He laid her in the cool, wet sand at the edge of the surf and covered her with his body. The foamy brine licked gently at her legs as she dug her heels into the sand and pushed up into him.

They did not speak. They only loved. Simply touching and learning each other. Words were too harmful and too much a source of misunderstanding. Words were for later. Much later. Now there was only love.

\*\*\*\*

"Have you always painted?" he asked, breaking their long silence with a safe topic. They had chosen to remain on foot while leading their horses toward home.

"Always." She looked out over the headlands. "At least for as long as I can remember." Olivia laughed, ducking her head. "I used to love the color purple. Everything I painted was some shade of purple. I remember painting an old yew tree near my home and proudly showing the picture to my governess. She was most displeased. 'There are no purple trees,' she said. And she tore it to bits."

She turned when Rhys made no rejoinder. He was looking at her oddly. "Your family employed a governess?"

"Oh—no—I misspoke." Suddenly finding a bit of sand still clinging to her skirts she brushed at it. Anything to avoid his eyes. "It was only a woman who sometimes taught the village children." She vaulted onto Opalina, her only thought escape. "Let us race!"

When Valmere was in sight, she could see Lord Bertram and Egg pacing near the stables. Olivia knew the instant her friend caught sight of her and Rhys. Egg stopped abruptly, placed her hands on her hips, and tucked her chin into her chest. Very much like a wet hen with a missing chick.

"Well, you see, Eglantine." Bertram folded her arm beneath his and patted her hand as Olivia and Rhys rode up. "There is no need to call out the hounds. Did I not tell you Roydan is quite capable of teaching one small female to swim?"

"Thank you, my lord, you did assure me. While I had no doubt of Mrs. Weston's capabilities, even if she is small and female,"—she gave Bertram a speaking look—"and certainly the duke is very…athletic, I only wondered at the time gone by and how wise it is to…" She frowned. "Swim, so long." Now that his lordship was put firmly in his place, she turned to Olivia. "How did you get on, my dear?" Egg pursed her lips and looked over her spectacles.

Olivia bit her lip and then laughed. "It was most delightful. I was swimming, dear—Lady Wiggins! I would not have thought I could make so much progress in one short day."

"Yes," the duke interceded, "Mrs. Weston is making tolerable progress." Thinking Rhys finished with his assessment; the two older people began their congratulations. But Rhys cleared his throat, "However, I believe she will need more instruction. I am thinking of one area in particular where more attention is needed if she is to become a true proficient."

Olivia could hardly look at him. He accomplished his speech without the smallest ghost of a smile. She wanted to shout "Bravo!" and roar with laughter. How could she ever think he was cold and humorless?

He made a brief bow to the company. "Tomorrow, at the same time, Mrs. Weston?" A real question in his eyes.

"Yes, Your Grace," she said, returning a curtsey. "I am looking forward to it."

She thought she heard his expelled breath as he strode off.

Olivia excused herself as well. She was too full and too transparent to remain with her friend. She took the opposite direction as she rode off.

The two older people were left, each staring after their loved ones.

"Well, it seems they were quite successful," Egg said almost to herself.

Bertram's thoughts were occupied along the same lines. "Yes, perhaps too successful."

They looked at each other and parted ways.

****

And so their affair began again, but this time, with no talk of contracts or of houses and carriages.

On fine days they rode, or more likely, met on the beach at their little cove. Even the unpredictable English weather seemed to be on their side. But when storms blew up, they would meet at Sea Cottage.

The room began to fill with small remembrances of their time together—a sprig of now-dried heather, a small collection of sea shells, a perfectly oval stone with two white rings around it.

They did not speak of the future or anything that might disturb the delicate balance of this fantasy world. They left those thoughts for the long dark nights.

But today was almost balmy and still. The tide had gone out, and the air was pure churned cream, thick and fresh with a hint of salt. Like a vanilla-ice custard Olivia had as a child.

She found his preserved footprints. A neat stitch along the ribbon of wet, silken sand. A smile tugged her lips. She removed her boots and gingerly stepped into his print. Her foot, small and slim, surrounded by his large and square one. It felt intimate. She wrapped her arms around herself, squeezing in her happiness. A silly goose. She quickly followed his trail, knowing it would lead her to treasure.

Rhys lay back on the sand, his hands behind his head in a cradle, staring up at the sky. He did not see her, lost in some private world.

She sat behind him, arms wrapped around her drawn up legs, chin resting on her knees. It was a rare treat to see him so relaxed and unconscious.

Then she saw a slight miracle.

He smiled.

It was by no means a full-fledged smile, but as he gazed intently up into the clouds, his lips curved and his eyes crinkled. It was *not* a grimace because there was no sun at the moment.

She followed his gaze, wanting to be a part of his world and happiness. But clearly his joy was of the internal variety, as she saw only clouds scuttling across the afternoon sky. She knew she should leave him to his thoughts and his peace, but she could not.

"What has made you smile?"

He jerked up. His face immediately shuttered.

Of course. *Damn, why couldn't she leave well enough alone?*

"It is nothing." He shifted toward her and kissed her. She gently pulled away.

"It is not nothing. It is *something*." She wanted to be let in. She wanted to know this man.

He was silent for a long while. Disappointed, with even silly tears threatening, she rose and began to shake out her skirts.

"It was only a silly game my mother and I used to play."

She waited.

"I was recalling it."

Still she waited.

He rose to his elbows and turned back to her. He pointed up above the cliffs.

"Do you see that cloud hanging to the right of the break in the cliff? It is at about two o'clock."

She leaned down to his level to better see his perspective and looked up.

"Do you see it looks a bit like a hare jumping over a huge rose?" When she did not answer, he continued, "Or at least it did a few moments ago." He idly scooped up a hand full of sand and slowly transferred it to the other.

Olivia softly sighed thinking she would get no more secrets, but he brushed his hands and spoke. "My mother would often take me to this beach, and we would make a game of finding pictures in the clouds. It is one of my strongest memories of her—that and her teaching me to swim." He looked at her shyly, as if he were gauging her interest level.

Apparently satisfied, he continued. "I always saw dragons and shields and great warriors. She saw fairies and goddesses with long flowing hair. But mostly she saw animals."

There was a long moment of the surf and gulls calling.

"That is why I…smiled."

Their eyes met. It was a gift. Granted, a small gift, but it was the best gift she had had in quite a while.

She was the first to break away. She sat on the sand next to him and looked up, pretending that the earth had not shaken and the planets were still in alignment.

"I rather think that gray bit of fluff at nine o'clock, looks quite like the great Egyptian Sphinx." She squinted and laughed. "Either that, or Sir Everett when he's deeply in his cups."

And so the game began.

He was quite competitive but scrupulously fair.

**** 

He was showing off for her. Olivia was sure of it.

He cut through the water, diving through waves and riding the surf. She imagined him as a little boy doing the very same thing, only instead of her calling out praise and caution, it had been his mother.

Each had lost their respective mothers at such tender ages. That single event had shaped both their lives so decisively. Like a grain of sand slipping between an oyster's fortress of shell to fester into a pearl—real and hard and beautiful. To remove the pearl, one must pry open the shell and expose its inner flesh and soft parts, otherwise the beauty remains hidden.

When Georgina Roydan died, her only son closed himself up. He became hard and withdrawn, a defense against the unbearable loss of the world as he had known it. And so the loving, sensitive, and shy boy of eight years had turned into a sober and reclusive Monk. Olivia knew this, as sure as she knew her name.

She hoped he would never return to that man—that monk.

He came toward her, shaking droplets of water like old Toby.

"Ugh! You will have me soaking in no time, Mr. Fish!"

"Madam Mermaid, I have not begun to soak you." Her jaw dropped open as he sank to his knees. "Let me commence now."

****

Olivia lay quietly, listening to the far off sea, its soft shush of waves blending with Rhys's breathing as he lay next to her. He was sleeping. She could tell by the evenness of his breath. His body spent, like the quietly disappearing foam left upon the shore after a huge wave.

Their love had been different this time. He was certainly a very clever pupil once he let his whirring mind stop questioning and his senses take over, but this time their loving contained a new element.

Today he had allowed her to kiss him in his most intimate places, even to suckle him there. As he spilled into her mouth, the sound from his own was like nothing she'd ever heard. It tore out of him like a wounded animal. He had pulled her up to him afterwards looking fiercely into her eyes and then oh-so-softly kissed her lips.

He had never talked about his aversion to this act, and she had never asked, but the memory must have been incredibly painful.

But today he had trusted her. Trusted she would

not hurt him. It had been a leap for both of them, like a needle through leather, painful yet clean and true. It had felt very much like love.

She dare not kiss him, not wanting to wake him...not yet. She would savor this delicious waiting. Her gaze raked his body, drinking it in with hedonistic pleasure, making an unhurried study of his beauty.

She began to mentally paint him, memorizing every line, every shadowed crevice. His portrait would require deep, dark undertones, and would be heavily layered to achieve the feeling of depth. But that would only be the base of the work; his true essence would be in the luminous highlights that would come later.

His hand lay half curled on his chest in a nest of dark, springy hair. She loved his hands. They were huge and square. Not a gentleman's hands at all. She remembered them on her body, dry and slightly abrasive. They had covered every inch of her, mapping her body. And then his mouth and tongue had followed...

She dragged her mind back to her task. She moved down, skipping over certain parts, for the relative safety of his legs. She had got the musculature wrong—they were longer, the muscles more fluid. She would remember that now. She longed to pull her hands down those legs, to feel as well as see, but there would be time for that later. Now she needed this moment to utterly fix him in her mind, storing the impressions for the time when she was gone. When this wondrous fantasy was over.

Her nose flared with that familiar tingle of tears. But this was *not* a time for tears. Those would be stored along with the imprint of his body for later—please

God, much later.

She returned her gaze to his mouth again, focusing on a sweet corner. Smooth cheek and rasp of new beard met the ripe opening of his honeyed, fleshy lip. A secret corner.

She pulled herself up next to him and flicked her tongue to taste salt and musky woman, her smell. A fan of breath brushed her lips as he expelled the air he had been holding. Ah, she wondered how long he had been pretending to sleep.

He looked up at her. What was in his eyes was enough. It was somehow enough.

She closed her eyes and lay back on the sand.

Rhys rose to his elbows and looked down at this gift, his Olivia with her open, waiting body. His emotions were spent long ago in the wake of her tender ministrations. Instinct took over—pure, sensual intuition his guide now. As if the world stopped spinning just for them; their bodies creating its only movement. They were gods. In a moment they would return to earth and the world would revolve on its own again. They would become mortal, but for this space of time, life was exquisite. He only needed to touch her for it to begin again.

And he did. His heart vanquished his head in a blaze of glorious love. Yes, love.

Chapter Twenty-One

Daria stared into the dregs of her now-cold tea, debating whether to ask for yet another pot. She squirmed. No, not a good idea.

Miss Arabella Campbell and her maid, Daisy was her name, had been closeted in this remote corner for nigh on an hour now. They seemed to be hiding. Little had been said beyond her ladyship's extreme boredom at hanging about London in the heat of the summer.

Frankly, Daria was tired of London as well, particularly skulking about for her new lover. Her latest task, to track the Campbell chit in the hope of her leading them to Roydan and ultimately to Weston, was proving as tedious as trying to mine gold from the duke.

Watching the maid now, it struck Daria that Daisy and Weston could be twins. However, closer inspection revealed this woman's nose was more upturned and her eyes closer together. Also, the voice was wrong.

Thank God Daria had not hied off to tell his lordship she had found Weston when she first saw this girl last week. She flexed her fingers. The swelling had subsided enough to don her glove, but the bruises still remained. He was not fond of wild goose chases. Well, it was not her fault Wilcove had told her the duke was in Scotland.

"Here you are." A flurry of movement descended on the scene in the form of Lady Campbell. Oh, not the mother, sighed Daria. "I got held up by that troll who owns the *Morning Chronicle*. Why, I wanted to—Daisy, you may leave us." The girl's mother practically sat on the poor maid so anxious was she to be alone with her daughter.

Daisy shot a glance at her mistress. "Very good, madam. I will be in the park across the way."

The mother pursed her lips as her narrowed gaze followed the maid's every move. "There is something about that girl I do not like. I can't quite put my finger on it...Well." She turned back to her daughter. "When you are a duchess we will employ a French maid. I believe Lady Schnobble can point me in the right direction.

"Did you not hear me?" Lady Campbell rapped a spoon on the table. "How can you sit there placidly eating? I will never understand you. But then you have never behaved like a normal girl." The young woman slumped as her mother reached into her reticule and retrieved a paper. A letter. Daria could see it clearly now. The woman flourished it like a flag in front of her daughter. "My dear, it has come!"

"What has come, Mamma?" A sigh accompanied a lazy spoonful of custard.

"Why, the duke's invitation, you silly chit!"

Visions of cream caramels disappeared and Daria perked up.

"Oh, my dear, we—you are to be a duchess! Her Grace, the sixth Duchess of Roydan. Does that not sound grand?" Lady Campbell clapped her hands in glee which thankfully disguised the slap of Daria's book as it hit the table. "Now, my dearest, you must not eat too many sweets." She looked at the girl like she was some sort of prized sow. "It is obvious he likes you well enough, but you know you have a tendency toward plumpness." She gave her daughter's arm a little pinch. Daria flinched. "I told you, you should have had more faith in Roydan's honor. I knew he would not forsake us, my dear. A mother always knows these things."

"Ah, no Italian counts then, Mamma?"

"Italian Counts?" The woman frowned and then humphed. "My dear as you will learn all too soon— please God—a good mother has to be prepared for all eventualities." Daria had to lean in to catch the woman's next comment. "Only think if Roydan had discarded you. No one would touch you. Indeed, I thought perhaps we would have to cut our losses and go to Italy. Imagine having to fire you off there." She affected a little shudder. "Those Italians will take anyone. Even Lady Ribble's girl—you know the unfortunate one with the harelip—got a husband there. I must write to her ladyship immediately and tell her of our news. I wonder if we will ever see that poor unlucky girl again?

"But that is neither here nor there. We have been summoned! Of course we will have St. George's for the church. Oh, won't Roydan be delicious in a coat of golden brocade with perhaps champagne-colored breeches."

Sweet Jezebel, the woman was utterly ridiculous, simpering and flirting as she peeped from behind the letter, as if Roydan were before her instead of her child.

"Hmm…" Lady Campbell frowned at her daughter's hair. "The seaside…not your best setting. We shall have to make sure Daisy brings the right pomades. But no matter, if that is where the duke is, then it is well enough with me."

Daria perked up. *The seaside? But where?* The duke had at least three estates near the sea. Oh, if she could only get her hands around the woman's neck and throttle the information out of her.

"Valmere," the woman said breathlessly, as if she had heard Daria's thoughts. "We are to travel to Valmere. Which I understand is one of his minor estates by the sea…"

Valmere. Of course. Daria should have known. Roydan disappeared for weeks on end during the summer months, touring his various estates. He never once brought her along, though she had hinted every year. He always returned to town too tanned for her liking and came to her bed like a cannon for those first few weeks.

"Though, to my mind"—Lady Campbell tapped one finger against the letter—"Beckham Abbey or even Waubeek Downs would have been more fitting for a proposal.

"Daisy! Where is that girl?" The woman rose gesturing for her daughter to follow. "We must begin packing. There is so very much to do. I wonder what one wears to the seaside these days?"

Arabella's head dropped as a faint sigh slipped from the girl.

"Yes, the pomades," the harpy continued. "We mustn't forget the pomades." The shrew sailed out still wielding her precious letter as if mere mortals could be struck down by its import. Her daughter released another sigh, gathered her reticule, and dutifully rose to go.

*Valmere. Weston is at Valmere.* Daria looked

283

longingly at the unfinished ice but rose as well. She should deliver her news. He was waiting. And she knew all too well he was not a patient man. But first she must use the necessary.

\*\*\*\*

Rhys held Olivia's hand as their horses danced impatiently beneath them. He had seen her halfway to the dower house but was loath to leave. Something nibbled at the back of his brain. Olivia laughed and pulled her hand from his.

"Silly man, I will see you in but a few hours." And she wheeled Opalina and took off across the field. She sat a horse as if she'd been born to it. Odd given her circumstances. He could no longer see her; she'd disappeared into the pollard trees.

Valmere's topmost chimneys peeked over the rise of the hill, growing like branchless trees till the roofline appeared. Rhys pushed Sid toward the stables. No time to curry the horse himself. Just enough time to bathe—

*Time!* He had forgotten to give her his gift. The watch lay ticking in his breast pocket, right over his heart. He pulled it out and ran his thumb over the case, still warm from his body.

He'd finished the piece only last night when sleep was impossible. It had looked as if it was never going to come together, but at the last moment everything slipped into place as if there had never been a struggle. The watch was exquisite, just like her, and he wanted her to have it—*his heart*. He flipped the case open—almost gone five. It suddenly seemed important she have it now, this instant.

As he clucked to Sid, wheeling him into a broad turn, he spied them. Three carriages stood in the stable yard.

Rhys shook his head. He would not let the grief in. He wheeled Sid around. And then around again, and again. Sid snorted in protest, but still the carriages would not disappear. *No!* He straightened Sid, and rode at a full charge to the stable yard. Hooves pounded the earth in concert with his breaking heart.

Stable boys and dogs scattered as Rhys raged into the paddock. He vaulted off Sid, throwing the reins to one of the braver lads.

"Who?" he said, his breath coming fast. "Who?" The word tore out of him. They all stood dumbly about like imbeciles. He grabbed the nearest boy and shook him. "Who!"

"The Campbells, Your Grace." Rhys stood with poor Matthew's shirt fisted in his hands. From the expression on the boy's face, he must look like the Devil incarnate. He made himself let go, took a step back, and swiped the spittle from his face. When he went to straighten the boy's collar, Matthew flinched. Rhys froze.

"Forgive me, Matty." He turned to go and realized he still held the watch. Turning back, he gestured for the boy's hand. Matty looked at the head groom who nodded, and he tentatively held out his hand. Rhys gently pressed the heart into it. He wanted to say something about taking care of it, but the words locked in his throat.

As he made for the house, the ducal mantle crashed back down on his shoulders and he stumbled. He could not go back; he must brave the future alone, without his heart.

"I am sorry, my boy, so very sorry. But it could not

be helped." He would not look at Uncle Bert. So his uncle continued, "It has simply gone too far. The papers continue to stir the pot of gossip, of course. But when Lady Campbell wrote that Miss Arabella was in despair and felt almost compromised, I knew what must be done."

*Compromised? He had hardly touched the girl!*

"I did not want to ambush you like this, but I saw your mind, lad, and I knew you would not be able to take the necessary step." Rhys spared his uncle a glance; the man grimaced as if he were being made to swallow cod-liver oil. "You know your duty. In your heart, you know this is the only way forward. This Gooden woman might very well be dead, but do you want to run that risk? You would not want to lose Valmere to this blasted codicil or disgrace the title by ruining the Campbell girl." His uncle paused but Rhys could not reply, his heart was too busy with the act of breaking.

"Besides, we do not even know the first thing about Olivia Weston and believe me, I have tried. Eglantine will tell me nothing of her circumstances. That in itself is quite damning. Surely her silence on the matter cannot bode well for Mrs. Weston's past?" Bertram compressed his lips. "However delightful, she is, unfortunately, unsuitable. It was well past time to contact the Campbells. It is expected. You have gone too far in securing their hopes."

His uncle's words felt like a battering ram, hammering away at Rhys's new and fragile world, till it lay smashed in pieces at his feet. He had no defense. He remained frozen to the ground, taking the hits.

Bertram's voice softened. "You must have known

it was impossible, lad."

The sound of pity penetrated worse than any blow.

"And what of *Lady* Wiggins?" His voice sounded like a rusty saw. "What do you really know of *her* past?" Rhys could not stop himself. He felt like a jealous child who wanted to smash a playfellow's favorite toy since he was being denied his own.

His uncle's eyebrows rose. "Eglantine? What has she to do with this?"

"Nothing." His mask went up, blocking the pain gathered in his throat—in his heart. "Your pardon, Uncle, I am not myself these days. I will see them at dinner." Rhys bowed and left the room.

****

Olivia found Egg having tea in the garden. She dropped a kiss on her head and collapsed into the chair opposite.

"Is the tea still hot, or should I fetch another pot?" Egg did not answer immediately; she seemed wholly occupied with arranging cubes of sugar.

"Egglet?"

"My dear—" Egg started and paused.

"Yes?" said Olivia, forgetting about the tea.

"My dear, the duke's guests have arrived," Egg finished, her voice full of unspoken sympathy.

"Guests?" Olivia gripped the edge of the tea table. How could one simple word annihilate her hope in one shattering blow? She did not know how she managed, but she plastered a smile on her face. This was the beginning of the end.

"Excuse me, Egg, dearest," she said, her smile fixed in place, "I think the tea is cold. I—excuse me—" And she left the garden.

But where to go? Where to take herself that would give any comfort? Where could she go to erase that word that doomed her happiness?

The answer was nowhere.

She found herself in a little-used parlor. It had never appealed to the women, being too dark and formal. The black and white checkered pattern of the marble floor blurred under a barrage of tears. She dashed them from her eyes.

How could she be so stupid? She dug her fingernails into the soft flesh of her palms. She pressed them harder, wanting to punish herself for being so ridiculous. She always knew she was the expendable piece in this game. A mere pawn in the machinations of the *ton*. Roydan was, and always would be, king. She was a hopeless fool to even pretend to play the queen.

It had all been a huge fairytale. Only her stupid heart did not seem to know it had all been a dream, for it was certainly breaking. But she did have one move left. She could cease to play.

She would leave. After all, there was no formal contract between them. Surely she had fulfilled her obligation? Besides, he was about to marry. She must try and save what little she had left of her pride. And in the end, she supposed, she would be saving him as well. But she would not think of that now. That pain could be left for later. Much later. Besides, she had much to do.

## Chapter Twenty-Two

Olivia could not get away that instant, as she had planned. She told herself she did not want to spoil Egg's delight over the mask and her anticipation of dancing with Lord Bertram, who seemed as in love with her as she with him. A letter must be composed to leave for Egg. Her things must be packed. But honestly, her few things could be gathered in an instant. The note to Egg would be harder, but it could be done. And though Egg would be worried and heartbroken at Olivia's disappearance, Eglantine Wiggins would survive.

In truth, Olivia stayed for one reason. The real reason. The terrible creeping hope that he would still choose her. That he would renounce the world and its rules and choose her.

Oh, how this awful hope pounded at her with every beat of her heart, every blink of her eyes, every breath she took. It was exhausting keeping this frail ember glowing. Better to stub it out, or drown it in a flood of tears, and be done with it. Yet she could not leave without *seeing*. She had to see the thing done. She had to have that picture to make hope finally die once and for all.

Only a few more hours to wait, to hope. Tomorrow evening would come soon enough. The ball was to be a masked affair, which certainly helped with Olivia's plans; no one would be able to tell if she was there or not.

Thus far she had managed to dodge the duke, as she now began calling him, even in her private thoughts. She and Egg had been invited up to the mansion for dinner, but Olivia could not face the role she would have to play, that of quiet companion while Miss Campbell and the duke played the happy couple. Instead, she pled a headache and took a long walk knowing she would not encounter him.

But after only an hour's time, a heavy rain drove her back inside. She nearly missed the letter on the hall table in her haste to get out of her wet outer garments, but the bold "Mrs. Weston" stopped her dead. There was no mistaking the duke's familiar hand. She ran into the parlor dreading yet, so foolishly, hoping to see him. She almost called his name.

"Stop," she said instead. "Stop." As if the command could quell her thundering heart, or possibly dam the tears that streamed down her face, or even still her shaking hands.

She was not thinking clearly. Of course he had sent Jonas or Albert; after all it would be the height of rudeness to leave his guests—his Arabella.

Would he learn to love this woman? This woman who was so unlike herself. Would he learn to touch Arabella Campbell in the same way he touched her? Whisper his wicked thoughts into an ear framed in gold instead of black? Would they have a child?

Only the clock striking ten made her pick herself up off the floor where she must have sunk she knew not how long ago. She stood before the narrow table, reaching out, feeling for the letter—like a coward, she could not look at that formal "Mrs. Weston" again—her fingers closed around the smooth heavy paper. Before she could bring it to her lips, she ran into the parlor, threw it in the fire, and hurried back out into the wet night.

\*\*\*\*

*Why did she not respond to him?*

Rhys had practically camped out at Sea Cottage for the past two days, but she never came. He ended by leaving another of his blasted notes. He had combed the coves and rocks, but she was never there. And Mrs. Wiggins gave him such dreadful looks on the four occasions he had been to the dower house, that he very much doubted she would tell him the truth, had Olivia even been within.

Bone tired and at his wit's end, he was almost looking forward to this damned charade of a betrothal and marriage so he could be with the woman he truly wanted, truly loved.

But time was running out. Would she have him? Surely after all they had shared there was some small space for them. If only he could know her mind. But the damned woman was nowhere to be found.

He was just closing the door to his study, another pointless note in his breast pocket, when he ran into something.

"Oof"

"Ohhhh!"

He stood face to face, well, face to chest with Arabella Campbell.

"Ah. Miss Campbell, have I injured you?"

"Only my nose, Your Grace, but I dare say, with a few days, it will be right as rain."

Was that meant to be a joke? He could not actually

be sure, she was frowning so.

"I do beg your pardon. May I get Shields to fetch some ice? Or perhaps you would like to lie down?"

The girl frowned even more. "No, Your Grace I would not like to lie down and no ice, I thank you."

Yet the girl stood mulishly in his path. *Damned infernal females, always wanting a fellow to be some sort of clairvoyant.* He switched tactics.

"Are you and your parents settled? Are your rooms acceptable?"

Miss Campbell replied with a tight, fixed smile, "Yes, Your Grace, we are quite settled, thank you. And our rooms are exceptional." Said as if exceptional was on par with hideous. What did the chit want of him? And when could he escape?

"I understand we have Lord Bertram to thank for our invitation." Rhys had no rejoinder, so he raised an eyebrow instead. "I was wondering if you might want to show me the gardens?" Her mind was as slippery as a fish. "Or perhaps the dower house?"

"The gardens…"

"And the dower house, Your Grace?"

The girl clearly had her ear to the ground, and it was patently obvious she did not wish to accompany him anywhere. They were both being played, forced into a conventional corner. He could not stand it. He had to get away. To save them both. He found and fiddled with his watch fob. His watch still lay in a drawer——he could not recall where. He glanced at the nearest window and then back to her. "You are well settled then?"

She thrust her jaw at him, sniffed, and left him. He bowed to her retreating back.

He felt for his watch again. Stupid. He had not checked the beach since this morning. Time was wasting. Lady Campbell's voice brought him up short as it came through the partially open library door.

"Roydan is too distracted. Believe me, all is not well."

Rhys wanted to move on—he was no eavesdropper—but he needed as much information as possible to make his way through these murky waters.

"And don't look at me like that, Kenneth, I *know* of what I speak," Lady Campbell continued ominously.

"Dismount, Gertrude." Lord Campbell sounded as though he had been drinking. "There is no reason to get on your high horse."

"She is our only child, sir, our one chance at getting her well settled. This marriage *must* happen."

Rhys pinched the bridge of his nose; he hated to think of hurting anyone in this tangled mess.

"Now settle, Gertie. I have made inquiries, and though Roydan's staff is quite close-mouthed, I believe there is a woman"—a gasp, from Lady Campbell—"who is, shall we say, distracting the duke. She is however, unsuitable. We have nothing to fear." There was quiet. "You will get your duchess or, by God, Roydan will see the back of my glove."

"Your Grace."

It was James. Rhys turned and moved to the hall entry door. James followed.

"There has been an accident, Your Grace. It is young Mathew, from the stables."

****

"There you are, Eglantine." Lord Bertram pushed his way into a thicket of wild brambles, and Olivia sank into the high back of her chair. "What are you doing in this tangle, Eglantine? I thought we had decided to let this section go for now." Egg did not answer. His lordship tried to move forward. but his long drab coattails snagged on a branch of thorns and pinned him in his place. He twisted, trying to extricate the fabric from a particularly nasty thorn, but the rip was inevitable. "Damn!" he muttered and turned to assess the damage. "My dear won't you come out of there so we can talk properly? I have the distinct notion you have been avoiding me."

"Nonsense, Lord Bertram." Eglantine spared him one look and a freezing smile and turned back to her work.

Oh dear, thought Olivia. My drama has spilled into Egg's bliss. Lord Bertram snorted when he realized he had been demoted to "Lord."

"Please, Eglantine, you will be torn to pieces in that mess. Let me call one of the gardeners to at least remove the most lethal bits."

"I will be quite well on my own here," Egg said, doing fierce battle with a stubborn root. "You don't want to be neglecting your guests." She gave a final yank and the root gave way. She held it up like a trophy before tossing it in with the other victims.

Poor Lord Bertram, no olive branch in sight.

Egg bent, prepared for yet another battle, and Olivia caught his lordship looking longingly at Eglantine's rounded backside.

Olivia wanted to reveal herself and tell him to retreat. She knew Egg and her moods, and he was not going to breach this one.

"Very well, my dear, I will see you tomorrow

evening. And remember, I have the first and the supper dance." Egg's only response was a grunt. His lordship "humphed" back—bless his heart—picked up his ruined coattails and took himself off.

Olivia decided to do the same.

She found herself on the beach. He had been there. His booted prints could still be seen in crazed patterns along the shore. But he had left. The maze of prints led up to a scuffle of horse hooves where they disappeared into the tall grasses.

She turned back to the sea. She was no longer alone. A woman had come from behind the rocks. Who would be on the beach at this time of day? There were no other guests staying at the mansion other than the Campbells, and she knew from the shape of the woman it could not be Arabella Campbell. Olivia had no wish for company, so she turned to go before she was spied.

"Mrs. Weston!" She was too late. "Ma'am, excuse me." Olivia turned back and blinked, and blinked again, and then caught her breath. The woman half-running toward her could have easily been her sister.

"I am sorry, I have startled you, and I'm sure you would have much rather I left you alone, but I could not. You see, I know—I know you and the… You must feel as hopeless as I."

"Who are you?" Olivia asked, still amazed at the likeness; even the woman's red, raw-looking eyes must mirror her own.

"Your pardon, ma'am, I am Daisy Taylor, Miss Arabella's maid."

Uncanny as the likeness was, Olivia had no wish to speak about Arabella Campbell or the duke or anything, for that matter. Her next words came out in a great rush.

"I am sorry I must leave you now. Lady Wiggins will be missing me, and I will be leaving quite soon to take another position. Good day."

A sob and the sound of a thud in the sand stopped her. Daisy Taylor lay in a pool of navy blue skirts, her head in her hands.

Olivia sniffed hard and clenched her fists. Oh, to turn and run and never stop. But instead, she dropped to her knees.

The poor woman immediately clung to her like a life line. Murmuring nonsense words of comfort, her own tears slid down her cheeks and fell onto the dark head cradled to her breast. Unbidden, an answering sob tore from her throat. Horrified at the sound, Olivia tried to pull back, but Daisy Taylor raised her grief stricken face and oh so gently touched Olivia's cheek.

She should have been appalled to be seen thus in front of a virtual stranger. Maybe it was the coming full moon? Maybe it was that she could not confide in Egg? Or maybe it was seeing this younger version of herself, so much like the sister she never had? But that one kind touch released a floodgate of emotion. To hold another being and empty that emotion into their arms was enormous.

Much later after they had used every inch of their handkerchiefs, Daisy looked out to the sea and shook her head.

"You see, Mrs. Weston, my case is a hopeless as yours. In fact, far worse, if you can imagine." She began crying again. "I will never even get a chance to mingle in company with my love. We are so very far apart in status."

Olivia asked who held her heart, but Daisy would

not say. They had sworn to keep their love a secret. "Will your love be attending the ball?" Olivia asked, the beginning of a plan forming in her head.

"Well, yes," was all Daisy said.

If she could not have her dream, then she would do her damnedest to make it happen for this lovely young woman. Yes, she would give Daisy one night of fantasy.

Chapter Twenty-Three

"It is truly remarkable. I am told only the Dowager Countess of Asterly has sent her regrets," Egg, stirred her tea. "And solely because the old woman, who is in her ninety-second year, had to be forcibly detained by her physician."

"Hunsford village has not a cone of sugar or an ounce of flour left within five miles, I vow," said the housekeeper, Mrs. Fields. "I have never seen such a swarm of locusts, if you'll pardon my saying so, my lady."

Egg laughed and leaned back in her chair. Olivia shifted from her place just outside the doorway to keep her friend in sight. But as she did, Egg's gaze must have caught the slight movement and her laughter trickled away.

"But I suppose it cannot be helped," Mrs. Fields continued, "what with His Grace all set to announce his betro—"

Egg coughed. Olivia bit her upper lip, glancing guiltily at Mrs. Fields as she revealed herself.

"Oh, I am sorry, my dear." Egg rose. "We did not see you there. Will you have a cup?" Mrs. Fields excused herself and immediately went to fetch more tea. "I'm afraid you have caught us gossiping like two old hens."

Olivia smiled. "Well, I don't know which is worse,

gossiping or eavesdropping." She swallowed the sudden lump in her throat. *Dearest Egg.* She looked so radiant these days, her cheeks filled out and rosy; the soft roundness had returned to her body making her seem almost youthful. Olivia drank the image in as if she were going into the desert and needed her fill of life-giving water before she left. After tonight, she did not know when she would see her again.

Olivia had been dogging her friend all day; no wonder Egg had sought a cup with Mrs. Fields in the housekeeper's room. She took both of Egg's hands, gently smoothing her thumbs over the glossy pink scars, and gave them a gentle squeeze. "Be easy, Egg, I will be fine."

Her friend's eyes widened, as if she somehow knew this was more than a simple assurance. Olivia touched her cheek and hurried to leave the room. She was almost out the door when she stopped. "Egglet…"

"Yes, my dear?"

"I always wanted to know. Was it red?"

Egg's brow creased and she shook her head. "Red? I'm afraid I do not understand, my dear."

Olivia forced the words out. "Jamie—my baby. Was Jamie's hair red?"

Grief washed over Egg's face, and she placed both hands over her breast. "Oh, my dear heart." Egg took a step forward, reaching for Olivia, but then stopped. "Yes, my dearest. It was the downiest wisp of red."

Olivia nodded and smiled as tears welled in her eyes. "Yes, I thought so. Wes would have been so pleased." And she ran out.

\*\*\*\*

"Well?"

Daria nearly missed the table as she tossed her reticule and shut the door. Hells Harpy, would she never get used to his stealthy comings and goings?

Oh please just let me have a drink. She could almost feel the round, golden brandy against her tongue, filling her mouth, and warming her empty belly.

His arm whipped out, staying her. No luck.

"Do not ignore me, my dove. I would think you'd have learnt that lesson by now. Is everything in place?"

She shivered despite the closeness of the small room. She had been damned lucky to get any accommodations. The village was crawling with lords and their ladies all a flutter over the duke's betrothal ball. The pressure on her arm increased. Dimly she wondered what dress she would wear to cover the inevitable bruise. "The footman has been hired. He has the powder and will make sure Roydan gets the champagne."

"And what of the morning ride?"

Daria eyed the brandy, only a few steps away, but so far. So very far now.

"Speak up woman."

"Roydan did not ride. His stable boy exercised the horse."

He was quiet, too quiet. Daria rushed in to fill the deadly silence. "I am not God almighty. I cannot order the duke to ride." She jerked out of his reach knowing she would pay for it later. "I tell you he is not behaving as he ought. Believe me when I tell you, I used to set my clock by him when he came to me every Thursday." Now, with her hand on the bottle and relief only a pour away, she felt stronger. "He *always* came to me at ten.

And he has *always* ridden in the early morning."

"Very well, we will move on to the second plan. In fact I think it is better that the ball come off. I always love a drama."

**\*\*\*\***

Mrs. Fields was correct; the mask was a veritable crush.

Never mind the invitations being issued only in the last week. Never mind that most of the *ton* had already scattered across the land to their own country estates, in deep rustication. Or the fact that it generally required several days of travel to get to anywhere *near* Valmere. These things were a mere trifle next to the prospect of being present when the monk finally shuffled off his cowl. Those few who were fortunate enough to receive an invitation, and who were close enough to attend, would surely dine on the retelling over the next few Seasons.

Olivia could see most of the ballroom from her spot in the corner beside one of the huge casement windows. She wore her darkest dress, a hooded cloak, and a mask just to be safe, but with all the humanity jockeying for position to see and be seen, no one would notice one dark wallflower. All her things were packed and the note to Egg waiting on her dressing table. All that remained was to see the betrothal done.

She watched her Egglet and Lord Bertram take the floor and wished the world were a different place for her dearest friend. A world where Eglantine Wiggins could have her Bertram. Could there be a chance for Egg to have some happiness?

Though the Campbells were much in evidence, she had yet to see Rh—the duke.

As if on cue a man's figure appeared high above in the minstrel's gallery. His white-gloved hands lay stark against the aged-black, intricately carved railing. Heavy arched beams soared thirty or more feet to the ceiling, framing his wide shoulders. And then his face, so pale in the surrounding gloom.

She could not make out its expression, but he looked to be searching. Dear God, he was searching for her. She ducked but realized he would not be looking for a woman dressed in black, hovering by the walls. Her fingers bit into the casement molding, stopping her from pushing through the crowd and running up the stairs to him. Something, or someone, caught his gaze in the room below. She tried to see who had so thoroughly commanded his attention, but a sea of bodies and masks blocked her view. When she looked back to the gallery, he had disappeared.

She did not have to wait long. The duke came striding into the main room, parting everyone in his path. That path led straight to—*Blast, this bloody potted palm.* A hush fell over the ballroom. Heedless of her vow to remain hidden, she stepped further into the room. Just in time to see His Grace, the sixth Duke of Roydan, lead a very beautiful looking—

*Daisy.* Of course, he thought Daisy was she. Olivia never dreamed he would dare to dance with her. The ember of hope fluttered with life as the duke nodded to the gallery and the musicians began a lively cotillion.

As the two began the dance, so striking, so beautifully matched, it was as if she were observing her own dream playing out before her. Her love dancing with…well, herself. Other couples joined the pair, and the magic diminished.

She spied Lord and Lady Campbell. His lordship had removed his mask, his color very high, and his lady, with her furiously nodding plumes and fluttering fan, looked as if she might take flight at any moment. Olivia could not blame them. The duke had not yet danced with his intended.

The music ended with the duke and Daisy stopping directly in front of Olivia. The pair bowed and curtsied to each other. So polite, so correct. Society's rules so firmly in place, while Olivia's hopeful ember fought for life.

*I am here. Can't you feel my love? Turn and you will know; you will know it's me, your true love. Oh, please turn—please see me waiting.* But instead he pulled off his mask and shook his head, staring into Daisy's eyes. Eyes so like the color of her own. But in the next moment, Lord Campbell had the duke's arm and, not so gently, pulled him away.

Arabella came from the opposite direction to confront her maid.

"Daisy!" said Arabella, "you certainly know how to make an entrance. Should I be jealous?" But Daisy only laughed. "Truly, you look beautiful."

Daisy regally inclined her head, playing the grand lady to the hilt. And even went so far as to teasingly rap her mistress with her fan. "Daisy? La, Miss you are too forward. I am Mrs. Weston. Mrs. Olivia Weston. But I am very pleased to make your acquaintance, Miss Campbell. Indeed, I have been looking forward to it all night." She sank into an elegant curtsey.

"Cheeky baggage!" Arabella said, but the reproof came with a dimpled smile.

"And may I return the compliment and say you

look rather lovely yourself." Daisy flicked her fan open. "You see, I was hoping to meet my love tonight."

"Really, Mrs. Weston." Arabella laughed. "I think I might be able to arrange that."

Olivia wanted to dislike this young woman, but watching the delight she took in her maid's obvious enjoyment, Olivia could not help but approve.

Arabella took Daisy's arm and spoke more seriously, "It will be soon enough, my dear. You must be ready."

"Oh, I am more than ready, my dearest."

"Miss Campbell, I believe this is my dance?" A gentleman in a chartreuse ensemble bowed over Arabella's hand and whisked her away. Daisy, after watching the couple for a moment, abruptly moved away.

"Oh!" Olivia stepped backward as a man nearly trod on her toes. She had been so fixated on the pair of women she had not realized he was so close.

"Your pardon, ma'am," he said, already moving off.

An icy cold feeling washed over her. Where had she seen that mask before? She mentally shook herself. Now I am imagining ghosts. *Get a hold of yourself, Olivia.*

The gentleman seemed intent on catching up with someone. He stopped before Daisy and bowed.

Olivia released her held breath. Heavens, the man was no evil fiend; he was Daisy's love. Likely the feeling he'd given Olivia was passion and excitement, not malevolence. Had her despair begun to color love to feel terrible and foreboding?

Daisy turned away from her satyr-man—ever the

flirt, thought Olivia. But the man caught her hand and pulled her to him in an embrace. Wrapping her against him, they made for the nearest French doors. The maid stumbled and seemed to want to remove her mask, but her love quickly steadied her and half-carried her out and into the night.

"Well, Daisy, my dear," Olivia said softly to herself, "he is certainly eager enough. I hope he is everything you ever wanted. I will live through you tonight."

The music had stopped, and Lord Campbell stepped onto a raised dais with his lady and their daughter. A sob caught in her throat as the room hushed. Oh, thank God Daisy had got her dream; her own were about to die. But where was the duke? She scanned the room for his dark head.

"Ladies and Gentlemen, I am sure you are aware tonight is a remarkable evening."

Olivia registered the general applause. Her heart hammered in her breast like a bellows keeping the tiny glow within her alive.

*Where was he?*

This was it. The announcement that would finally douse her fantastical dream.

She needed this. She had waited all night to brand this image and these words onto her heart. She could bear it. She *must* bear it. There must not be a shred of hope left to torment her in the years to come.

She willed herself to remember the smallest of details—the smell of beeswax candles mixed with the heavy scent of lilies and too many hot bodies pressed together. The breeze ruffling the palm fronds, making an ever-shifting web of shadow on the gold-colored walls. The feel of a marble side table, remarkably cool under her gloved hand. And finally, the picture of Lord and Lady Campbell with their daughter between them. Only the very tip of Arabella's elaborate Aurora headdress could be seen flashing between her parents' heads.

But the picture was not complete.

*Where was he?* He should be there. She needed him to complete this final tableau.

But his lordship was speaking. It would be over in only a moment.

"—however it is made even more remarkable because my only child, Arabella, has just consented to be the sixth Duchess of Roydan!"

A huge cheer rang out and there he was.

Time seemed to wind down. Rhys, half-running into the room. People rushing forward. Rhys now up on the dais with the Campbells. Removing his mask to look down at a smiling Arabella.

It was done. The ember extinguished to a charred nub. Olivia tore off her mask. Jewel-toned gowns blurred with dark evening ensembles till they became one big wash, like an overworked watercolor, muddy and lifeless.

She stumbled out of the casement door, heading for the side path to the stables, and to her new life without him.

**** 

He could not find Olivia—if that woman even *was* her. His mind was so damned fuzzy. She could not have simply vanished?

Rhys ran into the ballroom; the music had stopped and someone was making an announcement of some kind. *What the devil?*

The entire evening had been a strange dream starting with his dance with Olivia, who wasn't Olivia—or was she? Could his senses be so off from only a few days of not seeing her? The woman's coloring was Olivia's, she had the same stature and gracefulness, but somehow the woman was not *his* Olivia. The smell was wrong, the texture of her skin, not as fine. There was no getting a proper look at her what with their blasted masks and the relentless capering required to perform a country dance. He must have drunk too much. But he couldn't have. He had gulped one glass of champagne earlier in the evening and only because a hired servant had practically thrust it at him. The bitter taste still lingered in his mouth. Why could he not focus?

"...more remarkable because my only daughter, Arabella"—was that Lord Campbell speaking? Rhys made his way to the man's side—"has just consented to be the sixth Duchess of Roydan!"

The room exploded into a cacophony of sound and motion. The company rushed forward to take his hand and wish him happy. The room shifted, the great chandelier becoming only a blur of light. Someone grabbed his arm and steadied him. It was Lord Campbell. He and Lady Campbell were on either side of him, smiling and murmuring thanks to a sea of masks that seemed to float before him. He was about to shout it was a mistake, that there was no betrothal, but just as he got enough breath in his lungs, Miss Campbell was thrust next to him, and he saw her frozen smile.

All the air for his protestation knotted within his

chest. Dear God, she was an innocent in this terrible drama. It was all too horribly late. He would not humiliate and ruin her.

He must find Olivia and explain. He just needed to see her, to try to make her understand. If only he could get some air. He jerked off his mask. The whole room exploded in a deafening cheer. Masks and turbans came off as the *ton* took this as their cue to abandon all decorum.

He climbed on the nearest chair trying to get a better vantage point. The revelers yelled again, "Speech! A Speech, Your Grace!" They were all pushing against him; he could not keep his balance. The last thing he remembered as he fell was an evil-looking horned mask—a satyr.

Then everything went black.

Chapter Twenty-Four

Rhys raced to the dower house as soon as he could get away, but she was gone.

Her room, which he insisted on entering, was neat and empty feeling. He jerked open the armoire and hope sprung up, but only for an instant. The cupboard was full, but only with the dresses he had bought her. The few things of hers were gone.

Mrs. Wiggins remained very quiet. Perhaps it was shock, but he could not spare her his questions. Yes, she had got a note, but it said practically nothing, only for "Egg" not to worry, and Olivia would write again in a few weeks' time. Mrs. Wiggins had looked up into his eyes and told him quietly to let Olivia go.

Apparently, she'd escaped in one short hour. The groom said, "I'm very sorry, Your Grace, but I thought it nothing to let Mrs. Weston have the carriage. She said she needed to attend a sick friend."

Obviously she had been planning to run away. *Where was his note? Where was his farewell?*

He had followed her as far as London and then lost the trail. That had been weeks ago.

Now back at Valmere, he was hoping to find some peace, some way of getting beyond Olivia Weston. He would steep himself in the memories and finally purge himself of her. Hell, he knew the plan was ridiculous, but he had nothing else.

As mild as the summer had been, September blew in harsh and cold. Still, he spent long hours in their cove, putting his hands in tide pools she had touched. Ignoring the weather, as it suddenly blew hard and lightning ripped open the black sky, he plunged into the freezing water hoping he might not win against the huge pounding waves and the deadly rocks that lay beneath.

Utterly spent, he found himself pushing open the door of Sea Cottage.

After the timpani of the storm, the cottage sang its own more-muted song. The steady thrum of rain at the windows, the soft groan of ancient timbers, and the methodical drip that plopped from the chimney piece into the fire box, all served to heighten the emptiness of the room.

No one had been here. The square of paper he had wedged between the door and its frame had been firmly in place. He crushed it in his hand. Everything was as they had left it, a glass jar with its layers of colored sand, a wine bottle covered in runnels of wax, a nub of candle still in its neck. The shag feathers, collected one by one, and placed in a jar like a bouquet by the bed— so convenient for delicious torture. He stood dimly aware of a puddle forming around his boots. She had not cared how wet the floor got. They would clean it later...

He sagged, legs shaking. He longed to curl up on their bed, but could not bear to disturb its tidy coverlet, one she had smoothed with her own hands. Images of her—them—lying there streamed over him and settled around his heart, constricting it. And the rug before the fire was even more perilous with memories.

A sudden flash at the west window and thunder boomed, jarring him from his malaise; the paper he held dropped into the puddle. Rhys shivered as an icy trickle found his nape. No, he would not find rest here.

He ended up back at the dower house, now long empty, except for the small bedchamber he used to take his rest. Other than the drawing room, he had never really been here with her. He spent long hours wandering the gardens and the various rooms. He'd open her bedchamber door and imagine her at her dressing table, or run his hands over the gowns that still hung exactly where she had left them—well, all except the buttercup-yellow dress which he had taken and one of her chemises—one that still held a wisp of her scent.

About to turn for home, Rhys remembered the attics. He had never been up there. It seemed important he comb through every corner of the house so that no hint of her whereabouts might be left undiscovered.

He ascended the cramped stairway and opened the door. Hot, heavy air engulfed him, and his candle flame flickered and almost guttered. He pushed the door wider, hoping fresh air would save his light. Raising it high, he looked into the shadows. His hand jerked and he almost lost the light again. A ghostly ring surrounded him. It took a moment to recognize them as paintings, *her* paintings, propped on old chairs and broken easels, shrouded under white dust covers.

He did not want to look. It would be like ripping off a bandage where the wound had just begun to crust over. After a flurry of movement he stood utterly still among the wreckage of white pooled around his feet.

He had never seen paintings like this. They looked almost unfinished with their jarring slashes of pure color overlaying delicate washes. They were mostly land and seascapes—the cove, the west wing of Valmere with the sea below, a flock of shags taking flight over a placid sea.

He did not know how long he stood, soaking up their wild beauty. But eventually he moved further under the eaves, drawn to the very back of the room where, half hidden, a few canvases leaned against the wall.

One by one he turned them. They were her portraits. Mrs. Wiggins and her roses, a cat, Reverend Hargett with the Norman abbey as a backdrop, and even old Toby, his long nose settled between his paws. And then there was him.

He was naked, lying in the surf on the beach, his face thrust up to the waning sun. The picture was dark except for a bit of bright sun lighting half his face.

He finally reached out to touch the canvas; drawn to become one with that man who lay in darkness, but who looked toward hope and life.

He could not lose that hope. He must find her. He must.

\*\*\*\*

Olivia had taken the duke's carriage as far as Thetford and then changed to the mail coach. Once in London, she had sought out Hazel and Jeb, now newly married. They had immediately taken her in, but she knew she could not stay long. They could not afford to keep her, and Olivia had no money to contribute.

Busy with a bit of lace work, she startled when Hazel burst in the room and pushed the latest paper under Olivia's nose.

"He's getting pretty desperate now, I would say,"

she pointed to what must be the duke's latest notice. "I may not be able to read well, but I can certainly decipher a number, even one that high."

Olivia felt slightly nauseated. She had to get out of London as soon as possible. It would only be a matter of time before he found her. And she, most assuredly, did not want to be found.

The carefully folded bit of paper that announced the Duke of Roydan and Miss Arabella Campbell's betrothal lay in her pocket always within reach. Whenever she felt weak, she would take it out and make herself read every word. She would not be his mistress. She could not share him. Yet she would give just about anything to see his face once again.

Her eyelids closed but his image only became clearer. She shook her head and the news sheet in her hands rattled. *Enough.* She smoothed the paper and moved on... A name jumped out at her.

"The solicitors of Finney and Cobb are looking for a Mr. August Allen Hartner to assume the title of the Earl of Stokesly."

The paper dropped to her lap. Her father was dead.

\*\*\*\*

Heavily veiled, Olivia sat in Mr. Finney's office pleating her handkerchief into precise folds as the solicitor perused a sheaf of papers. Emotions shifted across his face, first concern, then incredulity, now sympathy, and finally back to concern. Olivia was ready to throttle the old fellow. Finally, he spoke.

"I am sorry to inform you, Mrs. Weston, but the earl, your father, left nothing but debts behind. Fortunately they will be the new heir's responsibility along with the heavily mortgaged estate."

"Do you know how he died? The papers gave no particulars."

The man sucked on his teeth and then looked down at his papers. "Yes, he had been out of the country for some time—nearly thirteen years." He looked up. "You must have been quite young."

"I was ten and seven years."

Shortly after her disastrous season. Her father's last words to her and her step-mama: *You both are worthless to me. One can't breed and the other can't catch a husband. I wish you both to the Devil.*

Mr. Finney's face folded itself back into concern. "He was found in the city of New Orleans. I am afraid the circumstances were not very honorable, Lady Olivia."

Lady Olivia…the title so utterly foreign to her ears.

"And my step-mother?

"She left the country six months ago. I know only because she came to me in March, claiming that your father must be dead, and she was surely entitled to some monies. When I told her there was nothing, she declared she would go abroad. I believe the countess settled in Canada. I can try to find a direction if you—"

"No. No, I thank you. That will not be necessary." Bile rose in her throat. She swallowed, remembering she had not had anything to eat today. She would risk going to a tea shop for a hot cup and a biscuit. She began to rise.

"However, Lady Olivia, your mother left you a small dowry and a parcel of land at the very corner of the estate, which is outside the entailment. We tried to find you, but your step-mama did not know of your where-a-bouts. I believe the plot contains a small

314

farmhouse and a barn," he said, consulting his notes.

The Point. Her mother had named it so. She had used some of her family's jewelry to buy the land. "Who needs baubles when one can have a garden full of carrots and a lovely chicken or two?" her mother had said. Olivia's father had been furious when he looked to sell the missing jewelry. But the scruffy barn and tiny cottage was her mother's haven. It was where Olivia had painted her purple tree...

*Was the old tree still there, and would it still look purple?*

Well, she sent up a silent prayer, she would soon find out.

****

The nearby church bell tolled three times. So late? Rhys reached for his fob out of habit. It was time for tea. He had eaten nothing since this morning, his breakfast being interrupted by his solicitors Fink and Ponzer. And then by Sir Richard of Bow Street.

Mrs. Dee Gooden had been found dead, her body tortured and mutilated. His father's codicil leaving Dee Gooden Valmere unless Rhys married had loomed over Rhys's life for almost a year. It now shrunk back down to a few harmless words conceived by a bitter, old man.

Rhys had never wanted his father's whore to get her hands on Valmere, but he could not wish for her death either. And such a terrible one. Apparently, the Reverend, her brother, had barely been able to recognize her, but in the end a clear identification was made. There had been no arrests and the Reverend, given Mrs. Gooden's past, was all too willing to put the matter to rest along with his sister.

Valmere was safe. But the fact left Rhys empty.

What did it matter now? The house and grounds were too full of memories. He had not been back since the wedding.

His stomach growled. The hunt for undiscovered treasures had lost its savor. Rhys raised his hand to signal his waiting servants who stood with the carriage farther down the block. Then he saw the painting.

He froze. He *knew* this painting.

He knew the bluffs and the way they jutted out over the sea. He knew the light at that time of day and how it caught the spray of the water where it pulsed into the cove crashing up onto a huge rock that lay in its mouth.

But even more than the landscape, he *knew* the figure standing on the bluff, the set and width of the shoulders, the length of the back, the stance. But mostly he knew the mind. Though the figure was murky and indistinct—almost anonymous—the artist had managed to capture its terrible anguish.

It was he.

And *she* had painted it.

Rhys heard a cough to his right. He jerked around spreading his arms, as if to protect the poor soul on the rock from prying eyes.

"Your Grace, will you come?" His footman held out his hand as if Rhys were some doddering old fool. He waved him off.

This was intolerable. Any passerby could see and know. Know that it was he there on display in all his vulnerability. Just like Hannah Humphrey's shop when she had exhibited that Gillray trash. Yet he saw no one, only his servants by the carriage whispering among themselves. He pushed into the shop.

The young clerk, startled by Rhys's abrupt entrance, nearly dropped his polishing cloth. Rhys reached into the window and yanked the painting out of the display.

The clerk, whom Rhys had never seen before, twisted his rag, clearly torn between summoning his employer, Mr. Bottoms, and trying to deal with Rhys himself. He had a chance to do neither.

"Where did you get this?"

The young man gaped like a fish. Rhys could see the poor boy registering Rhys's upper-class tones and authoritative bearing, juxtaposed against his rumpled linen and coat, his too-long hair and bristled face. Rhys allowed him to teeter for a moment.

Luckily for the young man, he correctly slid Rhys over into the category of Quality instead of riff-raff.

"Your lordship has a very good eye, why—"

"Where."

"Your pardon, sir, it is a new acquisition, I believe. A Monsieur Oy-eff is the painter if I am not mistaken, which means"—he paused, pulling his shoulders back to better demonstrate his acumen—"Egg in fren—"

"Get your employer."

Again, the fish mouth.

"Now." The mouth closed.

"Yes, your lordship. Right away, your lordship." He bowed and backed away, heading, as if his posterior had eyes of its own, directly for the shop's back room where he reached for the knob, still bent in supplication, and disappeared.

*Oeuf.* How clever.

By God, he could *feel* her.

As he stared at himself in the painting, he felt, if he

turned, she would be there, on the beach below with her canvas and brushes.

"Your Grace! What an honor." Mr. Atticus Bottoms's familiar pear-like figure minced into the room, his old-fashioned bob wig slightly askew, a crumb of pastry on his lips. "Gibbons, why did you not tell me that it was the duke who was waiting?"

The clerk attempted to stammer a rejoinder.

"Where did you acquire this?" Rhys asked for it seemed the thousandth time, his nerves severely stretched.

"Gibbons." The clerk jerked forward as if his employer held a leash. "Bring me the file on the seascape. His Grace would know all the particulars."

Once again, the young man bowed his way out, disappearing into the back room.

Mr. Bottoms smiled in anticipation. "A beauty, Your Grace. If I may be so bold, one feels the turmoil of the lone figure on the precipice, as if he is in the throes of some weighty—"

"Damn it, man, I am buying the thing. Spare me your salesmanship."

Mr. Bottoms attempted to speak again, but Rhys raised an eyebrow.

Blessed silence, except for the ticking of various clocks situated about the room. Their measured strokes usually steadied Rhys's nerves, rounding off the staccato edges of his thoughts, but now they only ratcheted them up. Suddenly the whir of gears yielded to a chorus of bongs as the clocks announced the top of the hour. A cuckoo, slightly late, warbled to finish off the cacophony.

Rhys curled his toes tightly within his boots.

Bottoms eyes shifted from the errant cuckoo, to the duke, and back. Gibbons appeared holding out one thin sheet of paper as if it were the Holy Grail.

Bottoms snatched it and fumbled for his spectacles.

"Ah yes, here we are, Your Grace. A Monsieur Oeuf. French for Egg, I believe." The shopkeeper looked up expectantly, as if to catch Rhys's approval. He received none. "Ahem…yes, Oeuf, very talented. It was brought in just last week."

"Where can I find Monsieur Oeuf?"

Mr. Bottoms scanned the paper, frowning.

"This is the second work we have acquired. The agent was no one I had ever dealt with before, and as you know, I am very careful with my acquisitions. After all, I have a reputation to maintain. Can't let just anyone in to ply his wares, don't you know. I was about to show him the door, but I happened to get a look at the painting as he was leaving, and I must say I was struck. It was another seascape, Your Grace, with two figures in the distance and a flock of birds which seemed to be following them—very riveting. Needless to say, I called him back."

"His name and direction."

"He would give no name, pardon, Your Grace, he said if I wanted the painting it would have to be on *his* terms. I almost showed him the door for a second time. I don't deal in stolen goods, Your Grace. I never have, never will. I always say, 'A man may not have much, but if he has his reputation he is well enough.'"

"Describe the man."

"Yes, well, let me see…a rather good-looking young chap, wouldn't you say, Gibbons?" The young man gave a reluctant nod. "About two and twenty, I would say…Possibly younger. Ginger-colored hair, one of these dandies you know. But there is no accounting for these young people's tastes these days."

Gibbons tapped his employer and whispered in his ear.

"Oh, yes, quite. I was getting to that, Gibbons." The clerk dutifully nodded. "He was sporting a beauty of a watch. An extremely fine Henlein with a pierced leaf design. Unparalleled to my view. Wouldn't sell, though. A pity, that."

Something of the man's description registered in Rhys's mind, but he could not spare the time to make the connection.

"You say he will be back with more work?"

"No doubt, Your Grace. I told him I had a prospective buyer for the painting already, and I would be very pleased to accept any others he cared to bring me, if they were of the same quality. I will be very happy to send word when another comes into the shop."

"Yes, do that. I want to know the minute the man returns." He turned to leave.

"Your Grace!"

Rhys turned back.

"Pardon, sir, I did not have a chance to tell you before, you seemed so immersed in the work, but I am very much afraid that particular painting has been sold."

"Sold?"

"Yes, as I mentioned, Your Grace, the gentleman who bought the first painting said he would take any others. I have yet to contact him about this newest offering—I must say I wanted to revel in its splendor before consigning it to a private home. The world should see this painting."

"What is his name?"

"I am afraid he did not give his name. But a woman was with him. It was she who gave me the draft for the painting. Indeed, I believe you may know the woman, Your Grace."

Rhys heart jumped in his throat. "Was the name Weston? Olivia Weston?"

"Weston? No, Your Grace. The name was Battersby. Daria Battersby."

Rhys tightened his grip on the painting. "Daria Battersby?"

"Yes, Your Grace"—another glance at the paper before him—"a Mrs. Daria Battersby."

Rhys forced himself to relax, schooling his features into a mask.

"I will deal with her and give you twice what she paid. And consider any others that come in to be sold to me." He started out of the shop but turned at the door. "I want to know the minute you see the red-headed man again. You will send word immediately."

****

Where was Jeb? Olivia pushed back the curtain and scanned the yard again. Likely all the rain had delayed him. Hazel, more impatient, had gone out to the woods to look for Dumpling, who had gone missing again. Somehow the bird always managed to escape the coop when the weather turned wet and muddy.

Olivia dipped her hand into her apron pocket, feeling the worn edge of Egg's letter. She had taken to carrying it, folded alongside the duke's betrothal announcement. She supposed it was silly, but she felt closer to Egg with the letter always within reach.

Poor Eglantine, with only that brief note Olivia left on the night of the ball and then one other written from London within the first week of her leaving. Jeb had posted it from Brompton and fifteen days later, to her utter surprise, she had received a letter in return.

They had just moved into the farmhouse and Hazel, who had been out with the cows had run in from the barn at Olivia's shriek.

"What? What's amiss?" She ran to Jeb, her apron dripping wet milk.

Jeb simply grinned.

"We have just received a letter from Lady Bertram!" Olivia laughed.

"Lady Bertram?" She looked between the two of them; sure she was part of a joke. "Who in the bloody blazes is Lady Bertram? And it better be good because I have just spilled half our morning's milk on the barn floor. Prudence and Chastity are sure to be in heaven."

"Perhaps I should say Eglantine Wiggins Merrick, Lady Bertram."

It was a good thing Hazel had left her milk pail in the barn with the cats, or Olivia was sure the other half would have been lost as well.

"Cor! You're jesting Miss O," she said, and then looked to Jeb who only grinned.

Olivia cleared her throat, smoothed the letter, and began to read.

"'I was so very worried when you left, and I did not know how or where you would live. The duke was—

"Never mind that." Olivia moved on.

"'I could not go on with my deception to Bertram, and so I told him all. He was very angry at first, and rightly so. He used the word 'betrayal' and I tell you the look on his dear face cleaved my heart in two. But, not long after, he came to me and said he could not abide a lie, and we would have to set about remedying that lie. You can imagine how very shocked I was when he got down on his knee and asked me to be his very own lady; his wife! We were married by special license on the fifteenth of September. I am going to trust that you will be well, as Bertram very much wants to show me Venice and Rome. We will likely be gone till the New Year, I suspect. Please, I beg you, to write me again as soon after that as you can. Indeed I will not be steady if I do not have a letter waiting for me. Your dearest, Egglet'"

The letter was a tattered and well-loved mess now, being nearly five months old. Egg would surely be back from her wedding trip soon, if not already. Jeb was to check the posting inn at Brompton when he left Mr. Bottoms's shop. Just another reason Olivia was on tenterhooks. While she longed for a letter from Egg, she dreaded what tidings the new Lady Bertram might have of the duke.

He was likely married by now, though she had heard nothing of the marriage. But then she had stopped getting the papers when they had moved to the Point. And news, even of that magnitude, would never find its way to their tiny corner of the world.

Olivia grabbed her cloak. She needed to get out of the house. Perhaps they would have chicken for dinner…

Chapter Twenty-Five

Daria's maid stood as sentinel, squarely in front of the door, but when she saw it was the duke, she quickly moved aside. The woman was fiercely loyal but never a fool.

He found Daria in the back sitting room next to a roaring fire.

She was much altered. She looked so much smaller. It had only been a few months, but her soft, fleshy roundness had collapsed, her skin falling into slack, watery folds. She sat huddled in a large shawl, though the room was quite warm.

"What have you to do with Olivia Weston?" he demanded.

"How dare you burst into my private rooms and talk to me of that harlot." But her voice sounded dull and lifeless.

"Have you forgotten, madam, I pay for this house?" He charged across the room to her writing desk and began to look through her mess of papers. "And isn't that rather the pot calling the kettle black?"

"You are in quite a state, Monsieur Monk."

There was nothing but bills and ladies magazines. Disgusted, Rhys crossed back to her and leaned over her chair. "I am not in the mood for your games, Daria. Tell me what you were doing purchasing a painting of Mrs. Weston's."

"You, my dear duke, have gone mad. I do not have the slightest notion of what you are ranting about. Now get out, you are blocking the fire." She reached for a bottle by her elbow.

Rhys stayed her hand. "You will answer me now, or shall I call in the Runners? It is your choice, but I warn you, you will fare much better talking to me."

"You wouldn't dare," she said, trying to get the bottle.

Clearly Daria had replaced food with drink. Rhys held the brandy away from her. "Then you had better not test me, woman. Speak up."

"I know nothing of a painting." She adjusted her shawl. "She came to me some months ago spouting some wild nonsense. She had the audacity to accuse me of starting that paltry fire at her shop. I sent her packing. I have not seen her since."

Rhys leaned in closer. "God help you if you did, Daria. God help you."

"Oh, do back away. You know I would never stoop to such loathsome dramatics." But her gaze would not meet his.

He backed away, afraid he might throttle her. "What do you know of a Monsieur Oeuf?"

"Monsieur Oeuf? As in Egg?"

"Yes, by God, the painter, Mr. Oeuf!"

She only gave him a blank look.

"Do you deny you were in Mr. Atticus Bottoms's shop last week and purchased a painting?"

"Oh that dreadful, dark thing? Lord, I would not have it on my walls for anything, all globs of paint slapped onto the poor canvas. You could not even tell if the people were meant to be lovers." She snorted and eyed the bottle, wetting her lips. "I don't know why he was so keen on the horrid thing. It was atrocious. I told him as much, but he insisted on having it."

Rhys set down the bottle, grasped the arms of her chair and leaned in. "Who insisted?"

Daria shut her mouth.

"Who was he, damn it? I know there was a man with you."

Daria drew herself up a little straighter in her chair. "A friend."

Rhys studied her for a long moment. Then he straightened and pulled the shawl from around her neck and shoulders. "Not much of a 'friend,' Daria. You are a fool to protect such a one."

Daria covered the bruises on her neck. Her other arm lay useless, encased in a sling.

"Dee Gooden is dead," He said and Daria's gaze snapped to his. The first sign of life he had seen in her. "The body was nearly unrecognizable. I have no idea if this 'friend' of yours is responsible, but make no mistake, I will find out. Are you sure you have nothing to tell me?"

She turned her head away from him and toward the fire. "Get out," she said quietly. "Get out and leave me alone. I will tell you nothing." She reached for the brandy.

He believed her. He turned and left the room.

As Rhys mounted his horse, he felt a tug on his cloak. He turned to see Foster, Daria's maid.

"It was Lord Biden, Your Grace," the maid said. "Oscar Biden. That's who done this to her."

*Oscar Biden?* Then it came to him. Lord Biden had been a favorite cohort of Rhys's father. Rhys nodded to the maid and shortened his reins. But the woman grabbed him again.

"You'll see that he pays, won't you, Your Grace?"

"You may be assured of that, Foster," he said, meeting her pleading gaze. "Thank you." And he set his heels to Sid.

"Biden," Rhys cursed under his breath. Daria had indeed, sunk low. He'd heard the rumors, like everyone else. What if the man had Olivia?

Rhys spurred Sid on, urging his mount to go faster through the gathering gloom.

At White's the majordomo had no information. "Lord Biden has not been a member for a number of years, Your Grace." The man's pursed lips made it very clear Biden had not chosen to quit the exclusive gentlemen's club. "We attempted to send several bills to a residence in Dudley Street, but we were told his lordship had long departed that particular house and the landlord had no information as to his new apartments."

Still, Rhys went to Dudley Street. The landlord mentioned having to turn away several unscrupulous characters who came to call upon Biden. None resembled Dee Gooden. He recognized one or two as moneylenders. Biden had departed in the middle of the night owing five months rent. The man frowned. "I cannot be sure, but I believe there was some rumor as to his leaving for the continent."

Rhys pushed on to some of the seedier Hells throughout the city asking about moneylenders, but no one he contacted had seen the man.

The next morning Rhys went to the docks, but if Biden had departed the country, he had not used his real name.

The next three days brought no new information to light. Rhys spent every night in some brothel or gambling Hell and his days in the City with moneylenders or haunting Mr. Bottoms's shop.

He had just come from seeing a Mr. Ephraim Kline who had lent Biden fifty pounds just over three months ago. Mr. Kline would pay good money to anyone who found Biden.

If only this infernal rain would stop. The London roads were like a stew—a thick brown gruel with bits of unrecognizable stuff sloshing up against one's boots. And with the turn of unseasonably warm weather, the stench of summer had returned. Rhys dumped his soaking greatcoat and beaver in Safley's arms. The butler frowned at the muddy puddle collecting on the floor.

"Your Grace." Wilcove held out a note. "This came for you about an hour and a quarter ago. The young man, Gibbons, I be—"

"Gibbons?" Rhys tore the note open. "I need a horse. Now!"

****

"Your Grace, I am desolate!" Mr. Bottoms yapped at Rhys's heels like a terrier after a rat. "The young rube did not know what he had. This piece was quite different from Monsieur Ouef's last works. It was pastoral and almost serene, but that is the impression only at first glance. One must look deeper and *feel* rather than *see* the turmoil hidden beneath the layers of paint." The duke stopped his pacing and turned to silence the man. But Mr. Bottoms, mistakenly thinking he finally had the duke's attention, spread his arms wide in a grand gesture and made his hands into claws

328

"That great yew tree crowded into the corner of the scene, yet lowering over the whole painting."

"Have done! How do you imagine the description of a bloody painting will help us?" Rhys began pacing again. How could one think with that man yammering about turmoil and trees? "The boy gave no hint as to his direction?"

"No, Your Grace. But I—that is Gibbons—" Mr. Bottoms pulled at one of the side curls of his wig, until it canted ridiculously over his ear.

"Go on, man. You must tell me everything."

"Well, Your Grace, Gibbons happened to let slip it was you who wanted the painting." Rhys took a step closer. Bottoms cringed as if preparing for an attack on his person, and his next words came in a rush. "When the boy heard that, he took off like a jack rabbit." Rhys wheeled away lest he actually give in to his urge to do damage to the man. "I immediately sent Gibbons to fetch you just as you directed," said Bottoms, nearly in tears. "I was unable to follow the lad. I could not leave the shop, and it was raining again. I was all on my own—"

But Rhys heard no more as he left the shop yet again. The door banged shut behind him, and the wind and wet took over. *Where to look?* He squinted through the rain, looking up and down and into the alley.

Nothing.

Then he saw it. A passing coach's lantern flared on the object. Rhys leapt toward the gutter, thrusting his hands into the muck before he lost his sense of the thing's placement.

It was a watch. Smashed and broken, but had been a fine piece. Dear God, he recalled something Bottoms had said about a fine watch.

Rhys rushed back into the shop. "Is this the young man's watch?"

Bottoms took only a moment. "Why yes, Your Grace! It is the Henlein I was telling you of. I was devastated not—"

Rhys flipped the case over. Blood. Bottoms gasped.

But Rhys was halfway across the shop, headed for the alleyway.

His brain went into an analytical frenzy. The watch had stopped at twelve. There was no minute hand on a watch this old, but Mr. Bottoms said the boy had arrived shortly after Gibbons had set out a pot of tea. They usually had tea at twelve. Bottoms had offered the young man refreshment in the hopes of prolonging his stay. But once spooked, the young man must have left within the next ten minutes or so, which would put the time at approximately a quarter past twelve. He would have been attacked within that hour. The dark, cave-like alley seemed the most logical place.

The rain had nearly stopped, now falling as only a soft tap onto his hat and into puddles. Rhys drew a knife from his boot and stepped into the mouth of the alley. Something skittered off to his left, and a dog barked in the distance.

Black eaves and jagged rooftops slanted over the narrow alleyway, blocking out what little light there was. A sudden wind blew and broken shutters creaked and flapped against the brick and mortar. But worse than the dark and eerie noises, was the smell of urine sharp in his nose, mixed with garbage so rank you could cut it with a knife. And something else...

*Was that a groan?* He turned toward the sound. Taking a few tentative steps, he slipped on some slimy filth. He reached out to catch an old sagging door, ripping it half off its hinges. The alley sprang to life like a candle's flare as disturbed creatures scurried from their hidden safety. Then, just as sudden, all was silent again.

The sweet smell of iron. Bile rose in his mouth and he swallowed. He had not slipped because of refuse. He needed no light to know he stood in a pool of blood. He had found the poor young man. His knife held before him, Rhys hefted the door back with his other hand.

*Oh, bloody Hell.* What he could see of the body before him was truly piteous.

Using the old door as a stretcher, he and Gibbons carried the boy into the shop, Mr. Bottoms fussing the entire way.

Rhys immediately sent Gibbons for the nearest doctor and then on to Roydan House for the duke's carriage and Dr. Asher.

Rhys did not know if the boy would live. As yet he had not regained consciousness.

"Hazel," the young man groaned.

Rhys leaned closer. "You are going to be fine, lad. We have the doctor on his way. All will be well."

"I must go—" He tried to rise, only to gasp in agony.

"You must not attempt to move. You have been badly beaten and likely have some broken ribs." Rhys leaned closer. "Can you tell me who did this to you?"

The young man's gaze focused on Rhys. "You are the duke, the Duke of Roydan." He tried to smile through his torn lips. "I did not tell him—" Then he lost consciousness again.

"Damnation!"

The doctor came, and the young man, Jeb, gained and lost consciousness several more times. Rhys was able to ascertain it was Biden who attacked Jeb, but the boy assured Rhys he had not told Biden where Miss Olivia was staying. He was quite proud of that.

"Young man." Mr. Bottoms hovered over the patient. "I was wondering if you might know the whereabouts of the painting you had been carrying?"

"Confound it, man"—Rhys nearly wrenched the man out of his wig—"have done with your nattering. Can't you see the poor boy is in a dire way? And you talk of paintings?"

"The painting!" Jeb jerked up, almost losing consciousness again.

Rhys turned back to the lad. "Settle yourself, boy. No one will hold you account—"

Jeb rolled his head back and forth, moaning. "Oh, God, you don't understand, he has the painting. The old tree and the—he knows where she is!" He tried to get up again.

"Be still!" Rhys barked. "What are you saying?"

"It's of the Point."

"The Point?"

"The painting is of the old tree and the farmhouse. Biden, he knows that house. He knows where she is." He sobbed. "God help her."

Rhys grabbed his shoulders, "Where?" Jeb winced, hissing in a breath. Rhys made his hands relax. He took a steadying breath. "Where Jeb, where is the Point?"

The boy blinked in obvious pain, fighting to remain conscious. Locking eyes with Jeb, Rhys willed his own strength to seep into the boy's broken body. *Please, God, don't let him pass out again.*

"Stokesly Hall. The Earl of Stokesly's estate. Near Twickham." Then Jeb collapsed.

Oh, God. Twickham was fourteen hours' hard ride from London.

## Chapter Twenty-Six

*Was he too late?*

He knew from the various inns where he had changed horses that he had been gaining on Biden, but was it enough? At the last posting house there had been only one horse to spare. Rhys decided to leave his curricle and ride the last leg of the journey. As he and his newest mount, June, rode up to Stokesly Hall, the house and yard were in chaos. A huge traveling coach and several others carrying baggage were bunched before the portico. Rhys did not even dismount.

"You there," he yelled to a young footman. "I am looking for a cottage somewhere at the edge of this property."

The servant's eyes scanned Rhys's mud-spattered boots and cloak, ending with his, no doubt, haggard face shadowed by whiskers. Rhys clenched his jaw. He wasn't used to being looked over and found wanting. But clearly the young man did not want to send a fox to a henhouse.

He seemed to have passed muster. "You'll be meaning the Point, sir."

Rhys nodded. "Yes, the Point. I need the direction."

"It's about sixteen or more miles down this road." The man pointed to a smallish track leading off the main drive. Rhys's hopes collapsed. Still so far to go.

The servant must have read his disappointment. "But you can get there in half the time if you go by the fields." Gesturing to the northwest, he pointed to the beginnings of a wilderness path to the left of the house. "You'll have to take a few fences though." The man gave June a dubious look.

"Hodgkins! Give a hand here with this trunk." The young man pulled his forelock. "Just be sure to keep the sun over your left shoulder, sir," and he turned to go.

"One more thing, man!" Rhys shouted. "Have you seen any other horse or equipage come this way?"

"No, sir, just the new earl's carriages."

Rhys dug in his purse and flipped him a coin. The young man caught it in a flash of his hand.

The weak sun had long disappeared in the cloud cover, but even if it had shown its face, he could not have seen it for the dense forest. Rhys reached for his watch, only to find his fob. "Damn it all."

June snorted and stumbled, the poor beast almost done. A while back she had balked at one of the fences, almost unseating him. Valuable time had been lost soothing her.

He had just decided he must try for the road, when he saw it—the huge yew—rising above the other trees. The cottage must be near. It *must* be. He picked his way through the trees, carefully marking the direction of the yew. The forest gave way to an open field. There it was, the old tree with a house beyond.

*But was he too late?*

Keeping to the tree line, no other horse or carriage appeared in the yard, he guided June to the barn. Shards of pain shot up from his feet as he hit the ground and his legs collapsed. He grabbed for a stirrup, and June sidled away in protest. His body cramped with fatigue but he pushed up on his legs and they held. Flipping the reins over June's neck, Rhys pushed her toward the water trough and pulled out his pistol.

He knew he should stop and take stock of the situation. He knew he should plan the best approach for the surest success, but all he could think of was getting to her, seeing her and holding her within his arms.

First staggering, and then, as his legs began working, running, he burst into the cottage. The painting lay on a large work table.

*He was too late.*

The blow came out of nowhere. His pistol dropped, clattering to the floor. Rhys slammed into something. Glass and crockery rained down on him. He shook his head, attempting to get his focus back, trying to blot out the pain. But worse than the physical pain, was the pain of disappointment. *He was too late.*

Blood ran into his eyes. He swiped at it with his forearm and blindly reached out, his fingers finding the shape of a broken bottle. Crouching he took a step forward, dimly registering the crunch of glass under his feet, as he waved the bottle in front of him. *Where was the bloody pistol? And where was Biden?*

The blood kept coming, running into his mouth and down his neck. His shin connected with a piece of furniture—a chair—he threw it aside.

"Where is she, you bloody bastard?" He needed Biden to say something, to gauge his whereabouts.

Floorboards creaked to the left of him—the gun must be in that direction.

Rhys charged toward the sound.

His shoulder caught a large body full in the chest

and smashed him into the far wall. A hand gripped his wrist and twisted; the bottle dropped and shattered. But Rhys landed a good uppercut to Biden's ribs and another to his face before Biden backed away.

"Oh, Roydan, you disappoint me. Such a shoddy show. I would have thought you would mount a much more strategic attack." Biden laughed. "You must be over your ears in love to forget yourself so."

Rhys ripped his shirt-tail out of his breeches and used it to wipe his eyes.

Biden. Definitely an older version, but looked to be very fit. Given Rhys's sluggish mind and extreme fatigue, it would be a very even fight.

The man leaned causally against the wall and smoothed his hair back, like some bored courtier. But on closer inspection perhaps his stance might have more to do with the damage to his ribs. Rhys hoped so.

The room was larger than he thought, but there were no hidden nooks where Olivia might hide. Stairs led up to what he supposed were bedchambers above. The door to the kitchen stood open. A patterned apron hung over a chair tucked beneath a large table. The pistol, nowhere.

"A pity we have no foils," Biden rubbed his jaw line as he pushed off the wall and circled to the large fireplace. "Now that would be a match."

Biden's eyes gave him away, glancing one too many times to the wood pile next to the hearth. He had spied the gun. Rhys dove and reached the pistol first.

"Ah, my dear boy." Biden held his hands before him as he backed away toward the door. "You would not dare to shoot a peer of the realm in cold blood, would you? No, it goes against your monkish tendencies." Biden smiled. "You are bluffing."

"On the contrary, Biden, when I see a rabid dog, I kill it without a qualm."

He cocked the trigger as a shadow filled the doorway.

*Olivia.*

His world wound down and time stuttered and then stopped altogether. The sun must be back out. It caught the edge of her hair making her into an angel. She was holding a basket—apples? The smell filled the air. With the sun behind her, her face was hidden in shadow. Oh, to see her smile at him. She stepped forward and there it was—

Olivia hitched the basket of apples to her other hip. Jeb was back early. The cottage door stood open. The old mare she had seen in the yard must be his newest rescue. After giving him a big hug, she would have to scold him for letting the heat out and possibly a chicken or two in.

Olivia blinked in the threshold of the doorway. The cottage light, or lack of it, was always an adjustment after being out-of-doors. "Jeb?" The shadowed man came into focus.

*Rhys.* Dear heavens, Rhys stood not ten feet from her.

Like the string of a child's top being pulled, the world whirled back to life. An arm snaked around her neck, another under her breasts, trapping her arms within her cloak. Apples spilled, rolling across the floor.

"Ah, my sweeting, you have arrived just in time to join our little party. Perhaps you would be so good, Roydan, as to lower that pistol. It is not a very mannerly way to greet our newest arrival, is it, my dear?"

That voice lisping next to her ear, where had she heard that voice? *My God, no. Hadn't he died that night?* She tried to turn her head, but his arm remained like a vise around her neck. Rhys, his face now a frozen mask, slowly lowered the gun. An apple rolled to rest against the leg of the table, a period to their hideous situation.

"Now, lay it on the floor, and slide it to me."

Rhys hesitated. The arm synched tighter around her neck. She gagged. Rhys's mask flinched. He bent and did as he was told. The gun skittered across the floor knocking a few apples out of its path. It lay a few feet in front of them.

"Very good. Now step back, all the way to the far wall." Rhys retreated.

He was hurt. Blood streaked his face and soaked his shirt. Likely from the glass that littered the floor.

Biden's hand found her jaw, and he squeezed it like a nut in a cracker. "I have waited a very long time for this reunion of ours, my dear, nearly thirteen years. And it's time my patience was rewarded." Hot sour breath fanned her cheek.

"You can be very provoking, sweeting. When I saw you at Parkington's mask, I could not believe my eyes."

Dear God, he was the man in the satyr mask. No wonder her skin had crawled.

"I would not have credited it except for the fact that—if you will recall, Roydan—her gown did not cover much, and I happened to spy that delectable birthmark hovering just above this delightful derrière."

The heavy ridge of his cock pressed against her. She closed her eyes as if to cocoon herself. She must remain calm.

"Ah, I see you are intimately familiar with that bit of flesh, Roydan. Looks a bit like a heart, doesn't it? You see," Biden lisped in her ear, "I had given up finding you, Olivia Jayne, and there you were right under my nose. I was rather hurt you did not recognize me, but then I was wearing a mask...not to mention being fully clothed." Biden laughed.

"I must say, I liked what I saw. And by God it's high time I got what was due me. Don't you think bets should be honored, Roydan? Ah, but you perhaps don't know the particulars? Tut-tut, Olivia Jayne." Biden turned her to him, his hand now fisted in her hair.

Long buried images rushed to fill her chest, making it hard to breathe. The candlestick heavy in her hand. The thud as it smashed into his head. The small pair of sewing scissors sinking into his breast. And then the blood, so much blood. She had watched mesmerized as it gushed out soaking her bedding. So sure she had killed him. He still bore the scar near his temple, the puckered skin marring his handsome face.

One cold, blue eye twitched and his hideous grin pulled into a thin line. "Have you not been completely forthright with our charming duke?" He used the hand in her hair to shake her head no. "Our *Mrs. Weston* has left out a few small details in her history. And you thought you knew our fair lady, Roydan. Quite a blood-thirsty little minx is our Olivia Jayne.

"But, we will fill the duke in soon enough, my love." He let go of her hair and held her by the throat again. "I hate to rush these delightful stories. They must be savored." Something cold and wet touched her ear. Her teeth met and she drew in a hiss of air. Dear God, his tongue.

Rhys fixed his gaze on her, as if willing her to trust him, trust that they *would* find a way through this horror. Olivia released her pent up breath and his nostrils flared, almost as if he were taking in her expelled air.

"I had hoped my little fire would do the trick."

*Fire? Was Biden responsible for the fire?*

"You disappointed me again, my dove. I sometimes marvel at why I still want you. You see, *I* was to be your rescuer. I would miraculously present myself just in the nick of time, and you were meant to come begging to *me!* But the gallant Duke of Roydan was there before me." He frowned as if he'd lost his place in some memory.

The gun lay only a few feet in front of her. Could she kick it toward Rhys? He was so far away.

"Yes, those damned poaching Roydans...like father, like son..." Biden shook his head, his fingers dug into her flesh. "And then you vanished yet again."

Rhys's gaze darted to the gun as well. He must be thinking the same as she.

"Ah, I almost forgot *this* in all the excitement. So kind of you to bring it to my attention, Roydan. Can't have these things lying around, can we?" His laugh, oddly high, like a young girl. "Firearms have a nasty tendency of going off unexpectedly." He bent to retrieve the gun pulling Olivia down with him. She tried to keep her cloak about her shoulders, but when Biden hoisted her back up against him, it slipped and dropped to the floor.

There was no time to prepare Rhys. No time for the words she had rehearsed so often in her fantasy. Still, Olivia tried to smile, her arms cradling her heavily rounded belly.

Rhys's frozen mask cracked and he gasped.

She opened her mouth to tell him of her joy. To tell him how many times she had imagined sharing this miracle child with him. Their miracle. But no words came. She could not make that joy fit this horrible scene.

"What have we here, my pet?"

A muscle jumped in Rhys's face and then hardened, his eyes once again shards of icy amber. She mouthed the word, no. Please, no. His steely face frightened Olivia more than any gun. What would he risk to protect her and his baby?

"Ahhhh…It seems you have been a naughty girl. No doubt lifting your skirts"—Biden turned from her to Rhys—"or all manner of trash. It will not do, my angel. I will not tolerate such tawdry behavior. But then again, you always were a whore, weren't you? Running off with that filthy soldier, Weston. Sullying yourself with half the regiment, I'll warrant. At least I had the pleasure of getting rid of him."

*What had he to do with Wes's death?*

"Settle, my love." The cold barrel stroked her jaw line. "It is not good to be overanxious, especially in your condition.

"Yes, the dear Major…Well, I suppose I cannot take *all* the credit. Your step-mama actually found the two of you, but once she established you were married, well you were of no use to her. But I could not be so lackadaisical. So I arranged the…little accident. It all went rather smoothly until I heard you were huge with his brat. I couldn't very well have you carried off with all those sentinels hovering about you. Billing and cooing."

*Biden had had Wes killed?* Olivia could not make these pieces fit together. The child within her stirred as if it could feel her distress. Shhh, she crooned over and over in her mind, willing it to calm.

"Yes, I truly thought I was done with you until I saw you at that mask with Roydan." Biden moved the pistol down her neck, over her breasts, to her belly. "Let's see…" His hand smoothed over her belly in a caressing motion, and then dipped down between her legs. Olivia braced herself, more fearful of what Rhys might do, than of her own revulsion. She shook her head minutely at Rhys, but his attention was wholly fixed on Biden. "Umm…she is quite…fecund. I suspect she must be very close to her time. I would guess only a few more weeks? What would you say, Roydan, does that sound about right? Is that your recollection as to when you fucked her?"

Rhys jerked forward. "You filthy—"

Biden pushed the gun to her belly. Olivia clamped her teeth together. Should she scream? Would Hazel be back from the far pasture? Could Olivia risk the girl being hurt?

"Oh, no, Roydan, you don't want to do that." Biden tsked. "Not when we are about to have some fun." He began to undo the buttons of his falls.

Olivia screamed.

The blow came harder than she expected, and she fought blackness. A hand covered her mouth. She bit down. "Bitch!" Biden jerked the gun up. The click of it cocking under her chin sounding overly loud. Rhys stood frozen halfway across the room.

"What is that old saying, Roydan? Two birds with one stone?" He laughed and the barrel pressed deeper into the soft flesh of her neck.

"How naughty of you, Olivia Jayne. But I am flattered you recall how I enjoy that bit of love play. However, we must be patient, my love. The biting will come later. Now hold still." The wool of her scarf burned the back of her neck as he whipped it off. He shoved the end into her bleeding mouth. He pushed more and more. "Yes, my dear, I'll wager you can take it all." She gagged.

"I am truly touched you remember that bit of fun. I thought you were quite comatose…but perhaps you only saw the teeth marks afterward?" He frowned and took the end of the scarf and dabbed the blood at the corner of her lip. "Never fear, we will remedy that soon enough. You will most assuredly be alert to all I have planned. You see, I haven't forgotten the marks you left upon me." He briefly touched his temple and then his chest. "So much blood from a paltry pair of sewing scissors. If your dear step-mama hadn't come in, I might have had to add murderess along with whore to your list of accomplishments."

He turned the gun from her onto Rhys and then untied his cravat with his free hand. "Clasp your hands together behind you like a good girl and hold this end," Her thoughts must have shown in her eyes. "I wouldn't risk it, my pet. While I am shivering with excitement at the thought of having you both to entertain me, it's you I want. The duke here is as expendable as having a second dessert."

She could not stop her hands from shaking as she clutched the bit of linen. The thin fabric bit into her wrists, and her fingers throbbed with pulsing blood. "There that is much better." Then he pulled her back to him. "So much to do. So many opportunities to explore."

He absently looped a strand of her hair slowly round his finger, his attention fixed on Rhys. "Hmm...you *are* a handsome lad, aren't you? Much like your dear father in looks but alas, not in tastes, I'll warrant. Too bad. I'd so enjoy a *ménage à trois*...But unfortunately, I only have two hands. And you my duke, I would speculate, are quite a handful if you are anything like your sire."

"Ahhhh!" Rhys lunged forward. Olivia cried out through the wad of wool as Biden pulled her squarely in front of him forcing her arms up behind her. She whimpered.

"I can see our friend Roydan is itching to spoil our fun, and that I will not tolerate. Let us subdue him, shall we, while still giving him an opportunity to view the entertainment.

"Ah, I have it—I can be so clever in a pinch. Lie down on the rug, Roydan." When Rhys hesitated, Biden savagely twisted her nipple. "See what trouble you cause by not following directions, Roydan?" Rhys, never breaking eye contact, did as Biden ordered. "Now, flip the end over on yourself." Rhys did so. "Arms by your sides, my boy. You look as if you still have a bit of strength in you and I do not like interruptions." Biden kicked the rug. "Now roll, boy." Rhys halted. He would be trapped, utterly. "I said, roll. Now!" Biden kicked again and Olivia stumbled. Rhys thrust his body, every roll of the rug imprisoning him further. Only his head and boots remained uncovered.

"Ah, one more turn so that the end is on top. That's it. And you can see properly? I will pull the end a bit." Biden pulled about three feet of the rug, enough so that Rhys faced Biden and Olivia. "And now I can set my chair right here so you will be locked up nice and tight." He dragged the chair's legs to rest on the edge of the rug and then sat, pulling Olivia onto his lap. "There now, that's so much better, don't you agree, my dear? Now, where were we? Ah, yes, I believe I had just discovered Lady Olivia Jayne's breast. She *did* tell you she is a lady didn't she?"

****

Rhys flexed every muscle till they cramped. So bloody helpless against this evil.

*How did he let things get this far? The babe—he had not been prepared. He had not been able to move for fear of Olivia. And then with the child—*

"—the old earl of Stokesly's only child." Biden was speaking. Rhys must pay attention. "You are a cunning little thing, aren't you, my dear? But I digress." He began to heft one of Olivia's breasts. Rhys's mind churned and writhed because his body couldn't. Her lips pressed into a thin, white line.

"Don't squirm, my love, I would hate to have to smash your pretty face." Olivia quieted. "That's my girl. Such an apt pupil. Now these are quite different from when I saw them last." He squeezed harder and despite her brave face, Olivia yelped. But Biden seemed not to hear; instead he frowned. "It is the bastard within you, I collect." He cocked his head thoughtfully. "They will be making milk soon. And since the brat will be

dead, I will be most happy to suckle you, my love."
Olivia moaned.

"No-o-o-o!" The sound erupted out of Rhys, filling
the room. Biden flung Olivia off his lap.

*Yes, come to me, you bastard!* Rhys tried to cover
his face but, of course nothing moved. Pain crashed in
killing all thought. He sucked in air, but the air was
blood. He spat. Something was being forced into his
mouth. He twisted his head, trying to jerk away, but
Biden wedged it deeper between his jaws. Blood filled
his nose. He snorted, blood spattering everywhere.
Blessed air.

"Have you guessed yet?" Biden's face filled his
vision. "I'll give you a tiny hint. You look very much
like a trussed goose."

*An apple?*

Biden clapped with childish delight. "That's it. I
knew you would get it."

Rhys tried to crush it, but it filled his mouth so
completely, wedged painfully between his over-
stretched jaws, his tongue trapped beneath. A gag rose
and he willed his jaws to relax.

The sound of crunching glass pulled him back to
the room. Olivia, hampered by her belly, skirts, and
bound hands, scrambled over the broken shards to the
door.

"Too many interruptions!" Biden raged. "You want
to act like a whore, groveling on the floor? I'll treat you
like a whore." He jerked her back by the hair and
pushed her to her knees between his legs.

Rhys rolled his head; No! He screamed but his
pitiful moan mocked him. Like a coward, he squeezed
his eyes shut. If only he could stop up his ears as easily,

blotting out Olivia's soft keening.

"That reminds me, Roydan, do you know I have had all three of your whores?" Rhys opened his eyes. "Yes, first, virgin Lady Olivia Jayne here," he began unbuttoning his falls, "and then"—another button slipped through—"Mrs. Dee Gooden." Rhys jerked his head to meet Biden's eyes. "Your father and I were bosom beaus. We used to share everything...That is, until he got greedy and stole the delightful Mrs. Gooden from me. No, old Roydan did not know how to play fair." A button popped off in Biden's hand. He looked at it as if it were something foreign. *Could the man be beginning to fray?* "That was not well done of him."

Biden rose, casting the button away, and turned as if toward some imaginary phantom. He was lost for a long moment. "As you know personally, she had a lovely mouth and knew how to use it." Biden bent and touched the rag in Olivia's mouth. He frowned but struggled on, as if he were trying to connect dots in a children's puzzle. However, in the blink of an eye, his face cleared, as if nothing was amiss. "But thankfully she is no longer able to tease any other poor unsuspecting gentleman with her tricks. Bitch was too far gone to be worth anything when I finally found her. She could barely string the words together to beg for a fix much less blackmail you. I did her a favor by putting her out of her misery."

He turned to Rhys. "And finally," he said, with a flourish of his arm, "we come to Mrs. Daria Battersby. Ha! Last and certainly least. I can see why you dumped that old bat, Roydan, I could barely stomach to have her suck me off, much less fuck her.

"But now we have the lovely Lady Olivia to

delight us. Come, my dear." He sat back down. Olivia craned her neck to look at Rhys, her gaze cutting to the end of the rug. By God, she had managed to push the legs of the chair off the edge of the rug.

Biden jerked her hair. "Blasted woman, look at me when I speak to you. It is time for Roydan's lesson. Dear Daria told me you would never allow this particular pleasure." He fumbled to release his cock and began to pull the wool from Olivia's mouth. His girlish, giggle shattered the quiet of the room, popping like ice encountering fire.

Would Biden's loss of control be their saving grace, or their doom? But Rhys had to take the chance. The time for thought ran out as Biden pushed Olivia's head toward his cock.

"Are you comfortable Roy—" Biden jerked to the door. "What now!"

The distraction was all Rhys needed. In a burst of energy, he thrust forward over the rug's unanchored edge. As it unrolled, images flashed like a Magic Lantern show. Biden throwing Olivia aside, the chair falling over as Rhys crashed into it. Next, a shovel glancing off Biden's shoulder, the gun clattering to the floor, and finally, Biden wresting the raised shovel from a young woman. Bringing it to her head—

*Slam!* Rhys barreled into Biden, clipping the backs of his legs and felling him.

Rhys leapt on the man. He saw only Biden's crazed eyes and a thin trickle of blood running from his mouth down his chin. Rhys heard nothing but roaring in his head and the sick thud of bone cracking against wood. The eyes were rolling back in the head now. Good. The blood leaked faster. Good.

Something pulled at him.

"No-o-o-o-o-o!' he shouted through the roar. *He was not finished. He needed to finish. Please God let him finish the bastard.* But he was too far away.

He heard crying. Someone was crying? *Who?* Finding that person was suddenly more important than anything else. Even more important than smashing that evil bastard. The world rushed back to him.

"Olivia!"

The woman who had the shovel was kneeling next to her softly crying. Crying? Rhys pulled free from the arms holding him and started toward the pair. The young woman's apron bloomed deep red, her hands covered in red, as she tried to staunch the flow of blood from Olivia's head.

## Chapter Twenty-Seven

Earthy leather, sweet tobacco, sandalwood, starch and—

She pushed into softness—a pillow—and turned toward the lovely smell, wanting to be closer. Could one smell in dreams? She couldn't remember, but it didn't seem possible. Images flashed over her memory, like a child's picture book. But the pages turned too fast, and she couldn't make sense of them—an older man with a bloody head, Egg weeping, a stranger with intense blue eyes and Rhys...

It must be a dream. A tear slipped from the corner of her eye, and she turned her head, pressing her eyes and nose into the pillow, blotting out the tears and smell of memories.

"Olivia?"

Hmm...now a warm pressure on her hand, smooth and paper dry. So real. And the voice...Another tear slipped out and a moan.

"You must awake now, my love. We have much to plan."

*My love?* Definitely a dream.

But the liquid voice and the small circles being drawn on her wrist felt so very real.

She steeled herself for disappointment and opened her eyes.

*Oh, sweet Saint Anne.* She shut them, sure when

she opened them again he would be gone. A fleeting mirage.

But he wasn't. He bent his dark head to brush warm breath and lips to her knuckles. She drank him in. His hair was longer, his skin paler than she remembered—

"The babe?" She pulled her hand from his to feel her belly. Fresh tears sprang to her eyes as she cradled the familiar and comforting swell. It was still there. She closed her eyelids, and she offered up a silent prayer.

When she opened them again his hand hovered over her belly, his eyes so intense, so haunted.

Looking at him now, she knew she was not strong enough to resist him. She would be *anything* to him if he only asked.

Abruptly he pulled away without touching her, his vulnerability snuffing out like a candle.

"Why did you not write to me?" His voice sounded rusty. He swallowed and his jawline flexed.

She swallowed too. She needed time to make sense of all this. She had so many questions herself.

"We must marry."

*Marry?* His declaration sounded harsh, almost an order. *What?* Besides he was already married. Wasn't he? She had the paper to prove it.

"What of your wife, Arabella Campbell? Your duchess?"

He waved his hand. "There was no marriage. She is gone."

*Gone?* It took but a moment for anger to replace confusion. But once she pushed the bewilderment away, rage flooded through her.

How dare he waltz in to play the hero? Obviously

something had gone wrong with his betrothal. But why now—other than the babe—why was she suddenly suitable? Ah, she had it.

"Now you have found out I am a lady, suddenly I am good enough for the great Duke of Roydan."

All she got for her sarcasm was that blasted raised eyebrow.

She tried again, wanting a real reaction from him. "Or is it because your pride won't tolerate a bastard?" She hated even saying the word—a word she would never associate with a child of hers—but she was so angry.

His jaw jumped, but otherwise, nothing. He drew himself up taller, if that were possible.

"I am not one of the clocks you unearth from a dusty heap, dissect, and put back together when the mood strikes you. I will not keep your bloody time!" Still nothing. He was looking at her as if she had two heads, but she would not back down. "So what is it, Your Grace? *Why* do you want to marry me? You *will* make me an answer."

He slowly flexed his hands and then tucked them behind him and rolled his shoulders.

"I thought I had made it perfectly clear, Mrs. Weston."

It was her turn to raise an eyebrow.

She watched him closely as he crossed to the window and looked out; she could not see his face; she could not tell any of what he was feeling. But, then again, could she ever? After a few very long moments, he spoke.

"Mrs. Weston"—he turned to her—"Olivia. I am a man of few words. Perhaps it is a fault, but I believe

353

actions to be the clearer indicator of feeling." He paused, and slowly closed his eyes as if to harness some enormous emotion. They opened; pools of warm honey. "I have made myself, and I dare say my servants and *certainly* poor Wilcove, half mad with searching for you these past five months, seventeen days, six hours and"—he glanced at the clock on the mantel—"forty-two minutes. I have given Lady Bertram no peace, even when it was clear the poor woman knew nothing of your whereabouts other than your being in London, and that I had to drag out of her, after reducing her to a quivering mess.

"My uncle finally threatened to call me out if I harassed her again. I believe I was one of the reasons they took their extended honeymoon. But I digress.

"I have hounded Sir Richard and various other Bow Street Runners till they refused to see me anymore, me, the Duke of Roydan.

"Tinsley has despaired of ever recovering me from the abyss to which I have sunk and has tendered his resignation on three separate occasions.

"My affairs are in shambles, I have not once been to the House of Lords, I have suffered being a laughingstock and the darling of that infernal Gillray once again for being 'thrown over' by Arabella Campbell, when, in fact, it was she who ran off with her maid—"

"*What?* Not Daisy?"

"Yes, I believe that is the name." He raised an increasingly dear, ducal eyebrow. "Please, if you will allow me to finish. After she ran off with…Daisy, I, of course, told her father I could not marry her. But I had determined that even before the debacle with the maid."

"But there was nothing in the papers!"

He gave her a quelling look. "The announcement of the break did not come for some two or more months after the event.

"The Campbells were, as you may imagine, extremely grieved and begged me to give them some time to recover their footing, as well as their daughter. I'm not sure they achieved either, but I did grant them the time and offered to have it come out that she threw me over. That is when my dear friend Gillray reared his ugly head again.

"So, my dear woman, I hope you will look at these actions and see the picture of a man...a man...quite hopelessly"—he knelt beside her—"and most desperately in love. You have me at your feet, Lady Olivia Jayne Ballard Weston, not that I give a damn if you have one ounce of blue blood, or that you are carrying my child—well, that is not strictly true—I cannot imagine a finer thing than you bearing my child. I will simply be no good to anyone if you will not have me. So will you please put me out of my misery and do me the great honor of becoming my wife and duchess?"

Realizing she had been gaping like a starved fledgling, she shut her mouth. This was the most she had heard him speak. Ever.

She looked deeply into his beautiful brandy eyes. "Why did you not say so in the beginning?" She could not help but tease him, if only a little.

"You will have me then?" He suddenly put her in mind of the little boy he must have been.

She smiled at him then and put both hands to his dear face. "Oh yes, most assuredly. But I must warn you, now that you have found me; you shall never be rid of me again."

Then, Rhys Alistair James Merrick, the great Duke of Roydan, with infinite gentleness, laid his hand reverently over their child, bent his head, and kissed the middle of her palm. She felt, rather than saw, his hot tears as they pooled in her open hand.

Epilogue

She had thrown him out!

*Slash*, went number forty-seven as he made a pass at the invisible fiend who was tormenting his wife upstairs. At one moment it was Dr. Asher, next it was Jeb and Albert who had been summoned to throw him out, then it was he, himself, for getting her in this predicament in the first place.

Yes, he ought to be skewered on old number forty-seven and roasted on a spit. He did not know how he was going to manage keeping his hands off his wife, but he—*slash*—would not—*slash*—risk having her go through this torment again.

Rhys jerked his head up. Yet another agonized moan from above.

He should be up there. *Slash!* With her. *Slash!* Helping. *Slash, slash!*

But she did not want him. She had actually shouted at him. Threatened to smash every one of his "bloody and infernal clocks and watches, if he did not stop reporting the time of every bloody contraction!"

Really, he was only trying to be useful. What could be so objectionable in that? And Dr. Asher had been very happy to give him something to do.

"My boy"—it was his uncle, who had long ago stopped cowering, and taken to heavy drinking instead—"do you imagine that your...efforts...are doing anything at all to help the duchess?"

*Slash!* The sword came within a hair's breadth of Uncle Bert's nose. Bertram did not even flinch; he merely drank deep.

"I don't see how you can sit there drinking, Uncle, when Olivia may very well be dying and the babe with her." Rhys felt for his watch, his fingers closing over its familiar heart shape, and pulled it out. "Bloody hell, it has been over forty-nine minutes since I was ousted. How long am I expected to endure?"

"I suppose, my dear boy, as long as your wife can," his uncle said wearily. "You will do yourself and your lady no good, not to mention Mrs. Cotton, by wearing a hole in the carpet."

Rhys snorted and sat heavily in the nearest chair only to rise again in the next moment and listen at the door.

"Uncle, did you not hear something?"

He had been assured on five separate occasions by five separate people that the moment Olivia delivered, Jeb would summon him immediately. But he didn't trust them. After all, they had the temerity to throw him out.

He caught a look at himself in the pier glass above the mantel. His eyes were wild, a sheen of sweat covered his forehead and neck, his hair hung in an unkempt mess about his eyes; in short, he was a wreck. He threw himself into the nearest chair and reached for his discarded glass.

Then he heard a cry.

It was more of a mewl.

His gut twisted. It was not the cry of his wife, or even one of her moans. No, this was a new sound. By

God, this was their child. His child.

He ran up the stairs three at a time, pounded down the hall, mowing down Jeb and nearly flattening Egg and Hazel as well, when he yanked open the door. Halfway into the room he slammed to a halt, computing the sight before him.

There she was, blotchy and sweating, holding a tiny, red-faced, wailing creature. He wanted to speak, but the flapping birds that had taken up residence in his heart now saw fit to move into his throat making it impossible to speak through their choking feathers.

She beckoned him to come. He did not know how he got to her side, but he supposed he walked like any other mortal.

She held the babe out to him. *Was he to take it? She would trust him with this most precious gift?* She nodded.

He wiped his hands over his breeches. Only dimly conscious of the bed sinking beneath him as he sat, he held out his arms.

It weighed almost nothing, its face not even the size of a tea saucer. An arm came loose from the linen, its tiny fist pumping. Startled, Rhys caught it.

Tiny fingers, soft as new-churned butter, gripped his own with surprising strength. Could there be anything more perfectly beautiful in this amazing world? Could God be so generous? Then his wife—his Olivia—looked up at him, closed her hand over theirs, and smiled. Yes, by heavens, the answer was a resounding yes.

# A word about the author...

As a girl Jess Russell escaped the world of rigorous ballet class and hideous math homework into the haven of toe-wriggling romance novels. She never imagined in her dyslexic brain she would ever come to write one, but a small scene grew into a story, and contest wins, and finally a contract. Dreams sometimes do come true, just like the happy ending in the stories she loves.

Jess lives in New York City with her husband and son and escapes to the Catskill Mountains whenever she can. She is a sometime actress, award-winning batik artist, and accomplished seamstress. Along with a sewing machine, she loves power tools and, what's more, she knows how to use them.

Jess is currently working on revamping her Manhattan kitchen as well as writing two other stories: (working titles) *Heart of Glass*, and *Mad for the Marquess*.

Please visit her at jessrussellromance.com

Thank you for purchasing
this publication of The Wild Rose Press, Inc.

If you enjoyed the story, we would appreciate
your letting others know by leaving a review.

For other wonderful stories,
please visit our on-line bookstore at
www.thewildrosepress.com.

For questions or more information
contact us at
info@thewildrosepress.com.

The Wild Rose Press, Inc.
www.thewildrosepress.com

Stay current with The Wild Rose Press, Inc.

Like us on Facebook
https://www.facebook.com/TheWildRosePress

And Follow us on Twitter

https://twitter.com/WildRosePress

13316206R00205

Printed in Great Britain
by Amazon.co.uk, Ltd.,
Marston Gate.